A NOVEL

NICOLE WILLIAMS

NEAR AND FAR
Copyright © 2013
Nicole Williams

ISBN-13: 978-1940448015
ISBN-10: 1940448018

Cover Design by Sarah Hansen of Okay Creations
Editing by Cassie Cox
Formatting by JT Formatting

chapter ONE

Jesse

SOMETIMES LOVE WAS about compromise, and sometimes it was about sacrifice. Most times, it was a little of both. I'd learned that the trial-and-error way.

One other thing I'd learned the trial-and-error way? I didn't care how much I had to compromise or sacrifice to be with Rowen Sterling. I'd do whatever I could to make her happy. To let her live her dreams. To feel fulfilled. To recognize she was so damn special to me, I ached—a deep, throbbing pain—whenever we were apart.

She was sacred to me.

I made it a priority to treat her as such. That's why I was on my second energy drink and had both windows in Old Bessie cranked down despite the near-freezing temperature.

It was Friday night. Scratch that. It was early, *early* Saturday morning . . . and I was heading west. Rowen didn't like me driving eight hours after a full day of ranch detail. Well, she didn't like me driving *any* distance in Old Bessie period, so we'd made one of those all-important compromises and settled on me leaving Saturday mornings for my monthly trips to Seattle.

One problem with that.

I wasn't willing to sacrifice a night with her, so I'd never really gone along with that compromise. I'd sacrificed sleep and pushed through exhaustion to get to her Saturday morning on every one of the six trips I'd made.

See? Sacrifice and compromise around every relationship corner.

She'd always grumble a little and try to pretend she was all put out I'd risked life and limb to get to her twenty hours sooner than planned, but one smile and shrug from me melted that act. She was a sucker for my smile. It got to her. Every. Single. Time. I wasn't above admitting I'd used that knowledge to my advantage when I found myself heading into deep-ish water with her. A smile, a shrug, and a shimmy, and she was putty in my hands.

Before anyone goes and thinks I'm not playing the love game fair, let me get it on record that I am—one hundred and twenty percent of the time—putty in Rowen Sterling's hands. No matter what she does, or what facial expression she makes, or what words she chooses, my steady state around her is putty. Pliable, gooey putty. I never thought I'd be so damn happy to be a glorified form of Play-Doh in a girl's hands. Life's ironies, right?

As I'm reaching for my third and last energy drink, I see my exit in the distance. As bushed as I am, I perk up instantly. I've driven that route enough to know Rowen's apartment is fifteen minutes away. Ten minutes if I really push Old Bessie to her upper limits. I pushed her to those upper limits every time, and so far, Old Bessie had never failed me.

I passed the sprawling community college Rowen attended. I'd walked around the campus with her a few times. It's a nice school, and the art building where she

2

basically lives when she's not working is impressive, even to someone like myself, who didn't know the difference between Monet and Manet until a certain impassioned someone took it upon herself to school me in art history. I'd learned more about art than anyone would guess some cowboy from Montana knew.

I loved that about Rowen. I loved that about *us.*

We took normal, average, and what was expected . . . and turned it upside down. We didn't do anything just because that was what society expected. We held to our own standards and didn't worry about meeting the expectations of some nameless majority.

By the time I pulled onto Rowen's street, I'd hit fifty miles per hour. I didn't even try to ease off the gas. I knew from previous attempts that trying to hold back would be a wasted effort. When I was that close to having Rowen in my arms, I couldn't pull back. When she was that close, I couldn't get to her fast enough.

Old Bessie practically got air when I pulled into the apartment complex's entrance. As I whipped through the complex's old buildings—that had enough wear and tear to look even older—I took note of every burnt-out light lining the sidewalk to Rowen's building.

She didn't have a car. She didn't do public transportation, except for the Greyhound bus she took once a month to come to Montana. What mode of transportation did my girlfriend choose to use in rainy, traffic-ridden Seattle?

A bike.

Yep, an old, single-gear bike she'd found at the apartment complex a week after she moved in. It made me uneasy in every way a guy could be. Every time I thought of her peddling to school or the funky doughnut shop she worked at that wasn't exactly on the low-crime side of town, I wanted to buy her a bus pass or a reliable little Honda.

She'd refused all of my suggestions about some kind, *any* kind, of transportation other than a bike. She was adamant I was being ridiculous. I was adamant she was being just as ridiculous. So what did I do when she thought she was right and I thought I was just as right?

I let it go.

Rowen rode a bike in a part of Seattle that made my stomach clench into knots when I thought about it. There was no compromise there. I had to sacrifice what I wanted for what she wanted, because ultimately, no one could control another person. The harder one tried, the more the other slipped through their fingers. I wasn't going to let Rowen slip through mine by being a controlling, over-bearing caveman.

I couldn't and—perhaps what was more essential—I *wouldn't* control her. So I controlled the few things I could when it came to her chosen mode of transportation. Like tending to burnt-out streetlights on the sidewalk to her apartment. Or checking her tires. Or greasing the chain. Or making sure she kept the can of mace I'd given her the day she'd moved-in in the side pocket of her backpack. I took care of the things I could control and didn't waste my time trying to control the things I couldn't.

It was an easier concept to accept than it was to execute.

Whipping into the first empty parking space I found, I didn't even bother grabbing my duffel bag from the bed of the truck. I almost forgot to turn off the engine and remove the keys from the ignition. Jogging to Rowen's first floor apartment, I fumbled with my key chain. She'd given me a spare key after clearing it with her roommate, Alex. I'd been relieved to discover Alex was short for Alexandria. Again, if Rowen had chosen to live with a male roommate, that wasn't something I could control. I wouldn't have liked it, but I trusted her.

Trust wasn't just something I gave someone; it was something they had to *prove*. And Rowen had proven it again and again.

Alex worked at the same doughnut shop Rowen did. She'd helped Rowen get the job there and, since it was a Friday night, she wouldn't come through the front door until the sun had come up. Alex lived life like it was going out of style, and weekends and all of the limitless adventures they held were not to be wasted.

After unlocking the door, I stepped inside and closed the door noiselessly. All of the lights were out except for the lava lamp bubbling in the window. The apartment was about the size of a shoe box, but Rowen and Alex had made good use of the space. Once I'd slipped off my boots at the door, I padded through the cubby-sized kitchen and headed for Rowen's bedroom.

She always burned a vanilla candle when she was drawing or painting or molding or whatever other medium she was hard at work on, and I could still smell it. I'd associated with that smell with coming home, with finding my way back to her.

Her door was cracked open, like she knew I'd be showing up and was waiting for me. I slipped inside and leaned into the wall. Rowen wasn't even ten feet in front of me, asleep in one of my white shirts that looked like a dress on her, her sheet tangled around her legs. I froze for a moment and just let myself . . . admire her.

That girl, that *woman,* was mine. And even though that was a hallmark I was intensely proud of, I was more sure and proud of something else.

I was hers.

It wasn't a question. It had never been an option. It was something set into motion the day the universe was created, and thousands of years later, there we were. We'd found each other. I was hers, she was mine, we were each other's. It was powerful stuff that hit me in moments like that. I knew it was the kind of profoundness that would get me labeled as a whipped sap, and I didn't give a damn.

If people wanted to call me a whipped sap because I loved—*loved*—the girl lying in front of me, then bring it on.

After another minute, that ache of separation reminded me of its presence. Watching and musing time was over; I needed to be close to her. My need to be with her became so urgent I didn't bother to slip out of my jeans. I just lowered onto the bed and slid across the mattress until every inch of me was curved around every inch of her. One arm slipped beneath her as the other one wrapped around her. I breathed the first full breath I'd taken since I'd said good-bye two weeks ago when she left Montana.

My intention wasn't to wake her, but she always did, almost like she was waiting for me in her dreams. "You weren't supposed to be here for another twenty hours," she said in a sleep heavy voice. "Sleep deprivation. Falling asleep at the wheel. I like you alive and in one piece."

I smiled and pressed my face into the curve of her neck. I inhaled, taking her in, and exhaled, letting her go.

"I know." I tightened my arms to feel her more solidly in them.

"You never listen to me." She sighed, and it was more a contented one than a disgruntled one.

My smile spread. "I know."

She twisted until her eyes locked onto mine. I couldn't breathe when she looked at me that way. I've never been able to when those blue eyes of hers held the emotion they were capable of. I was just leaning in to cover her mouth with mine when her hand pressed into the side of my neck, stalling me.

"I'm glad you don't."

"I know," I replied. "Me too." I held my smile for another second before my mouth dropped to hers. Rowen sighed again, and before I gave my body permission, I'd shifted until I was holding my weight above her. The pace of our kissing never slowed.

Her hands moved for the buckle of my belt at the same time mine moved for the hem of her shirt. Rowen was kissing me, touching me, and loving me in all the ways I could ever want to be loved. She was expressing her love in ways I'd never even known existed the first five years of my life.

She's love in human form, and even though I could tell she was still half-asleep and I was exhausted, I made love to her. We went slow and locked on to every touch like it was our first time all over again. When I moved inside of her, our combined sighs filled the room. And when our breathing turned into something heavier, I felt her unspoken words in her touch. She'd never loved, or never could love, anyone like she loved me.

Rowen Sterling consumed me.

chapter **TWO**

Rowen

IT WASN'T EVEN seven in the morning, and I was smiling. Actually, I was almost beaming.

I'd never been big on that whole "exuberant facial expression" thing. And then I met Jesse Walker. And now I beam at quarter to seven in the morning. I put all blame on him because I didn't think about it when he was around —smiling, that is—it's just something I'm simply incapable of not doing when he was close by. I'd fondly nicknamed it the Jesse Walker Smile Curse.

It wasn't a sickness I was searching out a cure for.

After "saying our hellos" last night, we both passed out about two heartbeats after. When I'd gotten up to start breakfast, Jesse hadn't even shifted. I almost checked his pulse he was sleeping so soundly. Sleeping in for Jesse was snoozing a few minutes past dawn. For him to still be asleep when it was rounding onto seven, the guy had to be about as beat as a person could be before keeling over from exhaustion.

As the bacon sizzled, I tried to work up some anger, or at least irritation, at Jesse making that five hundred mile drive after being awake for twelve hours. As usual, it didn't work. Truthfully, part of me was thrilled he'd defied exhaustion to get to me sooner. Another part of me, a part that seemed a bit larger, worried that one day, our luck would run out and something terrible would happen.

That whole "running out of luck" thing I worried about didn't only apply to Jesse driving across two state lines late at night. It plagued my nightmares and the darkest recesses of my mind when it came to Jesse's and my relationship. I tried to ignore it—that feeling that the bottom would surely fall out from beneath us any day— but it crept into my mind and spread like a cancer. I knew my natural mentality tended toward pessimism and that those premonitions stemmed from that, so I tried damn hard to suffocate the naysayer in my mind. It was a constant battle.

I'd never brought up my luck-running-out thoughts to Jesse, and I never wanted to. They were my demons to fight. It wasn't that I didn't want his help; it was just that I'd have to bring him into hell to be a part of the battle. Hell—my personal one or any other one—was no place for someone like Jesse Walker.

So I battled them on my own, swore to myself I wouldn't let the self-destructive person I'd locked up months ago out of her cage, and would do everything in my power to make sure I never ran out of luck when it came to Jesse. Whatever came, whatever obstacles we faced, one thing was certain: he was there now. He chose to give his love to me, and that had left me forever changed, no matter what happened.

"You make me breakfast when you come to Willow Springs, and you make me breakfast when I come here. You do realize you're spoiling me, right?"

My beam was back in all of its prior glory.

"I do." I turned off the burner before turning around. Jesse had managed to find his jeans, although the top button wasn't fastened, but he was still sans shirt. Probably because I'd tossed it behind the headboard when I peeled it off of him last night. "I kinda like spoiling you."

His eyes ran over me in a slow, purposeful way. Not in a lustful, I'm-going-to-take-you-right-now kind of way, but in a worshipful kind of way. I doubted I'd ever get used to him admiring me that way. "That can make a man weak."

"I know. That's all part of my evil plan." Whether it was the look in his eyes, or the way he looked in nothing else but a carelessly situated pair of tight jeans, I simply couldn't *not* approach him.

"What evil plan?" His arms tangled around me, and he drew me close to plant a kiss on my forehead.

"To make you so weak and spineless you'll cave to my every wish, whim, and want." I nestled my head into his chest as I wound my arms around him. His warmth spread to me, and I knew if there was one position I'd want to spend all of eternity in, that would be it.

"Hate to break it to you, but that evil plan has been working since last June, Rowen."

"Oh? Did I miss the memo?"

"I'm weak, spineless, and . . . *putty*"—I felt his smile curve into the top of my head—"to your every wish, whim, and want now. I have been. I always will be."

"That so?"

"For you only," he whispered into my hair. "For you, I'm a weak, weak man. I'm so weak for you that you could break me with one word. You could end me with one look. You could ruin me with one touch."

I thought we were born knowing how to breathe. It was an instinctive thing. But right then, I had to remind myself how to do it. "You're weak?" He was the strongest person I'd ever known. If he was weak, then I don't know what I was.

"Incredibly." He kissed my temple. "For you."

After a few moments of re-learning how to breathe—so much for "instinctive"—I wove out of his embrace to plate up our breakfast. "Well, damn. There goes my meticulously detailed evil plan."

Jesse chuckled. "What are you going to do with all of your free time now?"

Glancing over my shoulder, I gave him a once-over of my own. Mine wasn't nearly as innocent as his had been. "Other *evil* things." I lifted an eyebrow to fill in the blanks.

Jesse didn't blush. He didn't even blink. He did grin though. "Where do I sign up to take part in these other evil doings?"

I was about to forget all about breakfast and rush back to the bedroom—or hell, the table was faster—when the front door flew open. In dashed my quirky roommate with impeccably awful timing.

"ROWEN! Get your snarky ass out of bed! The day's a wastin'!" Alex's back was to us as she tugged off her knee-high, shiny black boots. Alex's wardrobe was hardcore. I don't think she owned a single thing that was cotton. She sported leather, silk, tulle, satin . . . did I mention *leather*? The girl was Hispanic, but she dressed like a Japanese anime character. Living with her was about as colorful and adventurous as her wardrobe.

"Hey. Alex. Lower it a notch or fifty," I said, waving a spatula at her. I was back to breakfast since getting hot and heavy with my boyfriend wasn't happening since Alex had arrived. "The landlord said if he gets another complaint from our neighbors about the noise coming from our apartment, we're getting an eviction notice."

Alex made an unimpressed sound as she wrestled off her other boot. "Puh-lease. He said that twelve warnings ago. Besides, if he evicted us, the sick perv couldn't get his daily jollies peeking on you when you pass by his window."

Jesse's forehead lined. He wasn't a jealous boyfriend, which was relieving in the way only a girl who'd been with a jealous, possessive asshole of a boyfriend could appreciate. However, he was a concerned boyfriend. To answer his silent concerns, I shook my head and rolled my eyes. Alex sold drama like it was running out.

After tossing her boots aside, she spun around and saw that I wasn't alone. Of course her gaze lingered over Jesse like mine had earlier. When I'd counted to five and she only looked about halfway done, I grabbed one of my pancakes and flung it her way. "Speaking of getting daily jollies . . ."

Alex dodged the flying pancake while managing to keep her eyes planted on Jesse. "Hot damn, I knew it!" A lesser man than Jesse would have squirmed from the way she was eye humping him.

"Knew what, sick perv?"

She rolled her eyes, *still* managing to keep them on Jesse. "There really is a God." She finally shifted her gaze to me. With a wink, she gave me a broad grin and sauntered toward the coffee pot. As she passed Jesse, she smacked his backside so hard it made both Jesse and me flinch. "And there's a devil, too." She waggled her eyebrows at me as she grabbed a coffee cup and filled it.

"Hey. Crazy. Keep your hands to yourself, or I'm getting a restraining order."

"What? You were keeping yours to yourself. Really, Rowen, when a half-naked man like this delicious boy-toy of yours is standing half-naked in the kitchen, *someone's* got to not keep their hands to themselves. Men like him weren't put on this planet so that women could keep their hands to themselves."

"Men like me can hear, you know," Jesse piped in good-naturedly. "We can even talk. You know, in case anyone wants to issue a *good morning* or a *hey, how are you?* before smacking my backside and making me feel like a piece of meat."

Alex rolled her eyes. "Good morning, Jesse. Hey, how are you?" Even she couldn't keep from smiling around Jesse. It was a bloody epidemic.

"I'm doing great, Alex. So nice of you to ask," Jesse replied.

"So what were you two freaks about to do with your morning before I burst in and objectified, sexually harass-ed, and assaulted your boyfriend?"

I sighed in exasperation as I carried Jesse's and my plates to the table. Living with Alex was like living with a one-woman circus. It was always loud, always intense, and always fun. "Something freaky."

She giggled into her coffee cup. "Please—*please*—don't let me stop you. I'm perfectly happy to watch what-ever freakiness you were about to partake in. Just pretend I'm not here." She hopped up onto the counter and got comfortable.

"Go medicate yourself or something." I was tempted

to throw another pancake at her, but I was hungry. I'd already wasted one pancake, and it hadn't even shut her up for a second.

"Come on! I wouldn't even say anything."

"Alex!" I shot a pathetic glare at Jesse, who was silently chuckling.

"What, Cranky Pants?"

"Medication. Now." I lifted my eyebrows and waited. Alex wasn't really on medication—contrary to popular belief—but we'd learned to build healthy boundaries so we didn't annoy the shit out of each other. She was about five seconds of stare-lusting over Jesse past annoying the shit out of me.

"Fine. Be selfish like that and keep him all to yourself." She slid off the counter, blew each of us a kiss, and headed for her room. "Damn. I hope I put Julio on the charger. I need my Julio action after walking in on that fine piece of cowboy ass."

I shook my head and dove into my pancakes.

"Julio?" Jesse asked, sounding like he was afraid to ask. He was right to be.

"Don't ask," I said, lifting my hand. The first week we'd lived in the apartment, I rushed into Alex's room after hearing her high-pitched screams. Let's just say there wasn't enough brain bleach to wipe that image from my mind. Ready to move on from the Julio, giant-hot-pink-vibrator conversation, I changed the topic. "How's the gang back home?"

Jesse's face ironed out, and his eyes went soft. "Home?" He dropped his forkful of pancake back on his plate.

I shrugged and gave him a look. Not that I was

complaining, but I didn't understand what I'd said or done to generate that warm expression.

"Do you think of Willow Springs like that? As your home?"

Ah. I got it. He'd gone all soft in the knees, eyes, and head because I'd called his home my home. Honestly, wherever he was or wherever he went was my home. I might have been too big of a chicken to admit that to him, but I suppose that without realizing it, I kind of just had. Damn my subconscious and its agenda.

"Mi casa es tu casa. Tu casa es mi casa. Right? In terms of Webster's definition of a home, I suppose Willow Springs is as close to one as I've ever had," I said with another shrug. I knew my answer was the reason his hopeful expression dropped ever so slightly. I also knew I'd just upgraded—or would it be downgraded?—my chicken status to coward status, but the overwhelming, at times stifling, feelings I had for Jesse were difficult to admit to myself, let alone to him.

I'd gone from living an anesthetized life in a black-and-white world to suddenly being thrust into an over-stimulating, overwhelming world in vivid Technicolor. It was a one-eighty that had taken place in barely six months. I hadn't adjusted yet, although each day I adapted a bit more.

Jesse's hand settled over mine. He squeezed gently. "You're right, Rowen. Your home is my home. And my home is yours."

I rotated my hand to tangle my fingers through his. "It sounds better in English."

"Nah. It sounded better when you said it." His eyes got all intentional again which, of course, made my stomach coil into a hundred little knots. Finally, he picked his fork back up and got after his breakfast. "Everyone's doing good," he said around a mouthful of pancake. "Mom and the girls all obviously miss you, and Dad misses you but tries not to be as obvious about it. Which, of course, makes it that much more obvious."

I laughed. Neil was a lot like Jesse. On the surface, he appeared to be a tough cowboy who'd never even considered crying, but deep down, they were both a couple of big softies. Hippies at heart, as Jesse had once described himself. "The feeling's mutual. Give your dad a hug for me when you get back. Just don't make it obvious."

Jesse waved his hand. "Obviously."

"Garth? Josie? Sunny? Cows?" Talking about Willow Springs always made me homesick. I liked Seattle and I loved studying art, but no place was like Willow Springs. I knew, deep down, no place ever would be either. I'd grown up in Portland, but it felt as much like home as a hotel. There was nothing in Portland I yearned for, nothing I missed. I hadn't heard from my mom since she drove away with the man who'd been the catalyst for my five years of self-destructive behavior. I'd cut off the dead branch in my life, and even though it wasn't an easy decision, it was the right one. The *healthy* one.

"Garth is . . . well, *Garth*," Jesse said with a shrug, "and I haven't seen a whole lot of Josie lately. I think she's been seeing one of the Mason brothers which, back to Garth, pisses him the hell off."

My eyebrows came together. "Why would Garth care who Josie is seeing or not seeing?"

"He wouldn't care if it wasn't a Mason."

"And these Masons must be . . . making and selling

16

meth out of a rundown trailer? Contract murderers? Raving lunatics?"

"They're a nice, down-to-earth family with a bit more money than the rest of us. A family who Garth is convinced not a single one of them knows the front of a horse from the back of one."

"So Garth hates them why?" My eyebrows were still pinched together.

"In case you haven't picked up on it yet . . . Garth's a bit of an asshole." Jesse winked as he took a sip of coffee.

"Now that you mention it, I believe I did pick up on that somewhere along the way." I tapped my chin, not masking my sarcasm.

"He's a subtle one."

"Just the word I'd use to describe Garth Black."

Jesse shook his head as he chuckled, making that sexy-as-all-hell hair of his fall across his forehead. It reminded me of the way I'd wove my fingers through it last night and tugged on it when—

"And Sunny boy misses you, too. Of course."

I cleared my throat and mind, and I reached for the glass of water in front of me. "Of course."

"The cows even miss you."

"The cows? Okay, now I know you're lying."

"What? They do." He stuffed a piece of bacon into his mouth and smiled at me as he chewed and swallowed. "They miss you because they can sense how much I do."

I rolled my eyes. "And they have this sixth sense to know you miss me?" I'd spent a lot of time around cows the past year. They didn't strike me as the "missing" kind of species.

"Cows are much smarter than people give them credit

for." Jesse tried to feign insult, but all he really managed was amused.

"Says the *cow*boy," I mumbled.

"Fine, fine. If you're going to insult my secretly intelligent cows, let's move on to something else." Jesse's voice, as it pretty much always stayed, was good-natured. On a rare handful of times, I'd heard him raise it. Whenever he did, I stopped and paid attention.

"What topic would you like to move onto?" I asked.

Jesse glanced at my half-empty coffee cup, and he was out of his seat and pulling the coffee pot out of its holder a moment later. "How about what *you* have on the docket for the day," he said as he topped off my cup. "Pike's Place? Alki Beach? Downtown?"

"Bed?" I suggested, although it was more of a request than a suggestion. When Jesse froze for a split second before his eyes went wide, I could tell he was all too eager to meet that request.

"Is this, like, an all-day event you have in mind? Should I pack some food and water to keep our energy levels high?" He was already grabbing a couple of sodas from the fridge before moving on to one of the cupboards. He pulled out an unopened box of granola bars.

"You'd better pack more than that, Cowboy, for what I've got planned."

Jesse swallowed, snagged the first food items his hands fell on, and raced behind me as I lunged toward the bedroom.

Of course, that's when my phone would ring.

"Oh, come on!" Jesse practically shouted as I checked my phone.

I frowned when I saw who was calling. Not because I

didn't like the person on the other end, but because I knew I had to take it. I *really* didn't want to have to take it.

"Ignore it." Jesse dropped his armful of snacks and drinks on my desk.

"I can't." I picked up the phone when it buzzed again.

He made a sad puppy face. "Please?"

"You don't play fair." That look really shouldn't have been allowed. I came so close to caving, hitting ignore, and carpe diem'ing.

"When a guy is literally two seconds from leaping into bed with his girlfriend, he doesn't have to play fair." Jesse settled into my desk chair, gave me a small smile, and nodded at my phone. "You better answer that."

"This isn't a cancellation of previously scheduled activities. It's just a momentary delay," I whispered right before answering the phone.

"What's a momentary delay?" said the voice on the phone.

Okay, so I guess I didn't get that last little bit in *before* answering the phone. "Errr, nothing. I was talking to someone else." I plopped down on the end of the bed and grinned at Jesse, who was spinning slow circles in my chair and tapping his wrist.

"Who? That crazy roommate of yours?"

"No. Not Alex. Jesse's in town. I was talking to him."

There was silence on the other end. "Who's Jesse?"

I sighed. Surely I'd been over it only a few dozen times that school year. "My boyfriend."

Another silence and then a small sound of recognition. "Oh, yeah. The hick from Montana, right?" I was starting to regret answering the call for other reasons than just delayed gratification. "Isn't Jesse a girl's name?"

I blew out a long breath before replying. Jesse keyed in on my irritated responses, and his brows knitted together as he studied me. "Is there a reason you're calling me a little after seven on a Saturday morning, Jax?" I asked.

Jesse's forehead lined suddenly, but it flattened back out almost as suddenly.

"Someone's not a morning person . . ." Jax muttered.

"Someone's about to get hung up on." My reply wasn't a mutter.

Jax's low laugh sounded. Jax Jones was a T.A. for some of the first-year art classes. He was an exceptionally talented artist who could have been studying alongside the best artists in the country. Why he'd chosen a community college in Seattle to attend, I didn't know, but the students fortunate enough to wind up with him as a T.A. learned more from Jax than they did from the professor.

Lucky for me—or not so lucky at the moment—Jax had been the T.A. for one of my classes each quarter. I had learned more from him than any other person, so I turned a blind eye to his faults and hoped some of his art genius would rub off. Everyone on campus knew Jax Jones's faults—he drank too much, screwed too many women, and probably did a little too much coke between classes—but he'd never crossed any of those lines with me, so I let the man have his faults. I wasn't going to be one of those who pointed a judgey finger his way. Lord knew I was a long-shot from sainthood.

Jax Jones was on the other end of spectrum from Jesse Walker. It might have taken me eighteen years, but I'd figured out I liked the Jesse Walkers of the world.

"What plans have you got for today?" Jax asked,

sounding almost excited. That got my attention. Jax did excited about as often as I did exuberant.

"Um—"

"Whatever it is, cancel it. Cancel it all," Jax interrupted. "I was able to line up an opportunity that a first-year student would slit throats for."

"What kind of an opportunity?" I asked slowly, keeping my eyes on Jesse. His eyes were on me, but his expression gave nothing away. He was so damn good at keeping his emotions locked away when he needed to. The only times he chose to do so were when one of those darker emotions was trying to push through.

"One of my old friends just bought the Underground. You've heard of the place, right?"

"Every college-aged student in the state has heard of it," I answered. It was a true "underground" kind of place. Guests got in by invitation only. Back alleys and an old elevator was the only way to get into the place, and it served up a party to end all parties every Friday and Saturday night. I'd never been, but I'd heard my fair share and then some about it.

"Well guess what college-aged student is going to have their art on display in the V.I.P. section for an entire month starting tonight?"

"Whoa. You are? That's huge, Jax. Congratulations." The Underground wasn't just a glorified meat market. It had been a springboard for dozens of artists' careers over the past couple of decades. Given the Underground saw more millionaires in their V.I.P. section than any Vegas casino did, a lot of starving artists with talent sold their entire collection and were put on the artsy upper-crust's radar.

"Not me, Rowen." He chuckled while I waited. "You. You're the budding artist whose dreams of fame and glory are about to come true."

I was too shocked to reply right away. I ran through Jax's words again. Had he really said my art would be on display at the Underground? Had he really said . . . "I don't have dreams of fame and glory." Yeah. That was the response I went with.

Jesse's forehead went back to creased.

"Sure, you do. You might not think you do, but somewhere deep inside of you, dreams of fame and glory are just waiting to burst free. We all have those kinds of dreams."

"I'm an artist," I replied.

"Then you *really* have dreams of fame and glory trying to bust out."

Okay, I wasn't going to argue. Besides, had he just said my art was going to be at the Underground . . . *tonight*? "I think I might have misunderstood you. It sounded like you said my art would be going up tonight? Did you mean next weekend? Or next month?" Usually, artists were commissioned for something like that months in advance to give them time to put together a balanced, cohesive display.

"I meant tonight."

Nope, I hadn't heard him wrong. "How in the world did that happen? Don't people normally wait years to get their stuff into the Underground? How in the hell am I going to put together a collection in, oh . . ." I checked the time on my phone. My eyes widened. "Just about twelve hours."

After my last outburst, Jesse came over and settled

beside me on the bed, dropping his arm around my waist. I took a breath, a full one. He always managed to calm the crazy a few crazy levels.

Jax chuckled again. "The guy who was supposed to have his art on display starting tonight O.D'd last night. When the guy who owns the club called me asking for a rising star to fill in the dead tweaker's spot, guess whose name was on the tip of my tongue?"

There was so much wrong in that sentence, I didn't know where to begin. So I kept my reply simple. "Eh, me?"

"Yep. Rowen Sterling. Rising star. Repressed feelings of fame and glory. Worst phone conversationalist ever. *You*."

The full weight of what was happening finally hit me. "Holy. Shit."

"Yep. Holy shit is probably the best kind of response to that."

I leaned my head onto Jesse's shoulder, trying to determine if it was all real. When his head tilted into mine, reality hit me. I wasn't dreaming. "So, what now?" I asked Jax, hoping he had a clue, because I had nothing.

"There's my girl." I heard the smile in Jax's voice. "I've already pulled some of your class projects that were lying around, but we're going to need more. We'll need at least a dozen different pieces, and we need to be at the Underground by six to get everything set up and ready before the doors open at nine."

My life had taken dozens of abrupt turns, so I'd think I'd be used to them. I wasn't. "Okay. Jesse and I will get ready and head to the school as soon as we can get there—"

"Why don't you leave the significant other behind? From my experience with my dozens of priors, they tend to get in the way and slow the process down. We'll work faster if it's just you and me. Not to scare you, but if we get this thing done tonight, it's going to be the miracle of the decade."

I grumbled, "Your confidence is inspiring."

"I'm just great like that."

"Letting Your Greatness go now. I'll be there in a half hour."

"I'll be waiting for you," Jax said before ending the call.

I tossed the phone onto the bed and tried to figure out what was happening. Then someone shifted beside me.

"Let me guess. Change of plans?" Jesse was smiling, but his voice betrayed his disappointment.

I nodded and gave him an apologetic look.

He gave the bed one longing look before cupping my face and pressing a soft kiss into my mouth. "There's always tomorrow."

Not that I needed a reminder, but moments like that, the unequivocal goodness that was Jesse Walker was glaringly obvious. "Tomorrow. You. Me. Bed. Not leaving it until you have to hit the road. Deal?"

Jesse's smile tilted higher on one side. "Like you even need to ask." One more kiss, that one lingering, and he stood up. "So. What can I do?"

My head was still reeling from that kiss, but a certain art exhibit at one of the country's most notorious clubs rushed to the forefront of my mind. "I've got to hop into the shower. Can you grab me some clothes and then a dress or something nice for later tonight?"

Jesse's eyebrows came together. I felt so transparent when I was with him that I forgot that he didn't know everything.

"That was Jax, one of the T.A.'s at school. He managed to get my art on display at this artist's dream of a nightclub. *Tonight*. And he needs me to get to the school right away and pull some things so we can get everything set up early." I was so busy rambling and rushing around the room, chucking random things into my purse, that it took me a few moments to notice the questions on his face.

I saw so many questions there, but I had so little time to answer them. Before I'd figured out if I needed to stay and answer his unsaid questions or if I needed to rush and get my butt to the school and answer Jesse's questions later, his face cleared. "Let me know what you need. When you can. Okay?"

I felt part relieved and part guilty that he'd shoved his questions aside. "Okay." I blew him a kiss before rushing for the bathroom.

"Sure you don't need any help in the shower?" I heard the hope in his tone.

Jesse was always hopeful when it came to a certain part of our relationship. "Not if I need to get to the school in under a half hour."

A long, tortured sigh followed me into the bathroom.

chapter **THREE**

Jesse

I GAVE MYSELF a few minutes to mourn what-could-have-been after Rowen took off in a mad rush, then hopped into the shower . . . that was still steamy and smelt like Rowen's herby shampoo. So I gave myself a few more pity minutes.

Then I sucked it up, told myself to stop acting like a whiny baby, and hopped out of the shower with an attitude adjustment. Really, I was happy for Rowen. Excited for her. We'd only had a few minutes to go over what had transpired on the phone, but from what she said, getting her art on display was pretty much the opportunity of a lifetime.

Barely one year in and she was already getting "opportunities of a lifetime." To say I was proud of her would be an understatement. Not just proud of what she created—I'd known how talented she was from the first time I sneaked a peak at her sketchbook last summer—but that she'd begun to realize how talented she was.

I was going to meet Rowen later at the Underground, and since I'd insisted she drive Old Bessie instead of her bike since it was pouring outside, I'd be hitching a ride with Alex. I liked Alex and all, but I didn't put it past her that we'd be literally "hitching a ride."

This morning, I'd replaced all of the burnt-out bulbs in the sidewalk lights, tuned up Rowen's bike, and fixed the dripping faucet in the kitchen. When I was done with all of that, it was only lunchtime. I still had another nine hours before I got to see Rowen again. After inhaling a couple of peanut butter sandwiches, I got creative. I didn't do "idle time" very well.

Since there wasn't a single thing left to do outside, I had no other choice than to get to work inside. I think I washed every piece of clothing Rowen owned. A mere five loads later, I'd folded, hung, and put away more girly clothing than I'd ever thought I could manage in a single day. When Alex stumbled into Rowen's room asking me if I knew where the C batteries were—I didn't, and I didn't want to know what she needed them for, per Rowen's warning last night—my face got red. Alex had found me layering Rowen's bras and panties into her dresser. I don't know why I went all "blushing school boy" because I'd been caught with a pair of panties in my hand. I mean, hell, I'd had my hands on about every single pair of panties Rowen owned, but the look Alex gave me made me feel like a particular brand of perv. Thankfully, after checking to make sure I didn't plan on trying them on, which only made me turn about five shades redder, Alex left the room in search of her much-needed batteries.

After laundry duty, I loaded, ran, and unloaded the dishwasher. I sprayed glass cleaner on all of the windows and mirrors in the apartment. I vacuumed, mopped the kitchen and bathroom, and I even had enough time to scrub out the tub.

Other than her clothes, I didn't touch Rowen's room.

Not because I didn't want to, but because I knew she wouldn't want me to. She wasn't messy, but she wasn't particularly organized either. She liked a little bit of chaos in her life, her room no exception. Scratch that: she liked a bit of *organized* chaos in her life.

I'd always been so busy doing something cattle related back at Willow Springs that I'd never delved into the domestic chores on the ranch. After that day, I had to admit the work Mom and my sisters did was harder than the work we guys did.

Actually, what they did made what I did seem like child's play.

After all of that, I needed another shower. It was a little past eight when I headed into the living room, hoping Alex was ready to head out. Work had done a decent job of keeping my mind off of Rowen, but since my hands weren't busy doing something, that ache of separation was coming back in full force.

Alex was sitting on the couch, one foot furiously tapping the floor, dressed in . . . well, I don't know exactly how to classify what she was wearing. She was dressed at least. Mostly.

She took one look at me, her eyes went wide as saucers, and she shook her head. "Uh-huh. No way. Turn around and go change," she ordered, waving me away. When I just stood there, unsure what to say or do, she added, "Now."

I glanced down to make sure I had on what I remembered changing into. Yep. Jeans, white tee, boots, and my hat.

"Listen, Sex God, you're fine and all, and I'm sure that look works when you're square dancing with Norma

Jean, but you have to go change. I will not be responsible for what happens to you if you go walking into that place dressed like that."

A five-second speech from Alex was like reading *Atlas Shrugged*. I was left with a whole lot of questions and didn't know which one to ask first. So instead of getting into an argument with her, I asked, "What do you want me to change into?"

"Something else. *Anything* else." Her nose curled as she inspected me again. Maybe she was allergic to cowboy. Good thing Rowen hadn't been.

Since I guessed nothing I'd packed would be up to Alex's standards, I decided to try to save some time. "Listen, I'm good. This is what I wear everywhere and, to my knowledge, I haven't heinously offended anyone to date."

"I find that hard to believe," Alex mumbled. "Now you listen to me." She wasn't mumbling anymore. "I'm not asking you to go change because I'm worried about you offending every Seattleite we pass—even though you would. I'm *telling* you to go change because if you walk into the Underground dressed like that . . . you are not coming out in one piece." She paused long enough to take a breath but not long enough for me to get a word out. "Those skinny emo guys might seem harmless, but they're vicious little bitches when they group together."

Ah. I got it. She was worried I would get my ass beat by guys who shopped at a different clothing store than I did. Alex might see the world one way, but I obviously saw it another way. Guys, at least the guys I'd met, didn't give a beating to someone else just because they didn't agree with each other's sense of style. If that was how it was there, I was in unchartered waters.

"Hey, I'm a lover, not a fighter. I'll be good. Really." I took a step for the door, hoping she'd follow me. That hope was wasted.

"Then you're *really* not going in there like that, Mr. Lover Not A Fighter. You need to get at least one good punch in before they kill you. That way you can die with honor."

She wasn't going to let it go. Obviously. If the quickest way to get us out of there was for me to get changed, then fine. I'd go change. I hoped a darker pair of jeans and a blue shirt would work for her because that was about as versatile as my wardrobe got. "Fine. I'll go get changed."

"Not so fast." She bounced up from the couch and followed me. "If you think I'm letting you dive back into that duffel filled with cowboy denim, you're got another thing coming." Grabbing my forearm, she steered me into her room.

It was more of a crypt than a room, and in the first few seconds, I saw so many props, costumes, and toys of a naughty nature that I doubted I'd ever be the same. As Alex tore through her closet, I did my best to focus on the empty patch of carpet in front of my boots. There were a pair of handcuffs to the left and a pair of underwear that really missed the memo on what underwear was intended to cover to the right, so I focused on that four by four inch span of carpet until I felt close to going cross-eyed.

"Here. These should work." Alex held out an armful of guy's clothing and waited for me to take it. "Brad wasn't quite as beefy as you, but he was about as tall."

"Brad?" I asked, realizing my mistake too late.

Alex sighed something that was too close to a moan

30

for my comfort level. "My old boyfriend. Four exes ago. He was a frickin' tomcat in the sack. He used to do this thing where he almost lifted me into the air before—"

"Thanks, Alex," I interrupted, heading for the door. I didn't need to hear any more about Brad and his mad tomcat skills in the sack. "I'll try these on and meet you in the living room in five." I was almost into the hall when Alex called after me.

"Ooooh, wait!" She rummaged around under her bed. "Boots!"

"I've already got boots," I replied right before she flung a pair of black ones my way. I managed to snag them before they clocked me in the face. Okay, so they were boots, but they were basically the polar opposite to the kind I wore—round toed, scuffed up, and a buckle below the ankle. Motorcycle boots? I think?

"Not all boots are created equal," Alex argued with my silent thoughts. "And those, Sex God, kick your boots's ass."

Again, I might have argued if I thought I had a remote chance of coming out the boot victor.

chapter FOUR

Jesse

I FELT LIKE I'd just been held down by a boy band and a motorcycle gang and what I was wearing and the way I looked was the scary result. The jeans were looser than I was used to, the long-sleeved shirt was tighter than I was used to, and the boots . . . well, they were nothing like what I was used to.

Not to mention my hair. When Alex came at me with a bottle of goop after I'd emerged from Rowen's room in foreign duds, I just clenched my jaw, closed my eyes, and prayed it would all be over soon. I still hadn't chanced a look in the mirror. If my hair looked anything like it felt, I didn't want to see it. I was clothed, but I felt naked. The missing hat might have had something to do with that feeling.

"I know you don't believe me, but you don't have to. Because you look hot. Like smokin', I-just-moistened-my-panties hot," Alex said, running a yellow light in her black El Camino. It was about as ancient as Old Bessie and had aged about as gracefully.

Some sweet, refurbished, classic cars turn every head when they pass by. Alex's El Camino wasn't one of those. It was rusted out, the engine made a noise like a jar of marbles had been dropped inside of it, and the rearview mirror hung on by a thread. And the interior's smell? Let's just say it was offensive enough that I'd been riding with my head half out the window in the chilly, rainy weather since we'd left the apartment.

"Thanks?" I replied, shifting for the hundredth time. What guys saw in loose jeans was lost on me. I'd never been in a more uncomfortable pair.

"Oh, come on, Sex God. Give it a break. The self-deprecation act is getting old fast. Just admit you dig that I decked you out in a little swagger, and let's get on with the night."

I knew Alex and I spoke the same language, but sometimes I wondered if we spoke different dialects because I didn't understand half of what she said most of the time. "Alex?"

"Sex God?" she mimicked.

I exhaled out my nose. "What's up with the nick-name?"

"What nickname?" She took a corner so sharply, I checked over my shoulder to make sure we hadn't lost the bumper or something.

"Sex God," I muttered.

"That's not a nickname. I thought that was your given name," she said with an evil grin.

I shot her an exasperated look.

She basked in my discomfort a few seconds longer before shrugging. "Truthfully? Because you are one."

My eyebrows came together. I hadn't realized that been one of my identifiers in the Jesse Walker fine print.

Suddenly, she smacked the back of my head. Not a hold-nothing-back whack, but hard enough it stung. I was about to unleash Rowen's favorite go-to phrase when her roommate went off the rails when she surprised me with one more whack.

Unstable was the first word that came to mind.

"Oww," I said, twisting in my seat so she couldn't surprise me with another one.

"I warned you to cut out the self-deprecation act. It was old two minutes ago. Now it's just making me violent."

I should have taken a cab. Or the bus. Or hell, hitched a ride like I was half-worried I'd be doing anyway.

"When I call you Sex God, that's because you are one. I don't give out compliments liberally, *especially* sex compliments. So stop acting like a humble douche, take Sex God like a man, and let yourself strut a bit."

My eyebrows came together again, but when Alex lifted her hand, that crease ironed our real fast.

"Good boy," she praised, returning her hand to the steering wheel. "Any man who can make a girl make the sounds I've heard coming from Rowen's room when you're in town is a bona fide Sex God. Any guy whose girl is still flushing the next morning is a certified Sex God. And any guy that can keep that look in Rowen's eyes even when he's away is the fucking king of Sex Gods."

I didn't know what to reply to that. That was standard when it came to my conversations with Alex.

"Any questions?" she said as I continued my temporary muteness.

"No," I said at last, wanting to steer the conversation far away from Rowen's and my relationship between the sheets. I wasn't sure how I felt about Alex hearing, witnessing, and knowing the things I did to Rowen, so I decided to take . . . *Sex God* as a compliment and move on. Hopefully we'd stay "moved on" from that conversation for the rest of eternity.

"Good. Because we don't really have time for questions." Alex sped up to an old warehouse and hit the brakes at the last possible second. Good God, it was a miracle we'd arrived in one piece.

"Why's that?"

"Because once we get inside, the music will be so loud the only way to communicate is through sign language, facial expressions, or bumping uglies."

Chalk up yet another cringe-worthy phrase from Alex.

"We're here?" I glanced at the warehouse again. It looked like no human had stepped foot in it in decades. No light streamed from any of the windows, and more of it seemed to be crumbling than standing. It was a horror movie director's dream.

"Welcome to the Underground. The most prestigious club in the city." A guy appeared at Alex's door and opened it. Valet parking? I hadn't seen that coming. "Not exactly what you were expecting?" Alex said before sliding out of her seat.

"Not exactly." I opened my door and got out.

"It's not much from the outside, but just wait until you get through the doors." Alex came up beside me and nudged me. "Haven't you ever heard it's what's on the inside that counts?"

I glanced at her. "I didn't realize that applied to clubs."

She wove her arm through mine and tugged me toward what I assumed was the entrance. "It applies to everything. Oh, and once we're inside, stay close, Cow-boy. You might be sporting different digs, but if the dudes even catch a whiff of cow shit on you, your ass is grass."

I rolled my eyes. "I can handle myself. This isn't my first rodeo."

"Yeah, saying 'rodeo' isn't going to make people believe you're not a hick."

"I'm not a hick," I said matter-of-factly.

Alex made a sound between exasperated and irritated. "No, you're a self-deprecating pain in my ass."

I smiled to myself. Alex was something of a pain in my ass too, but she was growing on me. "But you put up with me because I'm a Sex God. Right?"

"You're not *my* Sex God," she huffed. "Since I'm not reaping the benefits from your mad sexual skills, you'll only get a free pass from me for so long, so shape up or ship out, Cowboy."

"Yeah, Alex? You calling me Cowboy isn't going to convince anyone I'm not some dumb hick either."

"Whatever, Pain-In-My-Ass Walker," she muttered as the door swung open when we were a few feet in front of it. Either there was a camera on the door, a peephole, or a poltergeist was manning it. "And my warning to stay close wasn't just because the guys might go gang-busters on you. The girls in there are the biggest threat. They catch sight of you, and their grubby little paws will be all over you like you're a rung on the ladder to social climbing. And if anyone catches wind that you're the Sex God you are, I hope you've got stamina, Cowboy, because every last cock-crazy female in there will hold you down and do filthy, filthy things to you."

If there was a way to go back in time, I would have

travelled back ten seconds and stuck my fingers in my ears before Alex got out that last bit.

Thankfully, a guy who had to be almost twice my size stopped us just inside the door. He didn't say anything, but Alex obviously knew what he was waiting for. She fumbled around in her purse for her phone. Scrolling through her texts, she flashed one in front of the guy.

Without so much as a nod, he stepped aside and let us pass. We walked down a long, dark hall, and with every step we took, a beat that shook my insides grew heavier. I couldn't make out the music or if it was coming from above or below us, but when it started shaking the hallway walls, I knew Alex was right. It was going to be loud.

Finally, the hall ended at a row of elevators that look-ed somehow even older than the building. I followed Alex into the only one available—I wasn't sure if that was because the half dozen others were in use or because they were busted—and once I'd closed the metal screen door, Alex punched the B on the panel and the elevator jerked into motion.

"Hang on, Cowboy. We're not in Montana anymore."

Yep. Wherever we were, Montana felt like it was on the opposite side of the world.

The elevator screeched and jolted down for a couple more minutes. The music droned louder, and the air got heavier. Everything said that club was a place to run from, not run to, yet I was smiling. I was getting closer to Rowen. When the elevator jerked to a stop, Alex threw open the metal door, and I got a good look at the Under-ground. I realized that would be one of those times when I had to walk through hell to get to heaven.

"This is the place," Alex shouted above music

to the point I half-expected to see blood trickling ople's ears. I gave her a curious look. "Where the rabbit hole winds up taking you." She waved around the room. "You've arrived."

Because it felt wrong to scream at a woman, and a scream was the only way for her to hear me, I chose to flash her a thumbs-up instead. She rolled her eyes at my fake enthusiasm, grabbed my elbow, and steered us through the crowd. The Underground was . . . well, it was like nowhere I'd ever been before. Rowen had taken me to some funky, word-of-mouth places around Seattle, but nothing like that. I'd certainly never been to a place like it back in Montana. A big night out in Montana included a big barn, a rented dance floor, and a local country band.

The Underground was huge, probably the size of a couple of football fields put together. As big as it was, it still felt small since there was basically standing room only. There were thousands, maybe tens of thousands, of people bouncing to the music, swaying into the person next to them, moving like waves on the ocean. As if the mass of people and the volume of the music wasn't overwhelming enough, strobe lights went off around the entire room. It was different from anywhere I'd ever been, but the verdict was still out if it was a good or bad different.

"Pick your poison!" Alex called over to me once we'd worked our way to one of the bars. The music wasn't blasting quite as loudly there, but I still felt my brain vibrating against my skull.

"I'm only twenty." I leaned closer to Alex so I wouldn't have to shout. She gave me a *So?* look. "And I don't have a fake I.D."

One more *So?*. That one was more pronounced. After a few moments, she rolled her eyes. The way Alex had mastered the eye roll led me to the conclusion she thought humanity was clueless. Apparently she believed I was. "This isn't the kind of place that checks I.D.s." Indicating at the bartender who'd just meandered up to us, she winked up at him. "We've got an Underground first timer on our hands here."

The bartender's eyes sparkled as he turned his attention on me. A smile I wasn't used to having directed at me from a guy slowly moved into position. "He's getting his Underground cherry popped tonight, and I get the honor of serving him his first drink?" He flashed me a wink that made me guess he was more into my kind of equipment than Alex's.

Alex nodded and shoved my arm. "He might be now, but this guy's not leaving here a virgin."

I thanked her with a tight smile.

"Well, paint me Judy Garland and slap on some ruby red slippers because, honey, I've just landed myself in Oz," the bartender said with a wave.

I was just working through my options in the reply department—I was coming up on empty—when every nerve shot to attention. I'd been growing accustomed to that sensation, and it could only mean one thing.

Rowen was close by.

"You okay on your own for a while?" I asked Alex, who was ordering her drink.

She narrowed her eyes like my question was insulting. "Yeah, I think I can hold my own against Dorothy here." The bartender who shot me another wink when I glanced at him.

I certainly didn't need to worry about him taking advantage of Alex if I left the two of them alone. Me, on the other hand . . . Backing into the crowd, I waved at both of them. Their parting words?

"Hurry back."

"Away with you."

Spinning around, I wove through the mass of bodies, getting closer to Rowen with every step. I couldn't see her, but I didn't need to. The feeling inside of me told me all I needed to know. It wasn't like an invisible rope where when she pulled, I came, or when I pulled, she came. It was more like . . . a *magnetism.* The closer we were, the stronger the attraction became.

I followed that attraction to the other side of the club where a smaller room was separated from the rest of the place by a pair of sheer red curtains. That room was far better lit than the main room and nowhere near as packed. A few dozen people wandered around, inspecting some familiar and some not-so-familiar paintings and drawings.

That was when I saw her. She was standing in front of one of the paintings I hadn't seen yet talking to a middle-aged couple who was inspecting the piece like they were envisioning it above their fireplace. Rowen looked . . . well, she still made my heart hammer like she did when I first starting falling hard for her last summer. Falling like I couldn't even stop it if I wanted to.

She was in a black and silver beaded dress, the one she'd found at an antique store on Queen Mary Hill last month when I'd been over. She'd glommed onto that dress like it was a homing beacon. After admiring it for a while, she announced she was confident she must have owned the dress in a former life—apparently she'd been a flapper in the '20s—and that she had to buy it. Then she checked the price tag, frowned, and put it back. We walked out of the antique store without the dress, and Rowen headed for the nearest cafe to drown her sorrows in a cappuccino and a croissant. I'd excused myself to go to the restroom, returned ten minutes later to find her picking at a second croissant, and set the dress in her lap.

The look on her face that rainy afternoon? Yeah, it was one I'd never forget.

Other than the night I'd purchased it, I hadn't seen her in it. Even that night, the dress didn't exactly stay in place for long. Tonight, though, seeing her in that dress, smiling, talking, and showing off her artwork, so obviously in her element . . . She stole whatever fraction of a piece of my heart I might have still possessed. Rowen Sterling had every last piece of me, and I didn't want any of them back.

That magnetism jolted back to life in a staggering way. I couldn't *not* go to her. I'd gone two steps in the hundred left to go when my journey came to an abrupt end.

A man who made the guy guarding the front door seem like a kitten stepped in front of me. "This room's for V.I.P.s only."

I might not pour milk over my steak for breakfast in the morning, but I wasn't a weakling. When Big Boy rammed his chest into mine to stop me, I kid you not, I bounced back a good five feet. Okay, so manhandling hay bales, feed bags, and hundred-pound calves doesn't hold a candle to benching small SUVs. Noted.

The dude might have been Goliath's offspring, but Rowen was a mere dozen yards away. I wasn't going down with one warning. I advanced again, trying to step around him. That time, he grabbed my shoulders and shoved me back.

"V.I.P.s" he said slowly, half looking like he was hoping I'd try to charge past him again. "Not V.U.I.P.s."

I lifted an eyebrow. It seemed a lot of people didn't speak the same language as me around there.

"Very *un*-important people," King Kong clarified.

I let that insult roll off my back. I'd never cared about what strangers thought about me. Glancing over his shoulder, I caught another glimpse of Rowen. "My girl-friend's in there. She's the one whose art's on display."

Kong cracked his neck to one side, then the other. "Son"—I don't know where he got off calling me *son*. He couldn't have been more than a couple of years older than me—"even if that was your wife in there, your wife of twenty years who you'd just found out had been fucking your best friend in your own bed and you wanted to run in there and chew her a new one, you are not getting past me."

I inhaled. I exhaled. Something fired to life inside of me, something I generally did a good job of repressing. That act-first-think-second instinct. I took another full breath, set my hands on my hips, and tried to keep my voice level. "Would you please just go tell her"—I pointed at Rowen with my eyes—"that Jesse is outside? I'm sure she'll figure out a way to get me off of the V.U.I.P. list."

The bouncer twisted to look at Rowen. His look stayed locked on her long enough that my hands started to curl into fists of their own accord. "That's your girl-friend?" His eyes ran over Rowen in a way every guy could decipher. He was imagining her, right there, without her clothes on.

"Yes," I managed through a clenched jaw. That fire inside of me grew, spreading to every nerve.

He made an mm-mm-MMM sound, and that's when I felt it; that fire had just exploded past the point of my restraint. "Now that's a woman who's fucked her fair share of men. I wouldn't mind getting in that line."

I saw red. I felt red. I was a ball of emotion. I was a ball of . . . *rage*. One part of my mind still worked just enough to know I wasn't the type to swing first and ask questions later, but it was quickly and easily overpowered by the fury. "Wrong thing to say, big guy." My arm reached back automatically. "*Way* wrong thing to say."

It would have been a solid hit. The guy was still running his eyes all over Rowen like they were his hands —he didn't have a clue he was about to have a meeting with the business end of my fist—but someone ducked out from behind the curtains and stepped between us so casually I doubted he knew fists were about to start swinging.

"How's it going out here . . . ?" The new guy looked between the two of us, giving us both such condescending looks, he did little to unclench my fists. "I didn't catch you boys in the middle of anything, did I?"

Since it sounded like more of a rhetorical question, I ignored it. "Could you go get Rowen Sterling for me, please?"

The new guy inspected me closer. From his expression, it didn't look like he approved. "She's kind of in the middle of an art show right now. Not really the best time."

The guy had barely said three sentences to me, and everything about him grated on me. I generally wasn't the kind of person who found other people "grating." "I'm her boyfriend. Could you please just let her know I'm here?" I slid my phone out of my back pocket again to check it. Still no reception. Either we were so deep below the surface the cell towers didn't reach that far, or jamming devices had been installed in the club. I hadn't seen a single person with a phone to their ear or typing out a text.

"So. You're the boyfriend with a girl name."

I slid my phone back into my pocket and forced myself to bite back the fire begging to be released. After a moment, I felt mostly certain the words about to come out of my mouth wouldn't be ones I'd regret. "Yep. That's me. Jesse. Rowen's boyfriend. The boyfriend with a girl's name." Each word extinguished a bit more of the fire. Each "self-deprecating" word brought me back to the person I knew. Unlike the quivering rage machine I'd morphed into moments ago. Talk about bringing the Hulk out of the cowboy.

A smile broke out on the guy's face. I guessed he was pleased I'd agreed with the gender distinction of my name or that I didn't take myself too seriously. "Hey, I meant no offense. Or no *real* offense. I like getting under Rowen's skin, and mentioning her boyfriend with a girlfriend name really, really gets under her skin." He shrugged and gave a quick check over his shoulder. "I forgot she wasn't here glued to my hip the way we have been all day."

"You're Jax," I said.

"The one and only." He shook my hand when I extended it. I didn't make it a point to notice a man's handshake, but Dad had always told me that a man's handshake was an extension of himself. A two-second elevator speech without using words. He said the key was to make your handshake firm enough that the other person knew you were strong, but not so firm that it was a dead giveaway you were only *pretending* to be strong.

Jax's handshake was so damn firm, I felt like I was shaking a piece of wood.

He didn't hide his smile at the completion of our handshake. I did. His dad obviously hadn't taught him the finer points of the handshake. "Forget about the 'glued at the hip' comment. Don't worry about it. We weren't glued together at *both* hips." Jax chuckled and slapped my arm. He had a bad handshake *and* a bad sense of humor.

"I wasn't."

"You wasn't what?" Jax asked after waiting for me to elaborate.

"Worried. I wasn't worried when you made that comment."

"Oh?" Jax studied me again. I don't know what he was studying me for, but he didn't look like he was arriving at any answers. "Why not? You don't know anything about me. Maybe I'm the kind of guy who lives for going after other guys' girls." He was still smiling, like he was just messing with me, but something about Jax's eyes led me to believe he wasn't joking.

"You're right. I don't know you. I don't know what kind of guy you are." I stepped closer, making it obvious that I had Jax by a good three inches and thirty pounds. "But I don't need to know. Because I know what kind of girl Rowen is."

Jax waved off the giant who looked like he was ready to play hacky-sack with my head. "Rowen told me you were deep."

"That's great. Would you mind going and telling

Rowen her *deep* boyfriend is fifty feet away?" I peeked inside of the room. She was still by the same painting, talking to a new couple. I smiled.

Jax followed my gaze. "Sure, once I can pull her away for a moment, I'll let her know you're out here." His gaze lingered on Rowen too, but I didn't see the same flash in his eyes that I'd seen in the bouncer's. There was something else, something that almost made me as uncomfortable. "I'd let you in myself, but"—Jax hitched his thumb at the bouncer as he backed into the V.I.P. room—"rules are rules."

I flashed Jax a wave as he disappeared behind the curtains, and I waited for him to pull Rowen off to the side and tell her I was out there.

I was still waiting an hour later.

chapter **FIVE**

Rowen

WHERE WAS HE?

Those words consumed my mind as I smiled at strangers singing my pieces' praises. That night, career wise, pretty much defined epic, but I couldn't fully enjoy it without Jesse. The highs of life were always doubled when he was beside me experiencing them at the same time.

Alex had been texted the invite, so as long as Jesse was with her, he'd be able to get in. From there, all he'd have to do was ask around, and he'd be pointed in the right direction. If Jesse was at the Underground, he wasn't just leaning into a bar counter or sprawled out on one of the posh chairs waiting for me to come to him.

Jesse always came and found me. I'd grown so used to it, I'd almost started taking it for granted. I might not have been lost anymore, but I still liked Jesse Walker finding me. Even if it was only in a room of people.

"What was your inspiration for this one? It's exquisite." The woman of the couple I'd been tuning out for . . . how long? interrupted my thoughts.

I don't know why I glanced over my shoulder at the painting they were staring at—I knew exactly what was back there—but I still did. "Um . . . well, I guess you could say . . . *me*." I studied the painting for another moment then smiled. Displaying a picture like that, one that felt like such a window to my soul, made me feel like I was the naked person standing in the middle of a room of people staring and pointing. I didn't do transparent, I didn't *like* transparent, but I'd learned a lot about it from Jesse. I still wasn't big on it, but for him, I worked at it.

"How much is it going for?" the woman asked, lifting her expensive clutch like she was ready to fork out the dough right then and there.

"You'd have to check with Jax on that." I pointed at Jax, schmoozing it up with some richie-riches, decked out in his standard Jax attire. The guy dressed like he was an honorary member of the Rat Pack. He lifted his champagne glass when he noticed me. "He said there are several interested buyers, so he's taking bids. Or some-thing like that."

Truthfully, it was beyond me. When I'd painted that picture, I'd never intended it for anyone else's eyes but mine and Jesse's. The painting was more therapy, a healing journal entry, than a piece to be displayed and sold off to the highest bidder. When Jax and I were searching the art rooms in a crazed state earlier, praying we'd unveil some extra pieces I could display, he'd found it stuffed into the back of my storage area in the oil studio. He said it was brilliant and would have none of my pleas that it not be on display.

Jax always seemed to get his way. Or maybe I just never did. Whatever it was, the painting I'd wanted to stay hidden was the highlight of the night.

The woman grabbed her husband's arm and nearly bolted in Jax's direction.

I loved art. I loved studying it, pondering it, and creating it. I didn't, however, enjoy selling it. Or rubbing elbows with a bunch of people who'd spent more on their shoes than some families lived off of all year. It was part of the deal, though. Wealthy people didn't want to buy just a canvas; they wanted a story to go with it. They wanted to meet, shake the hand, and share the story with the artist behind the canvas. They wanted a story to tell the rest of their country club friends when they came over and coveted the canvas hanging on their wall.

Once Mr. and Mrs. Eager had scrambled over to Jax, I grabbed my phone and checked it. I didn't know what I was expecting—there never had been or probably never would be any reception in that place—but that didn't stop me from checking it for the four dozenth time in the past few hours.

No signal. Big surprise.

I blew out a frustrated breath and tried not to let my thoughts run away with me. The ones that suggested something had happened to him. That the brakes in Alex's piece of crap car had gone out and they'd runaway down the streets of Seattle until the car sped into the dark water of the Sound. Or that Alex had taken a wrong turn, confused another old warehouse with the Underground, wandered inside, and been jumped by a gang of street kids.

My mind was a runaway worry train. Loving someone as much as I did Jesse meant the darkness of the world seemed so black I never wanted to walk out the front door. Around every corner was some terror threatening to take away what I held most dear. I knew it probably shouldn't be that way, but the world had become scarier since I'd let love back into my life. Scary because of the fear of loss.

Of losing him. Of waking up to discover the one light shining bright in the dark night had been extinguished.

"Where are you, Jesse?" I whispered, chewing on my lip as I bit back the worst case scenario thoughts leaping to mind.

Then I felt him. Like he'd answered my question without using words. Jesse was close by, and everything inside of me heaved a sigh of relief. Scanning the room, I saw he wasn't there, which meant . . . My gaze shifted toward the entrance. The sheer red curtains were drawn closed, and I saw the shapes of two men standing behind them. One was the size of a damn tractor and the other was . . . a very familiar shape.

I rushed toward the entrance, avoiding eye contact with everyone I passed. I could not, I *would* not, answer any more questions about inspiration, where I saw my career in five years, or if I'd be interested in doing a nude of their wives. I burst through the curtains, trying to go slow since I was wearing heels. Heels and I weren't exactly copacetic. I should have gone slower.

I somehow managed to catch my toe on the floor, perform a clumsy spin, and was about to crash land face first when a lithe and strong pair of arms caught me. Those arms, or more like the owner behind them, had saved me from so many falls I'd lost count.

"You know I love it when you go and fall into my arms." Jesse righted me but kept me close. "It really feeds that hero complex I try to repress." He grinned the one that had made my stomach drop the first day we'd met. Almost one year later, my stomach did the same damn thing.

"And I kind of like it when you're around to catch me from falling. Because, don't tell, it really feeds that distressed damsel complex I trỳ so hard to repress."

"Our secrets and our repressed complexes are safe with each other."

I was going in to tap the rim of his hat when I stopped short. There was no hat. Lowering my hand to his hair, I ran my fingers through it. Did Jesse have *product* in his hair? I would have bet my left kidney Jesse didn't have a clue what product was. When my eyes went lower to find him in a long-sleeved henley with the couple top buttons undone, I wasn't sure who'd walked into an alternate reality: me or Jesse.

"What happened to you?" I ran my hands around to his back. They moved lower, and when I felt loose material around his backside, my eyes widened.

"Alex got a hold of me." Jesse shook his head then jolted when I slapped his butt. It didn't make the same sound, and it certainly didn't feel the same. When it came to Jesse Walker, it was tight jeans or no jeans.

"Alex," I said, followed by a sigh. "I'm sorry. I shouldn't have left you alone with her."

"No worries. It was an adventure, for sure, and I learned at least a dozen new phrases and words related to the acts leading up to, the parts involved, or the actual making of sex."

"Oh, God," I groaned. Jesse wasn't a prude, no where near it, but he was . . . *wholesome*. That was a rare trait and something to be protected. Spending an hour with Alex Diaz could obliterate that. "Next time, I promise I won't leave you behind with her. Wait. What am I saying? There won't be a next time. This whole night was one giant, unexpected surprise."

That was the first time I'd had a few minutes to take a

deep breath and let the last twelve hours catch up with me. Jax and I had pulled it off, barely, but sliding into the artist-of-the-month spot at the Underground as a college freshman wasn't the kind of thing that saw an encore.

"It looks like things are going great in there. I couldn't count how many people who stopped and stared at one of your pieces for five, ten, fifteen minutes at a time. One guy looked at one for so long, I started to wonder if he'd turned into a statue." Jesse looked at me with proud eyes. Genuine pride. I'd convinced myself for years that I didn't need anyone's approval or pride, but that wasn't the truth. I did care about those things, especially when they came from someone I loved and admired.

"It's been a good night," I replied, experiencing such an intense urge to kiss him I couldn't ignore it. So I didn't. Lifting up onto my tiptoes, I pressed my mouth to his until I felt it: the instant my whole body melted into him and I could no longer tell what part was Jesse and what part was me. I wasn't losing myself to him; I was *finding* myself in him. "And now it's a *great* night."

"Mm-hmm," Jesse hummed, smiling with his eyes still closed.

The bouncer shifted behind Jesse, reminding me of where we were, or rather, what side of the curtains we were on. "What are you doing out here?" I asked Jesse.

Jesse rubbed the back of his neck and looked to be searching for the right words. "Um . . . I wasn't exactly on the V.I.P. list."

"What?!" I made a face as I let out a mini shriek. "You're the only person I actually want to see, and they didn't put you on the V.I.P. list? Are you kidding me?"

Jesse still looked like he was trying to choose his

words carefully. "No?"

The anger I felt had nothing to do with him and everything to do with whoever's fault it was that Jesse's name hadn't been put on that list. "Why didn't you tell someone?"

Jesse indicated at the monster-sized bouncer. "I tried telling Kong, but I don't think he speaks. He just throws down the pain."

I sent a glare "Kong's" way, grabbed Jesse's arm, and marched through the curtains. When Kong stepped forward, I gave him a *do-it-I-dare-you* look. The only thing he did was step back and look away.

"God, Jesse, I'm so sorry. How long have you been waiting out there?"

He lifted a shoulder as he scanned the pictures. "Not long."

"Can *not long* be quantified?"

His gaze locked on one picture before guiding us toward it. I'd seen a lot of that picture already. "I don't know. An hour? Maybe two? It wasn't that long."

"An hour? Or two?" I was back to a mini shriek. "Why didn't you just bust through and come find me?"

Jesse stopped in front of the painting with a thoughtful expression. "I didn't want to make a scene. Tonight's all about you. Plus you've got a little too much faith in me if you think I could have gotten past Godzilla with tree stumps for arms."

I laughed and squeezed his hand. No one could shift my moods like Jesse. Anger one second, laughter the next.

He took a few steps closer, leaning in until it looked like he was studying each individual brush stroke. After a few minutes, he stepped back a few feet and took in the painting as a whole. His forehead was lined, his eyes curious, and his mouth flat, giving away nothing.

Dozens of people had inspected the same picture, and not once had my heart pounded the way it was then. Transparency was tough with anybody, but if a stranger saw into the depths of me and didn't like what they saw, brushing it off was easier. When someone I cared about, someone I cared about more than myself, saw into those same depths, their conclusion was *everything*.

Jesse knew the good, bad, and the ugly of me. He had for a while, and he'd never once turned his back and walked away. That felt different though. Those had been words, stories I'd told him, flashes in time I'd given him a front row seat to. He'd never *seen* the good, bad, and the ugly on canvas in paint form. I couldn't exactly tell you how it was different, but it was.

Right when the anxiety felt like it was about to rip me in half, Jesse's mouth lifted in a familiar way and his hand dropped from mine only to wind around my middle. "You're beautiful," he whispered, sweeping a kiss into my temple.

I choked on a laugh as a tear escaped my eye. "Which one?" I studied the picture with him.

His mouth moved from my temple to my ear. "Both of you."

Just like that, the anxiety was gone, chased away by the all-encompassing acceptance Jesse showed me. He'd accepted me as I'd been last summer, he accepted me for the woman I was today, and I knew he'd accept the woman I was in the future. His acceptance didn't come with an expiration date.

A figure slid in front of us. "Ah. You got in. Good for

you." Jax lifted his champagne glass at Jesse before taking a sip.

"Wait. You knew he was waiting out there?" I managed to hold back the flood of emotion until I received his response.

When Jax just lifted his eyebrows at me, I stopped holding the flood back. "And you didn't invite him in or, I don't know, tell me?" I crossed my arms and stepped toward Jax. I don't know what I was thinking, it wasn't like five foot not-a-whole-hell-of-a-lot in two-inch heels was intimidating, but I wanted to be in a position to intimidate. Jax Jones knew how much I wanted Jesse to be a part of the show, and apparently Jax Jones had also known Jesse was waiting just outside those curtains.

"It wouldn't have been right of me to invite him in, and you've been busy all night." Jax did that shrug of his that had never really bothered me before. If he did it again, I was going to go nuclear. Leaving my goddamned guest of honor outside for a couple of hours warranted a hell of a lot more than a shrug.

"Busy? Busy!?" I said, because once just wasn't enough. "Let me show you something. Pretty basic stuff here." Marching right up to Jax, I tapped his shoulder, lifted my eyebrows, and motioned toward the entrance. "'Hey, Rowen. Your boyfriend, you know, that guy you've been waiting for all night, is just outside. Why don't you go invite him in?'" My voice wasn't trembling —*yet*—but it was close. Jesse came up behind me and dropped his hands on my shoulders. It wasn't a *calm down* gesture. It was an *I've got your back* assurance.

Dammit, I loved that man, and he'd been left to just hang outside all night thanks to the guy in front of me with an amused expression that made me want to slap it off. Made me want to *punch* it off.

"I've dropped the ball on that basic stuff my whole life. Sorry, Rowen. Sorry, Rowen's Boyfriend." Jax lifted his champagne glass again and, that time, drained the entire thing.

My eyebrows came together. I'd met Jax in September, and we'd never had a problem. In fact, in a lot of ways, he'd seemed like the male version of me. Artistic, naturally cynical, dry sense of humor, same taste in music . . . but that night, he'd pissed me off big time. From that smug smile, he knew it, too. No apologies about it.

"That was an asshole move to pull." I glared at him, reaching for Jesse's hand to keep from shoving Jax.

"You know my reputation on campus?" Jax replied, his brown eyes darkening. "Why would you expect anything more than an asshole move from an asshole?"

I flinched like his words had been a slap. "What the hell is wrong with you? Did a wire trip in your brain in the past fifteen minutes?" Jesse's hands were still attached to my shoulders, but instead of holding me back, they were holding me steady.

"Yeah. A wire did trip in my brain." Jax drilled his index finger into his temple. "Forgive me for being human. I'm not your infallible, perfect cowboy." Without so much as a good-bye, Jax sped away from Jesse and me like we were radioactive.

"What in the hell is wrong with him?" I said more to myself than to Jesse.

"Long day. He's just tired. I'm sure tomorrow he'll wake up his usual Jax self—whoever that is—have a cup of coffee, call, and apologize. Then you two can get back to putting together kickass art shows."

My anger shut off like a switch had been hit. "Do you always have to see the good in everyone?"

"No, I don't have to. I just *choose* to."

I stepped into Jesse's arms. There wasn't a single wrinkle of concern on his forehead. Mine felt like it was pinched together with hundreds. "And you're with some- one like me because . . .?"

"Because I'm supposed to be with you." His answer came easily, effortlessly.

"What if tomorrow morning you wake up and *sup- posed to be* flies out the window?"

"No worries," he replied with a lift of his shoulder.

"'No worries'?" I rolled my eyes. "Really?"

"Really. Because whether *supposed to be* flies out the window tonight, or tomorrow, or fifty years from now, I'm not going anywhere because I'll always *want to be* with you."

I rested my head against his chest as a smile formed. "I feel like I should keep arguing because it's too soon to forfeit, but I think no matter what I argue back with, you've kind of got me on this."

"Yeah. You're right. I've really got you." One of Jesse's arms circled my waist as the other reached for my hand. "Dance with me." It wasn't a question. He was already moving to an imaginary beat.

"What? There's no dance floor. There's barely any music. There're bored millionaires wandering around just looking for something to lift their noses at." I liked danc- ing with Jesse. I might not readily admit it, but dancing with Jesse was one of the few things that gave me hope that the world wasn't eminently doomed.

"Come on. Dance with me." When he used that tone, the just-above-a-plea one, I'd learned months ago it was useless to put up a fight. I lost every time.

"Fine," I grumbled half-heartedly.

Staying right where we were, in front of the painting that made me as transparent as one person could be, he led me in a dance I knew I'd never forget. That was one of those moments that would be tattooed into my memory forever. I'd been living more and more of those since meeting Jesse Walker.

"You know I love to dance with you," he whispered, rubbing his thumb over the beading at my lower back.

"Remember our first dance?"

I felt his smile against my forehead. "How could I forget?"

chapter SIX

Rowen

SOMETIMES JESSE FELT very near, like last night when he curled around me in bed and held me until I fell asleep. And sometimes Jesse felt very far, like that morning when I woke up to an empty bed and cold sheets.

I didn't like him starting mile one of a five hundred mile trip at ten o'clock at night, but arguing with him was useless. Honestly, my heart was only half in the argument because extra time with Jesse was hard to argue with. Jesse had to be back on the ranch first thing Monday morning. When he didn't leave until Sunday night, he arrived back at Willow Springs barely in time for breakfast. That meant he went from driving for eight hours to working for twelve on no sleep. Not that I needed the confirmation, but Jesse Walker was some kind of superhuman.

Prying myself out of bed on those Monday mornings was always extra hard. I woke up knowing it could be upwards of a solid month before we saw each other again. I tried to make it to the ranch every month, but a couple of times work, school, or a combination of both had made those trips impossible. That Monday, however, was somewhat easier since spring break was less than two weeks away, and I'd get to spend a whole week at Willow

Springs. Just thinking about Willow Springs made me homesick. That might be silly given I'd only spent three months of my nineteen years there, but it was . . . *home.* At least by every definition of the word save for duration.

I wanted to give myself another minute to pout, but I forced my butt out of bed. The sooner I went to class, work, and my routine, the sooner spring break would get there. Hopefully. After getting showered and dressed, I sent Jesse a quick *Don't fall asleep in the cow pies. Miss you. Love you more.* text, I banged on Alex's bedroom door—I doubled as my roommate's alarm clock—before I unlocked my bike from the handrail just outside, and I was on my way. Jesse had worked his monthly magic on my bike. He must have replaced the brakes, too, because the lightest tap practically stopped me.

The ride to school only took about ten minutes, but on mornings like that, when the sky seemed to release a month's worth of rain in an hour, the ride felt a lot longer. Most days I was able to ignore the constant drizzle. No one complained about all the lush greenery, so I'd never understood why they threw such a fit about the rain that made it so green. Nothing beautiful had gotten that way without a little ugliness taking place behind the scenes.

When I pulled up to the art building, I don't think a single part of me was dry—my underwear included—but that didn't stop me from racing inside once I'd locked up my bike. I was so drenched, I sloshed—I actually *sloshed* —toward my first class. I don't think a single head didn't turn when I sloshed by. Most days, I didn't envy the kids who drove to school. That wasn't one of those days.

Art History of the Renaissance was my first class on Mondays, Wednesdays, and Fridays. Most history classes in high school had put me to sleep, but art history was totally different. It was a good-sized class, but the professor knew every one of our first names. As the T.A., Jax was available for regular study groups and test cram sessions.

I knew I was a few minutes late and prayed Professor Murray wouldn't issue his standard quip of *Nice of you to join us, Mr. or Mrs. such-and-such* before I scurried into a seat. When I eased the door open and took a tentative step inside, it looked like I was off the hook. No Professor Murray in one of his crazy bow-ties. Not one of the hundred students hunched into their seats. No one except for me . . . and someone who was neither a student nor a professor.

After Saturday night, he was someone I was not looking forward to seeing quite yet.

"Didn't you get the email?" Jax called to me from his desk. It looked like he was grading papers.

"What email? The one about you being an asshole?" Yeah, I was definitely not over it yet. "Because I definitely got that one."

He gave me that smug grin of his. "Haven't you heard? *Everyone's* gotten that email. But I was referring to the one about Professor Murray canceling class due to having a bad case of the flu."

"Well, I hadn't experienced your asshole ways up until Saturday night. I gave you the benefit of the doubt, and I now see the error of my ways." Those probably weren't wise words to aim at the man responsible for grading plenty of my papers, but I didn't care. If my G.P.A. took a dip, so be it. Telling him off was worth it.

"I am who I am. I make no excuses. I make no

apologies." Jax dropped his pen and rose from his seat. An expression I wasn't used to seeing on his face settled into place before he sighed. "I don't make apologies save for one exception."

I waited a minute for him to expound on that "one exception" thing, but my patience ran out. "I'm on pins and needles, Jax."

His eyes lifted to mine. A classroom separated us, but the look in them made me squirm. Too much intensity. "You. You're the one exception."

Those words did little to reassure me I was just misinterpreting his expression. "Do I want to know why?" I didn't really think so.

He shrugged. "Because you gave me the benefit of the doubt. You're the one exception because no one before you gave me that privilege." That was a bit too . . . *deep* for a Monday morning. "I'm sorry, Rowen. I *was* an asshole the other night, and even though some would argue that's my steady state, I try not to direct my asshole-ery your way."

As apologies go, it was a pretty good one, but I was having a tough time not laughing. "'Asshole-ery'?" I repeated, walking toward the front of the classroom. Well, *sloshing* toward the front of the classroom. "Where the hell did you pick up that gem?"

"The powers that be deemed asshole unfitting of someone of my level, so they created a whole new word just for me. Pretty special, right?"

He'd apologized, that heavy look in his eyes was gone, and he was back to exchanging witty banter with me. We were good.

"You're special, all right." I stopped a few feet in

front of him and bit my tongue to keep from teasing him about his outfit. Jax's motto wasn't just to *dress to impress;* he dressed to overwhelm. He wore slim-fit trousers, a tweed vest, and a checked skinny tie. His dark hair was meticulously styled, and not in the messy-I-just-rolled-out-of-bed-but-really-spent-a-half-hour-on-my-hair style. His hair was styled like a modernized version of Elvis's pompadour. Jax's skin was imperfection free, his nails never had dirt under them, and his dark eyes were ringed with a thick set of dark lashes. He was easy on the eyes—as dozens of girls who'd woken up next to him could attest to—but he wasn't what you'd call my cup of tea. I had a type, and Jax wasn't it.

Jesse was my type.

"Shit, Rowen. You're creating a lake." Jax took a few steps back, giving his shiny black boots a concerned look.

I glanced down and, sure enough, I was standing in an impressive puddle. From the looks of it, I'd leaked a solid gallon of rain water. "It's just water. Chill out."

"And these are *just* D&Gs." Jax rushed to the sink in the back and tore a handful of paper-towels free.

I shook my head, almost laughing. Jesse wore boots because they were meant to get dirty; I doubted Jax's boots had seen a speck of dirt.

Kneeling at my feet, Jax mopped up the puddle and then did something I wasn't expecting. After he'd tossed the wet paper-towels aside, he snagged his jacket hanging over the back of his chair and draped it over my shoulders. It was a nice jacket. Even someone like me, who'd purchased half of my wardrobe from second-hand stores, could see that.

"Better?" he asked.

"Yeah. Thanks." I hadn't expected his random act of concern, and it left me in unchartered territory.

"So . . . the artist and the cowboy, eh?"

Ah, there we were. Back in chartered waters. As obnoxious as he was, I'd take incorrigible Jax to concern-ed Jax any day. "Careful," I warned, giving him a look.

"The country boy and the city girl."

"Double careful."

"The good guy and the bad"—that time, I leveled him with a look—"the *great* girl," he corrected.

Before he went for another round, I crossed my arms and cleared my throat. "Haven't you ever heard that opposites attract?"

"I think I have heard that a time or two. You know what I've heard a lot more?" He didn't wait for me to reply. "Birds of a feather flock together."

He didn't have to waggle his finger between the two of us for his meaning to be obvious. That wasn't an argu-ment I was going to have with him. Opposites, identicals, and everything in between, that wasn't the be-all-end-all of why a couple got or stayed together. The X factor, the real binding agent, was in what couldn't be labeled, what couldn't be measured. Did Jesse and I make sense on paper? Probably not. Were Jesse and I about as different as two people could get? Probably.

Was I worried? Hell to the no.

What bound us together couldn't be seen or put into words. It was invisible. No word had been created for it. Fate, destiny, true love, soul mates were glorified, com-mercial terms that fell flat. I ascribed few words to what we shared, but one word I could, one word I felt the moment his fingers laced through mine, and that was . . .

eternal.

"I'm going now"—I hitched my thumb at the door as I backed toward it—"before we get back into asshole territory."

"Probably for the best. I wouldn't want my profound asshole-ery to ruin that equally profound once-in-a-lifetime apology I just made."

"I like the way you think." I slid off Jax's jacket and draped it over one of the chairs.

Jax tapped his temple before pointing my way. "I like the way *you* think." His dark eyes glimmered. "Birds of a feather, you know?"

"Bye, Jax." I didn't dim the irritation in my tone.

"You heard back yet on that internship at the museum?"

Only because his voice was clear again did I pause. "Not yet. I probably didn't get it. I think they would have let someone know by now." I'd applied to a summer internship position at one of the most prestigious museums in the Seattle area. I hadn't told anyone I'd applied, not even Jesse, because frankly, I felt silly. The paperwork stated clearly that they were looking for senior-level students, not to mention the mega-talented piece they'd said in a Human Resources friendly kind of way. Jax had learned about it because the museum had called to check my references and he'd been the one checking Professor Murray's messages that day.

"If they haven't called to tell you you've gotten it yet, then the position hasn't been filled."

I wished I had a hundredth of the confidence Jax had in my work. "Over-confident much?"

"I have to take up the slack for your utter lack of it,"

he replied, sliding his hands into his pockets. "You're talented, Rowen. You're a hell of a lot more talented than I was at your age." I fought the urge to roll my eyes. Jax was a T.A. for so many art classes because the professors were hoping even a smidgen of Jax's talent would rub off on the students. "You're the real deal. Don't let anyone, especially yourself, tell you you're anything less."

Since we were breeching into another topic I liked avoiding, I continued toward the door. "Bye, Jax."

"For real this time?" He started the morning with that smug smile, and he was ending it with the same one. I heard the damn thing in his voice.

"Bite me," I said with a bit more good-naturedness than I'd intended.

Jax chuckled. "Bye, Rowen."

chapter **SEVEN**

Jesse

"HEY, EARTH TO pussy-whipped Walker. Would you please stop leaving your balls in Seattle? I've been having nightmares ever since I saw those guys going at it in a tent in Brokeback. You gazing into a fire across from me with a dumb smile on your face while a tent looms off to the side isn't doing anything to ease my fears of getting Brokeback'ed out here."

I'd been in the middle of a daydream about Rowen and me in a happy place free of dickheads. Two seconds later, I was shaken free of that daydream to find I was across from one. "Filters." I picked up a twig and tossed it at him. "They'd make you a hell of a lot more pleasant to be around."

"Fuck filters," Garth said. "Filters are for guys who leave their testicles on their girlfriend's nightstand when they get up to leave."

I sighed and chugged the last of my Coke. Thanks to the unseasonably warm temperatures, calving season had started a few weeks earlier than normal which meant all of us at Willow Springs had to start our night watch rotation. I'd been the "lucky" one paired up with Garth, although I didn't think coincidence had anything to do with us being paired up like Dad had told me. I knew he hoped Garth and I would get back to being the kind of friends we'd been growing up, and against what I'd expected, Garth and I had made some progress in that whole forgive-and-forget thing. However, I guess Dad didn't think we'd made enough progress. Camping out with Garth Black a couple miles away from anything resembling human life was his way of forcing progress, I guess.

Dad and Mom still didn't know why Garth and I had fallen out. I hoped they'd never know. What was done was done, it was behind all of us, and the only thing that would come of them finding out about Garth and Josie was disappointment and maybe a bit of grudge holding.

That was all beside the point anyways. What had started as a tragedy had ended as a victory. I'd lost Josie. I'd lost my best friend. I'd found Rowen. Everything had worked out.

"Oh, and nice throw by the way." Garth threw the twig I'd tossed at him back at me. I leaned out of its way. "Given that girly throw, you must have left your dick behind, too."

"If I wanted to hit you, I would have."

Garth blew out a loud breath. "Please. Says the guy who didn't."

The next twig was an inch in front of his face before he noticed I'd moved. It bounced off the tip of his nose before tumbling to the ground.

Garth made a surprised huff while I laughed. "That was a bitch move, Walker." He rubbed his nose.

"Then stop saying stuff deserving of one."

"Damn." Garth acted like I'd just driven a knife into his face instead of a tiny twig. It had barely thumped him hard enough to leave a red mark. "Pussy-whipped little bitch."

"I can't decide if you're easier to deal with drunk or sober."

I stomped my empty Coke can and reached into the cooler for another one, offering Garth one, too. Dad didn't mind if the guys had a beer or two on night-watch, but Mom had packed Garth's and my cooler. She knew what I'd learned years ago: Garth didn't do moderation. At least not very well. It was all or nothing with Garth Black, and that was part of why being his friend was hard. It was also what made being his friend so much fun.

"Drunk. Sober. Doesn't matter. I'm not a fun person to be around."

"And here I thought we were having a blast."

Garth smiled tightly. "Fuck off, Walker."

Sunny picked that time to stomp his hoof back where he was grazing alongside Rebel, Garth's horse. Most of the time, Garth and I had to make sure to keep our horses apart because they'd get into it if one looked at the other the wrong way. At the end of the day, they seemed to work it out enough to graze alongside each other. Kind of like their human counterparts could sit across from each other at a campfire and talk "civilly."

"So? Rowen Sterling?" Garth's smile tipped up on one side. I didn't particularly like that smile when it followed the mention of my girlfriend. "How is the first girl in the history of the world to pick the good guy over the fiercely handsome, hung-like-a-stallion bad boy?"

"Rowen's good. Happy with her recent life choices. *Really* happy." I dodged the pebble Garth tossed my way.

"Sure she's not, shithead."

"Okay, the name-calling was endearing five hundred shitheads ago. One more, and you're going to start hurting my feelings."

"Sorry," Garth said, tilting his dark hat lower over his forehead. "Shithead."

Garth had always been the kind of guy who fit the *you can't teach an old dog new tricks* cliché, even when I'd met him when we were eight. Someone could devote their entire life to trying to change Garth, and it would be a wasted life. Garth changed for no one—not even for himself.

"Rowen's great, actually. She had a huge art show that kind of came up last minute when I was over there a couple of weekends ago. She sold almost every piece. A couple even went into a bidding war." I smiled into the fire. "God, Garth, she's so damn talented. You should have seen it. I know the general consensus is that we country folks are nothing but dumb hicks who wouldn't know Michelangelo from paint-by-numbers, but man. You could be the dumbest, blindest person on the planet and still feel something looking at one of her pieces."

"That art appreciation speech did nothing—*nothing*— to ease my Brokeback fears, Walker. Next time you decide to turn into a little girl, give me some warning, okay?"

Garth had been one of my best friends for over a decade, but most of the time, a rock would have been a better companion. "Don't make me drag you into that tent and do filthy cowboy things to you." I winked at him and blew a few air kisses.

Garth chuckled. "You are one sick son-of-a-bitch, Jess. I knew there was a reason we were friends."

"You mean it's not because we lift each other up and

bring out the best in the other?"

Garth almost choked on his sip of Coke. "No, that's definitely not the tie that binds because I think you suck. At everything. Hardcore."

"Thanks, friend."

Garth lifted the can my way. "So a big, fancy art show for Miss Sterling, eh? Not that I'm simpatico with art shows, but are most of them thrown together at the last minute?"

"No, I don't think so. I think they usually at least have longer than twelve hours to get it set up."

"Twelve hours, eh? And whose genius idea was that?"

"One of Rowen's T.A.s. Her friend Jax." Talking about Rowen made me miss her even more. Thank God spring break was a mere two days away.

"Is Jax a man or a woman?"

"A guy."

"And is this *guy* Jax . . . Rowen's T.A. or friend?" Garth's words were slow and deliberate. I didn't get where his sudden interest in Rowen's school life had come from.

I shrugged. "Both."

"Oh, hell no." Garth slapped his leg. "Please tell me you're not that dumb, Walker. Please don't tell me you believe this T.A. douche has weaseled his way into your girl's life because he really wants to be her friend."

"They *are* friends."

"Sure, friends to Rowen, but you know what he's after." Garth paused, waiting for something from me that never came. He rolled his eyes. "Jax the T.A. douche-packer is looking for a little friends-with-benefits action."

I felt my forehead wrinkle as I considered what he'd

just said. I wouldn't label Jax as upstanding, but he didn't seem like a snake either. Yeah, he'd been a bit of an asshole by not telling Rowen I was outside waiting for her, but that wasn't really a big deal.

Or was it?

Garth had planted a seed, and I was recalling that night with a whole new lens. Those lingering looks he'd given Rowen. The way he'd studied her hand in mine. Going out of his way to casually insult me and keep me out of the room. Did Jax have a thing for Rowen, or was it all a string of coincidences? I didn't know. I couldn't be sure. While I didn't like the idea of another guy putting the moves on Rowen, I trusted her implicitly.

"Shit. And I was the one who barely graduated high school. You might be book smart, Walker, but you are dumb as fuck when it comes to the rest."

"You graduated high school?" I made my best surprised face. I knew Garth had graduated. It was *just barely*, but that wasn't because he wasn't book smart. He just wanted everyone to think he wasn't. Well, that . . . and the girls. The girls were a definite distraction for Garth in high school. They still were.

"Go fuck yourself, Walker." Leaning into the pack behind him, Garth dropped his hat over his face. Guess I was taking the first shift.

"Do you have any other colorful vernacular in your vocabulary? Because when you use it every other sentence, *fuck* really loses its punch."

Garth sighed, muttering what sounded like another colorful vernacular. "Fine. Go *screw* yourself, Walker. How's that for packing more punch?"

"Better." I clapped a few times. "Bravo."

"We all know you've been doing plenty of screwing yourself with Rowen gone." He was muttering again, but he definitely meant for me to hear it. "So I suppose me telling you to go do it is redundant."

Sighing, I stood and stretched my arms above my head.

"Where the hell are you going?" Garth called as I headed into the field.

"Off to screw myself," I answered with a wave.

When Garth didn't have an immediate comeback, I glanced over my shoulder. He was sitting up, his expression a mixture of shock and disgust.

"Black, I'm kidding. I'm just checking on the horses."

"Dammit, Jess! Jerking off is not a joking matter!"

I chuckled as I approached Sunny and Rebel. They were munching away, content with their temporary truce.

"Back to the matter of spineless city boys moving in on one of our girls . . ." Garth was behind me, trekking through the tall grass with a couple of apples. Sunny and Rebel's heads snapped up. "You need to put that shithead in his place."

"And his place would be?"

Garth held out an apple to each horse and flashed me a wicked grin. "Beneath your boot."

"I'm not worried." That was a bit of a lie. The more I thought about it, the more Jax and his relationship with Rowen worried me.

"You should be."

"I trust Rowen."

"Good for you."

Garth's sarcasm was not lost on me. I'd had a decade

of it directed my way. "Black . . ."

"Listen, I'm not saying you shouldn't or you're wrong to trust Rowen. As far as girls go, she'd be the one to earn the trustworthy stamp. But that T.A. chump needs his ass kicked because not only is he not trustworthy, he's going to do anything and everything to seal the deal with Rowen."

I exhaled. "And you're so sure of this because?"

"He's a man. She's a woman. He's going out of his way for her." Garth counted off on his fingers. "A guy doesn't go out of his way like that unless he's hoping for, praying for, or expecting it to pay off in blow jobs."

"Garth!"

"Fine. Unless he's expecting it to pay off in fellatio." He nudged me. "Better?"

"No, not better. I'd prefer you to not mention Rowen, another guy, and . . . sexual favors in the same sentence ever again." That feeling, like my blood was heating, hit me again. I wasn't used to that sensation, but it had happened for the second time in two weeks. I didn't like feeling like a ball of instinct, but I couldn't control it. My body had declared war on my brain.

"I'm not trying to upset you, Jess. I'm trying to get you to pull your head out of your ass. I know you see the world as this place full of unicorns and rainbows and shit, but that's not reality. The world's mostly a nasty place with nasty people. Don't let your skewed view of it keep you from seeing a snake for what it really is." Garth paused for a few moments, and thank god he did, because he was saying a whole hell of a lot that took time to process. "Rowen loves the hell out of you, and I can see how much you love her. Part of loving someone is letting them do their own thing and trusting them. And part of loving someone is protecting them from the dark places and people." Garth clapped his hand over my shoulder. "So protect her from that piece of shit."

Garth thankfully gave me some space after dropping that mind-bender on me. He marched back to the fire, and I tried, failed, and tried again to work out what he'd just said. After a few minutes, I let out a long sigh and headed back. That wasn't something I'd work out in one night. That was something I'd need time to figure out. His advice went contrary to what I believed, but it made a hell of a lot of sense, too. Part of the job description in loving someone was protecting them. I knew that. I'd lived that. But had I, like Garth suggested, been blinded by a certain someone Rowen needed protecting from? Was Jax the kind of person she needed to be sheltered from?

Part of me said yes. Another part said no. I was pretty sure the intense internal battle would rip me in half if I didn't shelve the issue for a few hours. Either way, one thing was certain: I would pay a lot more attention. No more head up my ass where Jax was concerned.

Garth was sprawled on the ground on his pack, looking like he was hoping to squeeze in a nap, but I wasn't letting him sleep when he'd just gone and wound me up. I didn't want to talk about Jax anymore, but I wanted to talk about *something*. Talking was a great stress reliever for me, not to mention my favorite pastime.

"I saw Josie yesterday," I began, hoping to lure Garth in. Josie, Garth, and I had been inseparable until . . . well, until my best friend and my girlfriend slept together when I was out of town. "She stopped by to say hi to Jo."

"Good for Josie." Garth lowered his hat farther over

his face, his voice sharp.

"We all used to be friends. Why are you still so pissed at her? If anyone should still be pissed, it would be me."

He huffed. "Sorry, some of us don't follow that 'love and light' bullshit."

"And maybe some of us should . . ." I muttered as I dropped down to the ground.

Garth sat up suddenly, leveling me with a look. "Listen to me and listen to me good. I might have screwed her, but she *fucked* me. She fucked me up good, Walker." His voice was as dark as his last name. I couldn't often get a real emotional response from Garth, but that was one of the few times. "I don't want to think about Josie, and I sure as shit don't want to talk about her." Garth paused long enough to recompose himself. When he spoke again, all the emotion was gone. "I want to talk about that hot piece of ass you've got running around your house helping out your mom. Now that is a woman who looks like she knows the difference between screwing a guy and fucking him over, you know? You getting a little side action while Rowen's out of town?" He was back to his usual Garth self.

"Some of us believe in monogamy. Being faithful."

"Some of pretend to believe in it, but none of us really want to live that bullshit."

"Ever tried it?" I asked, tossing a few more pieces of wood into the fire.

"And ruin the good thing I've got going?" Garth extended his arms wide. "Why would I want to do that?"

"Because you have few redeeming qualities other than your dark charm and looks. And you're not getting any younger."

Garth replied with his middle finger. "Jess, Rowen's a solid girl. About as solid as I've ever met, and one of the few who'd even make me consider settling down, but we're twenty."

"So?"

Garth's eyes widened like I'd just gone mad. "You're telling me you're good with knowing your dick will never get up close and personal with another girl again? You're ready to throw away all of the fine conquests in your future for one girl?"

"Something tells me you think I'm the crazy one, but if you'd step into my boots for a second, you'd see that you are."

Garth made a face. "Whatever, Spineless."

"Whatever, Heartless." I leaned into the pack behind me. Maybe talking with Garth Black wasn't what I needed. Hoping to focus my attention on identifying constellations, I stared at the night sky for so long I was sure Garth was asleep.

"Just so you know, if you need a partner to kick city boy's ass into next year, I'm your man," Garth said over the dimming fire. "No one messes with my best friend."

"Best friend, eh?" I glanced over at him. He was still curled up, eyes closed and expressionless. Showing physical emotion was toxic to Garth.

"You're my only friend, Jess. You win the best title by default."

chapter **EIGHT**

Rowen

GIVEN THE HEALTH food madness rampant in America, a doughnut shop whose specialty was a bacon maple bar should not have been thriving. Especially in Seattle, where people rode bikes to work and ate kale chips for dinner. We should have had hoards of picketers out front preaching about how Mojo Doughnuts was clogging arteries in the Greater Seattle area and spreading diabetes like it was going out of style. I would have thought the whole food extremists would have burnt the place to the ground before allowing their children to enter a building where, no kidding, I got a sugar high just from sniffing the air.

But Mojo Doughnut was alive and well—it was Seattle's dirty little secret.

Alex had hooked me up with the job. She'd worked at Mojo through high school, and when she saw me filling out applications for the million and a half coffee shops in town, she uttered a *Hell, no*, ripped the stack into pieces, and basically dragged my butt to Mojo. She didn't ask the boss, she *told* the boss that I was working there. The boss, Sid, hadn't argued. He didn't even bat an eye. He told me I was starting that night.

Sid was a cool enough guy, I suppose. He was one of those rich Seattle people who paid a lot of money to look like they lived out of a tent. He lived in one of those modern condos down on the water and drove a brand new Volvo. He wore a lot of hemp, smoked a lot of pot, and his dreads were longer than my hair by a solid six inches. For a guy who sold close to four thousand doughnuts every day, he looked like he'd never eaten one. He wasn't scrawny, but if he lost ten pounds, he would have been.

Despite the I'm-homeless exterior and the fact he smelled like pot masked with patchouli, the guy was like damn catnip to women. Thankfully, not my kind of catnip. Even if I didn't have Jesse, if that was the brand of dude I was attracted to, I would have needed an exorcism.

Too bad my roommate didn't have the same opinion. Neither she nor Sid advertised their relationship—they were basically one relationship ring above fuck-buddies— but they sure as hell didn't do much to hide it, either.

As Alex, whose eyes were focused on Sid's closed office door, could confirm. I didn't mind working the late nights at Mojo, but I did mind closing with Sid and Alex. I shouldn't have to worry about feeling like a third-wheel at work . . .

Alex sashayed up to a life-size cardboard cutout. "Oh, Chewy, make wild Wookie love to me." Wrapping her leg around it, she gyrated against the cardboard to the beat of the disco music in the background.

I groaned and cleaned out the display cases of the remaining doughnuts. Whatever we didn't sell that day got tossed out. Every doughnut was made fresh that day.

"Chewbacca? Really?" I scanned the room that was as eclectic and strange as the doughnut selection. "You've got Luke. Han. Hell, even Vader"—I pointed at a few of the other Star Wars cutouts staggered around the room—"and you choose Chewy as your main squeeze?"

Alex couldn't have looked more offended. She draped her arm around the cutout that was a good foot taller than her and gave me a *Your point?* look.

"He doesn't even talk. He . . . roar-growls . . . or something like that." I'd seen Star Wars once and, after working at Mojo, I knew I'd never, ever want to watch it again. Sid was a hardcore movie paraphernalia collector—his favorite being Star Wars. I felt like I was living Star Wars thirty hours a week.

"He doesn't have to. His eyes say it all."

"Sure, they do."

Alex flounced by me, her outfit concocted of so many metals rings, grommets, and snaps she was a one-woman orchestra every time she moved. "You're lucky you make such kickass huevos rancheros or else you'd have earned the silent treatment after dissing my Chewy."

"Lucky me." I didn't hide my sarcasm.

When Alex kept heading for Sid's office door, I grabbed the remaining doughnuts double-time. Even with the disco music streaming through the place, I'd learned the hard way that I didn't want to be inside the same building when they got it on. I'd even tried earplugs, but I'd come to accept that they only way to save my inno-cent(ish) ears from that "earful" was to shove out the back door and wait in the alley until they came to their screech-ing, cursing end.

Alex had just closed the door when I snagged the garbage with one hand and the box of leftover doughnuts with the other. My pace quickened when I heard a growl coming from behind Sid's door. I couldn't tell if it was Sid or Alex. Scary.

Once I made it to the back door, I kicked it open and hustled into the alley. I made sure to prop open the door with a crumbling brick to keep from getting locked out. I sucked in a breath of the cool, rain-soaked air and felt excitement bubble up. I'd be breathing different air tomorrow night. We'd just had the last day of the quarter, which meant spring break was in session. If I could have caught a bus right after my classes, I would have. Unfortunately, the earliest bus to Montana wasn't scheduled to leave until the butt crack of dawn the next day.

Jesse. Willow Springs. One whole week. If there was a heaven, I was about to find it.

Snapping out of my daydreams, I heaved the bag of garbage into the dumpster. I was about to toss the box of doughnuts in when a strange and surprised sound came from inside the dumpster. A strange and surprised *human* sound.

Instead of running back inside Mojo, I grabbed hold of the rim of the dumpster and pulled myself up to peek inside. It maybe wasn't the smartest thing for a young woman in a dark alley all alone to do. Whatever had made that sound wasn't in a hurry to crawl out.

"Hello?" I called. The sight of the nastiness inside the dumpster was enough to level me, and that wasn't even taking into consideration the smell. Toxic sludge. That was the only explanation. "Anyone in there?"

Right then, the bag I'd just flung inside of it flew back out at me. I dropped down from the dumpster to avoid taking a direct hit.

"Yes! Someone is in here," a raspy female voice

called out. "And where do you get off thinking you can just toss your garbage anywhere you want?"

With so many out-of-the-norm things coming at me all at once, I couldn't decide what was the most odd. That someone was yelling at me from inside a dumpster, that someone had just used a bag of garbage as a weapon against me, or that I was accused of disposing of garbage in a . . . dumpster.

"Um, are you okay? Do you need a hand out or anything?" I wasn't used to talking to people camped out in dumpsters. I wasn't sure what common courtesies were customary.

"Since your hands are the ones that just dumped a sack of garbage on my head, no . . . no, I do not need a hand from you." Finally, a head appeared over the edge of the dumpster. Even though the alley was barely lit, I could still see that the woman had not seen the inside of a shower in weeks. Possibly even months.

"Oh my god. Are you okay?" I'd just tossed a bag of garbage on a person. I'd had plenty of low points, but that was another one to chalk up on the list.

"Do you see anything about me or my situation that would lead you to believe I'm *okay,* Girlie?"

I wasn't sure if she'd called me Girlie as a term of no-endearment, or because a few wires had been crossed and she thought that was the name on my name tag. That didn't seem like the time to clarify. Or correct her. "Here, let me give you a hand." I held up my hand and stepped closer.

"I don't think so. You've done enough." Then, in a not-so-graceful motion that had me biting my lower lip, she crawled up and over the lip of the dumpster. Her clothes were as dirty as she was, and they were really only hanging on by threads. Her canvas shoes were so worn her toes peeked through. Nothing about that woman, from her deep wrinkles to her emotionless eyes, said she'd lived anything but a hard life.

"Um . . . what were you doing in there?" My vocab skills were seriously lacking.

"Cleaning house," was her clipped response.

My face fell as my stomach twisted. "That's . . . that's your . . . *home*?" I'd been tossing garbage in that dumpster the entire school year. The thought that I'd been depositing refuse onto the poor woman's head for months did nothing to alleviate my upset stomach.

"Easy there, Girlie, before you pass out on me." The woman stepped toward me. "That's not my home; that was just my dinner reservation."

"Dinner reservation?" I said to myself, but she answered by pulling a half-eaten granola bar, a brown banana, and an almost-empty bag of sunflower seeds from the pocket of her worn trench coat. On their own, the snacks would have turned my stomach, but knowing where they'd come from made me feel the burn of bile rising in my throat.

"Are you hungry?" I was asking and saying some super stupid things.

"If I wasn't hungry, do you really think I'd be dumpster diving?"

"Probably not." I don't know if I was more bothered by her ironic tone or that I felt ashamed to have clean clothes and a full belly when people like her existed. My head dropped, and I noticed the box of marginally stale pastries between my hip and arm. "Here. Do you want these? They were made earlier this morning. I was just going to toss them." I didn't feel much better offering a hungry women a few dozen old doughnuts—what she needed was a balanced, nutritious meal—but it was all I had, and all of the fast food places within walking distance had closed a couple of hours earlier.

"What? Are those doughnuts?" The woman took a hesitant step forward, her eyes flicking my way every other blink. She almost reminded me of a feral cat, like she didn't trust anything or anyone.

"Yep." I held out the box.

Another careful step forward. "Are they . . . poison-ed?"

The skin between my eyebrows creased. "No."

"What's wrong with them then?" The woman inspect-ed them like every last doughnut was suspect.

I shrugged. "They're almost twenty-four hours old."

"That's all?" She said it like she didn't believe they were blemish free, but her hands were reaching for them.

"That's all. I swear."

When the box was about a foot from her hands, she lunged, snatched it right out of my hands, and dodged back toward the dumpster. She cradled the box like it was a baby and leaned into the dumpster. As she decided which doughnut to devour first, she kept one eye on me, watch-ing, waiting, like it wasn't a matter of if but *when* I'd do something underhanded to her. After settling on an apple fritter, she downed that sucker in three bites. She was on to her second fritter before I'd released the breath I'd been holding.

"If you're going to stand there gaping at me all night, talk or something." Chunks of doughnut shot out of her mouth.

"Talk about . . . *what*?" Dammit. I was seriously in the running for most moronic things to say to one person.

"Something. Anything. I don't care. I don't have conversations with a person on the other side that often, you know." Two doughnuts down, on to the third.

"A person on the other side?" I might as well keep with the moron-trend. "What other side?"

"Disillusionment." She actually stopped chewing to issue that show-stopper.

I thought over my response—I *really* thought it over—but one question kept sliding to the tip of my tongue. "And who's the one on the side of disillusionment?"

"The one who's convinced life can be a fairy tale."

I was silent for a few moments. Maybe she mistook that as me deciding how to form my rebuttal.

"In case you're trying to work out which one of us believes in fairy tales, let me tell you something, Girlie. Fairy tales have been dead to me since before you were even born."

"I don't believe in fairy tales. I believe in making my own damn tale."

The woman laughed manically between bites. "You and every one of us at some time. It doesn't last."

"What doesn't last? The idea or the reality?"

"Both."

I suppose if our roles were reversed and I was rolling around in a dumpster for dinner, I might have been just as doom and gloom. Hell, I'd been a numb version of doom and gloom a year ago. I wasn't that person anymore though, and I wouldn't go back.

"And don't get to kiddin' yourself that because

you've found a little patch of perfect that life's going to keep on keepin' on in the same way." I'd lost track of her doughnut count, but it certainly didn't look like she was slowing down. "Perfect isn't real."

"I've known that for a while. Perfect's fake." That wasn't a revelation.

"Not fake." For the first time, she lowered her doughnut and leveled me with a wild look in her eyes. "Just not of our world."

That was probably the point when I should have smiled, waved good-bye, and left the woman to her doughnuts. As time proved, I rarely went with what I "probably" should have done. "Perfect's not of . . . our world?"

She shook her head once, her eyes going up a notch on the wild scale.

"Then what world is perfect of?" It was official. I sounded like the newest member of the head-case club.

Clutching the doughnut box with one arm, she used her other to point at the ground. Her hand trembled.

"The asphalt? Perfect comes from the asphalt?" Yeah, I realized how stupid that sounded.

The woman's head shook as she pointed more firmly at the ground.

"The dirt?" One quick shake of her head. "The seismic plates?" Another shake. "The molten core of the earth?"

I knew with each guess I was getting farther and farther off my rocker, but I wasn't sure where she was going. For being such a chatty thing earlier, she wasn't saying much anymore.

She stuck her finger at the ground one last time before letting out a long sigh. I was obviously hopeless. "The dark place. The place of eternal damnation."

"Hell? Are you talking about hell?"

A nod. It was about time.

"Do you mean that in the figurative or literal sense?" I was almost afraid to have that question answered.

"Both."

And that was my crazy tolerance point. I didn't do the whole heaven and hell, saved and damned song and dance. She could keep up the conversation with the dozen dough- nuts I guessed she had left. I was just about back inside Mojo when she spoke again.

"Just because you refuse to see something doesn't mean it isn't real."

"And just because you think you see something doesn't mean it's real either." I wasn't racking up points in the let-crazy-be department, but something about her last words had unsettled me.

"At last, we agree, Girlie." Her voice wasn't shaking anymore. In fact, if I hadn't seen her before, with my back to her, I would have guessed she was a sweater-set wear- ing mom of three. "Just because you've convinced you love and are loved in a way that seems like it will go on forever doesn't mean it will. That's not real either. There's no such thing as expiration-free love."

I was really regretting not escaping when I'd gone for it. Why did crazy people have to make so much sense?

Oh, yeah. Because the world was one sick, crazy fuck most of the time.

chapter **NINE**

Rowen

I WOULD HAVE thought each twelve-hour trek on the good ol' Greyhound would get easier, or less traumatic at least, but the opposite seemed to be true. When I lumbered off the bus, I was half tempted to buy one of those reliable, five-hundred-thousand miles to the gallon cars Jesse had encouraged me to pick up at the beginning of the year. Anything to keep from cramming in between a couple of linebacker-sized guys who thought eau de funk was that season's scent.

I wasn't last off the bus, but I still received my share of stares. I didn't get nearly as many sideways glances when I was getting off in Seattle, but out there . . . well, my funky, dark style hadn't made its way east yet.

In honor of Montana, I had on the cowgirl boots Jesse had gotten me last summer. Since, wonder of wonders, the weather was almost summer-like, I had on a purple shift dress, the beat-to-shit motorcycle jacket I'd found at the Salvation Army last fall, and the denim ass purse (as I'd endearingly named it). After enduring two quarters of my natural hair color, I'd colored it darker again. Not black like before and not because I was trying to hide behind it. Because . . . well, I wanted to and I could. Jesse didn't care what color hair I had so long as I had some. Actually, he probably wouldn't have cared if my hair fell out. He was all noble like that.

I was the second to last person to step off the bus—small victories—and took in a long, deep breath. Montana still smelt a bit like cow shit, but nothing beat the feeling of stepping onto Montana soil and breathing its air while knowing my favorite people in the whole world were within arm's reach.

"There's a pair of legs a man could never forget."

Okay, *some* of my favorite people in the world. And some of my not-so-favorite.

"And there's a face a woman *wished* she could."

"Rowen Sterling," he said with his dark smile. In his dark clothes. With his dark ways.

"Garth Black. Minus the enthusiasm." I made sure not to return his smile. Garth and I had made some serious progress in the friendship department, but it was kind of a contest to see who'd blink first. Instead of blinking, the loser was the first one to smile . . . and not that curved-at-the-corners one he flashed most of the time. The emotion behind *that* was the opposite of a smile. We were talking about whoever cracked a real, honest-to-goodness smile aimed at the other person first. "Where's Jesse?" He'd always picked me up. He'd always been the first person I saw when I stepped off the bus. He would beam and wave, with a new white tee and still fresh from the shower. It was actually one of my favorite sights: Jesse Walker in all his glory waiting for me.

My second favorite sight? The view later that night when everyone else was asleep.

"Emergency." Garth lifted a shoulder and snagged my

giant black duffel from the storage compartment.

I froze. "What kind of emergency?" So many different kinds of emergencies could crop up from the kind of work he did that I'd started having recurring nightmares. Getting stampeded by the cattle, getting bucked off a horse over the edge of a cliff, and the most gruesome one of all gave away that I'd seen way too many horror movies in my lifetime—Jesse tripping and falling chest-first into a pitchfork. I woke up in a cold sweat whenever I had that one.

"Relax, señorita. No emergency involving Jesse or any part of his body you like to get freaky with."

His reassurance, pithy as it was, unfroze me. "What happened then? Who was involved? Are they going to be all right?" I slid up beside Garth and matched his pace into the parking lot.

"Don't know."

"You don't know."

"Nope."

"You didn't think to ask?" My eyes were scanning for Old Bessie. When I realized that would be the first drive from the bus station to Willow Springs I'd taken without the ancient rust-can, I felt a little . . . *sad.*

"Nope."

"Really?"

"Nope."

"Anything other than *nope* you'd like to add?"

"Nope," he replied, his eyes gleaming.

I groaned. Of course I'd be stuck with the most cryptic cowboy ever created when the words *Jesse* and *emergency* had come up. Again. It wasn't the first time those two words had been joined. Even though it didn't involve him directly, I hoped I'd never have to hear them combined again.

"Listen, before you go and start ripping out that once-again dark hair of yours, here's the deal. Jesse called me a couple of hours ago, said there'd been an emergency and he might not be able to get here soon enough to pick you up. He asked if yours truly,"—Garth stuck his thumb into his chest—"would swoop in, save the day, and pick you up. End of story. Any questions?"

I felt a little better. If the emergency Jesse was a by-stander in could be fixed in a couple hours, lost limbs, pints of blood loss, and bullets wouldn't have been involved. I hoped. "That's all he said? There wasn't anything else?"

We stopped at the tailgate of an older Ford pickup. From the color, I had a pretty good guess who its owner was.

"Yeah. There was something else." Garth lifted his brows and waited.

"I'm dying here, Black." I crossed my arms and lean-ed into the truck.

"He said to keep my hands, booze, and cock to myself or he'd rip me a new one."

I crossed my arms tighter and gave him a stern look.

"Fine. He didn't say *cock*. Only a real man with a legitimate one uses *cock* when speaking about what swings between the knees. I think Jesse said *little willy* or *wee one* or something like that."

"Anyone ever tell you you're way too fixated on what you *wish* swung between your knees?" I lifted a brow at him.

He lifted two at me. "Here's a secret, Rowen. All

men, every single one, are fixated on their johnsons. Anyone who tells you they aren't are full of bull—" Garth stopped himself, bit the inside of his cheek, and seemed to be working out something. "Full of it. Yeah, they're full of it."

"Thank you, edited version of Garth Black." I shot him a curious look. "If there's nothing else you'd like to add to this scintillating conversation, mind if we head out?" I started for the passenger door when Garth dramatically cleared his throat.

"Actually, there is something I'd like to add."

Of course there was. "What?"

"Wanna repeat that night of booze, lawn chairs, and moaning over an almost kiss?" His smile was so wide, his teeth lit up the night.

"Wanna keep your testicles?" I smiled a just as fake and overdone smile as the one coming at me.

"Only on days that end in *y.*" Garth chuckled and tossed my bag into the bed of his truck. It didn't make the thumping sound I was used to hearing when my bag was tossed into the bed of a truck. No, it made something more muffled, almost noiseless. I peeked in the back as I stepped up inside of the cab. Well, that would explain it.

"Dost my eyes deceive me or is that a mattress in the bed of your truck?"

"Your eyes dost not deceive you." Garth slid into the driver's seat.

"Why?" I asked needlessly, twisting around and fastening my belt.

Garth grinned into the windshield. "What do you think a guy like me would be doing with a mattress in the bed of my truck?"

My nose curled. "Filthy things, me thinks."

"The filthier the better." Garth waggled his eyebrows at me before peeling out of the parking lot. I might have missed Montana every minute I was away from it, but I did not miss the drivers.

A rare few minutes of silence passed. The dark roads and the truck's gentle vibrations were lulling me to sleep. Since I'd closed the night before at the doughnut shop, I hadn't gotten home until almost two in the morning. My bus left at seven, so that left three, maybe four hours of sleep time . . . which I had gotten maybe fifteen minutes of thanks to the crazy lady crawling out of the dumpster and saying bat-shit crazy things that kept me up all night.

"So? How are the nuptials coming along? Picked out your colors yet?"

I cranked the window down halfway. It was getting a little Garth heavy inside the cab. "So? How's your right hand? Fed up with you yet?"

"I'm left-handed."

I rolled my eyes. "How's your *left* hand?"

"Truthfully?" He lifted said hand and turned it over, inspecting it. "A little neglected."

"What poor girl are you seeing this month who's going to get a restraining order next month?"

Garth swung around a corner at such a hell-raising speed, I checked to make sure we hadn't lost my duffel. "You change that *girl* to the plural form, and I'll give you a list of names. The ones I remember."

"Wow. Someone's really taken their exaggeration tendencies to a whole new level."

Garth tilted his head back and laughed a few hard notes. "I don't know what we do without you, Rowen. My confidence was almost back to its prior glory before you stepped off that bus and started firing insult after insult my way."

"Someone has to keep that Zeus complex of yours from getting out of control."

"*Getting* out of control?" Garth's tone gave me the verbal equivalent of a nudge.

"Getting *more* out of control," I clarified.

"Speaking of getting out of control, that reminds me . . ." I was already cringing. I'd learned that when "that reminds me" came out of Garth Black's mouth with that level of sarcasm, nothing good could come of it. "Jesse mentioned a T.A. slash *friend* of yours who hooked you up with some last minute sweet art gig . . . show . . . rodeo . . . thing."

"Art rodeo? Really, Black?"

"I don't know what all you art people call your snooz-fest get-togethers. Give me a break, Rowen. I don't speak Lame."

"And I don't speak Idiot," I grumbled. Next time Jesse couldn't pick me up and Garth Black showed up in his place, I was hitching a ride back to Willow Springs. Or hoofing it.

"Your eagerness to dodge the topic leads me to the conclusion that you're uncomfortable talking about a certain T.A. slash friend."

Oh, dear sweet Jesus. "Jax?" I twisted in my seat. "Are you talking about Jax?"

"Yep. That's the one." Garth snapped his fingers. "That's the little fu . . ." Garth froze with his mouth open. The skin between his eyebrows came together. "Fu fu, fu, fu-fu-fu . . ." He was truly at a loss. It was a rare moment to witness with Garth Black. I was going to bask in it.

"Fu, fu, fu . . . *fucker*? Is that the word you were going for? Because that's one of the few that always seems to be on the tip of your tongue."

"That's the one," Garth said, able to form words again.

"And you were having a tough time saying it because . . .?"

After a few moments of deliberation, he hit the steering wheel. "Because Jesse and I made a bet."

"A bet?" Oh, great. That ought to be good.

"Yes. A bet. We've been sitting a lot of night-watches in the fields, and I guess he was worn out on my proclivity toward profanity and I was bored as all fu—" He caught himself again but just barely.

"I don't know whether to be more impressed that you haven't said your favorite word in the past twenty minutes or that you just used—*correctly*—the word proclivity."

"Be impressed by it all. There's plenty of it to go around when I'm close by."

"Enough self-trumpeting. Get back to this bet."

Garth sped through Willow Springs's front entrance so fast I almost missed it. "What's there to get back to? Jesse bet me I wouldn't be able to give up cussing for a whole month, and I bet him that he wouldn't be able to give up . . ." A lopsided smile twisted into place.

"That he wouldn't be able to give up what?"

"That's for me to know and you to find out. The important part is that I will be declared the victor come morning because there is no way Walker will be able to hold up his end of the bet tonight. The past couple of weeks, no big deal, but tonight? He's totally fu—" That was getting old fast. "*Foiled*. Tonight he's totally foiled."

"Foiled? What the hell, Black? Who are you and where did the hick go?"

"Oh, Rowen, finally. My self-esteem is back in the sewer where it belongs. Thank you." Garth slammed the truck's brakes in front of the house. The porch lights were glowing, and soft yellow light streamed from all of the windows. Even the one at the top, next to the chimney. I smiled, remembering dozens of the nights worth remembering. "Oh, and thank you for real for being the reason I'm going to wake up the winner of this bet. I owe you one."

"No, you won't owe me one. Now that I know about this bet between you boys, I'll do everything I can to make sure Jesse comes out on the winning side." I threw open the door and set foot on Willow Springs soil. I had to fight the urge to get down and kiss it.

"Fine. Fight it together. Stand by your man. Doesn't matter to me." Garth snatched my duffel out of the bed and grinned—I swear he actually grinned—at the mattress that was growing who knows what before sliding up beside me. "Come morning, y'all are going to be chanting *all hail the victor,* or you and Walker are going to be cross-eyed and tortured. I'm going to be laughing my way into next week."

"Two minutes. Quiet. Think you can manage?" Of course I already knew the answer.

"That's a negative. Besides, you haven't given me the juicy, illicit details about your relationship to the little Jax f'er."

Never had I climbed the steps to the Walker household in such a state of irritation. "What? He grades my papers? Sometimes we talk about what we did over the weekend? If you consider that juicy and illicit, then you really need to get out more, Black."

"Don't play the coy card with me, Ms. Worldly. You and I both know a guy doesn't ask a girl about her weekend if he doesn't have some shenanigans up his sleeve. Guys, straight ones, do not keep girls as friends unless they're hoping to get between their legs."

I let out an exasperated sigh. We were a few feet from the front door, so close I could hear and smell the sounds and scents of coming home . . . and someone's words were ruining the moment. "There's so much wrong with that last sentence I'm going to mentally repress it—for the rest of my life—and walk through that front door like you haven't been talking crazy all night long."

"To further prove my point that you're aware of Jax's underlying intentions. . . I present exhibit number one." Garth's hand flashed up and down at me. "Overly emotional."

"How's this for 'overly emotional'?" I waved my middle finger in front of his face.

"Proving my point even further."

"What? Is that what Jesse said? That he's concerned about Jax's and my relationship?" I couldn't really conceive of that. Jesse and jealousy lived on opposite ends of the galaxy.

"No, he didn't say that. *I* did." Garth's dark eyes flashed. "Just because Jesse likes to see the best in everyone doesn't mean I have to. He might not be concerned about the snake slithering toward his girl, but I am. I'm telling you, as a friend, as a guy, and as a fellow slithering snake"—I clapped a couple of times at his estimation of himself—"that this guy is up to no good. I'm not asking you to sock him in the jaw, I'm not asking you to twist his testes off, I'm asking that you have your guard up. Okay?"

Garth didn't only sound concerned; his expression actually matched his tone. I wasn't used to witnessing concern from Garth Black. It took me so off guard that might have been the only reason I agreed. "Okay. My guard's up." I smiled at him as I reached for the door handle. "Happy now?" I realized my mistake a second too late.

Garth beamed over at me. "I win."

My smile fell. "Bite me."

Garth bit the air in my direction. "All hail the victor."

I elbowed him in the stomach as I pushed through the door. I'd had enough Garth for the month. Garth had won our stupid, infantile game, but he sure as hell wasn't going to win whatever bet he had going with Jesse. I was making that a top priority.

The foyer was empty and quiet when we took our first step inside, but it wasn't by the time we took the second. A chorus of *She's here* echoed through the house. Clementine and Hyacinth skidded in from the living room, followed by Lily and Neil. Rose rushed in from the kitchen, a beater in her hand and flour dusting her face.

I braced myself as the two youngest Walkers tackled me. I might have been bigger than them, but they were five times as strong as me individually. When they came at me together, it felt like they were at least a hundred times stronger.

Garth backed away slowly like the squealing and tackle hugs were making him uncomfortable. In a prior life, the one I'd lived less than a year ago, they would have made me so uncomfortable I would have been permanent-ly scarred. I couldn't get enough of them now. I think I was making up for lost time.

"Quick, girls. Steal her away before Jesse gets back," Rose instructed. She managed to get an arm around me and slip in a squeeze. "When he gets here, he'll lock you away and we won't see you for a while. I didn't realize I'd raised such a selfish man." Flashing me a wink, Rose inclined her head toward the kitchen.

I was familiar with what came next. Even though the bus from Seattle arrived late, at least late for people who got up at four in the morning, Rose always had a warm plate of dinner waiting for me. While I gorged myself on a home-cooked meal, the rest of the family would gather around the kitchen table with a plate or bowl of whatever that night's dessert was, and we'd catch up until more yawns than words circled the table. Neil was always the first to "hit the hay" as he called it. Clementine and Hyacinth were close seconds, and I felt the only reason Lily and Rose finally headed to their bedrooms was so that Jesse and I could have some time alone.

Reunion night had become a time-honored tradition.

"How's school?" Rose asked as she pulled a Saran-covered plate from the microwave.

"Great. I just had a huge show and pretty much sold every piece."

Garth must have followed us because I heard him clear his throat loudly. I shot him a warning glare. He responded with a wink.

"Jesse told us about that. It sounded like it was quite the event, and he said the pieces you had on display were absolutely amazing." Rose set the steaming plate of enchiladas in front of *my* chair at the ginormous dining table. Yes, they'd designated me a seat. I knew they didn't think much of the gesture, but it had left me bleary-eyed when I'd found out.

"It was pretty awesome." I had to remove each Walker girl's death grip from my waist to sit down. They all clamored into their seats around me.

"I wish we could have seen it. I haven't been to Seattle since . . . well, since so long I can't even remember." Rose sat across from me and gave me one of those warm smiles I wasn't sure I'd ever get used to.

"We'll take the whole family over and make sure we hit the next one," Neil said. He approached the table with a plate of Rice Crispy treats in one hand and a cup of coffee in the other. When Neil wasn't working, he almost always had a cup of coffee in one hand. "What do you think, girls? You up for a trip to the big city next time Rowen has a big, fancy art show?"

Three heads bobbed eagerly.

"It's settled then. I hope you won't mind sharing your apartment with six more people, Rowen." Neil shot me a wink as he took his seat.

"Neil . . ." Rose settled a hand on her hip, giving him a look. "I know you're not a big fan of them and spend as little time in them as you can, but big cities have really great things known as hotels. Maybe we could rent a couple of rooms. Maybe we could go crazy and rent a couple of five star ones."

"Five star?" Neil's forehead lined.

"Never mind. The girls and I will handle all that."

"Has anyone heard from Jesse yet?" I knew it was an abrupt turn in the conversation. I'd tried to repress the question, but not knowing the details of the emergency Jesse was somehow involved in was making me uneasy. Everything must have been mostly okay or the Walkers wouldn't have been going about their business as usual, but I doubted I'd be able to eat a bite of dinner if I didn't find out what was going on.

"They should be pulling up any minute now. I got a call from Jo earlier saying they were coming home," Rose answered.

I sighed. He was on his way. Jesse would be there soon. Emergency situation had passed. "What happened?"

"Jo can't chew gum and walk at the same time," Garth muttered. He was sitting down at the other end of the table.

Rose gave him a look that I think was meant to be intimidating, but it was more filled with maternal amuse-ment. "Sprained ankle, it sounds like. We were worried something had broken, so a minor sprain was a relief."

"Who's Jo? Jo as in Josie?" I'd gotten to know all of the ranch hands, and Jo wasn't one of them.

"No, not Josie. Someone I just brought on to help me and the girls out," Rose answered.

"Wow. Go, Jo. I need to meet this guy who's up to the challenge of keeping up with the four Walker women." That was when I heard a familiar sound. A rumbling, sputtering noise accompanied by the sound of crunching gravel. Only one truck in the world could make that pathetic of a sound and still manage to get me all worked up.

"You can definitely meet Jo, but I think you're going to be disappointed if you're looking to meet a guy," Rose replied.

I stopped chewing. "Jo's not a guy?"

"No. Jo is *definitely* not a guy," Garth said. I wasn't looking at him, but I didn't need to be to know what smile was on Garth's face.

"We call her Jo, but her name's Jolene. She's only been with us for a few weeks, so that's why you haven't had a chance to meet her yet."

"And that's who Jesse took to the emergency room tonight?"

Lily nodded. "She was out delivering the guys' dinner when she tripped into a gopher hole or something like that."

"And Jesse was the only one around to take her to the emergency room?"

"No, but he was the only one around who was brave enough to drive Old Bessie through the fields and into town."

I set my fork down on my plate. "Jo was driving Old Bessie?"

"She drives it all the time when she takes out the guys' meals." Lily gave me a confused look like she couldn't understand why I seemed so surprised.

"She drives Old Bessie," I repeated, more to myself than anyone else. I don't know why that was so upsetting. Maybe because I thought Jesse and I were the only people brave enough to drive it, or maybe because—from the way Garth's had voice had basically made love to Jo's name—I didn't like the idea of some goddess in cowgirl boots driving my boyfriend's truck.

"She also was Miss Montana last year. Just in case you were wondering, or hoping, she fell from the ugly tree"—Garth was eating up my discomfort—"she didn't.

Not even close."

I wished innocent eyes and ears weren't close by, keeping me from saying and doing the things I wanted to.

"She's also a gymnast. Flexible. *Super* flexible." Garth clasped his hands on the table and leaned in. "And she has a thing for cowboys. Blond, strapping, smiling-idiot variety cowboys . . . so you girls already have something in common."

Those enchiladas were not looking so appetizing anymore. Other than throwing them at Garth's smug face, I didn't have much use for them. I was at the point between considering and acting out on my enchilada-tossing fantasy when I heard a pair of footsteps coming up the front steps. One set sounded sure, the other set . . . hobbled.

"Sounds like that's all the Rowen hoarding we'll get tonight." Rose stood from her chair. I shot out of mine. We made like a caravan and headed for the front door. That time, Garth wasn't taking up the rear; he was leading the stampede.

Opportunistic bastard.

I barely had a second to suck in a breath and roll back my shoulders before Clementine threw open the door. "Jesse!" She screeched her standard brother-worship greeting. It didn't matter if she'd gone days or seconds without seeing him. Her greeting always held the same level of enthusiasm.

Jesse had just scaled the top step and was slowly making his way through the door. He wasn't alone. A chick who I assumed was Jo had one arm draped over his shoulders as she hobbled pathetically beside him. I'd sprained my ankle a few times before and never once had a sprain constituted clinging to a person that way. The way she clutched his shoulder and looked at him with those big doe eyes of hers made my claws come out. When she giggled as they wove through the front door, my claws were ready for some serious slashing.

"See what I mean? That is definitely not a man," Garth whispered to me, nudging me in the ribs.

"Oh, go and have relations with your left hand," I snapped quietly enough the girls wouldn't hear me.

"I'd rather have relations with her"—Garth lifted his chin toward Jo—"but something tells me she'd rather have relations with a different cowboy. Heads up, Rowen. That goes for your *and* Jesse's affairs." With one last nudge, Garth wove through the Walkers toward Jesse and Jo.

As soon as they were in the foyer, Jesse's eyes searched for me. They locked on me almost immediately, and his smile moved into place. The one that chased away any and every doubt and insecurity I had festering inside of me.

Garth moved up beside Jo to relieve Jesse, and before Garth's arm had wrapped around Jo's waist, Jesse was lunging toward me. I had time to give Garth an apprecia-tive smile and notice the look of disappointment on Jo's face. The chick really did have a thing for my boyfriend. Not good.

But then all was good again. Jesse's arms wound around me before lifting me. "I'm so sorry I missed you earlier. It killed me not being there to pick you up."

I'd forgive a million times over when he hugged me that way. "Being trapped inside a moving vehicle with Garth Black almost killed me too."

Jesse chuckled into the bend of my neck, gave me one

more squeeze, then set me back down. "It won't happen again."

"Let's hope not. Let's hope you can't sprain the same ankle twice." I moved just far enough to the side to lock eyes with a certain someone who seemed unable to pry hers from a certain part of Jesse that made me every shade of territorial.

I knew every last female who wasn't related to him checked out Jesse's backside when he passed by—hell, I'd probably been the worst offender—but that girl . . . well, for some reason, her checking out Jesse's backside got under my skin more than the rest.

Jesse and I didn't do territorial. Or at least, we *hadn't*. It looked like I would be the one to break that rule.

"Oh, hi. You must be the Rowen this guy can't shut up about." Jo circled her finger Jesse's direction.

"I must be." I stepped out from behind Jesse and angled myself in front of him. Yeah, because my hundred and twenty pounds could protect him from whatever I suddenly felt he needed protecting from. "I don't know who you are, though. Jesse hasn't mentioned you."

Garth let out a low, "Meeeooow," and tried to hide his smile.

If my arms were long enough, I would have bitch-slapped that smirk off his face.

"Oh, my gosh. Where are my manners?" When she hobbled my way, I noticed she wasn't clinging to Garth like she had Jesse. In fact, she was barely using him at all. Much to Garth's dismay. "I'm Jolene. It's great to finally meet you." The miraculously cured girl stopped in front of me and smiled, and dammit if it didn't look like a genuine one. If it was one of the syrupy fake ones begging to form on my own face, it would have been easier to hate her guts. That smile, along with the biggest pair of brown eyes I'd ever seen, made gut-hating hard to attain. When her gaze flicked to Jesse and that smile grew, it became a little easier again.

What I really wanted to do was wave, grab Jesse, and do things to him all night that would make me blush in the morning. Because the Walkers were staring at me with growing concern and Garth was practically holding his breath for a girl-e-girl cat fight, I forced a smile. "It's nice to meet you, too."

"Jesse tells me you're going to school in Seattle?" As soon as I nodded, she added, "At a community college, right?"

That was true, and I wasn't ashamed I was attending a community college while I stowed away money for a four-year school, but the way Miss High Horse had said it . . . well, it certainly sounded like she meant it as a jab. Or was I way off?

"That's an affirmative." I teetered back and forth on my heels and toes, a sure sign I was getting worked up. "I also work at a nutty doughnut shop where I make minimum wage, and I ride a bike older than me since I don't own a car. Oh, and almost my entire outfit came from a thrift store." There. If she was throwing a jab with the community college comment, I'd just glazed over a few other hot topics.

"Are you kidding me? That outfit is from a thrift store? No way. I never find anything good or in my size."

Since her size was rail thin with jumbo tits, I figured she had a tough time finding stuff in her size anywhere.

"And wait . . . is that . . ." She zoomed in on my

denim bag.

"Yep. It is." I patted it possessively. "Rose made it for me out of a pair of Jesse's old jeans."

And she started eye-molesting my bag. "I thought that looked like a familiar sight."

I exhaled slowly. A *familiar sight* was visiting the same vacation place every year; the way Jolene was mind-fucking Jesse's ass was something else entirely. "So you're working here? Helping out Rose and the girls?" I felt another twinge of possessiveness. "No community college for you then, eh?"

"I just got back from almost a year-long Peace Corps mission, and since I've got a few months before I head out on my next one and I had plenty of time on my hands, Rose asked if I'd help out." Jolene smiled at Rose, who was watching us just like everyone else in the room was: with guarded interest. "I'm thrilled to be working at one of the most renowned ranches in the state."

Two words. Kiss. Up.

Then something else registered. "Did you just say Peace Corps? As in you're a member?"

Her smile turned my way, and she bobbed her head. "For the past year."

Yeah. I was going to hell. "Is that like a lifelong career sort of thing?" I'd graduated with a couple of kids heading off to join the Peace Corps. They were rich kids who thought they were above the material, capitalist, American mentality, but really, they just wanted to piss off their parents. Both of them were back in Portland and working a Starbucks drive-through a month later.

"Well, it can be. I'm just planning on doing it for a couple of years. I wanted to give something back before I did something selfish and committed to seven years of school."

Neil had drifted back into the kitchen, probably because the Rice Crispy treats were calling his name, and Clementine followed. Everyone else was still staggered around the foyer, letting Jolene and I own the conversation.

"Do most people go to school for seven years?" Of course, the pessimistic critic inside of me picked that one thing to run with. Not the unselfish, Peace Corps part.

"The ones who want to become doctors do."

Her smile was rubbing me the wrong way. Big time. It might have been real, but I was about to really remove it if she didn't dim it a few hundred volts. Peace Corps. Future M. D. Gorgeous to the tenth degree. A kiss up to the hundredth. Oh yeah, and she was so hot for my boyfriend I could feel her ovaries pulsing. What Jesse Walker saw in me over someone who redefined perfect, I didn't know, but I wasn't going to waste any more time fleshing it out.

Jesse said, "It's been a long day for all of us. I'd say it's about time to wrap it up." My god, that man had impeccable timing.

I'd been in front of him for close to five minutes and we had yet to kiss. That was unacceptable. Sure, his family was staggered around the room, but we'd never let that stop us. We toned it down to a PG level when they were around, but the whole reason I'd failed to kiss the man who made ovaries pulse near and far was because I'd let some real-life Sleeping Beauty lookalike mess with my head. No more messin'. Wait, scratch that. No more messin' unless it included messin' around with Jesse

Walker.

"And by wrap it up, you mean it's time for *us* to wrap it up." Rose circled her fingers to include everyone in the foyer except for Jesse and me.

Jesse's dimple formed as he gave his mom a sheepish look. "Maybe?"

"Oh, fine. I suppose you've earned a quiet night with Rowen to yourself, but tomorrow I won't give up so easily."

"Thanks, Mom." Jesse's hands formed over my shoulders, and he guided me to the front door. Someone was a little eager and unconcerned about showing it.

"Thanks, Mom," I said, lowering my voice in a bad attempt to mimic Jesse. I managed to give Hyacinth and Lily quick hugs before Jesse sped me through the door. "I've got presents for all of you. Let's have a girls' get-together tomorrow. No boys allowed." I elbowed Jesse's ribs lightly. He groaned like it was anything but. "Sound good?"

"Sounds great," Lily replied, tucking her hair behind her ears.

"Especially the no boys allowed part," Hyacinth added, giving Jesse an accusing look.

"Oo, that sounds like fun. I can't wait," Jolene squee'd, clapping her hands.

I suppose I should have clarified the girls' get-together rules, like thou shalt not covet the other girls' boyfriends. I wondered if I could get that stamped onto a shirt I could wear around a certain someone.

"You kids be good now. I'd hate to win a bet this easily." Garth winked as we passed him and Jolene.

"You're not winning *another* thing tonight, Black.

Get that through your dark skull and darker head now."

Rose was following the girls into the kitchen when Jesse whacked Garth in the stomach. "Go cuss already. You know you're about to die from keeping-it-all-inside poisoning."

"Nah, I don't think so. Tonight's the first night of the past two weeks I'm actually tickled pink we made that little bet."

"Tickled pink? What the hell, Black? What has happened to you?" I asked.

Jesse moved his mouth outside my ear. "See? It's already happening. Talking in little girl words is the first sign he's about to keel over from poisoning." Jesse wrapped his arms around my waist and continued for the door. "Come on, Black. Just get it out. It will all be over soon, and I promise, I won't gloat in my win. Too much."

Garth made a crude motion with his hand. Jolene cringed and moved away as he continued pumping his fist in front of his crotch. "Take notes, Walker. That's the only action you're going to be getting for a while."

"And that's our cue to leave." Jesse guided me the rest of the way onto the porch.

"Good night, Jesse! Thanks so much for taking such good care of me." Nails on a chalkboard—that's exactly what Jolene's words sounded like to me. "See you at breakfast."

"Night, night, Jolene. Keep that ankle elevated. You wouldn't want to spend the summer with one nasty cankle," I replied before Jesse had a chance. "It was *really* great to meet you." I knew my sarcasm wasn't lost on Jesse or Garth, but neither of them let on that my farewell was anything but genuine.

"So great to meet you too, Rowen. Have a nice night." When a hobbling cast sounded like it was moving our way, I hurried to shut the door.

"Oh, I plan to." Making sure the door was closed—*firmly*—I wrapped my arms around Jesse's waist.

"Plan to what?" He tilted his hat back and leaned in. The look in his eyes made my stomach bottom out.

"Have a nice night. Have the nicest kind of night a girl could have with a guy like you."

"I like where this is going."

"You better. Because we're not going far." I shoved Jesse until the backs of his legs ran into one of the porch swings. Yep, that would do. It would have to because my need for the man had burst free. Keeping it bottled when he was within arm's reach was a chore, and it was utterly impossible when we were alone and he graced me with that look. I was straddling his lap before he'd fully collapsed into the swing.

"I *really* like where you're going with this."

Grinning at him, I slid off his hat and wove my fingers into his hair. "I missed you."

His eyes closed as I massaged his scalp. "Good."

"Good? You're glad I missed you so bad I almost skipped class for a few days to hop on a bus just so I could see you for a couple hours before I had to turn around and get back to reality?"

"Yeah, I am glad."

That was the first time Jesse had admitted to being glad about me being uncomfortable. I had to be missing something. "Why?"

His eyes opened and locked onto mine. "Because, Rowen. Because the day you don't miss me is the day we're doomed."

Jesse's words never failed to amaze me. He saw everything a bit differently than everyone else . . . but what he saw was so right. "In that case I missed, missed, missed, missed, *missed* you." Leaning in, I kissed the tip of his nose.

"And I've never been happier to know that you missed, missed, *missed* me."

"You missed a couple misses in there."

Jesse's smile spread. "So I'm forgiven for not picking you up tonight at the very place we met?"

A Greyhound station smack in the middle of Montana. The place we'd met. It might not have been ideal for most romances, but it was *our* place, and that trumped everything else. "That depends," I said before skimming my lips up his jaw.

He shuddered. "Depends on what?"

"On how persuasive you can be?" My mouth moved to the other side of his jaw.

"Oh, I can be persuasive." His voice was rougher. Rough enough I knew what he wanted to do, which made it that much harder to keep restraining myself.

When my mouth was just outside his ear, I kissed his earlobe. "Show, don't tell."

Jesse's hands formed over my hips as he shifted me into a more *suitable* position. "Showing."

His head turned, his mouth searching for mine. When he found it, the weeks of separation and torture of anticipation poured out in one kiss. Jesse expressed his love through his touch, as opposed to the boys before him who had merely used "love" as a justification to touch. When Jesse's mouth moved with mine, I sensed exactly how he felt about me. It didn't matter how many times I'd kissed him; I never got used to the magnitude of it. I knew it was something a person never could get used to, so I did my best to enjoy it and be in the moment.

My fingers curled into his shirt and pulled it free of his jeans. His hands slid up my legs, past the hem of my dress. We were on the porch swing, one wall separating us from whoever was still in the kitchen, but getting caught seemed less irresponsible than stopping the ride we were on. I might have actually died from the disappointment if Jesse's hand had lowered and his lips stopped. So I pressed on, my lips unyielding against his. Just as I was tugging his shirt over his head, the front door swung open.

The figure stepping out onto the porch was enough to freeze us in place. The porch lights flickered back on, and a grin as wide and maniacal as the Joker's formed on Garth's face. Shutting the door first, he ambled our way. "Looks like I was about two minutes early to walking in on you losing our bet, Walker."

I, like the frozen idiot I was, kept Jesse's shirt three-quarters of the way up his back. Jesse's hands slid down my legs, out of the "danger zone," and they paused just above my knees. "Get out of here, Black. Go find someone else to harass. I'm busy."

"Oh, I can see just how *busy* you are." Garth winked at me for a grand total of fifty thousand times. "Carry on. I can wait until morning to be declared the winner."

He was swaggering his way down the stairs when Jesse called out, "Come on. You and I both know there's no way you've gone two weeks without cussing. It's impossible for you, Garth."

"Is it?" Garth paused and cocked a brow. "But

enough about me. Let's talk about you and how it's a *physical* impossibility for you to carry out your end of the bet. Especially now that your precious, hot-for-you Rowen is here." Garth took another long look at Jesse's and my position, smiled, and headed for his truck. Jesse was mid-groan when Garth whistled. "Might I suggest ice? A large bag of it. Apply directly to the groin area, and that might help with the level of blue your balls are going to get if you consider stopping your johnson mid-game."

The pieces fell into place about Jesse's bet when Garth's truck fired to life. By the time he'd peeled down the driveway, I'd directed as stern a look as I could manage at Jesse. "You made a bet with Garth Black that you could go longer without sex than he could without cussing?"

"Maybe?"

"Maybe?" I screeched. "*Maybe?* What kind of an answer is that, Jesse Walker?"

Half of Jesse's face wrinkled. "It seemed safer than an outright *yes*."

I let out a long sigh. Not only was I beyond irritated at Garth, but I was still so wound tight with want for Jesse, my thighs were practically trembling around his lap. Yeah, our position wasn't doing anything to calm my hormones hitting hyperdrive. "What in the world possessed you to make that kind of depraved bet with him?"

"I told him one night I bet he couldn't go without cussing for a day, and he turned around and said he bet I couldn't go without sex for a day." Jesse lifted one shoulder. "That was two weeks ago. I knew the sex part was a non-issue . . . until you got here. Never once did I think Garth Black could go a solid two weeks without dropping a profanity along the way."

Fantastic. I wasn't going to get laid by my positively lay-worthy boyfriend because two boys had behaved like idiots.

When I moved to shift off of him, he stalled my efforts. When my lap crashed down on his, heat jolted up into my stomach. "What Garth Black doesn't know . . . he *doesn't* know." Jesse's hand formed around my face, and he brought me closer. "Just like I have no clue if he's been whipping off profanities when he's alone, he won't know how unlucky or lucky I'm getting when I am."

When Jesse's lips settled over mine, mine took a while to unfreeze. Once they did, I came so close to tossing my resolve right over my shoulder. When his fingers wove into my hair, giving it the slightest tug as his tongue moved into my mouth, I nearly forgot my name, let alone the resolve blossoming somewhere inside. The resolve that had everything to do with not wanting Garth Black to win. Jesse's other hand was skimming past the hem of my dress when I found the strength to pull back. That feat alone should have earned me the gold in willpower.

If a young cowboy could have looked more disappointed, I hadn't seen it.

"This isn't about me not wanting you this way, that way, and every way until you made me scream your name at least five different times like I *hoped* we'd be spending the night," I said. Okay, that look of disappointment just went a few notches higher. "This is about not letting that smirking, swaggering, infuriating Garth Black win."

"Let him win. I don't care." Jesse tried to pull me back to him. *Tried* being the operative word. "However, I do care about this. Us. What you were about to do to me five different times tonight apparently."

I gave myself the satisfaction of a small smile. Although I didn't love frustrating Jesse, I did love knowing I had power over him. It was the same power he had over me.

"Good night, Jesse." I planted a quick kiss on his cheek before moving off of the swing. We were at a stalemate. No amount of arguing from him would change my mind, and it was obvious no amount of argument from me would change his.

"Really?" His hand reached for mine, and he looked like he couldn't believe the night had taken such a drastic turn.

"Really." I looked him in the eye so he could see how serious I was. Let that be a lesson: Don't make bets with Garth Black having anything to do with Jesse's and my sex life.

He held my hand and gaze for a few more seconds, likely hoping I would change my mind. When that proved wishful thinking, he pulled me back down to him and scooted to the end of the swing. "Come here. Just because we can't, or you won't allow, us to continue what we were doing doesn't mean we have to retreat to opposite ends of the house." He patted the space beside him. "I don't want to waste our time together spending it apart. We spend too much time like that already."

Truer words had never been said. "You sure have a way with words, Walker. If I wasn't fully committed to not letting you lose this bet with Garth, you'd be getting so lucky right now."

He groaned so loudly the ranch hands in the bunk house probably heard it. "Not the thing to say to a guy who's holding on by a thread."

I curled into a ball on the swing and dropped my head on his lap. Best pillow ever.

We were quiet for a while, just the occasional creak of the swing as Jesse rocked us and the distant echo of the cattle. I was at my favorite place in the whole world, beside my favorite person in the universe . . . I felt a rare form of contentment in moments like those. Like there was nothing more I could want. Like death could come knocking on my door and I'd cross into the hereafter knowing I'd lived a full life.

Feeling those kinds of things for one person was different, and intense, and even a bit scary at times, but no matter what, I knew it was one thing above all: special. So much that I'd lump it into the category of sacred.

Jesse Walker was sacred to me.

"I love you, Rowen." So much silence had passed that his words came over me like a tsunami.

I tangled my fingers with his and smiled in my half-asleep state. "I love you, too, Jesse." I nudged his leg with my shoulder. "But you're still not getting laid tonight."

"Yeah, yeah. I know." He chuckled softly and gave my fingers a squeeze. "But this isn't exactly a poor substitute."

After that, I surrendered to sleep quickly. I never had bad dreams when Jesse was close by. He chased them all away.

chapter TEN

Jesse

I WAS DREAMING. I knew what was happening wasn't real. It might have been real years ago, but it wasn't my reality anymore. The scared boy chained to the water pipe in that dark, wet basement wasn't me anymore. The boy covered in his own filth, more animal than human, wasn't the man I'd grown into. The boy guarding the only thing he could claim as his own, ready and willing to tear into whomever or whatever might try to take it from him, had been my life at one time. It wasn't any longer.

I'd gone for years without dreaming of my life before my real family had found me. My true family. But the dreams had come back. In the past couple of weeks, they'd increased in frequency. I'd never had one while sleeping beside Rowen . . . but that had changed.

I jolted awake in a cold sweat, almost panting. It took me a minute to realize I was safe and another minute to remember where I was. My gaze jumped to Rowen, and my arms tightened protectively around her. She was still curled up, asleep, and half on the swing, half on my lap. A peaceful expression covered her face. The blanket I'd grabbed from the chest on the porch had slipped almost completely off of her. I grabbed the corner and pulled it up, tucking it under her chin.

I studied her for a minute, unable to shake my growing sense of protectiveness. As someone who cared about Rowen, of course I was concerned with keeping her safe, but my desperation went beyond that. It was something a bit darker, something not quite so benign and selfless. I'd warred with it in the past, that protectiveness that toed the line of possessiveness. My protective feelings for her didn't just stem from her benefit, as they had until recently. The new sense of protection cropped up from feeling like she was mine, no one else's, and not wanting anything else to find out about her for fear of her being taken away.

I recognized that staggering feeling as a demon from my past. One I thought I'd buried. One I obviously hadn't. It unsettled me to the core, but I reassured myself that I'd caught the demon before it had taken over. Knowledge was power, and knowing that the little boy of my past was trying to possess Rowen in a way that wasn't acceptable or healthy meant I would be on my guard to stop it from going any further. I'd rather remove myself from her life completely than strangle the life right out of Rowen. I'd kill myself trying if need be. I wouldn't go back to that life. I wouldn't drag what was most special to me back either.

"You look like you need this, sweetie." A steaming cup of coffee appeared in front of my face. "And this, too. It might be unseasonably warm, but the nights are still plenty chilly." A heavy blanket dropped over me.

"Thanks, Mom." I yawned, took the cup of coffee, and forced the dark thoughts back where they belonged: in the grave I'd buried them in years ago.

"Look at that hair." Mom teased with a few pieces,

trying to get them to behave, then gave up. "It didn't matter what I put in your hair when you were younger; it always had a mind of its own."

"Good thing I pretty much live in a hat." I took a long drink of coffee, retrieved my hat from where it had fallen off last night, and slid it into position.

"Did you two stay out here all night?"

I nodded. "All night. I've got the bug bites and frost bite to prove it."

"Good thing you're a rough and tough cowboy then." Mom gave me a smile before sipping her own coffee.

"Good thing." I stretched my arms high above my head. I was stiff, too. "What time is it?"

"Almost six."

"Was there a day off announced I wasn't made aware of?" The fact that I hadn't been woken up with a cold bucket of water meant I'd missed some kind of memo.

"Not so much a day off, but your dad decided today would be a fun day to have all the guys make breakfast for us girls." Just then, a crashing sound came from the kitchen. "They're working a bit slower than we do. Breakfast might be ready by dinnertime." Another crash, that one even louder. Mom grimaced. "Or maybe in time for tomorrow's breakfast."

"Sounds like I'd better get in there and throw my pathetic cooking skills into the mix. I'm pretty sure I can manage to not ruin toast."

"No. Stay." Mom shoved off the railing like she was going to physically stop me if I tried moving. "It's nice to see you like this. When she's with you."

It was kind of nice to feel like this when Rowen was around. "What? Am I hopeless or something the rest of the time?"

She laughed a few notes, her smile shifting from me to Rowen. "Not hopeless. Just kind of . . . lost."

"I feel a bit lost when she's not around." My arms tightened around her instinctually. I couldn't decide if that was the possessiveness from my past or of today.

"I know you do, Jess." The corners of Mom's eyes creased, like she was concentrating on what to say, but after a moment, they ironed out.

When she didn't speak, I said, "Well, it will be summer break soon, and she'll be back for a long time. You won't have to put up with me wandering around like a lost puppy dog."

"And after summer break? What then?"

"Then she'll go back to school. We'll see each other as often as we can, and the rest of the time, I'll be a lost puppy."

Mom took a long drink of her coffee. She didn't normally down it in one long sip like the guys, which meant she was stalling. She was looking for just the right way to word what she wanted to say. "And when Rowen finishes up school in a few years . . . then what?"

I had a reply on the tip of my tongue for most any question—I'd been given the gift of gab after all—but that one stumped me. I had given it plenty of thought, but I didn't have an answer to that question. I knew what I wanted. I also knew what Rowen wanted. Pretty much most of her wants and my wants aligned, but our commitments columns had a tough time aligning.

I worked at Willow Springs. Ranching was what I knew. It was in my blood, and I knew it always would be. Rowen lived, breathed, and dreamed art. That's what she knew, and that's what was in her blood. If five hundred miles of land separating us decided to up and relocate one day, that would make Rowen's and my future a lot easier to piece together. If Seattle and its vibrant art scene was an easy drive from Willow Springs, our problems would be solved. Maybe not all of them, but at least some of them.

"I guess we haven't really worked out the details yet," I answered Mom. I would have scratched my head if it hadn't been such a terrible cliché.

"It's time you start thinking about what you *think* you can't live without and what you *actually* can't live without." When Mom's face got all serious like that, I'd learned to sit up and listen.

"I knew I must have inherited my genius from you."

Her face softened when she smiled. "And your dashing good looks."

I motioned between Mom and me who were, as two people could go, about as opposite as opposite could get. I doubted we had a single strand of DNA that was even close to matching. "Obviously."

She patted my cheek as she headed for the door. "I'll let you get back to your bug bites and frost bite, sweetie."

"Mom?" I glanced down at Rowen and swallowed.

She paused with her hand on the door and smiled, waiting. I wanted to tell her about the dreams . . . the nightmares. I wanted to admit my fears about why they'd come back. I wanted her to comfort me the way she had that first year I'd come to Willow Springs and woken up every night screaming. I wanted someone to know . . .

But admitting them out loud to another person seemed like I was giving power to my fears. If I kept them to myself, would they eventually die off? Or would keeping them to myself make them that much worse? I didn't know, and I hated that feeling. So instead of bringing Mom into the dark world I'd resurrected, I forced a smile. "Never mind."

She was observant, though. Always had been, and my weak attempt to reassure her had done nothing but put her on alert. Just then, another loud sound came from the kitchen: shattering. Mom and I winced.

"I'd better get in there." I shifted nice and slow so I didn't disturb Rowen, who hadn't even stirred from the noise. "If everything turns into a burnt, inedible mess, I'll at least make sure there's toast and coffee."

Mom wiped her brow. "You're a good son."

Before heading through the door, I glanced back at Rowen, peaceful, resting, not a worry in the world. And there I was—anxious, troubled, unsure.

Not wanting to give it any more thought, I headed for the kitchen. None of the smells I associated with breakfast were present when I stepped into the kitchen-slash-chaos room. The air was permeated with the scent of burnt, and the smoke curling from the fry pan and toaster oven told the rest of the story. That wasn't breakfast; it was a massacre.

We hadn't hired on all of our hands for the summer yet, so about ten guys, plus Dad and Garth, were fumbling around like *domestic* was a foreign concept.

"It's breakfast, guys. Not open heart surgery." I went to the sink to wash my hands, dodging piles of batter and raw egg on the floor. By the time all was said and done, Mom and the girls had about ten times as much work whenever us guys made them breakfast. Mom had complained about finding dried pancake batter weeks after the last breakfast we'd "made."

"Says the guy standing there doing nothing." Garth didn't take his eyes off of the pan on the stove. I think he was attempting to scramble eggs. The only thing that looked scrambled, though, was his expression.

"Nice to see you preparing for your future. Behind an oven, spatula in hand." I clapped my hands over Garth's shoulders and gave them a hard squeeze.

He shrugged me off. "Go blank off, Walker."

"Touchy. Even you must recognize there's a kernel of truth in what I just said." I poured a glass of orange juice, downed it in one long gulp, then poured another. I needed my Vitamin C and energy to survive one of the all-time worst breakfasts in history.

"At least I'm living it up now and saving my pussy-whipped period for when I'm old and ugly. Unlike some-one else I know."

"Are you calling me old and ugly?" I asked with a straight face.

"Yes. And pussy-whipped." Garth poked at the eggs with the spatula like he was afraid they were about to come to life.

"I love you too, Black." Finishing my second glass of orange juice, I dropped the glass in the sink.

Garth mumbled his response while I shouldered up beside Dad. He had a grave expression as he manned the griddle.

"Where do you need me, Captain? I'm suited up and ready to go." I had to nudge him before he acknowledged me.

"Oh. Hey, Jess." Dad's gaze didn't shift from the handful of runny pancakes on the griddle. "Sleep good?"

I grinned, remembering who I'd gotten to sleep with. "Slept *great*." Then I remembered the nightmare that had jolted me awake. My smile fell, but I didn't let it disappear completely.

"Pussy-whipped," Garth said with a loud cough.

"Good, good. Glad to hear it." Dad stepped aside and handed me the spatula. "Why don't you take over? See if you can get those devil pancakes to behave."

"How long have you been cooking them?" I tried to keep my amusement contained. Watching a man like my dad, who I'd watched leap in front of a charging horse, back away from an electric kitchen device like it was the most frightening thing he'd ever seen was all kinds of funny.

"Twenty minutes. Maybe thirty."

I didn't know jack about cooking, but I knew enough to realize something was way wrong if pancakes were taking a half hour to cook. Studying the griddle, I saw the problem. "It helps if you turn it on, Dad."

"I plugged it in," Dad said, sounding almost defensive.

I reminded myself not to smile. "And for that, you get partial credit. To get full credit, you needed to turn the dial on."

Dad scowled at the griddle. "Okay, since you're the expert, you're on pancake detail. I'll go man the coffee."

I chuckled and turned the dial to the right heat setting. "You mean you'll *drink* the coffee."

"Someone's got to be in charge of quality control."

I'd just wrestled away one of the spatulas Garth was hoarding when the back screen door whooshed open. A familiar voice exclaimed, "Holy cows on crack! Are you frying up entrails or something because the smell coming from this kitchen was burning my nose before I even stepped out of my truck."

I was about to greet Josie when a yelp sounded beside me. Garth was shaking his hand furiously and glaring at the fry pan. He was biting his tongue so hard to keep from swearing, he looked close to drawing blood.

"There's no shame in losing. You've put up a good fight, but how much longer are you going to torture yourself?" I said. After putting up with a hefty dose of abstinence last night, I knew there was no way I could go another night.

"I'm going to torture myself a whole two seconds longer than you, Walker. Just long enough to bask in my victory. Then I'm letting loose every last word I've been holding back."

He really was the most stubborn person I'd come across. "I don't know that waving your hand around like that is doing much good. Other than making the rest of us laugh."

Garth stopped waving his hand, shot me a glare, and stormed over to the fridge. "Where's the butter?"

Josie intercepted Garth at the fridge, grabbed his wrist, and marched him over to the sink. "Butter?! No, absolutely not. That is, like, the worst possible thing to put on a burn."

"Hey, Pushy, think you could lock that chick-crazy instinct inside long enough to let me tend to my wounds?" Garth tried to pull his hand out of her grasp, but all that did was make Josie tighten her hold.

"Hey, Asshole, think you could shut the snarky up and let someone actually help you for once in your life?"

Josie cranked on the faucet and tested the water with her wrist before guiding Garth's palm beneath it.

"Cold water? Really? No, butter's what you put on burns." Even though he was still fighting, I could see relief flood Garth's face as the cold water streamed on his hand.

"Says who?"

"Says my dad."

Josie practically snorted. "Yeah, and we all know your dad deserves the father of the year award."

Garth's whole body went stiff right before he snapped his hand out of Josie's grip. "I think I've had enough of you and your *help* for two lifetimes."

Josie didn't flinch like most people would have. She didn't even blink when Garth turned his most potent glare on her. "And I've had enough of you and your lack of help for three lifetimes."

"No arguing in my kitchen. It's a rule." Mom and the girls entered the kitchen, doing their best to not look appalled. The expression on Clem's face made up for the absence of one on the rest of theirs. From her utter horror, anyone would have thought she'd just walked in on us shaving a litter of puppies.

"Sorry, Mrs. Walker. There's just something about Garth that brings out the worst in me." Josie shut off the sink and glared at Garth's back.

"At last. A compliment." Garth stopped in front of the oven again, grabbing the spatula like it was a weapon and the fry pan was the enemy.

"I didn't realize it was the guys' attempt and sequential failure"—Josie practically spat the last word at Garth —"to cook this morning. I just stopped by to check on Jo. Is she up yet?"

"I've been up for two hours, thank you very much," Jolene said as she joined everyone in the kitchen.

When Josie passed me, she gave me her greeting slug. "Two hours? What in the world have you been doing for two hours? Lord knows you weren't out collecting eggs or cleaning out stalls."

"Getting ready."

"For what? You expecting it to rain Hollywood hotties this afternoon or something?" Josie was in a mood. She was about as stubborn as Garth and could be as moody too. When both of them were like that, it was best to keep all things of a breakable nature out of arm's reach.

"No, but a girl never knows when her future husband might lay eyes on her for the first time. If that day were today, I sure wouldn't want him to see nothing but a country bumpkin." Jolene came up beside me. I was watching the pancakes like a hawk. If nothing else, the pancakes would be edible. "Hey, Jesse."

I nodded my acknowledgement. "Hi, Jolene. How's the ankle?" I took a brief look at her bandaged ankle. It looked pretty swollen, but at least it was just a sprain. After the fall she'd taken, I was afraid she might have broken her leg.

"It's just peachy. Thanks to my hero making sure I got such speedy medical attention." Jolene leaned in closer.

Scared she was going to injure herself yet again, I slid the griddle down the counter and myself along with it. The girl was accident prone.

"Do you need any help with those?" Jolene hobbled a couple steps closer. There was no more cord for me to scoot it any farther out of the way.

"Nah, I think I've got it. Why don't you sit down and get comfortable with the rest of the girls? It's our morning to serve you all. Or at least *try* to serve." Looking around at the breakfast efforts, I thought maybe it was time to throw in the white flag.

Jolene stepped closer. At that proximity, her arm was literally half a foot away from sizzling against the fry pan. I wasn't in the mood for another E.R. visit. Maybe Garth would fill-in. Oh, wait. No, not likely. I felt like Jolene was waiting for me to look at her, but the pancakes were so close to being done that I couldn't spare one moment of distraction.

Her hand curled around my forearm. "And what if I want to serve you?"

I don't know what I was more confused by: her words or her hand on my arm. How in the world was I supposed to respond? I don't know if it was Jolene or women in general, but I never seemed to get what they were saying between the lines. I was just looking to Garth for a little help when I felt that familiar jolt. I actually sighed with relief. I dropped the spatula, forgot about the pancakes, and turned to find Rowen hovering in the kitchen doorway. Her gaze wasn't on me—it was on Jolene, and she didn't look especially thrilled. When her attention moved my way, her whole face changed. Mine mirrored hers.

"Hey, Cowboy. You haven't said good morning yet." Rowen crossed the kitchen toward me like a woman on a mission.

I shoved off of the counter and wrapped my arms around her once she was close enough. "Good—" That was all I got out before Rowen's mouth crushed into mine. I was self-conscious about kissing—well, *making out*—

with my girlfriend in front of twenty people for about two seconds before everything faded away. All that was left was Rowen, me, and that kiss. Her fingers played with the hair at the nape of my neck as mine focused on holding her as close as one person could be against another.

"Go get a room. It's going to be hard enough to hold this breakfast down without having you two sucking face two feet in front of me."

I heard Garth's words, but his message didn't register until he hurled a spoonful of pancake batter at my face. That was enough to bring me back to reality, and a smirking cowboy over my girlfriend's shoulder wasn't the reality I wanted to be in. Especially after that last one I'd been enjoying.

"Jealous?" I glared at Garth, keeping Rowen close.

"Not even close."

"Here you go, Jesse. Let me get that off for you." Jolene lifted a wet washcloth.

Rowen's arm flashed in front of Jolene, stopping her and the washcloth. "I got this, Jolene. If you want something to wipe clean, why don't you wipe that smirk off of Black's face?" Then, wiping some of the batter from my face, Rowen lifted her finger to her mouth. Giving me a coy smile, she slipped her finger in her mouth and sucked the batter right off. *Slowly* sucked it off.

A shiver ran down my back. Sliding her finger free, she leaned in and whispered, "The pancakes are burning." She shot me a wink before heading over to the table to take a seat. "Oh"—she stopped, snapping her fingers— "and good morning."

Putty in her hands. From the smile she gave me, she knew it, too.

Once Rowen had taken a seat and I was able to move again, I rushed to the griddle to discover that the pancakes weren't just burning. They were burnt to a crisp. So buttered toast and coffee it would be. It was pretty pathetic that that was the best a handful of guys who'd been hard at work for an hour could come up with.

"Hey, Dad? Do you think it would be all right if I did a half day today?" I tossed half a dozen slices of bread in the industrial-sized toaster while Dad and a few of the guys poured coffee.

"Sure. It should be quiet enough around here that I was planning on giving everyone a half day. Even you." Dad almost dumped a full cup of coffee on Josie, but thankfully, she was ready for the worst. She grabbed the cup with both hands, gave Dad a half smile, and lowered it to the table. Carefully.

"What did you have planned for this afternoon, Jess?" Josie asked, taking a sip of her coffee before handing it to Rowen to share. Someone had forgotten to give her a cup.

"I wanted to take Rowen down to the swimming hole."

"It's going to be freezing this time of year. Why in the world would you want to do that?" Josie gave an exaggerated shiver.

Because I want to be with my girlfriend, alone, and I wouldn't mind repeating some of the things we've done there before. Like skinny-dipping. And what follows skinny -dipping . . .

"Sounds like fun. Sign me up." From Rowen's twist-ed smile, I knew she and I were on the same wavelength. For the love of God, I hoped she'd changed her mind about the whole "not letting Garth win" thing. What Garth didn't know didn't have to affect the bet.

"That's sounds fun to me, too. What time's everyone going?" Jolene said.

Rowen visibly prickled at Jolene's words, but I tried not to be so obvious. What part of taking *Rowen* to the swimming hole hadn't been clear? I guess if you were Jolene, none of it.

"Well, I was kind of thinking just Rowen and—"

"You know what, that does sound like a good time. I'm in too." Garth smiled widely when I glared at him. I knew he wasn't oblivious; he was just being obnoxious.

"Okay, fine. I'm in, too," Josie added. "I'll just make sure to wear my snowsuit."

Jolene clapped. "Yay. This will be fun."

Rowen grimaced like the clapping or excitement or the combination was worse than nails clawing down a chalkboard.

"This will be fun." Garth elbowed me in the ribs as he headed to the garbage can. Turning the fry pan upside down, the scrambled eggs that could have been dropped inside.

I worked my jaw. "Can't. Wait." I'd just gone from having the entire afternoon and evening open to spend with Rowen to adding a couple more to the mix.

The day pretty much had to be uphill from there, right?

"I hope you like your toast black, ladies, because that's the way Jesse here likes to make it." Garth tossed a piece of charred toast at me, and I caught it before it slapped my cheek.

On second thought, uphill might not be the state of things.

chapter ELEVEN

Rowen

I WAS IN one of my favorite spots in the world—pressed tight against Jesse—as Old Bessie rumbled down a country road and Johnny Cash flowed in the background. What was to my left and in front of me was as good as it got. What was to my right and behind me . . . not even close. So much for an afternoon alone.

Garth stuck his head through the open rear window, and he had no qualms about hollering six inches away from my ear. "Think you can get this beater past twenty? I'm going to grow a full beard before we get to the swimming hole at this pace!"

"Your mother should have drowned you at birth," I said, thumping Garth's hat over his eyes.

"She tried. Didn't work."

"Obviously *and* unfortunately."

"So much anger toward me. If I didn't know better, I'd think you had a crush on me or something." Garth did that eyebrow wiggle that had driven me up a wall so many times I'd seriously considered shaving off his eyebrows while he slept.

"Okay. Enough. I have to put up with you for the rest of the day, but I'm not going to put up with you irritating

Rowen." Jesse shoved Garth's face through the window before sliding it closed. For the fifth or sixth time. No matter how many times we slammed the thing closed on him, the crazy SOB wouldn't take a hint.

"Josie, you really must be one of my best friends." I threw a warning look at Garth when he went for the window again. So help me . . . One more time and I would crawl into the bed of the truck and toss him over the side. Right after I pushed Miss Montana out. I doubted she had blinked while eyeing Jesse through the window. After the stunts she'd pulled that morning at breakfast, she was seriously on my shit list.

"Duh." Josie rolled her eyes. "But what's making you bring it up?"

"Because if you weren't, I would hate you right now for inviting yourself and the two tagalongs in the back."

"Garth, A.K.A. The Ass of Hole, invited himself. And Jo I couldn't really un-invite." Josie stuck out her lower lip and even made it wobble. "And I'm sorry, I know I shouldn't have invited myself like that, but you're one of my best friends too, you know? It's not fair that Jesse hogs you the whole time you're here."

"I feel like I should apologize for that, but it wouldn't exactly be a heartfelt one," Jesse said, slinging his arm around my neck before whipping down another country road. It was so overrun I could barely make out which part was road and which part wasn't.

I knew Josie was mostly teasing but not completely. My visits to Willow Springs had been few and short, and I only had a handful of hours to spend with Jesse before I had to get back on that bus to Seattle. But Josie was right; it wasn't fair. Even though I knew fair wasn't a guarantee in life, I tried to even the score whenever I could.

Winding my arm around Josie's neck like Jesse's was around mine, I gave her a squeeze. "Two things. Actually three. I'm sorry I haven't made time for one of my best friends this year. I *suppose* I'm glad you're going to the swimming hole with us even though I was planning on making up for lost time with my boyfriend." I nudged her as she giggled. "But I do not and cannot understand why you couldn't un-invite Jolene. It's not like she's your best friend or family." I was cool with Josie tagging along. Garth . . . well, I'd accepted it. But Jolene the Jesse Worshipper? I don't think so.

"Actually, we're both."

"You're both what?"

"Best friends and family," Josie answered with a shrug.

"You're shittin' me, right?" I glanced between Josie and Jolene.

"Shittin' you not. We're cousins."

Well, shit.

"We're only best friends because when you share every summer together with another girl, sharing the kinds of things girls share, well . . . you kind of become best friends by default."

"Did you know this?" I looked at Jesse, still baffled.

He lifted a shoulder. "Yeah. I mean, Jolene's stayed with Josie's family every summer, except last year when she was with the Peace Corps. You're the same age, too, right?"

"Save for three months," Josie said.

"My, aren't you the Jolene expert," I grumbled. I wasn't really upset with him but with the situation. The girl I was sure I didn't want within a ten-foot pole of my boyfriend was pretty much tied to him by circumstance. "And Jolene comes here every summer because . . . she likes the scenery?" That last part wasn't exactly a question. It was obvious how much she enjoyed the "scenery".

"She grew up in Missoula but likes spending her summers in the country. She usually just spends the summer messing around with me, but when she found out Mrs. Walker needed a hand this season, she practically jumped at the opportunity."

I slumped a little farther into my seat. "I bet she did."

The window whooshed open again. "Hey. My dick is about to fall off from underuse back here. Think we could speed it up and arrive sometime this year?"

"Good-bye, Garth and Garth's dick. Rest in peace." I didn't bother to make sure his face was out of the way before sliding the glass closed. "Josie, you're telling me every morning, Jolene gets up and drives close to twenty miles to slave away in a kitchen because she couldn't think of a better way to spend her summer?" Not. Buying. It.

"She isn't staying at my place, Moody." Josie looked between me and Jesse like we were clueless.

"Then where the hell's she staying? In a tent?" Maybe that was the Peace Corps way. To cut down on carbon emissions or something like that.

"She's staying at the Walkers. Where did you think she'd be staying? You ought to know. You were the one working there last year."

"But I stayed there because my home was two states away, Josie. They had to go out of their way to make a room for me . . ." And then something I really didn't want to click into place did. I twisted in my seat all the way so I could look at Jesse full on who was humming along to Johnny Cash, trying to stay out of the conversation. "Oh, hell no. Tell me—please tell me—she is not sleeping in your room."

"It's not really my room anymore," Jesse replied, looking like he was putting his answer together carefully. "I haven't slept in it since last spring before you came. The only person that's been sleeping in it is—"

"Me!" I didn't mean to snap, but I still did. "Where am I supposed to sleep now? Or am I being kicked out? Maybe I can set up a cot in the barn or something. Next to the horses."

Both Josie and Jesse looked at me like I'd lost my mind. Even in my impassioned state, I knew I was close to it. The room was just . . . special. It felt like mine, like ours, and knowing that someone else was living in it made me feel a bunch of things I didn't like: anger, jealousy, sadness, and even a little bit hopeless. The last one scared me the most.

"What? Rowen, no, of course not. Calm down." Jesse's hand dropped to my leg. "You're taking my room and I'm sleeping in the bunkhouse with the rest of the guys. I should have told you that last night, but we didn't exactly make it to bed . . ."

Josie looked out the window and shifted.

I huffed, "Trust me, we were doing nothing last night to make you shift in your seat. And we won't be doing anything tonight thanks to a certain bet that still stands."

"What bet?" Josie piped in.

"Bet or no bet, we couldn't do anything this afternoon either thanks to the company of best friends, pity friends" —I grabbed the window right before Garth got it open—

"and arch nemeses. Lucky us."

"What bet?" Josie repeated.

"Forget about it. To your knowledge, and I wish to my knowledge, there is no bet." I really, really wished I didn't know about that asinine bet. "I'm still trying to wrap my head around how you and Montana Barbie are cousins and, in one fell swoop, she displaced me. Of my bedroom," I added when Jesse let out a long sigh.

"Listen, I know she's a bit of an acquired taste, but give Jolene a chance, Rowen. You and I didn't exactly get off on the right foot and look where we are now." Draping her arm around me, Josie gave me a nasty noogie.

"Yeah, yeah. What would I do without friends like you?" I patted my hair back into place once she was done disheveling it. "And what are you talking about right and wrong foots with us? We got along swimmingly from the very start."

"Whatever, Rowen. You might not have come right out and said what you were thinking, but the look in your eyes did. You hated me hardcore because you thought Jesse and I were still together. Face it—you were a bitch."

My eyes widened. "What? I was not. I was completely civil."

Josie snorted. "Yeah, civil by Henry Tudor's standards."

"Henry Tudor? Really, Josie? If you're going to enter an argument with me, you better bring your A game."

Jesse was smiling. I could feel it rolling off of him.

"Rowen. You're a bitch. Not all the time and not with everyone, but we all know you do bitch well when you have to."

I wanted to pull her braided pigtails until that smirk

came off of her face. "Jesse . . ."

"No, no. Don't you bring him into this." Josie waved her finger in my face. "This is between you and me."

I stayed silent for a minute, not because I was trying to build my argument against her, but because I knew she was partly right. Okay, *mostly* right. I was a bitch to her at first. I'd covered it up with a smile—a whole lot of no good that did me—and I knew Josie hadn't been the first to form the B opinion about me. I'd developed that part of me as a defense mechanism. I'd let people into my life for temporary periods, but I'd never let them get to know the real Rowen. Not until last summer. Then I'd dropped the walls I'd hidden behind for so long. Even though every day was a struggle to keep them lowered, I knew I'd never regret fighting that battle. I'd shed so many of my dark layers that I might as well shake loose another one.

So yes, Rowen Sterling had been a bona fide bitch. Rowen Sterling didn't need to stay one. At least not to the nth degree. I'd still reserve a little bit to keep things interesting.

"Fine. I was a bitch. What can I ever do to earn your forgiveness?" My overdone apology was interrupted when Josie threw her arms around me and hugged me tightly.

"You just earned it," she said with a sniffle.

I patted her back and did my best not to squirm. Random acts of physical affection still threw me. There was only one exception to that: Jesse. No matter how many times he sneaked up behind me to throw me over his shoulder or leaned in unexpectedly to kiss the corner of my mouth, I didn't squirm under his touch. Josie's, along with everyone else's, I was still getting used to.

"Just let your bitch relax and get to know Jolene.

She's really not that bad, I promise," Josie said. I made an uncertain face, earning a pinch from her. "Behave."

"So, Jesse . . ." I started. He braced himself. "What do you think of Jolene?"

He was nearing a wince when he answered, "I have a feeling no matter what answer I give you, I'm going to be in trouble."

"You're probably right. So why don't you just go with the honest one?" I arched my eyebrows and waited.

He shifted in his seat and cleared his throat. "She's okay, seems nice enough. She hasn't spilt coffee on my lap yet, so that's a point in her corner, but she did detain me from picking you up last night, so that's, like, negative a hundred in the other."

I knew that wouldn't be romantic to plenty of women, but to me? It was the ultimate aphrodisiac. "Pull over."

"Why?" he asked, already doing it.

"Just do it."

Before Jesse came to a complete stop, I had my seat belt off and was crawling over his lap. His eyes went wide right before my mouth covered his, then they closed and his lips moved against mine in eager, long pulls. When I felt three pairs of eyes on us, and when Jesse's and my bodies were starting to run away from us, I pulled back and slid back into my seat.

"What was that for?" he asked, breathless.

I snapped my belt back into place. "For being so god-damned, amazingly you."

Jesse shook his head a few times, and a loud thud sounded above us. Like something pounding the top of the cab. Or someone.

"That's it. I'm walking. I'll see you all when you

finally get there," Garth shouted, driving his fists into Old Bessie one last time before hopping out of the bed and marching down the road. All three of us inside the cab laughed.

"Hey, Garth?" I hollered, hanging my head out Jesse's open window. "Am I a bitch?"

"Ha!" he shouted as he kept on trucking down the road, blazing his own path.

"Was that a *Ha* of outrageous disagreement or non-committal, partial agreement?"

Jesse had pulled Old Bessie back onto the road and had caught up to Garth.

Garth scowled at us, quickening his pace. "That was a *Ha!* of utter, total, and unwavering agreement."

My glare had barely formed when Jesse punched the gas so hard Old Bessie actually fish-tailed on the gravel road.

"What was that for, Speedy Gonzalez?" I asked.

Jesse grinned widely as he checked the rearview mirror. "For every action, there is an opposite and equal reaction."

"Yeah, Jesse, I know you're the valedictorian of Willow Springs High, but what does that physics gem have to do with peeling out on some backwoods road?"

"That was my reaction to Garth's action." His eyes flickered to the rearview again. Something really interesting seemed to be keeping his attention.

"So Garth's action was implying I was a bitch . . ." I twisted to find a serious cloud of dust obscuring the whole road. It was so thick, I couldn't make out Garth anywhere in it.

"And my reaction was giving him a dirt and gravel

shower."

"Would you quit being so perfect already? It's really getting old." Giving Jesse my own devilish grin, we both started laughing. I was going to have to keep that action/reaction reminder in mind when dealing with Garth. Or any other a-hole, for that matter.

"You're not just going to leave him, are you?" Josie piped up.

"We really just are," Jesse replied.

"What? You can't do that. It's still another couple miles to the swimming hole."

I gave Josie a look. Since when did she care about Garth's well-being? In fact, I'd been sure up until then that her name would have been the first on the petition to banish Garth Black from the face of the earth.

"Exactly. So by the time he makes it, maybe he'll remember some of his manners." Jesse urged Old Bessie along. Since we'd dropped the baggage, we were cruising.

"Manners? Garth Black?" Josie said the words, but they were the exact ones on my mind.

Jesse's face scrunched up as he considered that. "Yeah, you're right. But if nothing else, at least it will piss him the hell off and give us a little bit of Garth-Black-free time."

Josie sighed. "You are an animal, Jesse Walker."

"Whoa, whoa, whoa." I waved my hands in front of me. "Did you just say Jesse's an animal? And if my ears doth not deceive me, then what—in a world where the Jesse Walkers are animals—are the Garth Blacks?"

"Your words, expressions, and hand gestures doth annoy me, so I shalt not give you a response."

"You and I might be the two most opposite chicks

alive, but at least we've got Shakespeare in common."

Finally, a smile cracked Josie's face. "There is that."

A couple minutes later, Jesse pulled off to the side of the overgrown road into a parking space that was doubly as overgrown. I couldn't see the swimming hole, even though it was less than fifty yards in front of us because a ring of giant willow trees lined the entire shore. There was one tight spot a person could squeeze through, and an ancient dock that was just barely floating extended into the water there. The mass of giant trees seemed like it was protecting whatever was inside from the outside world. When Jesse had taken me there the first time last summer, I'd straight out refused when he told me that we'd have to walk through because it looked a little creepy from an outsiders' perspective. Then he stripped down for his "swim," and my feet magically followed him.

Once I'd made it past the willow tree perimeter and was looking at it from the inside out, back-floating in the middle of the water, well . . . it was magical. It had become a favorite of Jesse's and mine. That was the first time we'd been able to swim since I left for school, but we'd made plenty of visits just to curl up in a blanket on the dock.

"Let's hurry up and enjoy some Garth-free time." Jesse shoved his door open and grabbed my hand to help me out.

"I enjoy all of my Garth-free time."

Josie moved to the tailgate to open it for Jolene. "How you doing back here, Gimpy?"

"Stuck, I think. Garth had to help me in. Someone else is going to have to help me out since he's probably still coughing up dust." Jolene's eyes landed on my certain *someone.*

"Well, don't look at me. I'm not going to sprain my ankle helping your gimp ankle out." Josie crossed her arms and took a couple steps back. Some best friend-slash-cousin.

"Jesse?" Jolene said slowly, expectantly. "Mind being your usual gentlemanly self and sweeping a girl off her feet?"

I didn't even try to keep from rolling my eyes. Whenever that chick opened her mouth, an eye roll came standard.

"Sure. No problem." Jesse shot me a nervous glance before moving toward the tailgate. I wasn't irritated with Jesse. His willingness to help anyone at any time was one of the things I loved most about him. I was irritated with those who took advantage of his selfless qualities.

Jolene really ate up the whole thing, winding her arm around his neck, snuggling in nice and tight against his chest, making those damn Bambi eyes at him like he was the be-all-end-all in all maledom . . . which Jesse was. But that was for me to know and no one else to find out.

Jesse did his good deed of the day, kept his hands and arms to all of Jolene's super safe areas—yes, I was watching—and was just about to lower her to the ground when she clung a little tighter. Subtlety was a nuance lost on that one.

"That's a long trek down some treacherous terrain. Mind carrying me the rest of the way?" she asked, practically batting her lashes. "I'd hate to sprain the other ankle or see those muscles of yours go to waste."

If I wasn't seeing a special shade of pissed, I might have gagged a little.

"Um . . . are you sure you can't make it? It's really not that bad . . ." Jesse didn't need to look at me to feel me seething. I'm sure he could feel it rolling off me in radioactive waves.

"Oh. I'm sure."

Oh, I knew she was.

"Okay, well . . ." Jesse turned slowly, partially wincing like he was bracing himself. "Will you be okay if I walk Jolene down real quick and come back for you and Josie?" I knew he was really asking *Are you going to be pissed beyond the point of appeasing if I do this?*

The answer to that was yes. And no. Jolene might have made the list after that morning's shenanigans, but she'd just landed the number one spot on my shit list. Jesse . . . he'd never been anywhere close to it. I doubted he could do anything to wind up on that list. Just because a scheming little trollop was using his goodness against him didn't mean I was going to hold him responsible.

"Yeah. We'll be great." I shot him a thumbs-up.

Jesse's whole body relaxed. "Be right back." He managed to press a quick kiss into my lips as he walked by. Jolene's Barbie-doll hair came dangerously close to my hands. So close that I had to fight the urge to yank a chunk of it.

I only watched Jesse and Jolene walk away for a second because I realized it was a real-life vision for a secret fear: Jesse walking away with a girl as seemingly perfect as him and leaving me behind to wonder if my time with him had been nothing but a dream. It was baseless and unfair and gave away just how insecure I could still be, but it was there.

"Put your kitty claws away, Feisty." Josie nudged me

as I yanked my beach bag from the truck.

"You still can look me in the eye and tell me your sweet and innocent cousin is not head over heels in panting lust-love with my boyfriend? I mean, come on, Dolly Parton wrote a goddamned song about some girl named Jolene sauntering in and taking some lesser woman's man. I don't want to be the girl whose man leaves her for some flaming locks of auburn-haired girl." How a forty-year-old country song could seem so prophetic I don't know, but damn if it didn't seem to be telling my life story at that juncture. That I knew who Dolly Parton was and what songs she sang gave away just how much time I'd spent at Willow Springs and just how much they loved their iconic country singers.

Josie yanked off her tank top and adjusted her bikini, bouncing her boobs into position. "You're so melodramatic, Rowen. Anyone ever tell you that?"

In fact, someone had. On my first day at Willow Springs, a certain cowboy might have accused me of such.

"No. Never," I lied. "Anyone ever tell you you've got your damn head in the clouds?"

"I've been accused of that plenty of times, for sure." Josie laughed as she shrugged out of her cutoffs. Stripping down by the truck was easier. Less to pack down to the swimming hole. "Okay, I'll give you Jolene is flirting with Jesse. But that's who she is. She's the girl who flirts with every single guy she comes in contact with. She's been doing it for so long she doesn't even know she's doing it anymore."

I tugged off my slip dress and tossed it into the cab. "*That* isn't flirting. *That* isn't even an innocent crush." I waved my hands toward the spot Jesse and Jolene had disappeared into the trees. "That's a bad case of I-want-to-build-a-shrine-to-you-and-have-a-dozen-of-your-babies."

"Please, Rowen, give me a little credit here. One, I'd know if my cousin was wanting to have wild-monkey sex with your boyfriend because the girl can't keep a secret to save her life, and two, there's a code between relatives out here."

"A code?" I adjusted my own swimsuit top, although I didn't have as much filling mine as Josie did. My black bandeau top didn't do anything to enhance what I had either.

"Yeah, a code. You don't date each other's exes."

I wasn't familiar with that code, but Montana people did things a bit differently. "What's the time period on that? Weeks? Months?"

Josie got in my face and clapped her hands over my shoulders. "Ever."

"Like never ever?"

"Is there another kind I'm unaware of?"

I let that settle in for a moment. I wasn't sure if I bought it, but Josie clearly did, and she was no fool. I might have had a few more points I wanted to clarify, but a cowboy hustling his way back up the hill came within earshot.

"How was that for record time?" He stopped in his tracks at the front of Old Bessie when it registered I was in nothing but my swimsuit. A slow smile fell into place. A smile that made me feel things I shouldn't be feeling with that stupid bet hanging above us.

"How's Jolene?" I asked.

Jesse shrugged. "Good. I'm not really sure why she was so excited to come. She doesn't want to even get in the water. Something about not wanting to get her hair wet."

If Jesse truly was stumped as to why Jolene was so eager to come, men really were a clueless species.

"I don't know about you two, but I don't want to sit up here and melt any longer. I'm diving in." Josie plunked her red sunglasses on and started down the trail toward the swimming hole.

It was hot. So hot, I felt sweat beading on the back of my neck. "Hey, wait up. We're coming!"

Jesse peeled off his shirt and was stepping out of his boots when I passed him. Not missing an opportunity, I slapped his backside. "Come on, Cowboy. Time for a swim."

"Right behind you. Just have to get my shorts on."

Jesse was working his belt free when I caught up to Josie. She arched an eyebrow, her gaze fixated on him. "You need any help over there, Jesse, let us know. My guess is that you've got three willing and eager female volunteers."

"Get going, man-ogler." I shoved Josie's shoulder then gave her another one when she glanced over her shoulder one more time. "I think that flirt gene runs in the family."

"You think right," Josie replied, wiggling her butt and shaking her arms to an imaginary beat the rest of the way down the trail.

I didn't know if I attracted the crazy ones or they were attracted to me, but I had plenty of friends who fit into the escaped-from-the-psych-unit category.

"So you really think Garth will be all right?" Josie asked as we wove through the willow trees.

"I think Garth Black would be all right even if he was injected with Ebola virus. The mean ones just keep on keepin' on. Kind of like the Energizer bunny."

"Spoken like someone who knows." Josie let a curtain of willow branches fall in my face.

"Hold up. Are you calling me mean now too? I guess informing me I was a bitch just wasn't enough for one afternoon—now you have to drop the mean card on me?" I shoved the branches aside and glared at her back.

"Stop glaring daggers at my back. Meanie," she tacked on.

"For future reference, honesty is overrated. Way overrated in your case."

Josie laughed and paused long enough to let me catch up. She planted a surprise kiss on my cheek. "Good thing you love me."

I wiped my cheek and tried to snatch my elbow away when she wove her arm through it. I should have known better than to put up a fight. "Good thing," I sighed, letting her pull me along the rest of the way.

After being whipped, smacked, and assaulted by an army of willow branches, we broke free of the tree wall. The swimming hole was so flat it didn't even look like water. The willow leaves were just starting to bud and the water looked dark, almost black, without the usual rainbow of green. Absence of color or not, it was still beautiful. Then a figure waved from the dock, and the beautiful moment was pretty much ruined.

"'Bout time you showed up. What took you so long?" Jolene called.

"We were having a threesome. Sorry," I piped up, making Josie choke on her gum. "Jesse's an animal. Just

149

ask Josie."

Jolene laughed nervously. She hadn't been immersed in my dry sense of humor like Josie had. "Where's Jesse?"

"With Garth now." That time, Jolene did choke. "Kidding. No sexual acts, favors, or advances were made. After you left." I just couldn't help myself on the last part.

Josie hissed at me as she jogged down to the dock. "Did you forget your swimsuit, Jo? After all that deliberating and trying on five hundred this morning?"

"No. I've got it on," Jo said, setting down the magazine she was flipping through.

"What is the girl who hates tan-lines waiting for then?" Josie plopped down next to her cousin and scooted onto a corner of her beach towel.

Jolene caught sight of something over my shoulder. I didn't need to check who it was. The smile about to tear her face apart gave it away.

"I wasn't waiting for anything. I just hadn't gotten around to it yet." Jolene hobbled to a pathetic stand and did her wiggle, shimmy strip tease. The one where the chick with the perfect body takes her time sliding off her clothes, adjusting her swimsuit just so, making sure every last eye on the beach is on her. The one that makes every guy's throat dry and makes him roll onto his stomach to keep his "approval" from showing. Yep, that was the one Jolene was unearthing with my boyfriend getting closer.

I should have shoved the bitch into the lake when I had the chance. Before Jesse was there to witness it. Despite knowing Jesse would be in his swim shorts—and the less clothing that covered Jesse Walker, the better—I didn't want to turn around. I didn't want to see him staring at another girl as she stripped a few yards in front of him. I didn't want to see him wipe drool from the corner of his mouth. No man alive could keep his eyes diverted when a girl like Jolene was stripping down to her spandex underpants, so I wouldn't blame him. It was just that . . . well, it would break a little piece of my heart. Stupid and cliché, I know, but I already felt that painful ache in my chest.

When I found the courage to turn around, my eyes locked on his . . . and his eyes locked on mine too. Grinning, he jogged until he was right in front of me. His eyes didn't leave mine the entire journey. I wanted to cry with relief. I wanted to cry with the love I had for the guy standing in front of me, a love that, inconceivably, grew each day.

"Go for a swim with me," Jesse said, grabbing me and hoisting me up until my legs tangled around his waist.

"Now? No sun tanning to warm us up before we jump into that glacial water?"

"Nope. I need to go in now."

I grabbed Jesse's upper arms and held on as he started toward the end of the dock. When we passed Jolene, he acted like he didn't even know she was there. Her on the other hand? She definitely knew he was there. She was running those eyes all over *there* again.

"Why? What's the rush, Walker?" Not that I cared, but we both knew the water would feel like tiny needles pricking our skin until it went numb.

"I need to cool down."

My eyebrows pinched together in confusion. His hips rocked gently into me, and I understood. "Super. Now I'm in need of cooling down."

"Good timing, then."

"Good timing for what?"

Jesse's arms tightened around me before he leapt into the air. "For this!"

That water wasn't just glacial; it was something else. My skin was unable to decide if it was closer to burning or freezing, but I couldn't have cared less if my skin was actually on fire. When Jesse held me that close, nothing else seemed important. When our heads burst to the surface, we sucked in gulp of air. Jesse let me have a second breath before his mouth covered mine. I didn't even realize we were in water anymore, let alone that it was freezing cold. I loosened my legs around him just enough to drop a few inches. From the feel of it, the water wasn't *cooling* him down much.

"Hey! I didn't sign up to watch the two of you suck face all afternoon. Detach and behave yourselves," Josie shouted from the dock.

"Then don't watch!" I broke away from Jesse long enough to yell back. "We didn't sign up to have a third wheel times three this afternoon!"

Josie waved dismissively. "Whatevs. Get over yourselves and your all-consuming love for each other thingy. We get it already." Josie stood, stretched, and tested the water with her toes. "Let's do something fun." Jesse and I lifted her eyebrows. "Fun for *all* of us. Not just the horndogs in the bunch."

"You look like you're having a blast up there on that dock," I said.

"I'm bored, and we've been here a grand total of two minutes."

I don't know why Josie had been so eager to tag along. She knew we were going to the swimming hole. As far as entertainment went, she needed to get creative.

"What did you have in mind, Josie?" Jesse asked, swimming us toward the shore until we could touch bottom.

"Ooo, I know!" Jolene interjected in her excited voice, with her excited face and her excited eyes. Excited. Bleh. "Let's have a camel fight."

Could the girl get anymore Girls Gone Wild? First the slow, porn-quality strip, and now this? A camel fight? Jiminy Christmas.

"Sold. That sounds ten times better than sitting on this rickety old dock just waiting for it to sink." With that, Josie tossed her sunglasses aside and jumped in.

Jolene took a minute longer, having to take off her ankle wrap and pull her hair into a bun. After adjusting her swimsuit—for the bajillionth time—she hurried to the shallow end of the dock and stepped in where the water was at knee level. The way she'd booked it down the dock further confirmed my theory that she was milking her ankle injury for all it was worth. Especially if it was worth a ride in Jesse Walker's arms.

"Are we really doing this?" I asked Josie when she paddled up to Jesse and me.

"You better believe your grumpy ass we are."

"I call shoulders since I'm temporarily handicapped," Jolene said, wading toward us.

She was going to wind up permanently handicapped before the week was over.

"Well you're not riding my shoulders because that ass of yours might be bony, but you're as tall as an Amazon. Find another pair of shoulders," Josie said.

"Looks like it's you and me then, Jesse."

And just like that, we'd all walked right into her web.

"Hello." I waved. "There is one other person here." As much as I knew she'd like to ignore me.

"Oh. Yeah. I know. Sorry, Rowen, and no offense, but"—Jolene's smile screamed condescension—"you're the littlest of us. I didn't think you'd be strong enough to take me. Why don't you ride on Josie's shoulders?"

I had to bite my lip. I had to bite it so damn hard to keep from spewing what I wanted to reply. I hadn't missed her choice of wording with *take me,* and from the tilt of her brow, she hadn't wanted me to miss it either.

"Lean down a bit, Jesse." Practically shoving onto his shoulders, Jolene finagled her way up them in two seconds flat. Sprained ankle, my ass. "Hold on tight to my legs. The tighter the better because I do not, and I repeat *do not*, want to get my hair wet."

Jolene was just rising to every one of my cliché standards for her.

Jesse gave me that look, one I was getting familiar with. The look that said *Is this okay?* The one that asked *What do you want me to do?* That look endeared him to me that much more.

Replying with one nod, I practically dunked Josie while climbing on her shoulders. Josie grumbled a few words, gave me a hard pinch, and grabbed hold of my knees.

"I hope you don't mind the wet poodle look," I warned Jolene. I capped my warning with a smile as Josie marched toward Jesse and Jolene.

"You obviously don't." Jolene capped hers with just as overdone a smile.

Jesse was holding her ankles and his forehead was wrinkled like he wasn't sure there'd ever been such a bad idea.

"You're going down." I extended my arms, eager to knock Jolene from her high tower atop my man's shoulders.

"No. You are." With that, Jolene's arms thrust forward, and her hands landed square above my swimsuit top. I was falling through the water before I'd even gotten out a scream.

When I resurfaced, Jesse was rushing my way with Jolene still atop him. "Rowen? Are you okay?"

Josie sputtered to the surface beside me. "I'm okay," I said, spitting out a liter of lake water.

"She's okay," Jolene repeated, grinning down at me. "Again?"

"Again." Climbing on top of Josie again, I felt something new trickle into my veins. Revenge? Resolve? I didn't know, but it couldn't hurt. "Hold on tighter, Josie."

Josie huffed. "Yeah. And don't take a direct hit like that next time."

"One, two, three, four. I declare a camel-fight war," Jolene sing-sung as Josie and I came at them.

"It's war, all right." That time, I wouldn't underestimate how long her go-go-gadget arms were. Or her strength. She might have puny arms, but I'd forgotten how strong ranch life made a person.

"Yes, it is"—Jolene dodged my arms when they came at her—"and you're the loser."

That time, I took the hit to my abdomen. My back actually stung from how hard I slapped the water. I'd never felt anger how I felt it when I broke through the surface. I ignored Jesse's concern and Jolene's triumphant expression when I climbed on top of Josie for the third time. I wouldn't be the first to go down again. That was final. I didn't care if she ripped out my hair or broke my collar bone. I wasn't losing to Jolene.

"Get that bitch off her high horse, Rowen," Josie muttered up at me, sliding wet streaks of hair from her face. "Or off your hot boyfriend."

"Planning on it."

Jolene had her hands on her hips as Josie and I came at them. "If you could'a, you would'a."

That time when I came at her, she came at me. My hands locked on her shoulders and hers shoved into my collar bone. I might not have been too far off on that whole collar bone-breaking premonition.

I pushed her with all I had; she shoved at me with all she had. Just when I was sure she was about to topple back, she righted herself. Same went for me. We were at it for a good minute, at an obvious stalemate, when one of her hands moved lower. The next thing I knew, I was topless, and Jolene was swinging my bandeau top over her head.

Jesse's eyes bulged as mine narrowed.

My instinct was to cover my chest, and that's what I did for a few moments. Sitting like that, I was an easy target. Forgoing all pride and inhibition, I dropped my arms and sharpened my glower.

Giving my top one last twirl, she flung it behind her. "Oops." Pasting on an all too familiar smile, Jolene wove her fingers into Jesse's hair. The hair that I was all kinds of territorial over.

Bad move.

I let out a low growl, urged Josie forward, and went at that smiling, hair-petting bimbo with both arms. I was about a foot away from making contact when Jolene toppled off of Jesse's back. Her shriek right before she crashed into the water was one of the sweetest sounds I'd ever heard.

When I glanced down at a sheepish cowboy, I found Jesse's hands still open where they'd just been fixed around Jolene's ankles. Shrugging, he winked up at me. "No one messes with my girl."

When Jolene surfaced, I gave her one of my own smiles of victory. So much for not getting her hair wet. Josie bounced up and down in celebration, which was all well and fine except . . . I was still topless.

Of course, that would be the moment Garth emerged from the willow trees, and, of course, me and my bare chest would be the first thing he'd zero in on. "Woohoo! Just in time for the free show! Good timing on my part!" Garth shouted, cupping his hands around his mouth.

"Go to hell, Garth!" I yelled back, covering myself a moment before Jesse's hands were about to do the same.

"Now why would I do that when I just landed myself in heaven?" Garth had lost his shirt somewhere along the way. Stepping out of his boots, he hung his hat on a branch before sauntering down the dock. "Jess, I'm disappointed. You never told me Rowen had such a fine rack."

"Black . . ." Jesse warned, heading toward Garth.

"Walker," Garth mimicked. "I mean, those are a pair of serious fun-bags if I've ever seen some."

Moving so fast he was a blur, Jesse grabbed Garth's calf and pulled him into the water. Garth toppled into the water, miraculously managing not to utter a curse. Josie and I cheered. When Garth kicked to the surface and Jesse was ready and dunked him, we cheered even louder.

"I'm going to kick your backside!" If hearing Garth substituting "backside" for "ass" wasn't funny enough, hearing him do it while sputtering out water was even better.

"Not before I dunk yours."

Jesse and Garth continued with their man war while I dropped into the water. Time to look for a missing swimsuit top.

"Hey, Jolene. Mind telling me where my top is?" I swam toward her.

Jolene pulled the rubber-band from her hair and ran her fingers through it. She hitched her thumb over her shoulder. "Back there."

"Yeah, I guessed that since you hurled it over your back. Mind going and finding it?"

"Yeah. I do mind. I'm not the one who lost it." She was furiously working to make her hair less of a soaking wet mess.

"No, you're the one who tore it off and tossed it into dark water."

Without so much as a screw you or a good-bye, Jolene headed for the shore.

Jesse and Garth were about to have company duking it out in the water.

Josie swam up beside me. "Come on. I'll help you find it. She must be hardcore PMS'ing."

"Or has a hardcore crush on my boyfriend who she's realizing is hardcore in love with me."

Josie flicked her fingers in my face, splashing me. "After that bout of bitchiness, I'm beginning to wonder."

"Why wonder when it's so obvious?"

Josie and I swam in the general direction of where my

top had gone under, and someone kicked up beside us. "Helloooo, ladies." Jesse had an exuberant expression which meant he must have come out the victor in the dunking war. "Need some help?"

"Yeah. Finding my top," I said.

Jesse's eyes twinkled. "I believe I have some experience with that."

If I was a blusher, I might have just from the look he gave me. "You're a regular search and rescue pro."

"I got this, Josie. Why don't you go save your cousin from Garth? He's got that look in his eye."

Josie's head whipped back. "If he even thinks about getting that look in his eye with Jolene, I might take Rowen up on her idea and inject him with the Ebola virus."

Jesse quirked a brow at me.

"It was a figure of speech. That's not how I meant it," I called after Josie, who was paddling back. Garth had pulled himself out of the water and was helping Jolene out with, indeed, that certain look in his eyes.

"That's how I took it," Josie shouted back. From her tone, I guessed Josie hadn't missed that gleam in Garth's eyes either.

"Let's see if we can find your top. As much as I might not want to." Jesse winked before disappearing into the water.

We'd swam so far away from the dock we were almost to the other side of the swimming hole. A curtain of willow branches draped into the water . . . and that's when I got an idea. I was already swimming toward the branches when Jesse resurfaced.

"Nothing."

"I think it's more this way," I replied, smiling.

"What? Really? You think it flew that far?" Jesse paddled after me.

"Farther." When I was a couple of feet in front of the branches, I dove and swam a few strokes before coming back up. The branches extended so far into the water, they created a good-sized pool. They provided such a barrier I could barely make out Jesse on the other side, let alone the three back on the dock. If I couldn't see them, that meant they couldn't see us . . . I'd just moved a bit closer to shore when Jesse joined me inside the private world.

"There's no way it went this far," he said, moving my way.

"I know." Jesse gave me a confused look. "Use your imagination."

"Oh, I am. Big time." He was grinning like the devil when he stopped in front of me. His arms went around my waist, and he pulled me close. "But you know, my male, hormone-driven imagination might not be syncing with your much more innocent and sweet one."

"I doubt that," I whispered right before covering his mouth with mine. Tracing the seam of his lips with my tongue, I waited for him to respond. I didn't wait long.

One hand went lower and the other went higher, and when they both found what they were looking for and gave a gentle squeeze, I swore I was about to drop my head back and cry out. Last night's abstinence was making the afternoon's make-up session especially intense.

When Jesse's mouth lowered to my neck, I wove my fingers into his wet hair. "I bet you're all right with my swimsuit top going missing now, right?"

"I really can't imagine being more all right with

anything else right now," he said against my neck, giving another gentle squeeze to prove his point.

That time, a moan escaped my mouth. When Jesse's grip tightened over my backside, successfully fitting my southerly region tighter against his, I came so close to orgasming, I could have been labeled the female two-pump-chump equivalent. "Jesse, oh my god, yes."

I felt his tell-tale smile move into place, and then his hand left my breast. Practically dying from the anticipation of where it would move to next, I hadn't expected the alternative: it had been busy removing his swim trunks. When his fingers slid my swimsuit bottoms aside and I felt something that, yet again, put me one second away from orgasming, I flinched my hips back.

How my brain was able to remember anything right then, I didn't know, but it was all curse and no blessing. "Jesse," I hissed.

"Yeah?" The skin between his eyebrows lined as deep as I'd ever seen it go. Understandably so. When it came to that piece of our relationship, I'd never been one to hit the brakes. Or I hadn't been until last night.

"Forgetting a certain bet you made with a certain someone?"

Jesse grimaced. "I was about point two seconds away from forgetting my first name."

That would make two of us.

"Come on, Rowen. He won't know. I won't tell, you won't tell, and even if he did find out, who cares? It's just some stupid bet."

"Some stupid bet you agreed to with a guy I can't let win at anything. It's in my genetic code or something."

He sighed. "Just forget I ever mentioned it. There's

no bet. I don't even know a guy who would be so idiotic to enter into such a bet." Jesse's arms tightened around me, pulling me back into position. "I need to be close to you, Rowen."

"It feels more like you *really* need to be close to me," I said, gliding my hand down him. His eyes might have rolled back in his head. I jolted when Jesse's finger slid just inside my bottoms, circling a certain spot.

"And it feels like you need to be really, *really* close to me."

I didn't have a single doubt if I flat-out told Jesse I wasn't in the mood to have sex, he would have backed off immediately. He would have switched from high-drive to being happy making out or just lounging beside me. He'd never forced, guilted, or manipulated me into having sex, and I knew he never would. His tortured look and reaction was a result of him wanting to have sex with me. Wanting and waiting.

The thing was, I really wanted to have sex with him. He'd been correct when he said really, *really*. It wasn't just about satisfying an overwhelming desire either, though that was present. It was about feeling his love. It was about feeling the physical expression of love that was for no one's eyes but ours. It was about me worshipping him and him worshipping me, and the two of us finding a release together that we couldn't experience apart. At least not in the same way.

It was about being in the moment, and living that moment to its fullest. It was about feeling infinite in those few moments we rarely got to share together due to location and obligation. It was about loving each other in such a way we could have been drowning in it.

"Hold that thought." I lifted my finger as my desperate mind searched for a solution to the whole "bet" mess.

Jesse gave me a look as I swam the opposite direction of where he obviously wanted me to be going. "Looks like I'll be holding something."

I tried to stifle my laugh, but I guess I wasn't really up to the task of stifling. "Just a minute. I'll be right back."

"Don't worry. I'll be fine. I'll just be here. Wet. Naked." Jesse moved into shallower water so I had a nice view of that wet nakedness. "Ready." Turning to face me, he gave me another view of the "ready" part.

I glanced away and swallowed the flames crawling up my throat. "Well, it looks like you'll have plenty to entertain yourself with while I'm gone."

"I'd rather have you entertain myself," he called before I dropped below the surface.

I wasn't a good swimmer. Decent sure, but I wouldn't have received any medals for form. Speed, however, was a different story. Especially when the faster I swam, the faster I'd be able to get back to what I was practically trembling to get back to.

Another flash of the wet nakedness waiting for me fifty yards back urged me ahead even faster. The threesome Jesse and I had escaped from were spread out on the dock, soaking in some sun. Josie and Jolene were sharing a towel, and Garth was sprawled out on the splintery wood.

"Hey, Black!" I hollered when I was a dozen strokes back.

"Hey what?" he replied, sitting up. He was still in his tight, black jeans. Even his belt buckle was still in place.

"Forget your swimming trunks?"

"No. I don't wear trunks, shorts, or anything else that

might think it's okay to go above my ankle. I'm a cowboy, god dammit. We don't wear shorts. Might want to relay that to the swim short wonder over there in the trees. What a disgrace."

"As much fun as this little spat could be—because, come on, you and I know we could go on and on about this real cowboys don't wear shorts thing—I'm kind of pressed for time." Pressure definitely had something to do with me searching out Garth. Swimming up beside him, I crossed my arms over the dock and met his stare. "I need you to do something for me."

Garth smiled like the Grinch hatching his Christmas Eve plan of terror. "I'd ask what that favor would be, but given you're still topless and I'm guessing the poser in hiding's probably lost his shorts, I think I know what's on your mind. Plus, you've got that general look about you that says your head's going to explode if you don't get a little vitamin J in you soon."

I splashed Garth in the face, thankful Josie and Jolene had their earbuds in. At least they were able to block out the filth that came from Garth's mouth. "Cuss, already. You know you want to. I can tell from that look on your face that says your head's going to explode if you don't scream a FUCK YOU! at the world soon."

Hearing those two words, Garth almost sighed in contentment, followed by a small tremble. Probably from withdrawal. "Now why would I want to do that when I'd say you and Jesse are about one bikini bottom of restraint away from giving me the win?"

"Cuss, Garth."

"No."

"Garth . . ."

"Rowen," he deadpanned back. "Either go enjoy Jesse or yourself because I am not losing this close to the end. I cuss now, and two weeks of not cussing will be for nothing. I'm not losing because not only would the losing part suck, but then you two would celebrate your win by playing hide the snake. Where's the fairness in all that?"

"Garth . . ." My nails were digging into my palms so hard I had to be close to drawing blood.

"Rowen," he mimicked, sticking out his tongue.

"Dammit! Why do you have to be so difficult?"

"Are you looking for an actual explanation? Or was that one of those rhetorical questions?"

Unbelievable. He was smiling, all calm like.

"That was an I-don't-care-why-you're-so-difficult-just-show-me-how-I-can-beat-it-out-of-you kind of question."

"I'm sorry, ma'am, I'm fresh out of I-give-a-darn. Why don't you check back next century?" Garth tilted his head and waved.

"Fuck you."

He lifted his eyebrows. "My, oh, my. You suck your boyfriend with that filthy mouth?"

That earned him another splash. "Go to hell, Black."

"Lucky Jesse," Garth said with a wink.

I was obviously getting nowhere with Garth. Actually, I was obviously getting somewhere—backwards. Not the direction I'd been hoping to go. Taking a handful of slow, not-quite-soothing breaths, I decided to do something high on my list of Never Want to Do: swallow my pride in front of Garth Black. The one thing higher on that list? Delaying sex with Jesse Walker.

"Please?" Yeah, it was as hard as I imagined it would

be. Just one word in and it had already singed my throat. "From one misunderstood, glass-half-empty misfit to another . . . please?"

The cocky smile fell right off Garth's face. It was working. My momentary lapse into sincerity was doing exactly what I hoped it would do: throw Garth for a loop. He studied my face for a few more seconds, trying so hard to glare at me his brow almost broke out in a sweat. Then he let out one long sigh, slid his hat low on his brow, and shook his head. "You women and your pouty faces are going to be the death of me."

"Was that what I thought it was?" I bit my lip to keep my excitement contained.

"Yeah, it was. That was me slitting my own throat when I had my opponent right where I wanted him. That was one misfit taking one for the misfit team."

I'd known it all along. I forgot it along the way some-times, but Garth wasn't the hard shell of a man he liked us all to believe he was.

"Thank you." I beamed at him. "So, so much."

"Yeah, yeah." He waved at me dismissively. "Get the fuck out of here and go fuck your boyfriend already."

Well, the redeeming thing had been nice while it lasted.

"Fuck, that felt good." Garth hopped up like new life had just burst into him. Arching his head back, he cupped his hands around his mouth. "FUCK, FUCK, FUCK!!! FUCKITY FUCK, FUCKERY, FUCKER!"

Jolene and Josie must have had their music blasting or were comatose because Garth was shouting so loudly, the next zip code could have heard him.

"FUCK!!!"

"Done?" I twisted my finger into my ear.

"Just getting warmed up, Topless-Wonder."

"I'll leave you to it then. Have fun." I shoved away from the dock and started swimming for a certain clump of trees in the distance. I'd only gotten a few yards when I stopped. "Hey, Garth?" He looked like he was about to break into another chorus of curses. "Thanks. For a self-proclaimed asshole, you're a pretty decent guy. From one misfit to another, I'm glad we're on the same team."

From the looks of it, Garth would have been more comfortable having his nether-region waxed than receiving a compliment. He looked off in the distance and scratched the back of his neck for a moment, at a total loss. How could someone render a man like Garth Black speechless? Give him a compliment.

Finally, he glanced my way. "Rowen. Go fuck your-self." His words were softened with a smile and a wink. In terms of endearment, that was the pinnacle in Garth's world.

Before things got any more record-breaking with Garth, I continued my swim back to Jesse. If I thought I'd swam fast the previous one-way, that had nothing on the return trip. Not only had Garth just fallen on his own bet sword, but Jesse was a few more kicks away, naked and still hopefully . . . *ready*.

When I resurfaced after my dive beneath the willow branches, I didn't see anything naked or ready waiting for me. In fact, I was beginning to wonder if I'd picked the wrong section of trees when someone bubbled to the sur-face behind me. I almost burst out of my skin in surprise before those strong, familiar arms wound around me.

"Looking for someone?" Jesse lowered his mouth to

my ear.

"Yeah. But you'll do."

"I know I should at least pretend that hurt my feelings, but I need to confirm something first."

I rolled my head back and let it rest against Jesse's shoulders as his hands traveled up and down my body. "What do you need confirmed?"

"Was that what I thought I heard coming from Black's mouth?"

"Yes. And from the sounds of it, it's what's still coming from his mouth." Garth sounded like he wasn't only making up for lost time, he was making up for future time as well.

"And am I right to guess you might have had something to do with that?" Jesse's hands stopped moving, but his fingers started, and they were about to send me right over the edge.

"Yes," I sighed, draping an arm behind his neck. "Yes, you're . . . oh my god, you're good." He chuckled against my neck, his pace slowing. "I mean, yes, oh my god, you're *right*." Come on, he knew better than to expect a logical string of words to come from my mouth when he was doing those kinds of things to me.

"Why? Why was it so important to you that I not lose? Why beg Garth to let me win?" His fingers stopped altogether, and while I could at least think, that wasn't what I wanted to concentrate my efforts on.

"For the same reason it was so important to you that I didn't lose to Jolene back there. For the same reason you pretty much shoved her off your back. We're a team." I twisted until I was facing him. Cupping his face, I kissed him softly. "Win or lose, we're in it together. Right?"

168

Leaning his forehead into mine, Jesse's eyes went soft. "Win, lose, on top of the world, or at rock bottom . . . I'm with you, Rowen Sterling. To the very end."

It was my turn for my eyes to go soft, although mine went so far they formed tears. "To the very end."

Maybe there was more I wanted to say, and maybe there was more he did too, but when Jesse's mouth crashed into mine as he shifted me above him, there were no words left. When Jesse entered me, I lost everything. All the words on the tip of my tongue. All the thoughts swirling through my head. All control. The only thing I felt was Jesse and his love.

I kissed him back, moving against him, hoping that was all he felt too. It didn't take either of us long, but when we did fall apart around each other, the last thing I remembered thinking before crying out and the first thing I remembered at the end of it was that surely no one had ever loved another person the way I loved Jesse Walker.

chapter TWELVE

Rowen

THINGS CAN CHANGE so fast. Too fast.

Example?

Spring break felt like it would last forever one Sunday afternoon while making love, and in what seemed like a blink later, I was on a bus heading west. Things changed too goddamned fast. Especially the good things.

That afternoon at the swimming hole had been the high point, the twelve-hour ride home the following Sunday had been the low, and for some sick, unfair reason, my low point followed me into Monday. Well, I guess it was actually Tuesday since we'd passed the midnight mark.

Alex had just flipped off the Open sign and was pouring herself another cup of coffee while I emptied the display of the remaining doughnuts. I'd been moving like a slug all day long, at barely half time. Even the first day of spring quarter hadn't cheered me up, and I'd gotten every single class I'd signed up for. Art, art, and more art. Did I mention art?

I was doing what I loved and excelling at it. I was in the running for one of the most prestigious internships in the city. I had good friends who were always willing to share a laugh. I was healthy, living independently, and had managed to move forward from my past.

And there was one other thing. A *monumental* thing. I had the love of a guy who redefined what a good man was. I had the world at my fingertips.

So why couldn't I shake the feeling that something was about to change? Like I'd come home to spring in Seattle to find my own personal winter about to set in? Why did I feel like I was walking around like I was waiting for the ground to fall out from beneath me? Why did I feel like the one person I cared about most was about to slip through my fingers?

Probably because I'd had to say a teary good-bye to him yesterday morning while knowing it would be another two weeks before I saw him next. I was pre-menstrual, and the clouds had been leaking rain non-stop since I'd pulled into the bus station. It was crazy how hormones and the weather could change a person's entire outlook.

"So this Jolene chick pretty much followed you two around all week?" Alex plopped down on the display case I was cleaning, picking up our conversation from earlier. It had started out with what we'd done over spring break, then turned into a Jolene this, Jolene that fest.

"The only place we were safe was the other side of his bedroom door." I smiled at a few memories as my heart ached. "So we spent a lot of time behind closed doors."

"You saucy little sex-pot you." Alex patted my head.

"Thanks?"

"So what are you going to do about this Jolene chick now that you're hundreds of miles away from your boyfriend who she is probably, at present, knocking over the head with a fry pan so she can drag him into her bed and have her way with him?"

I slapped her hand away from where it was still patting my head. "So glad I told you. I feel *so* much better. So reassured right now."

Alex laughed and twirled one of the chains coming off her black vinyl bustier. It was the first day of a new quarter. Chains, vinyl, and torn-up fishnets were the obvious choice. "Calm down, little kitten."

"I might if you weren't here, doing the opposite of calming me with your opposite of reassuring premonitions."

She laughed again then cut it short when she saw my face. "Okay, let's approach this rationally since approaching it emotionally is making you an angry cat." She tapped her chin for a few seconds, then her eyes widened. "Are you worried about Jesse actually going for Jolene?"

After deciding that Alex was serious, I gave her question some thought. I didn't need to give it much. "No." It was a simple, truthful answer. Jesse didn't possess a non-loyal bone in his body.

"Are you worried about him getting drunk off his ass and jumping into bed with her in his drunken haze?"

I rolled my eyes. Jesse did drunk about as often as he did disloyalty. "No."

"Then what are you worried about exactly?"

That was the question that sent the proverbial punch to my gut. What in the hell was I so worried about? Why had I wasted precious time fuming over some inconsequential person? The lines in my forehead felt close to becoming permanent. "I don't know."

Alex's eyes met mine. "So you're not worried about

Jolene and Jesse's future relationship. Good, we got to the bottom of that. But, and this is one big but you better pay attention to, girl, because it's a doozy . . . *but* you should be worried about Jesse's and yours. Because this little jealous, insecure thing you're dealing with will only hurt the two of you."

And round two of the proverbial gut punch.

I thought about what Alex had just said for so long, the doughnut in my hand came close to petrifying. She was right on every single level I'd been wrong on. How had I missed that? What had clouded me to seeing it? Was it my tendency to glom on to the bad in life? Shit, I hoped not. Or was it because I loved Jesse so much I'd become a crazed person boiled down to raw emotion and instinct? I wasn't eager for either of those possibilities to come out on top.

"Damn. How did you get so smart?" I stood up feeling like the epiphany dump had put me in need of some fresh air.

Alex hopped down from the counter. "Making a bunch of mistakes."

"If that's the measure of a person's smartness, I should be a regular Einstein and a half."

"Okay, well I lived and I learned."

My brows came together. "Are you implying I haven't?"

Alex paused on her way down the hallway, probably heading for Sid's office. "We'll see." She gave me a small smile before—yep—rounding into Sid's office and closing the door.

I was going to need that fresh air for more than one reason.

Grabbing the trash with one hand, I carried the old doughnuts in my other and break-necked for the back door. It was still raining, but at least it'd slowed to a drizzle. Between the events of the past twenty-four hours, the rain, and sheer exhaustion, I couldn't go another step. The dumpster wasn't even ten feet away, but it might as well have been ten miles. I was spent.

Setting down the garbage bag, I leaned into the brick wall and tried to calm my mind. Confusion had set in, and it was moving fast, its contagion spreading. Even standing became too much. After dropping to the ground, I buried my head between my knees and focused on breathing. For no solid reason I could point to, my world felt like it was crumbling, piece by piece. Either I needed to get a concentrated dose of Midol injected in my ass or get a solid eight hours of sleep and wake up feeling normal. Or normal for me, at least.

"Where have you been all week?"

As yet another sign that I was a mess, I barely even flinched when that strange voice hollered at me. I rubbed my eyes before looking up. No tears, but they'd been close. It probably shouldn't have surprised me to see the homeless woman from last week coming toward me, but it did. I'd almost convinced myself she and what she'd said had all been a hallucination.

"Girlie? Did you hear me?"

"Spring break. I was in Montana." My voice was robotic, and my movements felt the same.

"Doing what?" The woman stopped in front of me. The expectation in her eyes told me what she was looking and hoping for. I held out the box of doughnuts. She snatched the box out of my hands, backed into the wall, and was one doughnut in before I'd worked up a reply.

"Seeing my boyfriend. Seeing his family and friends, too." A heavy dose of home sickness stabbed at me. I loved my life in Seattle, but I never longed for it or ached for it like I did Willow Springs.

"How was it?" she asked around a jelly doughnut.

I didn't know why I was sitting there having a semi-personal conversation with a homeless person who had scared the crap out of me, but I needed to talk to someone. Thankfully, she seemed to be firmly back in her rocker.

"Great. I had an amazing week."

She finished the rest of the jelly doughnut before asking her next question. "Then why are you in an alley all alone looking like you're about to start crying?"

I literally couldn't escape perceptive people. Not even in a garbage-ridden alley on the scary side of Seattle. "I'm confused."

"Confused about what?"

I swallowed. "So many things."

"Things about your boyfriend?"

"Maybe . . . Yes." I sighed and scuffed the tip of my boot against the asphalt. "I don't know." Those three words summed up my current state of mind. It seemed, after nineteen years of life, I didn't know shit. I felt like I'd known some yesterday, but today was a whole other story. I didn't know why I was so upset or why that anxiety had settled over me, and I really didn't know why I was having a conversation with a stranger. One who ate a box of doughnuts for dinner.

"Excuse me for saying, Girlie," she started, her eyes boring into mine, "but love doesn't seem like it should be so confusing. It doesn't seem like it should be so hard."

175

"Why not?" I wasn't agreeing or disagreeing; the verdict was still out.

"Because it's *love*," she said with a shrug. "It should come easy."

I sat there a while longer, reeling over what she'd just said. Part of me knew that was true. Another part of me screamed it was a lie. Should love be easy? Or should it be hard? Should it even be either?

In twenty-four hours, my mind had become a giant mass of confusion.

chapter **THIRTEEN**

Jesse

THE NIGHTMARES WERE coming every night, and what was worse than their frequency was that Rowen has somehow made her way into them. That's a world and a part of my life I didn't want her anywhere close to. I'd protect her from it at all costs.

I'd bolted awake last night after a repeat dream. I was in the basement again, chained to the pipe, more animal than boy, but I wasn't alone. I heard another chain clinking against a pipe across the room. When I saw her, there was no denying it was a young Rowen. She was crying, curled up into a ball, and trembling. No matter how many times I called out to her, or how loud, she didn't hear me. She didn't know I was chained on the opposite side of the room from her. Then the basement door opened, and I heard familiar shoes coming down the stairs. When the shoes stopped on the basement floor, they paused. When they started moving again, they weren't coming my way. They were going toward Rowen. I fought against my restraint so savagely, the leather around my neck rubbed the skin raw. Drops of blood dotted the floor when I heard the first scream come from the other side of the room.

And then, mercifully, I was ripped awake.

THE LAST TWO weeks were long. Partly because I hadn't seen Rowen and partly because I hadn't slept more than a couple hours a night. What was waiting for me the moment my eyes closed and my brain drifted off made me force myself to stay awake. My first five years of life, I'd done the opposite because any dream world was an improvement.

Rowen and I'd talked every day since she left at the end of spring break, but she seemed different. A bit removed or preoccupied.

Or maybe her seeming removed and preoccupied had nothing to do with her and everything to do with me. I certainly wasn't the carefree Jesse everyone was used to, although I tried to play the part. Most people accepted the facade, but a few—my mom, Lily, and Josie—saw through it. They're too perceptive, and part of me was irritated by that. And part of me was grateful because I knew if and when I did need to talk to someone about my reincarnated demons, I'd have someone. Of course Rowen was the person I'd go to first with anything. . . but not that. I didn't want her in that world. She's been through so much, and it was my job to protect her from any more darkness.

So, yeah, the last two weeks had been bad, but things were looking up. The next day was Friday, and I had the weekend off to go visit Rowen. I would work through whatever was going on in my head, Rowen would be none the wiser, and everything would be just fine.

It sounded easy enough, but I knew doing it would be the opposite.

The afternoon chores were done, and I was up in my attic bedroom changing into fresh clothes. After Jolene had stumbled in on me three different times while I was changing in the laundry room, Mom and I decided my bedroom might be a better place to change. At least until Jolene learned to knock.

After clasping my belt into place, I grabbed my wallet out of my dirty pants. I was about to slide it into my back pocket when I paused. For months, I couldn't go longer than an hour without checking to make sure it was still there. Then I'd gone months without checking. I couldn't even recall the last time I'd checked to make sure it was still tucked into the last card slot of my wallet. I had a sudden urge to check. That unsettled me. A lot. The frantic feeling jolting through me was foreign, yet familiar. I'd lived that frantic feeling in a past life. I didn't want to live, or even revisit, it in this life.

I inhaled as I opened my wallet. Slipping my little finger into the last slot, I slid it along the bottom. My throat went dry. I slid my finger back again, making sure I hadn't missed it. Surely it was still in there. After sliding my finger back and forth a couple dozen times, I emptied the entire contents of my wallet. Maybe it had fallen into a different slot. My driver's license, a few dollar bills, and a photo of Rowen fell to the floor. My wallet dropped beside the mess a moment later.

Hitching my hands on my hips, I scanned my room. It wasn't meticulous, but it was clean by guy standards. Something that small could be anywhere though: buried in the floor planks, hidden between the sheets of my bed, hiding beneath my boots in the closet. It *could* have been anywhere, but I didn't unleash a full-fledged search and rescue because I knew it wasn't there. I could feel it. Or I suppose what was more true was that I *couldn't* feel it.

The connection between myself and an inanimate

object making itself known again terrified me more than any of my nightmares. Unlike the nightmares, that was real. That was happening. I was feeling a familiar pang of obsession, my heart racing as I grew more frantic, feeling an actual connection to something I didn't want to feel a connection to.

If ever a person could regress so quickly, it was me. Weeks ago, I wouldn't have believed it, but there I was living it.

I didn't know how long I stood in my room, inhaling and exhaling, trying to fight back the feelings crashing over me like waves, one right after the other. But I failed. Nothing could pull me off the runaway train I was on, at least not yet.

The next night, though . . . the next night, I'd be with Rowen. If anything or anyone could get my mind off of it and give me some clarity, it would be her. I'd be okay. Tomorrow, things would be so much better.

Having no other assurances to give myself, I put my wallet back together, slid it into my back pocket, and left my room. I had an hour before dinner, and I was going to use it to clear my head. In Rowen's absence, the best substitute was saddling up Sunny and tearing through a few miles of countryside.

I was just shoving through the front door when Dad called me into his office.

"Hey, Dad. What's up?" I hovered inside the office doorway, trying to sound and look like carefree Jesse Walker.

"I was just talking to your mom, and she mentioned you were planning on heading to Seattle for the weekend." Dad slid off his hat and dropped it on the desk. "Is that right?"

I nodded. "That's right. I figured I'd leave as soon as we finished up tomorrow afternoon." Just thinking about spending the next night with Rowen beside me calmed me. Not all the way, but enough so I felt like I could breathe again.

Dad sighed. "I was afraid of that. It's probably my fault for not coming out and saying it, but, Jess . . . this is calving season. I know it's early this year thanks to the warm weather, but nonetheless, this is when I need you most, son. It's go time now through the end of summer, and after fifteen years of this, you know there's no such thing as days, let alone weekends, off." Dad's hard words were softened by his voice and expression, but still . . .

"Wait. What? Are you saying I can't leave to see Rowen tomorrow?" That's what it had sounded like, but in my current state, I needed everything spelled out.

Dad's forehead lined. "I'm sorry, Jess."

I braced myself in the doorway. "Just like that? You're going to tell me I can't go see her? Dad, I'm not a little boy you can tell what to do and not to do. I'm twenty years old. I get to decide who I want to see and when I want to see them." I'd never spoken to my dad like that before. I might not have been blatantly disrespectful, but I was bordering on it. I didn't look up to anyone on earth as much as I looked up to my dad, but him telling me I couldn't see the person I wanted to see, fresh on the heels of that wave of emotions, made me feel like a cornered dog. I needed out of the corner no matter what.

"I'm not telling you this as your father, Jesse. I'm telling you this as your employer. The height of our season has started, and I need you here. You've got responsibilities and obligations to fulfill, Jess."

"I've got responsibilities and obligations to Rowen, too."

"That's right. You do. And you've got them here at Willow Springs." Dad stood behind his desk chair, his arms folded over the top of it, watching me carefully. "Life's about figuring out how to manage and balance your responsibilities and obligations."

"How do I balance the fact that Rowen is expecting me in Seattle this weekend and you're expecting me here?"

Dad quirked a brow. "Son, that's easy. Rowen, thank god, loves you so much she'll forgive you and wait for you. The cows? They won't wait when a hundred-pound calf is ready to push its way into the world."

I thought about that for a minute. As much as I didn't want to admit it, I knew Dad was right. I'd been the idiot for thinking that even though Willow Springs was in firing-on-all-engines mode, I'd be able to take a few days off and head to Seattle. I'd ignored or played ignorant to the truth because I hadn't wanted to see it. I didn't want to think that anything would keep me away from Rowen. I still didn't want to think about it, but I couldn't claim ignorance anymore.

"Shit," I muttered, propping my forehead on the doorway. That pretty much summed up the whole day.

"Jesse—"

"Sorry. I just . . . Today hasn't exactly been made of win, if you know what I mean."

"First, no need to apologize. Shit, and worse, pretty much sums up the difficulties of a long-distance relation-ship." Dad moved to the front of his desk and leaned into it. He'd had the chair and desk for over a decade, and I'd never once seen him actually sit in the chair. We were too restless a breed to sit comfortably behind a desk. "Second, is something troubling you, son? I know I may not be the most sensitive person on this ranch, but you've seemed a little . . . *off* lately. Anything you want to talk about?"

There was so much I wanted to talk about, but I didn't know where to begin. Once I opened up about it, I couldn't pretend it would all magically disappear. "No, I'm good. You know how it is sometimes. Too many thoughts, too little gray matter." I tapped my temple and forced a smile. I was just heading off to make my nightly call to someone —the first nightly call I wasn't looking forward to—when dad cleared his throat.

"Jess, I'm sorry. You know I think the world of Rowen, and the fact that she thinks the world of you puts her that much higher in my esteem. Maybe she can visit here instead. You know she's welcome anytime, and I'll try to give you as much free time as I can when she comes. It wasn't too long ago when I was a young cowboy trying to making things work with a vivacious city girl."

"How did that work out for you?" I asked.

"Truthfully? It was hard as hell, and there were more days I thought we'd never make it than days I thought we would."

Just the reassuring words I needed to hear at that stage in my life.

"But you want to know what?" Dad lifted his left hand and pointed at his ring finger. "I've still got this on my finger twenty plus years later, and I wouldn't trade a day of hardship with your mom for a day of easy-breezy with someone else."

"How do you think she feels?"

Dad chuckled. "You'll have to ask her. I learned a long time ago that answering for your mom adds another day of hardship to the running tally." Grabbing his hat off the desk, he slid it on and beelined out of there. I didn't know why, but Dad went a little stir crazy if he was trapped in his office for more than a few minutes. "You're a good man. You've got a good woman. You live a good life. Why the long face?"

I didn't want to tell him it was because I was afraid the drain was about to be pulled. I didn't want to say I was worried all the good in my life had just hit its expiration date. I didn't want to admit any of that, so I forced a smile and slugged him lightly in the arm as he passed by. "I'm not so sure I've got a *good* employer."

"You're right. You don't," Dad said as he headed out the front door. "You've got a *great* one."

I wanted to stall. I never wanted to make the call I needed to make. I didn't want to disappoint her. My afternoon had taken on a whole new level of suck; how much worse could it get? Pulling my phone from my pocket, I was about to find out.

Rowen picked up on the second ring. "Hey, you."

God. Just hearing her voice made my day about a hundred times better. "I miss you, Rowen. I miss you so damn much." It wasn't exactly a greeting, but it was all I could get out.

"What a coincidence. I miss you so damn much too. Good thing for both of us we get to spend the weekend together."

I bit the inside of my cheek. "Actually, that's why I'm calling. There's been a change of plans." Keeping my voice strong when I felt anything but was hard.

"Change of plans? What change?" That right there, Rowen's voice dropping in disappointment, was what I'd give my right leg to keep from ever hearing again.

"I can't come this weekend. Dad needs me here." Keeping my answers short was the only way to keep up the strong act.

"You're not coming . . ." It sounded like she was talking to herself, but those words sliced through me.

"I'm sorry. I'm so, so sorry. You have no idea how bad I want to be there, Rowen. How bad I *need* to see you." I dropped into the chair close by and waited for her reply.

"You have no idea how bad I need to see you either." She paused suddenly, like she was choking on something. She was quiet for so long I checked to make sure I hadn't lost the call. "Oh, well. I guess we'll just have to suck it up and make due, right?"

Truly, a horse kicking me square in the stomach would have been less painful. I half-wished one would kick me to help dull the other pain trickling into my veins. "Can you come here instead? I'll be busy, but I'll sneak away when no one's looking. At least we'll have a couple nights together, and I promise not to sleep a wink. At least when I fall asleep in the saddle, I'll fall off with a grin on my face."

"Jesse—"

"Come on. Just say you'll come. It won't make any difference that our plans changed so long as we're together. Come." I was one more *come* away from begging, but that was all right. I wasn't above begging. Rowen was quiet for so long, I convinced myself she was working it all out in her head.

And that was when she sighed. "I can't."

"You can't?"

"I've got work, Jesse. I'd planned on you being here, so I got scheduled for a shift. I have a school project due on Monday I haven't even started yet."

"Can't you get someone to cover for you? And bring your project, and I'll help you with it. Hell, I'll do it for you. Just come. Please." There I was, Jesse Walker, a desperate man.

"Jesse, I can't—"

"Rowen—"

"Dammit, Jesse, I've got a life too, you know. I can't just up and cancel it all because you changed plans. I can't plan my life around yours, and you shouldn't expect me to." I couldn't tell if Rowen was more upset or angry. I'd learned that, a lot of times, she disguised one with the other.

"You're right, you're right. I'm sorry. That's not how I meant it." I lowered my head into my hand. Words had always been my ally, but they seemed to have become my enemy. "I don't expect you to put your life on hold for mine. I'd *never* ask you to do that. It's just—"

"Then what were you just asking me to do, Jesse?"

I rubbed my temples and took my time answering. "To come visit me. If you were available."

"I'm not."

"I know. I shouldn't have assumed you would be."

"Good thing for you I love you, so you're forgiven." The lightness of Rowen's voice was returning, but a darkness consumed me. "I wish I could, though. I wish I could just drop everything and come."

"Yeah. I wish I could, too."

Rowen and I talked for a couple more minutes. For the first time, I felt worse at the end of our call than I had at the start.

chapter **FOURTEEN**

Jesse

ANOTHER WEEK DOWN. One more to go before Rowen would be there. Three weeks was a long time to go without seeing each other. We'd gone longer, but no stretch had ever felt so long. I knew that had a lot to do with my state of mind and how "unsettled" seemed to be my new normal.

It didn't help that Rowen seemed to be slipping through my fingers. She hadn't said anything outright, but something was off. So I was off, Rowen was off, and we were off. My whole life was off.

If I didn't get a grip and focus, I was about to fall off of Sunny too.

"Jesus, Walker! Pull your head out because I am not saving your sorry ass if you go and break your other arm!" Garth was about twenty yards ahead of me on Rebel, weaving through the herd.

"Why don't you mind your business and I'll mind mine?" I shouted back, reining Sunny in. Garth and I were taking the late afternoon watch, and a couple of the other guys would be relieving us for night watch. Dad had been right about calving season setting in early. Three-quarters of the year's calves had been born in the past week, and with so many young, awkward animals grazing in the wide open, there was an increased risk of predators taking out a few. There were plenty of coyotes around, but to my knowledge, none had ever taken down one of our calves. The rest of the herd would have crushed the hell out of a coyote if it had tried. I'd never *seen* a mountain lion take down one of ours—they were sneaky creatures that stayed far away from people—but we'd lost at least two of our calves to mountain lions. What posed the most risk were the wolf packs. They'd taken close to a dozen of our herd—adult and calf—and I'd seen them do it once before, too.

Garth had been with me. We were thirteen, had the afternoon off, and were doing our usual trying-to-one-up-the-other routine when we heard the spine-chilling sound. By the time we'd raced Sunny and Rebel there, the pack was already ripping apart what was left of a calf and carrying it away. The wolves had shown no real fear of us, and that was the most frightening part of the whole ordeal. I'd realized that I wasn't the top of the food chain out there like I'd assumed.

I hadn't seen a wolf pack since, but I'd heard them plenty of times, and I'd had to account for a handful of the herd they'd taken out too. To Dad, it was just a part of the business. We'd lose some to natural causes, sickness, and predators; that was the price of being in the cattle business. But to me, it somehow seemed more personal. A formidable, strong predator going after an innocent calf. I'd been ranching a long time, and I knew it was part of the great circle, but my heart didn't quite accept it. See? Damn hippy heart . . .

"You know, I'd love to mind my own business.

That's what I normally do because that's what I'm good at." Garth and Rebel bumped up beside Sunny and me as we finished checking the herd. "But you know what happened when I was minding my own business last summer? I got a call to come help find poor little Jesse Walker who might have gone over Suicide Ridge."

"No one twisted your arm."

"No, no one did. But who else was going to save you if it wasn't me? Because, let's face it, I'm the biggest, baddest badass out there, Walker. You want me on your side when you tumble over Suicide Ridge."

Surprisingly, doing watches with Garth the past month had been nice. The one up side to him running his mouth all the time was that it kept my mind off of other things.

"I don't know, Black. I seem to remember a girl beating you to the saving-me punch."

"Yeah, a girl who didn't have a rope or any other way to actually get you or her out of that ravine."

I shoved him hard enough he slid in his saddle but not so hard he fell right off of it. "Fine. I'll admit it. I'm glad you're on my side."

"Speaking of on your side . . ." Garth lifted his chin, looking over my shoulder.

Glancing over, I saw Old Bessie bouncing through the field, heading our way. I sighed. I really didn't like it when Jolene drove Old Bessie. Not because I was chauvinistic and didn't want a woman driving my truck, but because it smelt like her for a solid week afterward. That fruity perfume she liked always overpowered Rowen's softer, earthier scent, and I didn't like that. I might be pathetic, but I'd take Rowen however I could get her, even if that was just from her scent permeating my truck.

But now it would smell like Jolene. Fruity. Over-powering. Solid week. Plus, I still hadn't quite gotten over her top-snatching stunt at the swimming hole.

I sighed. "Why does she always have to drive my truck?"

"Because at least she gets to go for a ride in or on something of yours," Garth replied instantly, right before shoving me. A much harder shove than I'd just given him.

Before I knew it, I was crashing into the dirt. Thank-fully, I'd fallen on my good arm. "Shit, Garth"—I sat up and dusted myself off—"I take back that whole 'I want you on my side' thing." Sunny had spooked a bit when I'd flown off but hadn't gone far.

"Oh, my goodness! Jesse, are you okay?" Jolene flew out of Old Bessie, sprinting my way like I'd just lost a limb.

"Oh, no, Jesse. Are you okay?" Garth matched Jolene's voice . . . or at least tried to. "What can I do to help you? Massage your sore, bruised muscles? Ride your stallion stick until you're red in the face? Motorboat my huge titties in your face until your pain goes away? What can I do to be of service?"

"Do me a favor and shut the hell up, Black?" I said, standing.

"Shutting up? Not my strong suit."

"Ha. Name one strong suit you have other than cussing, drinking, and getting women into your bed."

Garth's smile stretched wide. "Shoving your ass off your horse."

I moved lightning fast, but Garth had been expecting it and reined Rebel to the side. He wasn't fast enough. I caught his leg, gave it a hard tug, and Garth Black was eating some dirt for dinner, too.

"I hate you, Walker." Garth spit dirt from his mouth, rolling onto his back.

"I love you too, buddy."

"Scratch that. I *fucking* hate you."

"Aww, sweetie. You're so thoughtful." Patting his cheek, I jumped out of the way as his leg swung at me. "Be a good boy and stay put while I go get dinner."

"And you be a bad boy and get an extra blow for me from Miss Hooter-ific bouncing your way. Damn, I love a girl who believes the less support when it comes to her bra, the better."

I went to intercept Jolene since she must have been bringing dinner, although she was still jogging my way with a worried look. I didn't feel like dealing with her never-ending conversations, her urge to touch me at any and every whim, or her asking me every five seconds about how Rowen and I were doing. Jolene was a nice girl and all, but she didn't exactly get the concept of personal space, physically or emotionally. I didn't want to talk about my girlfriend with some acquaintance, and I didn't want to be hugged every time I said something funny. Not to mention, Jolene had walked in on me changing so many times, I was pretty sure she knew what my butt looked like better than I did.

Jolene stopped jogging when she was a few yards in front of me. "Are you okay? That was a nasty spill!"

"Yeah, I'm fine. That was nothing." I'd fallen off a horse as many times as I'd mowed the lawn. It came with the territory.

"Is there anything I can do? I've got a first aid kit

with me . . . and I've been told I can work some serious magic with these fingers." Jolene stepped behind me, dropped her hands on my shoulders, and rolled my muscles between her fingers. Not only was it a strange thing to suggest after someone had just fallen off a horse—a massage, really?—but it made me uncomfortable. I wasn't used to another woman's touch, and having her hands on me felt strange.

"I'll go grab dinner." I stepped away from Jolene's hands and headed for Old Bessie.

"I'll help." Jolene jogged beside me. "How's Rowen doing? I haven't seen her in a while. You two okay?"

I worked my tongue into my cheek so I wouldn't reply immediately. I tried to speak respectfully to everyone, with maybe Garth as the exception. That was just the way I'd been brought up, but Jolene was making it very hard. She'd asked me not even two days ago how Rowen and I were doing. My answer was the same. "She's doing great. *We're* doing great. Thanks for asking."

"Oh. Well that's good." Her voice had lost all of its bubbliness. "Are you going to marry her?"

"Jolene," I warned, stopping in place. I didn't want to have that conversation with her or anyone.

"Well? Are you?" She was dead serious.

"Why do you want to know? What difference does it make to you?"

"Because I want to know," she said with a shrug. "And yes, it does make a difference."

I generally found myself confused somewhere along the way when I talked with Jolene, but it had barely taken thirty seconds to get me stumped during that conversation. "Why? What possible difference could it make to you if I do or do not want to marry Rowen?'"

Jolene's face fell. "Are you serious? You really don't know?"

I pinched the bridge of my nose and exhaled. "No, I really don't know. Why in the world would I?" *Women are a complicated species.* Dad had drilled that into me—and then I'd learned it on my own—but damn if that woman and that conversation didn't bring that complicated attribute to new levels.

Jolene studied me for a few more seconds, searching me for something. Finally, she dropped her gaze, crossed her arms, and marched over to the driver's side door. "Your dinner's in the bed. You can get it yourself."

And I'd pissed her off. I was really winning at life these days.

Only because it was my truck did I kick the tire when I came around the bed. I grabbed the couple of paper bags of food but would have to come back from the cooler since it didn't look like Jolene was planning on leaving the cab. I'd definitely pissed her off . . . although I didn't know what I'd said or done exactly to do so.

When I made it to the tree where Garth was camped out enjoying some shade, I dropped the bags on his lap. "Thanks for the help."

Garth shoved the bags aside and waved his finger at me. "You've got all the help any man could possibly need stewing over there in your truck."

I double checked to make sure Garth and I were seeing the same thing. Yep, Jolene was still pissed. "In case you're losing your vision, that's not a look of helpfulness on Jolene's face. She is most definitely not in a helping mood right now." I rubbed the back of my neck, wondering if I should go apologize. "I said something to upset her . . . but I don't know what."

"Shit, Jess. You weren't over there for longer than two minutes. What were you chatting about that could have hurt poor Jolene's feeling so?" Garth kicked out his legs, crossed his ankles, and laid down like he was ready for a nap.

"I don't know. All we did was talk about dinner, Rowen, and if I wanted to marry her one day."

"Marry who?"

I gave him a look. He knew who I was talking about and was just messing with me.

"Marry. Who?" Garth repeated.

"Marry you, shithead," I said, kicking the heel of his boot. "Rowen. Marry *Rowen*." I couldn't believe I had to clarify that.

"Oh, well that's why."

"That's why *what*?"

Garth rolled his eyes before closing them. "That's why Miss Peace Corps Montana is pissed. You mentioned marriage and Rowen in the same sentence, and I'm guessing there was no addition of polygamy and Jolene."

"No. No mention of Jolene or polygamy."

"Hmm, you know, it's too bad it's not legal in this state because I might actually turn into the marrying type if I could have a dozen wives."

"You can't even take care of yourself. How do you think you'd be able to take care of twelve wives?"

Garth shrugged. "I don't know. But I sure wouldn't mind trying."

"Nice digression, there, but could we get back on point, please? What would make Jolene so upset about me mentioning I want to marry Rowen one day?" I knew she wasn't the biggest fan of Rowen, and Rowen of her. Some personalities just didn't click. Rowen's and Jolene's definitely didn't *click*.

"Questions like that one really make me question your intelligence, Walker." Garth's eyes opened just long enough to say the next part. "Jolene likes you. That's why she's got her panties in a bunch because you mentioned Rowen and the M word."

"I know she likes me. I'm a likable guy."

"Oh my god, shit-for-brains. Jolene doesn't just like you because you're a 'likable guy'"—seeing Garth make air quotes almost made me laugh—"she likes you because she wants you to hump her this way, that way, and another way you didn't even dream was possible. Oh, and after that, she wants you to put a ring on her finger and let her play house."

I shook my head. How else could a person respond to that? "Jolene doesn't like me like that."

"Uh . . . yes, she does."

I crossed my arms. "No, she doesn't."

Garth studied me for a few seconds, then sat up. "You really are clueless when it comes to the female species, Jess. You know that?"

"I suppose entrusting my girlfriend to my best friend a couple of years ago should have clued me into that." I gave him an accusatory look.

Garth raised his middle finger at me. "That should have been a big clue, and you not picking up on Jolene's borderline *Fatal Attraction* toward you is another."

I settled my hands on my hips and exhaled. "You really think Jolene likes me . . . in *that* way." I didn't want to bring up the hump, hump, dream hump, ring analogy again.

"Jess, I'm ninety-nine percent she already has your wedding date set and your kids' names picked out."

As much as I wanted to believe Garth was wrong, he usually wasn't about that type of things. Plus, even though she hadn't outright said it, Rowen didn't like Jolene and obviously had something against her. Could her knowing Jolene had a thing for me be the reason why? The longer I thought about it, the more it made sense. The longer I thought about it, the more I wondered how I'd been so oblivious. I'd been preoccupied lately, but really, I probably hadn't noticed because I wasn't concerned about what Jolene said or did. I didn't notice because I wasn't in a noticing frame of mind with her. I *noticed* Rowen, every single thing she did, and every undertone and hidden meaning in what she said. My mind was trained to notice her, not Jolene, and perhaps that was why I'd missed it.

"You're positive?"

Garth chuckled darkly. "The only thing I've been more positive about is that I'm better looking than you."

"Says no female in existence." Narrowly missing his kick, I headed back toward Old Bessie and an even more complicated situation.

"Where you going, ugly?"

"Clearing something up."

"When you're done with that, let her know I'm available if she wants to work out any angst or frustration," Garth said.

Jolene was still gripping the steering wheel and glaring out the windshield when I approached. It didn't look like she was going to acknowledge me, and that was okay. She didn't need to; she just needed to hear me.

I took a deep breath. "I'm sorry for upsetting you, Jolene. I'm sorry for hurting your feelings too, if I did that."

"You did," she replied slowly.

"I'm sorry for that. But I thought you knew. I thought it was obvious." I leaned inside the passenger window. My truck was, as I guessed, overpowered by that fruity, sweet perfume.

"What did you think was obvious?" She still wouldn't look at me.

"That I want to spend the rest of my life with Rowen." It was sure obvious to everyone else. I don't know why it hadn't been to Jolene.

"You've made that pretty damn obvious," Jolene huffed, giving me a sideways glare. "But you know, what if Rowen doesn't feel the same way? What if one day she wakes up and decides she doesn't want to spend the rest of her life with you?"

I didn't want to think about that at all, but I had the answer. "Then I'll die a single man."

Jolene laughed a few strained notes.

"It's her or no one for me, Jolene. I've known that for a while now. I can't control Rowen's future, but I can control mine. If she decides she doesn't want me to be a part of hers one day, I'm going to wind up a lonely man." I sighed, wishing the pain in my chest would go away. "It's a better option than pretending with someone else."

Jolene shook her head. "You'd really rather be alone than pretend with someone else?"

"Yes." It was the obvious choice for me.

She turned the ignition and Old Bessie fired to life. I

snagged the cooler out of the bed before she tore off. "You and I really are two totally different people, Jesse. Enjoy your life." She finally looked over at me. Her eyes were shiny, which made me feel even worse than I already did. "I don't want you to live alone, but something tells me you're going to with the woman you've picked. A girl like that doesn't want to be tied down to anything or anyone. A girl like that doesn't know how to give real love because she's never been able to accept it."

My body went rigid. "A girl like Rowen knows something about real love that a girl like you could never understand, Jolene. And that's all I'm going to mention about Rowen around you again. I think it's best you leave now. We've both said more than enough, I think."

My words hadn't been kind ones, I knew that, but neither had hers. I normally didn't adhere to the repay fire with fire motto, but Jolene saying that Rowen didn't know how to give or receive real love had angered me in a way that felt unbridled. Even though Rowen was hundreds of miles away and Jolene's words would never make their way back to her, I still felt an overwhelming need to protect her.

"It looks like you and I finally agree on something, Jesse," Jolene replied, before punching the gas. Old Bessie bounced through the field so furiously, I was certain the fender was going to pop off again, but it never did. Or at least not that I saw.

When I made my way back to Garth, he'd already dove into dinner. "So? How did it go?" He wasn't even trying to keep his smile contained.

I dropped down beside him. "Shut up."

BY THE TIME Garth and I'd been relieved and we'd made it back to Willow Springs, it was past ten. Rowen and I usually talked around nine her time since that was her break time if she was working and it was a little before I went to bed. Hey, don't judge; when a person gets up at four in the morning, they can't stay up until two . . . at least not every night.

I couldn't remember if Rowen was working that night, though. That worried me. I always remembered what shifts she worked. Not because I needed to know where she was every minute of every day, but because I liked to know what she was doing hundreds of miles away. When I was out checking the fence, or hauling feed, or lately, up to my elbows in cow placenta, I liked to imagine for a few minutes what she was doing. Was she in class? Painting a picture, half of her face scrunched up as she decided what it was missing? Out with her friends, taking advantage of all Seattle had to offer? Or was she selling crazy doughnuts, turning down the music every time she passed the stereo system?

Usually I had to guess what she might be up to, and that was all part of the fun, but on the nights she was working, I could almost imagine exactly what she was doing. I'd watched her from the back table for so many hours, I think I knew her job almost as well as she did. But I didn't know if she was working. I couldn't remember, and that upset me more than it should have. I knew it had a lot to do with everything that had been going on in my head lately; my mind had felt like a never-ending maze of dominos tumbling over for the past month.

After getting Sunny taken care of for the night, I grabbed my phone from the small barn office and checked for missed calls. Sure enough, I had one and a voice mail.

"Have a nice night of phone sex." Garth smacked my arm as he passed by. "Say hi to Rowen for me."

I had the phone to my ear, waiting for the voice mail to start, so I gave Garth a reply in sign language.

"Sorry. I meant, *moan* hi to Rowen for me." Garth gave me a thumbs-up as he left the barn.

I'd had my fill of Garth Black for one day three hours ago. Finally, I was getting a reprieve.

"Hey, Jesse, it's me." Rowen's voice put an instant smile on my face. "So it looks like I missed you. Again. I know you've been really busy." There was a long pause, long enough it made me freeze. "So, I really didn't want to tell you this on a voice mail, but since I missed you last night and you missed me tonight, I have to tell you some way . . . I won't be able to come out next weekend." My smile was gone. So far gone. "I didn't realize it when we made plans for me to come visit, but that's the same weekend as the Spring Art Show. Since I guess I'm on the committee, I can't really miss it." Rowen sighed, sounding as bad as I felt. "And even though I know you can't come see me with everything you've got going on, I'm still going to be selfish and ask if you can. Because I want to see you, Jesse. I want to see you so bad I'm half tempted to just drop out of school so I don't have to be at this Spring Art Show thingie. Okay, so I'm exaggerating. A little." Another long sigh. "I'm sorry. I suck as a girlfriend and, apparently, I suck at keeping a calendar. All right, I'll stop taking up your time with my ramblings and let you get to bed. I know you've got to be exhausted. I'll try calling about the same time tomorrow night. Okay?"

I was already trying to remember which button I

needed to punch to replay the message because, even though it was just a voice mail, it was Rowen. It was a piece of her I could have and hold on to.

"I'm just getting ready to head out with Jax and the other person on the committee so we can get this sucker planned, but I couldn't go a night without talking to you. Or at least, talking to your recording." That time, I sighed with her. "I miss you, Jesse. Right now, it almost feels like I miss you as much as I love you . . . and you know how much that is. Sleep tight and sweet dreams. Sweet dreams of me, okay?" She ended her call with an air kiss, and I hit the replay button immediately.

So many things unsettled me about that message. I also knew there were just as many things that should have reassured me, and the old me would have focused on the good and barely noticed the bad. But the other person, the Jesse that was caught in a tug-of-war between the old and new, was only concerned with the unsettling parts. That, of course, unsettled me even more.

I left the barn listening to Rowen's message again and wishing I could will her there. For one minute even. Just so I could hold her and she could hold me and I would know everything would be all right. I'd remind myself of the man she saw when she looked at me and remember why it was so important that I overcome my internal battle. I couldn't seem to win the war for myself, but I believed I could for her. I'd do anything for Rowen, including caging demons I'd unknowingly set free. I just needed to see her. To feel her close. I needed more than a message left on my phone. I wished I didn't, I wished a few voice mails and a couple of phone calls could be enough, but I knew it wasn't. I wasn't as strong as I thought, and realizing that was terrifying.

Heading up the porch steps, I was about to hit replay for the third time when I noticed something moving from the corner of my eye. Mom was on one of the swings, a plastic bin in her lap, smiling gently at me.

"Hey, sweetheart. How are you doing?" Mom's voice always had an undercurrent of concern—that's part of what made her such an incredible mother and person—but her greeting held more concern than normal. She knew something was up with me, but she'd given me my space. She'd always known what I needed, even during those first few years.

"Hey, Mom . . . um . . . I'm . . . I'm doing . . ." I'd been putting up a good front, but I guess my *I'm fine* facade was taking a temporary break.

"Yeah, Jess. I know." Moving a couple of the bins from beside her, she patted the freed space. "Come keep me company. The girls get enough of me during the day, and your dad has been snoring for two hours now."

I wanted to sit and talk with Mom . . . and I didn't want to sit and talk with Mom. Experience had proven she could get to the bottom of what was troubling me in a short, innocent-seeming conversation. I wasn't ready for her to work her magic yet. I wasn't ready to speak openly about it; I still hadn't let go of the hope that it would go away on its own.

However, at the end of the day, I could say *no* to my mom about as often as I could to Rowen. "What are you doing out here?" I asked, approaching the swing.

"Sorting through old pictures. I've gotten way behind on getting things labeled and into albums. Obviously," she said, motioning at the bins filled to capacity with photos.

"Yeah, but why are you doing it out here? Inside's a little warmer." I was just unzipping my heavy Carhartt jacket when she shook her head.

"You keep that on, sweetie. Thank you, though. Besides, it's nice being outside in the cool every now and then when you spend your days in a hot kitchen." I settled into the swing beside her and lifted my brows. "Okay. I might be out here because I was waiting for you."

"You almost had me convinced with the photo bins, Mom. Really."

"Not quite, though?"

"Given none of them were open, that kind of gave you away." I couldn't tell how many deep conversations Mom and I'd gotten into when I thought she needed nothing more than help drying the dishes, or plucking green beans, or any one of the other everyday tasks she liked to use as a gateway to something big.

"I think I'm losing my touch." She shook her head.

"So why were you waiting up for me?" I said, not wasting any time.

Mom reached back and grabbed something off of the table beside her. "I made your favorite dessert." She held out the steaming piece of apple pie, and waited.

"Thanks, Mom." I took the pie and rested the plate on my lap. On any other day, I would have been inhaling it and going in search of another piece in thirty seconds, but eating was the furthest thing from my mind. "Pie? This was the reason you were camped out on the porch waiting for me?"

She folded her hands in her lap and cleared her throat. "Well, there may have been one other reason I was waiting for you."

"Go ahead, Mom. I promise I won't go run off and hide out in my tree house like I did after you explained, in detail, the male and female reproductive organs." I gave her a wry smile.

"You totally over-reacted."

"Mom, you used a banana, a couple of limes, and a pomegranate." Every teenage boy's worst nightmare? Having his mom teach him the ins and outs of sex education.

"That was what the online home-schooling lesson plan suggested."

"I was twelve."

Mom lifted an eyebrow at me. "Are you trying to tell me twelve-year-old boys are impervious to sexual urges?"

I shifted on the swing. Eight years later and I was almost as uncomfortable as I'd first been when the words "penis" and "vagina" came out of my mom's mouth. "You probably could have waited a few more years for the whole condom-over-the-banana demonstration. You know, just in case you and Dad are planning on raising any more sons."

Mom scoffed at me. "I may wash dishes by hand and make my own piecrusts, but I'm not fool enough to be old-fashioned about some things. I've tried to be . . . *practical* . . . with raising all of my children, and I wasn't eager to think of my baby raising one. Thus the banana and condom demonstration."

I smiled into my lap. How many twenty-year-old guys had conversations like that with their mothers? Yeah, probably none but me. "Is that what you're waiting to talk with me about? Fruit and prophylactics? Because I think I've got both areas covered now . . ."

Mom reached for her tea cup and saucer and took a couple of sips. "I couldn't help hearing your phone call with Rowen a few nights ago."

That's where I figured the conversation would be heading. "Yeah?"

"Things sounds a little . . . *strained*, maybe?"

I set the pie down on the table beside me. With what we were talking about, I wouldn't be up for eating anytime soon. "Yeah."

"What's going on?"

So damn much. "Just lots of things," I answered with a shrug.

"The distance? Is being apart so much taking a toll?"

"That's part of it. It's not the main issue, though." I clenched my phone. I'd held it twice as much as I'd held Rowen's hand that year. "But being apart definitely makes it that much harder to work out the other things."

"What other things?"

Part of what I loved about my mom was her ability to deliver a question so succinctly. She didn't soften it or wrap it up in a bunch of fluff. Right then, though, I wouldn't have minded her questions not being so direct.

"Things I'm not ready to talk about yet, Mom," I admitted, dropping my gaze.

There was a good minute of silence before Mom draped her arm over my shoulders. "You love Rowen, and she loves you. Hold on to that, and work out the rest. Just don't assume that these issues, whatever they are, will fix themselves or disappear on their own. Work them out. Don't let them create a wedge between you two."

"And what if you have no idea how to go about working them out?"

"Then get an idea. The answers don't come easy, Jesse. God knows the questions sure do, but the answers never come easy. You have to work for them, and in my experience, you have to work *hard* for them."

Having my mom's arm around me still managed to soothe me, almost to the point of wanting to admit everything that had been bothering me. "I guess I should have known better than to assume that once I'd found the woman I wanted to spend my life with, everything else would just fall into place."

Mom laughed softly, patting my shoulder. "Honey, if it was easy, they wouldn't call it love."

"Yeah. I'm figuring that out."

Setting down her tea, she twisted toward me. "What about you, Jess? How have *you* been?"

I swallowed. That topic was even more touchy than the last one. That topic was one that scared the shit out of me. I kept my eyes forward when I answered. "Okay. Why?"

"You've just seemed a little . . . in your head, you know?"

Mom had nailed it. I'd been so in my head I was close to driving myself crazy. I knew exactly what she was asking—*is your past back to haunt you?*—and I know exactly how I wanted to answer—*yes, please help me beat this*—but the words wouldn't form. I simply couldn't admit all that I was struggling with: the ghosts of my past, my fears of one day not being enough for Rowen—would she outgrow me?—my growing fears of Jax and his motives for being in her life . . . insecurity after insecurity, fear after fear. The obstacles were so thick around me, I hadn't been able to move—to *breathe*—in weeks. Nothing came easy anymore. Everything was a struggle.

"I'll be okay, Mom." I sounded more convincing than I felt.

"I know you will, Jesse. You're one of the strongest people I know. I'm just worried about everything you might lose before you get back to being okay."

I stood up. I couldn't talk about any of it anymore. It was too much, too fast. "I've got this, Mom. It's going to be all right."

"Don't let the things you *think* you need to do keep you from doing the things you *actually* need to. Okay? Fight for the things that matter—don't waste your energy on the rest."

I nodded and headed for the front door. "Thanks for the pie. I'll have to have a piece for breakfast."

"Jesse?" Mom said. I paused with my hand on the door. "You know I'm here whenever you need to talk, right?"

I was suddenly so exhausted, I could have collapsed right there. The day, the week, and the whole month had suddenly caught up to me, and the weight of it all was almost too much to bear. I needed to crawl into bed and sleep for five days straight . . . and then I remembered all that was waiting for me when I did fall asleep. I wanted to chug coffee to keep away from those dark places. "And you know that when I'm ready to talk, I will."

chapter **FIFTEEN**

Rowen

SOME PEOPLE JUST seemed to come into my life exactly when I needed them. It's like the universe's way of handing me a solution to a problem in the form of a person. Like a homeless, slightly deranged woman who talks a little too much like one of those fire and brimstone TV evangelists.

So maybe my "solution" from the universe wasn't exactly firing on all cylinders, but Mar said a lot of things I needed to hear, just when I needed to hear them. She was like a homeless, American Buddha. We'd had so many late-night alley conversations that I'd started inviting her inside Mojo during business hours so we could share my lunch and chat. As far as atmosphere went, Mojo left a lot to be desired, but it was a hell of a lot better than a sitting in a dirty alley next to a putrid dumpster.

"And you've been with this boy for almost a year now?" Mar asked, waving half of my peanut butter sandwich at me.

"Yep. Pretty close." I thanked Alex for filling our coffee cups by giving her a chunk of my Kit-Kat. Sid was not a big fan of me inviting a vagrant into his doughnut shop to "shoot the shit," but after a little *convincing* from

Alex, he'd turned a blind eye. Besides, half of his customers, including Sid, dressed like they'd dived their fair
share of dumpsters. He couldn't really turn his nose up at
the real deal or else I was calling bullshit.

"You're serious about this boy?" Mar asked.

I nodded and crunched into a carrot stick. I generally
tried to keep my relationship with Jesse off the table with
Mar. Not because I was ashamed or uncomfortable talking
about Jesse and our relationship, but because I was afraid
of what she'd say. She had a kernel of wisdom for every
bloody topic in the universe, significant others especially.
If the conversation even started veering toward love,
marriage, and everything in between, oh, brother. I knew
to sit back and strap in because Mar could have filled an
encyclopedia by the time she'd stopped talking.

"How *serious* serious?" Mar shoved the rest of the
sandwich in her mouth and moved on to the bag of chips.

"Serious enough I can't imagine being with anybody
else. Serious enough I can't imagine spending my life
without him." I set my carrot stick aside and slumped into
the booth. Talking about Jesse, even thinking about him,
had been putting me into a sad, depressed mood for a
while. I knew what the gloominess stemmed from—not
getting to see him and missing him like mad—but sad and
depressed weren't exactly feelings I wanted to have when I
thought of my boyfriend.

"You mean to tell me you're actually considering
marrying this country boy one day?" Mar froze in the
middle of opening the chips.

"Well . . . yeah."

"Oh, Girlie. You are not nearly as smart as I thought
you were," Mar said, whipping her head from side to side.

"Nope. Not even close."

At first, her unexpected insults had almost hurt my feelings. Now, they pretty much ran off my back since I'd heard a dozen different ones each time we talked. "And why does wanting to marry some amazing guy make me the dumbest person on the planet?"

"I don't care how amazing this boy is. I don't care how many gold stars he's earned. You can't expect someone like you to be happy settling down with one man." Mar was wagging her finger at me. Her head started bobbing too, almost like a nervous tic. It only got that way when she was getting worked up about something.

"Who is someone like me exactly?" I felt like I had a general understanding, and what I knew of myself didn't clash with the concept of spending my life with Jesse. Apparently Mar saw me in a different light. I was curious to know what she saw.

"An artist. A woman who needs to stay inspired. A creative person who needs to *create* to stay fulfilled."

"And why does being with Jesse make none of these things possible?" I asked, taking a sip of coffee.

"You need someone to keep you inspired. You need a muse. No muse, no art." Mar crunched into a chip, her head bobbing.

"Jesse is my muse. He keeps me inspired."

"Oh, yeah, I'm sure he was. At first. The beginning of every relationship is the best we can ever expect out of one. It never gets any better than that first year. After that, it's a slow, downward spiral."

"Thanks for the uplifting words," I mumbled.

"Prove me wrong," she said, shaking her finger at me. "I bet some of the best art you've created was when you and your boyfriend were first together. Some true master-pieces came out of that early stage of your relationship." Mar paused, letting that set in. "Am I right?"

I thought about it and, as much as I didn't want to agree with her and her crazy theory, I nodded.

"And what about now? Compare what you were creating six months ago to what you're creating today. How does it compare?"

Okay, I really wanted off her crazy train before it went any farther down the loony tracks. I might have thought Mar made a lot of sense at one time, but right then . . . I really wanted to believe she was full of shit. I wanted to believe she was the insane person I'd originally thought because then I could brush off what she'd just said. The questions she'd just asked.

I had not, in two weeks, been able to put a single brushstroke on canvas, nor had I been able to put charcoal to paper. It was like my creativity tank had suddenly run dry, and I didn't know why or how to fill it back up again. I was an artist who could no longer create.

I'd been avoiding the reasons behind my dry spell, much preferring to believe I'd hit a wall or was burnt out after a busy year, but really . . . I knew the reason for my creativity hiatus. Jesse. I knew, in some way, he was connected to it.

I wasn't blaming him, but whatever we were going through was what set the whole thing in motion. We hadn't seen each other in weeks, we'd been missing each other's phone calls, and when we did manage to connect, he was distant. I could feel his distance. Five hundred miles separated us, and I'd never felt far from him when we talked on the phone. Up until the past month.

Some things were still the same. I still loved him past the point of logic, and I knew he felt the same about me. Things just didn't *feel* the same. The worries I tried to keep locked in the back of my mind were becoming more and more in-my-face with every passing day. I could almost feel Jesse slipping away from me, and since I had no idea why he was, I couldn't stop it. I didn't know how I was losing him, just that I was. Bit by tiny bit.

If I lost Jesse Walker, I wasn't sure I'd be able to keep myself from the same fate.

"Take it from me. You don't want to settle down with one man. You need a new man, a new adventure every year to keep the muse alive. You marry this boy, and mark my words, you'll kiss your art career good-bye."

When my phone buzzed, I came close to sighing from relief. I didn't want to think anymore about what Mar said or how much sense she made. I checked the phone, hoping it was Jesse. That time, I did sigh when I saw it wasn't.

"Hey, Jax," I greeted, shoving the rest of my uneaten lunch at Mar. My appetite was gone. It had been gone so much lately, my clothes were getting a little loose.

"Where are you?" Jax sounded breathless, almost like he was . . . excited.

"At work. Why?"

"Good. Stay there. I'll be there in five minutes."

"What? No, tell me whatever you're coming here to tell me on the phone. I hate suspense." Plus, I didn't need another stomach ulcer.

"Not even. I want to see your face when I tell you this."

"Jax—"

"See you soon." The line went dead.

I groaned. The night had started out strong. I'd packed my favorite candy bar, I'd gotten a hold of Jesse for a few minutes before starting my shift, and Sid had announced I'd be getting a fifty cent an hour raise starting next week. Yet there it was, not even ten o'clock, and I had Mar preaching to me about not marrying the man I loved or else, Jax pulling a hurry up and wait on the phone, and I wouldn't even enjoy a stick of my Kit-Kat because Mar had just downed the rest of it in two bites.

Night fail.

"Was that a former muse or a future muse?" Mar asked, the melted chocolate of my coveted candy bar coating her teeth.

"Neither," I grumbled.

"You want to talk about it—"

"No," I almost snapped. I was in a pissy mood, and I couldn't even blame part of it on PMS.

Mar stayed quiet for a couple of minutes, devouring what was left of my lunch. The whole time, I sat there stewing and getting angrier and angrier. Angry because of what she'd said? Maybe. Angry because of what she'd implied? Probably. Angry because, deep down, I was worried she was right? That, *that* question was the one that made me angrier just thinking about it. I tried to not think about it, I didn't allow myself to answer it, but it wouldn't go away. It had leeched to my brain and wouldn't stop sucking the life out of it.

Before I knew it, the anger was spilling from my mouth. "Where do you get off giving me relationship advice anyways? What makes you think you've got all the answers and I've got none? What makes you so sure the man I'm with is so wrong for me?"

Mar popped the last chip in her mouth and watched me with an unfazed expression as she swallowed. "Experience."

"Experience? Please. We've all got experience." That was the laziest excuse for making one a know-it-all on life.

"Maybe. But not all experiences are created equal, Girlie." She waved her finger at me again.

"And what makes your experiences superior to mine?"

Mar extended her arms to the sides and ran her eyes down herself purposefully. "My experiences left me penniless, homeless, broken-hearted, and alone. Does that answer your question?"

I bit my lip, feeling the slightest bit of regret for going off on her. Her rhetorical question got me thinking. I didn't know much of Mar's past, just like she knew little of mine. We really just talked about everyday things, along with her peppering in her random gems of wisdom and the occasional pointing and staring wide-eyed at the ground like she half-expected little demons to come crawling from it. I'd guessed she had a tumultuous past, but I didn't know the details surrounding my assumptions. Or if they were even true. "What happened to you?"

Mar's head bobbing picked up. God, the neck pain that woman must get. "A man."

"A . . . man?" I suppose that explained why she spoke so bitterly about them.

"I was an artist like you when I was young. I wanted to create something the world had never seen before. Something it would never see again. I wanted to paint billboards around the country, a new one every month. I wanted to share what was inside of me. I wanted to share the gift I'd been born with."

"You wanted to share your art?" I asked to make sure I was tracking. Mar was getting that crazed look in her eyes she got when she was about to start talking about the land of fire and judgment just below our feet. I always boogied out when the conversation went that direction. That special brand of crazy was only meant for a psychiatrist's ears.

Mar nodded. "But then I met a man, and he ruined my life. Right before running away once it was good and ruined."

Shit. A chill just ran down my back. I couldn't tell if it was from her words, her tone, or that look on her face. It was probably the combination of all three. Mar was opening her mouth to continue, and I was on the edge of my seat, when Jax burst through Mojo's front door.

"Rowen!" he shouted, jogging my way.

From the corner of my eye, I noticed Sid give him an annoyed look before turning it my way. I guess Sid wasn't down with me having more visitors than he had customers.

"What's the big surprise, for crying out loud?" I asked, glancing over at Mar. She was talking to herself and her eyes were bouncing like pinballs.

"Are you sitting down?" Jax skidded to a stop in front of the table.

I lifted an eyebrow at him and waved my hand elaborately at the booth I was seated at.

"Fine. Why don't you stand up just so I can watch you pass out when I tell you?"

Jax rarely did excited, probably because he thought he was above such a passé and overused emotion. Also because Jax Jones was an arrogant, elitist ass. For him to be as close to excited as I'd ever seen him meant one thing. "What Playmate did you lure into your bed now?"

Two months ago, it had been a runway model. Last month, a fashion model. Sticking with what I knew of Jax's preferences, and that each girl had larger breasts than the last, a Playmate was the logical guess. And yes, that I was thinking that hot on the heels of being so upset about my relationship just proved how much I was trying to repress those gloomy feelings.

"Rowen . . ."

"Fine. Which *two* did you lure into your bed?"

"My god, you are a royal pain in my ass."

"My sentiments exactly," I grumbled.

"Rowen Sterling, would you shut it for five seconds so I can get out what I need to tell you?" I was just about to answer him when he clamped his hand over my mouth. "No response is required. A simple nod will do." I gave him a "simple" nod. Jax's hands gripped both of my shoulders as he kneeled in front of me. "Guess who just landed the hottest internship in the Seattle art community?"

My breath caught in my chest. "Since those are pretty much the same words you said to me when I found out about the art show at the Underground—"

"And you guessed wrong that time."

"I'm going to go with"—I stabbed my index finger into my chest—"*me*?"

Jax's smile stretched into position. "Yes." He gave my shoulders a shake since I was frozen. "*You*."

I knew my first reaction should have been exhilaration because, really, every single one of those interns had gone on to become highly celebrated artists. I'd just landed myself the golden ticket, for all intents and purposes. So why did I only feel dread? With a big side of despair?

I knew the answer. He was the answer to all of the questions I'd been wrestling with all month. Jesse. I still hadn't told him about applying for the internship. If I decided to take it, and I'd be a stupid, stupid fool not to, how could I break the news to him? How could I tell him I'd let some summer job get in the way of spending a summer—a whole three months—with him? How could I admit that an internship took priority over quality time with him?

That's not the way I felt about it—Jesse came number one on all of my priority lists—but I knew how it would seem. I was choosing the job over him. I was re-prioritizing, and he wasn't in the number one spot anymore. Just thinking about all the explaining and heartache was enough to make me light-headed, and I had yet to even accept or decline the internship.

"Rowen? It's okay to say something now. Let your snark run wild." Jax was waiting for me to jump up on the table and do a celebratory dance. That's what people did when they found out they'd been chosen for that position. Why was I partly hoping the floor would open up and swallow me?

"Um . . . wow?" That was all the excitement I could muster.

"You did hear what I just said, right? The gravity of what is about to happen to your career is computing? Nod once for yes. Twice for no." To Jax's credit, he did actually sound concerned. He wasn't just being a wiseass. He flashed three fingers in front of my face. "How many fingers am I holding up?"

I promptly slapped them away. "I heard you. It's just taking a minute to set in." The longer it settled in, the more unsure I felt.

"I'm just going to tell myself you're in shock and unable to show your unbridled excitement."

"Jax—"

"Just let me live in this alternate reality for a while."

"Jax—" My uncertainty started to switch to irritation.

"I'm taking you out to celebrate. Right now." Jax grabbed my hand and gave it a tug.

I tugged back harder. "I'm at work. I couldn't just up and leave to go 'celebrate' with you even if I wanted to." Which I didn't. I wasn't in the mood to celebrate with anyone.

"You really don't think your boss would let you leave early? You just landed probably one of the top hundred internships in the whole damn country." Jax still hadn't let go of my hand; he still hadn't given up hope.

"Have you met my boss? No, he definitely wouldn't be cool with me leaving in the middle of a shift." Actually, Sid might have been okay with it.

"Fine. What time do you get off? I'll pick you up, and *then* we'll celebrate."

I couldn't tell if it was persistence or good old-fashioned pushiness, but he was really starting to tick me off. "Jax. I'm not in the mood to celebrate."

His eyebrows came together. "Why not?"

The disco music in the background, the unyielding stares of Mar and Jax, the internship I'd been offered . . . all of it started messing with my head. The room started spinning, one movie poster and cardboard cutout at a time. "Because . . ."

"Because? That's all you've got for me? Really?" Jax ran his hand through his hair.

"Be. Cause."

"Rowen? What's the deal? I give you a piece of news that should have you dancing a goddamned leprechaun jig right now, and instead, you look like you're about to go to your best friend's funeral. I'm not following."

I took two full breaths. "Jax, thank you for the news, and I'm sorry I'm not living up to your expectations in the reaction department. I need some time to myself right now. Some time to think."

Jax's eyes turned to Mar, who'd been watching the whole exchange with rapt interest.

"She was visiting me during my break. But I've got to get back to work now." I still had a few hours left of my shift, but I was going to ask Sid if he'd let me leave early. I needed to sort out some stuff, and something about doughnuts, disco, and Sid and Alex's evening "exchanges" told me sorting stuff out at Mojo would be impossible.

"I don't think I've had the pleasure of meeting . . ." Jax glanced at Mar and waited for me to make the introductions. Jax would not take a hint.

"Jax, meet Mar. Mar, meet Jax." I waved my hand between the two and slid out of the booth.

"Pleasure," Jax said, his expression the opposite of his greeting.

Mar nodded at Jax then stood. "Thanks for the dinner, Girlie."

"You're welcome." I stood and crossed my arms.

Taking one long look at Jax, she gave me a purposeful look. "Now that's a muse."

As Mar shoved through the front door, Jax shouldered

up beside me and watched her. "Wow. I gotta give it you to, Rowen. You *do* know how to pick them. A hick for a boyfriend and a homeless woman as your lunch buddy."

I found Jax's snide comments hard to swallow on a normal day, but right then? I couldn't deal. "There's the door, Jax." I thrust my finger toward it.

"I know where it is. I came through it." He looked at me, and from his lack of concern, I guessed the way I felt hadn't made its way to my outside yet. "Why are you in such a hurry for me to leave? I just got here."

"Because I'm not in the mood for adding a misdemeanor to my record tonight." I quirked an eyebrow, and a moment later, Jax got it.

"That's the last time I'm bringing you good news," he said, stuffing his hands in his jacket pocket and marching for the door.

"Promise?"

As he shoved out the door, Jax paused. "Shit, Rowen. What the hell is wrong with you?"

That was the million dollar question.

chapter **SIXTEEN**

Jesse

I'VE HAD ONE priority for the past month, and that's keeping Rowen in the dark about what I've been battling. I don't want her to know. I don't want her to be a part of it. I don't want her *near* it. I want her as far away from the poison flowing through me as I can keep her.

But after the nightmare I had last night, I couldn't keep that a priority any longer. I gave myself a minute to calm down when I jolted awake. I wiped the sweat from my face and waited for my heart rate to return to an almost normal beat. Then I reached for my phone on the floor beside me and punched in her number without thinking. It was early, just past four in the morning, and even though I knew my call would wake her, I can't not make it. After the dream I had, I can't not hear her voice and know she's safe. Her piercing screams had repeated my name in my sleep all night, over and over again, calling for me, waiting for me. I'd struggled to get to her, I'd fought against my restraints until I'd blacked out, but I couldn't get to her. I couldn't save her from the pain. I couldn't save her from the horror I'd unknowingly dragged her into.

My breathing was still ragged at the first ring. It hadn't calmed down any by the second. When she answered on the third, it stopped altogether.

"Jesse?"

Oh, god. She wasn't asleep at all. Her voice was strained, exactly how it'd been in my dream. That jacked my heartbeat right back up to its former level. "Rowen? What's the matter?" There was silence on the other end. So much that I threw off the covers and reached for my jeans. "Rowen? Are you okay?"

I heard a muffled sound, like a sob she tried to stop short but sneaked out anyways. "I don't know," she said, her voice quiet and hoarse . . . and well, it terrified me.

I was no longer sure if I was in a real or dream world, but I didn't care. All I knew was that Rowen was hurting and I was restraint free. I could get to her. I *had* to get to her. "Are you hurt? Do you need the police or medical attention?" It took everything inside of me to keep my voice level and strong. I felt the total opposite, but I managed it for her. She needed me to stay together.

"Jesse, no. No, I'm fine." She sniffled and cleared her throat. When she spoke again, her voice was a bit more composed. "I'm sorry. I'm fine. Really. You just caught me at a bad time."

I felt a fraction better knowing she was safe and unharmed, at least physically. "What's wrong, Rowen? Tell me." It was no longer a question of if something was wrong.

"I just . . . we need to . . . I need to talk to you."

I could feel the battle she was fighting trying to get out each word. I kept up the strong act even though the uncertainty of what she wanted to talk about strangled me. "I'm here now, free as long as you need me. What do you need to talk about?"

"Not on the phone. I don't want to say this without being able to look into your eyes."

That admission doesn't set me any more at ease. I balanced the phone between my ear and shoulder and slid into my jeans. "I'm coming. I'm on my way." I buttoned them and grabbed a T-shirt from the stack in my dresser.

"What? No, Jesse, you can't drop everything and come see me. Don't be ridiculous." Rowen's voice was getting back to normal, but I couldn't shake the way it had sounded when she'd first answered. I'd never forget it. "I'll be out in a couple weekends, and we can talk then. Really, it can wait. You just caught me in a weak moment."

If she thought I would be okay waiting almost two weeks to know what was upsetting her, she really hadn't figured me out. There was no way I could just go about my day like everything was fine with her when something clearly wasn't. "Rowen, I'm coming. I'm leaving in the next five minutes."

"Jesse—"

"I love you. I'll see you soon." I pulled on my socks and boots and slid on my hat before yanking open my bedroom door.

She let out a long sigh. "I love you, too. But really, I'm okay now."

From the way she'd sounded, I doubted it; even if she was okay, I wasn't. I had to see her. It had been too long, and we were both obviously going through some big things.

After Rowen and I said our good-byes and she again tried to discourage me from coming and I again discouraged her from continuing to discourage me, I charged down the stairs. I was headed for the front door when someone emerged from the kitchen.

"Hitting the morning chores a little early, aren't you, sweetie?"

"I'm going to see Rowen, Mom." I grabbed my jacket from the coat rack and threw it on. "I know you and Dad need me here right now, and I know this probably seems incredibly irresponsible and impulsive, but I need to get to her. I need to get to her now."

Mom leaned into the kitchen doorway and smiled. "Jess, that's the first *responsible* thing I've heard you say in weeks."

I smiled back at Mom. No one could have stopped me, but getting through the front door without a fight was a weight off my shoulders. "Will you tell Dad? I'll call you tonight once I get there and know how long I'll be."

"I'll tell him."

Needing to get behind the wheel and start ticking off some miles, I opened the front door.

"Wait! If you think I'm letting you drive ten hours nonstop like I know you will"—she gave me an accusatory look—"with an empty stomach, you really don't know the woman who raised you." After rushing into the kitchen, Mom hurried back with a lunch box and a thermos. "Since my summer help up and quit with no notice last night, I had to get up early to make breakfast burritos. I already have half a batch done, so you're in luck. The coffee's fresh and strong." She winked and handed me a road-trip breakfast, lunch, and hopefully not dinner. If I pushed it, I'd be in Seattle before five.

"About Jolene . . . I'm sorry, Mom." I didn't realize she would quit after our conversation last night, but maybe

I should have. I hated that it put my mom and my sisters in a tough spot.

"No apologies, sweetie. I think it was pretty obvious to all of us why Jolene took the job. And it sure wasn't for the dish washing."

I sighed, not sure what else I could say. All I'd done was make a mess of things lately. Shooting her a small smile of apology, I continued out the door.

"Good luck, Jess," she called after me. "Don't be afraid to pay Rowen back the favor she gave you last summer."

I hopped in Old Bessie, pausing long enough to give her a confused look.

"Opening up." She stared at me like she was trying to really drill that one in and headed back inside.

I fired up the engine and was too impatient to let it warm up before punching the gas. Every trip past, I'd felt a bit lighter with every mile that brought me closer to Rowen. That trip, though, I felt like a band was tightening around my chest with every mile. I didn't know why or what that meant, but I pressed on. I'd face my worst nightmares ten times over to get to Rowen.

chapter **SEVENTEEN**

Rowen

IF THEY HANDED out awards for Worst Girlfriend of the Month, I'd be the front runner.

I couldn't believe I fell apart like that on the phone with Jesse. I suppose it was all thanks to the perfect storm of bad timing. Jesse had enough on his plate; he didn't need to deal with me losing my shit when he was hundreds of miles away.

I could tell something had been going on with him, but every time I'd tried to bring it up, I couldn't figure out how to fit it into the conversation. As his girlfriend, I *should* be able to figure out how to ask him how he's doing, call bullshit when he says fine, and wait in stubborn silence until he 'fessed up. Not getting to the bottom of what Jesse was dealing with was one of the many reasons I should be preparing my acceptance speech for the Worst Girlfriend of the Month award.

Another reason? Answering the phone when I'd been up all night crying my bloody eyes out. That was one giant "my bad" on my part. After closing Mojo last night, I'd gotten home a little after two in the morning, tried going to bed, and failed. Then I proceeded to have the most legendary meltdown of my life. Everything I'd been holding at bay the past month, everything I'd stuck my head in the sand at, flooded over me, and it was too much. Too much times twenty. I cried, I sobbed, hell, I even wailed. Alex was with Sid, probably still locked away in his office doing lord knows what to each other, so I hadn't needed to worry about waking anyone with my dying cat cries. As a policy, I didn't do crying all that often, but when I did, I didn't mess around. I was the best crier out there when it came time to let loose.

So why had I answered Jesse's call early this morning after sobbing into my pillow so long it was soggy? Because I couldn't ignore it. Because I felt like Jesse knew I needed him. Because he was the only person who could comfort me. Because I *had* to answer that phone call. It wasn't a logical string of thoughts; it was all instinctive.

Hearing his voice had been a relief, hearing the solid strength that had been lacking lately. His voice soothed me. Until he said he was getting in his truck and heading west. I already felt bad—for the reasons already mentioned—but knowing he was dropping all of his responsibilities because I'd gotten weepy made me feel like I might just secure the Worst Girlfriend title for two months instead of one. I was just that bad of a girlfriend.

Neil and Rose depended on him. Willow Springs depended on him. His fellow ranch hands depended on him. Hell, the cattle depended on him. And letting my iron wall fall had made him drop it all.

Another part of me was scared of him showing up because I knew I'd have to tell him about the internship. I'd have to admit that I'd been hiding it from him, expecting to never get it, and I knew he'd want to know what my plans were. Would I take it? Stay in Seattle for the summer? He deserved answers. The problem was, I didn't have answers to give him yet. I had no clue what I was going to do, and I wasn't sure if having Jesse there would help me make up my mind or make it harder.

So, last night had been a mess. Early that morning had been a mess. Then later morning rolled around, and Jax's phone calls started coming in. One right after the other, every five minutes it seemed. When I ignored those, the texts came. *Have you decided? You want me to tell them you'll take it, right? Are you ignoring me? Why are you ignoring me? You're taking the internship. I'm telling them yes if you don't get back to me by tomorrow morning.*

After that last text, I'd powered down my phone, thrown my pillow over my head, and gone to sleep instead of my morning classes. I was still sleeping during my afternoon classes, but I forced myself out of bed when it was time to head to work. I could jeopardize my own future by not going to classes, but I couldn't jeopardize Sid's and Mojo's. That was a whole heap of bad karma I didn't need poured on me.

Coming up on nine, I started to accept that Jesse had changed his mind. Really, that was the responsible thing to do, and I was fine for the most part. I tried to convince myself to be glad he'd stayed behind because I knew that was the right decision, but even at my most convincing, I couldn't chase away the pang of disappointment.

A part of me had clung to the hope that I'd be able to put my arms around Jesse in the flesh and blood. Accepting that wasn't going to happen was disappointing in a way I couldn't describe. I felt like I'd swallowed an iron ball and it was trapped in my stomach, making it difficult to take each step.

Realizing Jesse had probably been trying to call me

all day to tell me about the change in plans, I was heading to the back room to get my phone when Mojo's door swung open. I had my back to it, but I knew who'd just rushed inside. I was smiling before I spun around.

I'd never seen Jesse so disheveled. I didn't think it was possible. I'd seen him dirty and mussed after a long day on the ranch, but his appearance went beyond that. Combined with the anxious expression on his face and in his eyes, it *scared* me.

"Thank god," he said, striding my way. Before I could ask if he was okay or why he looked like he'd just crawled out of hell, he had me in his arms. He pulled me to him, almost clinging to me, like I could slip away in an instant.

I exhaled, letting out a day's worth of worry. Right then, everything was fine. Nothing stood in Jesse's and my way. Nothing threatened to tear us apart. I wiped the tear that had slipped from my eye before he could see it. Apparently the flood gates hadn't been completely lifted. "You came."

Lifting his hands to my face, he lowered his forehead to mine. "Did you really think I wouldn't?"

When I thought about that, *really* thought about it, I knew the answer. "No, I didn't."

"Are you okay?" He scanned me with a furrowed brow.

"I am now," I replied truthfully. A month's worth of separation, weeks' worth of worry . . . it all vanished with his touch. Somewhere along the way, I'd forgotten that Jesse's touch was some powerful stuff. I could only hope mine provided him even half the relief.

I was glad that Mojo was pretty quiet, not that it

would have stopped me. I lifted my mouth to Jesse's, braced my arms around his neck, and got after making up for lost time. He didn't seem to have any objections.

His hands fisted into my shirt, and he kissed me back, hard and unyielding. Our chests rose and fell in time, reminding me that when we were together, everything made sense. Life didn't seem so confusing; the answers didn't seem so complex. When Jesse and I were close enough to share the same breath, confusion and uncertainty were distant memories. We didn't stop until oxygen, or lack thereof, became a concern.

Jesse's lips pressed into mine one more time before a contented smile moved into place. "It's been so long, I almost forgot how good you taste."

As the haze of that kiss lifted, I noticed something too. "It's been a while, but I don't remember you tasting like . . . like"—I tasted my lips, my face crinkling—"like *motor oil.*"

"Do I want to know how you know what motor oil tastes like?" Jesse leaned back enough that I could see what was responsible for the bitter taste. A good quarter of Jesse's face was streaked with black lines and fingerprints. Motor oil.

"Probably not," I answered. "But enough about me and motor oil . . . I want to know about you and motor oil and why you're covered in it." After I took a small step back, I saw that the same went for his clothes and the rest of his body. Black streaks and smudges ran all over him. Truthfully, it was kinda hot in a way that would only work on Jesse Walker.

"Well"—he rubbed the back of his neck and gave me a sheepish look—"it turns out you were right all along."

"Right about what exactly?"

"Old Bessie. She broke down on me about halfway through the panhandle of Idaho. And you were right about something else—North Idaho is its own country. A marginally terrifying one." He was still smiling, but I could tell it was mask to cover his sadness that his truck had finally given out on him. Beyond explanation, I was kind of sad, too.

"Old Bessie finally pooped out on you, eh?"

Jesse nodded.

Trying to lighten the mood, I said in my best funeral voice, "She lived a full, happy life. I know it's difficult, but during these trying times, try to focus on the happy memories. The reminder that Old Bessie is in truck heaven."

"It's been so long, I'd almost forgotten this, too."

"Forgot what?" I asked, not missing the smile he was fighting.

"This!" Holding me tight, Jesse's fingers pinched and prodded at my sides until tears were about to run down my face from the laughter.

"Stop it!" I laughed, trying to swat away his hands. "Stop it, Jesse!"

After another moment, his hands mercifully stopped. "You're still a wiseass," he said affectionately, kissing the tip of my nose.

"Ditto that, Walker." Since we were still embracing smack in the middle of Mojo and had the attention of every one of the five customers, I grabbed Jesse's hand and pulled him toward a table. "So what happened? How did you get here? Oh, and by the way"—I kissed him full on the lips one more time—"however you did it, thank you for coming *here*. I'm glad you came."

"Not as glad as I am." His arm wound around my shoulders after I slid into the booth beside him, and he dropped his hat on the table. "So after Old Bessie sputtered her last meter, I pulled over and tried all the usual and not so usual tricks to get her to start again."

"I'm guessing the not so usual is why you're covered in black?"

"Pretty much. Old Bessie was having none of it. I couldn't even get the engine to turn over. After accepting if I wanted to get to Seattle, it wouldn't be in Old Bessie, I grabbed my bag and started hitching down the highway." Jesse's smile went higher on one side, like he found that secretly amusing for some reason.

"You hitchhiked? From Idaho?" My stomach hit the floor. I'd lived a wild life and did some crazy shit that most people would never think of, let alone actually do, but hitchhiking hadn't been one of them. Everyone knew that only people who hitched or picked up hitchhikers were mentally deranged. It was a commonly known fact.

Except, apparently, known by my wholesome, Montanan boyfriend.

"I did."

"Who picked you up?" God, I was about to break out in hives thinking about it. Jesse was a strong guy, and I didn't doubt he could kick the ass of ninety-nine percent of guys, but all that muscle and strength came up with a big goose-egg against a gun. Or a huge knife. Or a Taser. Or any one of the dozens of weapons carried by people who picked up hitchhikers.

"The first time it was an old couple. They were on their way to their first great-grandchild's christening in

Spokane. They were from Missoula, and they said they could recognize another Montanan, so that's why they stopped."

I interrupted him. I had to. "The *first* time?"

Jesse lifted a shoulder. "Well, yeah. The Kleins' drove me from Kellogg to Spokane. Then a few guys heading to a rodeo in Wenatchee offered me a ride. They were Wyoming cowboys, so they made me ride in the horse trailer." My mouth dropped open. "To their credit, there wasn't any room in their truck, and their horses were probably better company than they would have been."

"Why's that?" Having been raised with a menagerie of them, Jesse loved animals. However, he also loved to talk and, other than Mister Ed, I had yet to meet a talking horse.

"Because a Wyoming boy is cowboy on the outside . . . but a Montana boy bleeds cowboy."

I rolled my eyes. "I can tell someone's been spending a lot of time with Garth Black."

"So much time, I think I've earned my sainthood by now."

By my standards, he'd earned that a long time ago. "So how did you get from Wenatchee to here?"

"Uh . . . well . . ." Jesse searched the ceiling for an answer. Never a good sign. "A team bus picked me up." Jesse had a tough time lying, and he had a harder time buffering the truth. The poor guy was squirming.

"What kind of team?"

"A *dance* team."

"And was this dance team male or female?"

I would have thought the world's fate was riding on his shoulders from his anxious expression. "It was a female dance team."

Of course a bus full of girls would pull over when they saw Jesse hitching. That was more fact than the theory of relativity. A woman, especially a band of them, didn't just drive by Jesse Walker without staring, stopping, or offering him a ride if he needed one.

"What kind of dancers were they?" Knowing they were girls and dancers had been enough information for me, but from the way Jesse was chewing at his lip, I knew there was more.

"The *dancing* kind of dancers." I lifted an eyebrow and waited. He exhaled. "The kind that use a pole."

Opportunistic, pole-humping bitches. After I got that out of my system, I laughed. Laughed hard and loud and like I wouldn't be able to stop. Jesse's overwhelming hesitancy to admit that he'd been picked up by a bus full of pole dancers endeared him even more to me. The fact that he was embarrassed by it was the cherry on top.

Jesse chuckled with me, and the two of us made such a laughing raucous that Sid emerged from his office. Alex wasn't working, so I guessed he was actually able to do some paperwork.

"Hey, Jesse! What's up, my country brother?" His face lit up when he saw us. Sid had a soft spot for Jesse. Along with every single person who'd ever met him. As Sid came closer, his eyes widened. "What the hell happened to you?"

"My truck threw up on me. Then it died."

"That sucks, man. You really need to consider picking up one of those little hybrids. Better for the environment, and let me tell you, my Prius is a fricking machine."

I wanted to, but I didn't roll my eyes. Sid didn't drive

a Prius because he was all environmentally conscious. He drove one because he liked the way it "labeled" him one of those hippy, earthy types.

"How does it do pulling a horse trailer?" Jesse asked, keeping a straight face.

"I'd wager a little better than that gas-guzzling truck that's about to become scrap metal."

Jesse pumped his fist over his heart. "Ouch, Sid. The pain is still fresh."

"Sorry, I forget the gritty cowboy is sensitive. Especially when you're all coated in grease." Sid looked like he was about to shake Jesse's hand, then saw how filthy it was and decided against it. "I've got a pile of paperwork I've got to get back to, but it's good seeing you again. Don't stay away so long next time, okay? I think our Rowen here was about to take a plunge into the Sound, if you know what I mean."

"Staying away isn't something I'm very good at. Obviously." Jesse's arm tightened around me as he waved at Sid.

"Get that boy a doughnut and some coffee, Rowen. And a washcloth," Sid added, disappearing into his office.

"Bacon maple bar?" I didn't know why I bothered asking; Jesse inhaled a few of them every time he visited.

"I need my protein. I'm a growing boy." Jesse grinned as I pulled a couple of bacon maple bars from the case.

"So these pole dancers . . ." I said. Jesse's face dropped while I poured a cup of coffee. "Do they normally travel in a team bus? Because, from what I know about pole dancing, it's more of an individual event. At least that's the way it was when I was doing it."

Jesse smiled at me humorlessly. "Ha. Ha. I don't

know. I guess they were going to some kind of competition or something here."

"So if you go missing, I know where to look?" I was being an insufferable smart-ass, but in all fairness, Jesse knew what he was getting into with me. Something about the way his eyes always lit up when I gave him a hard time told me he didn't mind much.

"Yeah. Look in your bed."

"Looking forward to that." I set the coffee and doughnuts in front of him, along with a damp washcloth, then went to grab my lunch from the fridge. It was a little early for my break, but if Sid didn't like it . . . too bad. I hadn't seen my boyfriend in a month, and I'd never missed a shift at Mojo. He'd have to deal. When I returned to the table, Jesse hadn't touched the coffee or doughnuts. His face was drawn together in seriousness. I rested my hand on his shoulder and scooted close. "Jesse?"

"What's the matter, Rowen? Why were you so upset this morning?" His eyes stayed locked on the table, but his hand found mine.

"Not now. I don't want to talk about that here. We'll talk after work." I'd been so caught up in our reunion, I'd forgotten why I'd been so upset earlier. There was nothing about that confession I was looking forward to. Not even the relief I assumed I'd feel because I knew my relief meant he'd feel like he'd been blindsided by a semi.

"Why not? I've been driving myself crazy all day wondering what's the matter." His words were needless. I could tell from his expression alone that the day had been torture.

"Because I want to give you my undivided attention. Because I don't want to be interrupted every two minutes to ring up a maple bar. Because I want privacy, and I want to be able to go to bed with you right after and make love until the sun rises." There were dozens of *becauses*, but really, I was scared. I wanted a little more time with him, another hour or two of him looking at me with love, not betrayal.

"All right, when you put it that way . . ." Jesse nudged me, the seriousness dimming from his face. "Could you just promise me something? It will make me feel ten times better while waiting."

I'd seldom been able to deny Jesse anything. I nodded once.

"Promise me that when you're done telling me what you need to, that we'll be okay. Promise me nothing's going to change between us. Promise me that, and I know I can deal with anything." That strong, certain voice of his wavered a bit. Just barely, but it caught my attention.

I wanted to promise him that, God knew I'd never wanted to make a promise to anyone the way I wanted to promise Jesse that. But how could I promise when I didn't know? Nothing would change the way I felt about him, the way I felt about *us,* but I couldn't promise when I didn't know how he'd feel once I told him about the internship. I was figuring out a way to answer him when the door opened and a couple headed for the display case. I couldn't imagine being as relieved as I was to be interrupted when I was with Jesse.

Lifting my index finger to Jesse, I rushed to the counter to help the couple. I'd be lying if I said I hurried with their order. I took my time wrapping up their Nirvana By Chocolate and Afternoon Delight doughnuts. I felt Jesse's eyes on me the entire time. Once I'd rung them up and I really couldn't stall any longer, I inhaled and headed back to Jesse. He was still watching me, but his forehead was lined and there was something in his eyes. Something I used to see when I looked in the mirror, but I'd rarely, if ever, seen in Jesse's eyes: uncertainty. Anxiety. And maybe, just maybe, a hint of fear.

I'd been picking up on those things on the phone with him lately, but I had yet to see them play out in front of me. It shook me to see the man I loved—who'd always seemed like a rock, as close to invincible as a mortal could be—that undone. Seeing him unsettled did the same to me.

"Jesse, I'll tell you what's been going on with me, but I need you to tell me what's been going on with you too. I know something's been bothering you, but I don't know what." I scooted beside him and grabbed his hand. I wasn't sure if it was more for his support or mine. "But I *want* to know. I want to be able to help you. I want to be strong for you the way you've been strong for me. I want to help you with whatever this is."

"I'm fine—"

"Don't. Just don't," I practically snapped. "Give me a little more credit than that. I know when the person I love most in the world is struggling with something. I mean, shit, I used to be the reigning queen of struggling through life. Don't treat me like I can be appeased with a *I'm fine* or that I'm happy to play ignorant and accept what you want me to believe. I'm not that person, Jesse. I'm the person who's willing to walk through hell with you because I know the way. I'm the person who will be with you the whole way until you come out on the other side. Got it?" I hadn't been expecting that impassioned speech to just pour from me, but apparently I'd been bottling it up.

It actually felt like a relief to get it out.

Jesse sighed. "Rowen, I can't—"

"Can't or won't?"

"Both," he admitted with another sigh.

I shook my head. "And who does that sound like? Who does that remind you of? Because it sure as hell reminds me of a certain someone sitting beside you who didn't want to open up to anybody last summer. Who did everything she could to push people away." I nudged Jesse and squeezed his hand. "Until another certain someone said too bad, got her to open up, and wouldn't let her push him away."

"What are you saying, Rowen? I got a little confused with all of the *certain someones*." Jesse managed a small smile.

"I'm saying it's time for me to repay the favor, buddy. So be prepared."

Jesse's arm went around my neck, and he pulled me close. Pressing his lips to my forehead, he kept them there for a few breaths. "I just fell a little more in love with you."

"That was the whole point."

We sat like that for a few minutes. Silent and still, content just to be near one another. Then I heard Jesse's stomach grumble. Actually, I felt it, too.

"Holy . . . Either you swallowed an angry gnome or your stomach is staging a revolt." I patted his stomach. "When did you eat last?"

"Um . . . six this morning. Maybe seven?"

"Jesse Walker! You need to take better care of yourself. You're a growing boy, you know." Grabbing my lunch bag, I upended its contents onto the table. "Here.

Eat." I pulled out my peanut butter sandwich and handed it to him, ready to hold him down and force feed him if necessary.

Then, because life was too short and those kinds of moments were too few, I smashed the sandwich into his mouth like we'd just cut into our wedding cake and I was *that* bride.

Jesse's eyes went wide with surprise, but it didn't take him long to catch up. He was used to those random moments of crazy from me. Grabbing my wrist, Jesse moved it away from his face toward mine.

"No, Jesse. Don't you dare!" I laughed, trying to dodge the smashed peanut butter sandwich. Just as I was certain I was going to take it in the face, he let go of my wrist. Instead of peanut butter, his lips covered my mouth. Because Jesse Walker was *that* kind of groom.

Although, since his mouth was covered with peanut butter, I suppose he still got a bit of payback. When Jesse's mouth left mine, I held out the mangled sandwich. "Eat your dinner, Casanova."

Jesse laughed, took the sandwich half, and devoured it in two bites. "I guess I was hungrier than I thought."

"I better save the Cheetos for Mar, just in case she shows up tonight."

Jesse stopped chewing the carrot he'd just popped in his mouth. His face froze up again.

"What's up?" I asked, dropping my hand on his forearm. "Bad carrot?"

He gave his head a swift shake, clearing his face a bit. "Something like that."

"Don't eat any more of those little bastard carrots then," I teased, exchanging the baggie of carrots for an

241

apple.

Jesse forced out a laugh, but it was strained. "So . . . Mar? That's her name?" He paused, looking like he'd just bitten into something sour. "This is the homeless lady who's been giving you so much self, life, and relationship advice?"

"Hey, she might not have a fancy degree, but you can't frame a real-life experience certificate. I don't agree with everything she says, but she makes some valid points." I'd mentioned Mar to Jesse a few times over the past month. He hadn't been thrilled that I was hanging with a homeless lady and, even though he'd never outright said it, I knew he was concerned that I was taking her advice to heart. Especially when it came to the relationship advice she was always so eager to shell out.

"Valid points about what? Settling down too young? Not being tied down to anything or anyone? Moving to Tahiti and selling coconut juice from a beachside trailer?" Jesse's mouth curved up on one side before biting into the apple.

"Okay, every point but that last one was totally whack. Because, really, everyone knows you haven't lived until you've sold overpriced, water-downed coconut juice to wealthy tourists from a sweltering tin-can of a trailer."

"Everyone knows that," Jesse said around a bite of apple.

"Mar is mad smart."

"Have you talked to Mar about us?"

"A little, not too much." Mar knew I had a boyfriend, but I kept the specifics to myself—I hadn't even told her his name. But that didn't keep her from making assumptions about us and doling out words of wisdom based on those assumptions. Jesse nodded, working something out in his head. "What? Tell me."

Jesse set down the apple and twisted toward me. "I don't know. It just seems weird that you're talking about us with a woman you know next to nothing about."

My eyebrows came together. "Why?"

"Some things you need to keep protected, you know? Some things you don't share with just anybody. You choose the people in your life you open up to about the sacred things because those are the people truly invested and concerned about your life. Anyone you run into will be eager to give you advice, but are they really taking your best interests into consideration? Or are they simply letting their own experiences and biases mold the advice they give you?"

I let all of that digest before replying. "Shouldn't they? I mean, aren't we all shaped by our experiences and biases?"

"Yes, of course, and someone who truly knows and loves you will give you advice, but it will be after taking *you* into consideration, not *themselves*."

Well, crap. That made a whole lot of sense. "I suppose I shouldn't be surprised that you've given this so much thought."

"I give everything a whole lot of thought. Especially when it's related to you and me."

"I'm such an under-thinking slacker," I muttered, tearing a corner off one of Jesse's maple bars. The non-bacon corner.

"No, you're not. I'm just a paranoid over-thinker."

"Maybe just a little." I pinched the air in front of him, making him laugh.

"Come here." He kissed me softly, barely a peck, but it felt so damn good. "Just be careful who you open up to. That's all I'm saying. In fact, that's what I should have just said instead of giving you a five-minute presentation."

"Wait, are you now telling me to not open up so much? Is this the same guy who, not even a year ago, was hounding me for two months straight about opening up and letting people in?"

Jesse gave me a *Give me a break* look. "I'm saying there are extremes on either end of the opening up spectrum. Being at the so-open-your-brains-are-going-to-fall-out spot is just as unhealthy as opening up for no one, not even yourself."

I pulled another piece of maple bar and popped it into my mouth, giving Jesse's words some thought. I saw his point—I always did—but I couldn't get completely on board with it. I talked about Jesse with friends and acquaintances because he played such an important role in my life. What could I do if those people took it upon themselves to offer their two cents worth? Stuff a sock in their mouths? Clamp my hands over my ears and walk away? No. People liked to give advice; that was human nature. As the saying went, *Opinions are like assholes; everyone's got one*. So what if someone offered me some misguided advice? I didn't have to listen and let it affect my relationship with Jesse.

I hadn't been doing that . . .

Or had I?

Everything became a bit blurred the longer I thought about it, so I decided to shelve it and come back to it later. Too much thinking, not enough kissing.

"It seems I'm destined to be unhealthy no matter what

I do. I think I need help," I teased, though only partly so. Everyone needed a little, or in my case, *a lot*, of help to get through life.

"That's what I'm here for. I'm here to help you when and if you need it."

I twisted in the booth to make sure I was looking at him straight on. "You know that goes both ways right? I'm here to help you when and if you need it. And maybe even if you won't admit you need help, I'll do it anyways because I'm all pushy like that." My words made Jesse's forehead wrinkle, as I'd expected they would. I should have just leaned in and kissed him. Kissed the living breath out of him. Kissed him until he forgot who he was and where he was.

I should have, but the moment passed us by when the door jingled open again.

"That would have been one hell of a kiss," Jesse said, his eyes dropping to my mouth.

"Probably the kiss to end all kisses." I played along. "Eat your bacon maple bars and I'll go help the customers, and then maybe we can pick up right where we almost left off." I winked as I slid out of the booth.

Jesse groaned in torture.

I laughed and glanced at the customer heading toward us. "Hey, you're early."

"I'd say I'm too late," Mar replied, inspecting the empty baggies on the table. From the looks of it, she'd had a shower. Well, and from the smell of it, too. A woman's shelter nearby opened up once a week to offer showers, lunch, and an activity to the homeless in the city. I'd looked it up and told Mar about it, and she'd been going for the past few weeks. I think the weekly showers were the only reason Sid allowed her in the shop.

"Don't worry. We saved you some. And this is great timing because I really wanted you to meet someone."

"Who? The boy I've been warning you against settling down with? Sure, I'll meet him. I'll tell him to get lost unless he wants to see your future ruined."

My mouth opened in shock. Mar had said some odd things in my weeks of knowing her, but never anything quite so cruel. Jesse, who was back to working on the apple, went rail stiff in the booth. Obviously her words had shocked him as much as they had me.

"Um . . . maybe you should leave, Mar?" I didn't want to manhandle her out, but I would if she didn't leave.

"No. Why doesn't he?"

I glanced at Jesse, who was slowly twisting in his seat. When his eyes locked on Mar, his entire face fell and went ash white. His hands curled into fists and it looked like he'd stopped breathing. He didn't just look like he was staring at a ghost . . . he looked like he was staring at the devil.

"What's the matter with you, boy? Dumb as you look? Or do you know that I'm right and you're going to do nothing but drag this girl down with you?"

"Mar. Leave." I motioned toward the door, keeping one eye on Jesse.

He was still frozen, but he blinked a couple of times like he was trying to clear his vision. When he stopped blinking and saw that Mar was still hovering in front of him, he shoved out of the seat so fast he was a blur. His eyes dropped from Mar as he lunged away from her, keeping as much distance as he could. He headed for the door.

"Jesse!" I called, but it was like he couldn't hear me. It was like I wasn't even there. He was in another world, and even I couldn't get through to him. "Jesse, stop!" He shoved through the door and broke into a run the instant he was outside.

"Jesse? Is that his name?"

I nodded automatically, biting my lip. Tears were already welling. I had no idea what had happened or how to make it right.

Mar huffed. "Small world. I had a son named Jesse. He was just as worthless as your Jesse, so I suppose we've got something in common."

My breath caught at the same time my legs wobbled. Something hit me with such force, I almost fell to my knees. Something, so intense I had to wrap my arms around my stomach, told me why Jesse had just behaved the way he had.

"Mar? How old is your son?" I bit the inside of my cheek and focused on the spot where Jesse had just been because I couldn't look at her.

"Hell if I know. I got rid of him years ago," she snapped.

Bile rose up my throat. I felt the chunks of maple bar begging to come out. I had to grip the edge of the table to keep from going down. Oh my god. What had I done? "How old was he when you . . . when you . . ."—I couldn't make myself repeat her words—" . . . saw him last?"

From the corner of my eye, I saw Mar's head start to bob. "Five years old."

That was when I lost it. My dinner, the tears I'd been holding back, my composure, my strength. I lost it all right there on the floor of Mojo Doughnuts.

chapter EIGHTEEN

Rowen

I'D KNOWN DARKNESS in my life. *That* though, that was something else completely.

After Sid peeled me off the floor at Mojo, he had to hold me back. As soon as I saw Mar's face, my strength surged into my muscles ten times over. I suppose it was a good thing Sid held me back. If I had gotten my hands on Mar, I don't know if I would have been able to stop. I didn't know the finer details of the abuse Jesse underwent as a young boy, but I knew enough to know that people who'd done those things to him should be serving life sentences or rotting away in an unmarked grave. My fists wanted to deal out a sentence right then, but after shrieking that I'd been possessed by the dark man—or some crazy other shit—Mar scurried out of Mojo.

I knew she didn't have a clue why I'd transformed into a wild person wanting to wrap my fingers around her neck. She didn't know the young man she'd insulted was the baby she'd given birth to twenty years ago. I knew that when she'd looked into his eyes, the same flicker of recognition that flashed in Jesse's wasn't in hers. She hadn't even known the flesh and blood she'd abused was right in front of her. That right there, that she'd already forgotten the face of the person who'd never be able to forget her face, sent me over the edge. That was when Sid almost lost his hold on me.

Once Mar was gone, I calmed down, although not a lot. After telling Sid an emergency had come up and I needed to cut out early, I grabbed my purse and phone and called Jesse. I must have called him close to a hundred times with no answer. As soon as his voice mail picked up, I hit redial. I did that the entire bike ride back to my apartment. I knew it was unlikely he'd be there, but at least I could ditch my bike and borrow Alex's El Camino for my search.

I tried to keep my mind focused on the ride, avoiding potholes, and getting a hold of Jesse, but I couldn't stop thinking about Mar. I couldn't comprehend how the minuscule chance of running into my boyfriend's abusive birth mother—who, by the way, was a homeless lunatic— had worked its way into my life. I tried to steer clear of those thoughts, but I couldn't help feeling like wherever I went, bad shit followed. How else could I explain what had happened?

A coincidence?

A small world?

Not even. It had happened because the nasty things of the universe were attracted to me. Even though my views on myself might have changed, that didn't mean what followed me had. I'd brought that on Jesse because I was . . . cursed. I brought it on him because I'd let someone I knew nothing about into my life, and I'd given her a front row seat to the intimate, special pieces of it. I'd opened up too much and, like Jesse had said, it was just as unhealthy as the other way around. But my error hadn't hurt me the way it had hurt him. I felt like a mini wrecking ball was going to work on my insides—one bone at a time, one organ right after the other—but I knew after witnessing the look on Jesse's face, my pain was nothing compared to his.

I'd been crushed. He'd been *ruined*.

As I pedaled into my apartment complex, I tried to push all thought from my mind. All the regret, the what-ifs, and what-nows. I needed to focus on finding Jesse. That was all that mattered. Finding him and offering him whatever comfort he'd accept from me at that point. I didn't bother to lock up my bike. I just rushed to the door, fumbling around for my keys.

The door swung open before I could get my key in the lock. Alex pulled me inside, looking frantic. "Oh, god, Rowen. I was just getting ready to call you. Shit, I don't know what's wrong. I just got home a few minutes ago. The front door was open, so I thought maybe someone had broken in." My heart was in my throat as Alex and I rushed through the apartment. "I was checking all the rooms, all the closets . . . and that's when I found him."

"Is he still here? Where's Jesse?"

Alex's head bobbed as she pointed down the hallway. "In your room. Something's wrong, Rowen. He isn't saying anything. I don't think he even knew I was in front of him when I found him. I was about to call 911."

"I got this, Alex. Thank you." I gave her a quick side hug before running down the hallway.

"What's wrong, Rowen? What's going on?"

"I'll explain later," I said because, even if I knew how to fully explain it all right then, which I didn't, there wasn't time. I needed to get to Jesse. I needed to know if the damage I'd unwillingly inflicted could ever be undone.

I paused just long enough outside my bedroom door to suck in a deep breath. I knew I would need it, and I didn't know when I'd be able to breathe deeply again. Stepping inside, I didn't need to scan the room to find him. My eyes found him like they were trained to find nothing else. What I saw made me wish I'd never been born with the gift of sight. I would swear that going through life blind would be better than having to live with that image of Jesse.

He was pressed into the back corner of my room, his back fitted tightly into it. His head was curled into his bent knees, and his arms were limp at his sides. He wasn't moving. The only sign of life was the infinitesimal rising and falling of his back.

"Jesse?" I took a hesitant step forward. He didn't move. There was no response. Wherever Jesse was, I needed to work my way into that place. I couldn't let him be alone. "Jesse, it's me. Rowen."

Still nothing.

Choking back a sob, I unglued my feet and rushed to him. I wasn't sure how he'd react to my touch, or if he'd react to it at all, but I had to put my arms around him. I had to hold him like he'd held me so many times, almost like he was holding me together. I crouched down beside him and scooted into the corner until my body was pressed into the side of his. Slowly, I wound my arms around him and drew him close. It was hard to describe, because he was still six-foot and two hundred pounds of muscle and bone, but somehow Jesse felt . . . frail. For the first time and what I hoped would be the last time. There were lapses of momentary weakness, and then there was frail. Like one gust of wind could blow him away from me.

"Jesse. Come back to me." I was trembling from keeping my emotions contained. "Please. I love you. You're safe. Just . . . come back to me. I *need* you." A sob sneaked out at the last part and another was about to when Jesse's body flinched.

"Rowen," he whispered as one arm circled me.

His whole body was so tense it looked as if some of his muscles were about to burst through the skin, but I sighed in relief at that one word. It was to date, and probably for every date forward, the most incredible sound I'd ever heard. Jesse was back. Wherever he'd gone, whatever dark place he'd been trapped in, he was back.

"Oh my god, are you okay? Wait. Stupid question." Tucking my chin over his head, I held him close and rocked him in my arms. "What can I do? What do you need?" I didn't know what to say, and in my loss of knowing *exactly* what to say, I ended up unable to shut up.

"Just this." His head was still curled into his knees, but his body relaxed little by little with every passing second. The more he relaxed, the tighter my arms went. When his head finally lifted, his gaze shifted my way. His eyes didn't give away that he'd been crying, but they did look different. Almost . . . hollow. Void. I would have preferred to see devastation or rage. "I shouldn't have run off like that. I shouldn't have left you alone. I'm sorry." Jesse's voice was strained, almost raspy, like each word was a fight to form.

I whipped my head from side to side. "Why are you apologizing to *me*? I'm the one who needs to apologize. I'm the one who's going to need to apologize to you for the rest of my life." I fitted my hand to his face, touching my thumb to the corner of his lips. "I'm so sorry, Jesse. I fucked up. I fucked up big time. I had no idea that . . . *that woman* . . . was your birth mother."

"Don't use that word. Please don't use that word." I must have looked confused. "That woman was never a mother to me. She never showed an ounce of love, or compassion, or nurturing. She doesn't deserve that title. Even with 'birth' preceding it."

I stared at the most incredible man in the world. A man who'd showed me unparalleled love, who was hard working, respected, and had a heart bigger than the giant state he lived in. I stared at an exceptional man who'd been hurt by awful people. The unfairness of it all made me so mad I wanted to hit something. I wanted to hit it until my knuckles bled and my tears were gone. I knew the laws of the spherical mass we lived on; I knew them because I'd tried to break just about every one and failed. I knew the rule was that life wasn't fair and one was a fool to expect it, but the Jesse Walkers of the world should have been the exception. People who were so good they didn't seem like they were of our world shouldn't have been punished by the heinous rules of it.

I wanted to hit something . . .

So I curled my fingers deeper into Jesse and let that be my outlet. "What can I do?" Having no clue how to ease his pain was almost as bad as knowing I was responsible for it.

"Just . . . let me figure all this out for a while. Let me process before you start firing off questions because I'm sure you've got hundreds."

I did have hundreds. Possibly thousands and, hard as it would be, that was a request I could accommodate. "Do you want me to go?" The thought made me sick. I didn't want to leave him—I wasn't sure if I could—but if that's what he needed, I'd just have to. I'd brought that mess on him; I would do whatever it took to clean it up.

If it even could be cleaned up . . .

"No. Stay." The arm around me tightened, and I breathed my second breath of relief in five minutes.

We sat like that for a while, or maybe it wasn't long at all. I couldn't tell. I'd lost all understanding of time. So many questions flew through my mind; so many almost burst free. The only thing that slipped free, the only thing I couldn't hold back, was, "I'm sorry."

"Don't, Rowen. This isn't your fault, and it isn't about you. This is about me and dealing with"—Jesse sighed, looking like he was fighting to find the right words —"dealing with something I thought I'd left behind . . ." He had to stop again. His chest was rising and falling hard again, and his face was twisted in pain.

I kissed the spot below his ear. "It's all right, Jesse. I can handle it. You can tell me whatever it is."

I was going to add more, but a couple of raised voices caught my attention. They were growing louder. Alex kept saying that now wasn't a good time, now was a very bad time. When I deciphered the other voice, I swallowed. It was too late to rush to the door and lock it. Not that that would have stopped Jax.

"Chill out, Alex. I'm not here with a chainsaw. I'm just here to talk to her."

Jesse's head whipped up right as Jax stormed inside. Such bad timing.

"Oh, well, sure. Boyfriend's in town. That explains why you've been avoiding my calls."

"What the hell are you doing here? And who the hell do you think you are bursting into my room? Why don't you get the hell out?" Apparently, I was in a hell raising kind of mood.

"Nice to see you, too, Cupcake."

Jesse's body stiffened. "Jax, I don't have anything against you, but I'm about to. Rowen asked you to leave. Either be a man and listen to her, or I'll have to be the man for both of us and show you the way out." Jesse's voice was low and level, making it a thousand times scarier than if he was yelling.

"Easy, Cowboy. I don't do the testosterone-fueled intimidation thing, and from the looks of it, you've already been in the middle of something today." Jax looked purposefully at Jesse's black-smudged clothing.

"Jax. Leave," I ordered, standing. "And, trust me, if I'm the one who has to make you go, you're going to *wish* Jesse had gotten to you first."

"Unlikely." Jesse stood beside me and crossed his arms. He'd taken a one-eighty from the broken form on the ground he'd been moments ago.

"Down, boy. And girl." Jax's smile curled in amusement as he inspected me. "I just have one quick question to ask you, and then I'll be happy to show myself to the door."

I knew what that question was. I knew the words about to come from Jax's mouth would undo Jesse all over again. I knew my betrayal, hot on the heels of being brought face to face with his childhood abuser, could send Jesse into another tailspin. The next one even worse.

"Jax . . ." I gave my head a small shake and pleaded with my eyes. "Don't."

"Have you decided on that internship yet, Rowen? How much longer do you think the museum is going to wait? After all, this is pretty much the opportunity of a lifetime and there are dozens, if not hundreds, of applicants in line behind you." Jax's smile was still in place. After that stunt, I'd normally want to slap it off of him. Instead, I felt deflated. Utterly and totally depleted of everything.

That probably had a lot to do with the way Jesse was looking at me. Not with betrayal but with confusion. "You got an internship?"

"I haven't accepted it yet." I studied the floor, unable to look him in the eyes.

"When did you apply?" His arms uncrossed and he stepped in front of me.

None of the answers would be easy ones, so I forced myself to go with the honest ones. "At the start of the school year."

"The *first week* of the school year," Jax chimed in.

I looked up long enough to glare at him over Jesse's shoulder.

"Why didn't you tell me?"

"Probably because she was scared you wouldn't support her."

I might have felt like a deflated balloon, but so help me god, if Jax opened his mouth to say something like that again, I could find the strength to punch him square in his smiling mouth. "It wasn't that I was scared you wouldn't support me. I was more scared of what it meant and what might happen if I got it."

"I don't get what you're saying, Rowen. Exactly why didn't you tell me . . . Because you were scared of what might happen? What were you scared of happening?" Jesse's hand settled into the bend of my neck, trying to get me to look at him.

I couldn't, though. I couldn't look him in the eye and say what I needed to say. "I was afraid of this happening. I was afraid of getting it. I was afraid of you finding out and feeling betrayed. I was afraid of what would happen to us if I took the internship." I was turning into a rambling mess. "I was afraid of so many things."

"Hey, it's okay. We'll work this out," Jesse reassured me when I should have been the one reassuring him. "If you take the internship, when would you start?"

I paused. That was the worst part. I knew that would be the part that would be the hardest for him to accept.

"The day *after* school ends," Jax said when I stayed quiet.

Jesse glanced back over his shoulder, probably glaring at Jax the same way I wanted to.

"And when does it end?" Jesse asked me, trying to keep his voice level.

Scratch that former thought. *That* answer was going to be the worst part.

"The day *before* school starts in the fall."

I wasn't focused on Jax anymore. I'd forgotten he was there. The only thing that had my attention was Jesse. My gaze had slowly lifted until my eyes locked with his. What I saw in them sucked the oxygen from my lungs.

"The whole summer?" One fraction of his expression still looked hopeful, like he was waiting for me to correct Jax.

I'd lied by omission all year. I wasn't going to lie to his face. "The whole summer." My voice was as small as I felt.

That last remaining scrap of hope left Jesse's face. Lowering his gaze, Jesse's hand fell from my neck. He pinched the bridge of his nose and squeezed his eyes shut. He'd gone from one nightmare to the next, and I was the one responsible for bringing him to the portal of each one.

"I need to leave," Jesse announced suddenly, starting for the door.

"Wait. Don't go." I grabbed for his arm. "Stay and let's talk this out, Jesse." I gave his arm a tug, but my efforts were nothing when Jesse moved with that kind of purpose.

"No, Rowen. I don't want to talk this out right now. I can't." He continued toward the door, refusing to look at me.

"Jesse—"

"Don't, Rowen. Just don't." He paused and gave me a brief glance. What I saw on his face was something I'd never forget. Never. "I'm losing everything. That should earn a person some time alone."

I didn't want to let him go. I wanted to throw myself in the doorway and hold him captive if I had to. I didn't want to let him go because I was terrified if Jesse walked out of my bedroom door, he'd never walk in it again. It would be the last I'd see of him. I didn't want to let him go . . . but I needed to. I knew I didn't want to let him go for selfish reasons. I didn't want him to go because that was what *I* wanted. My selfishness had done enough. Had done more than enough.

I had to let him go because that was what *he* wanted.

I let him go because that was what was best for Jesse.

It was one of the hardest things I'd ever had to do.

As soon as my hands dropped from his arm, Jesse continued for the door, shouldering roughly past Jax. Jesse didn't say another word. He never even looked back. It was like he'd already put me behind him, like I'd always feared he would, and come tomorrow, he wouldn't be able to remember my first name.

I'd always known that day was coming. As much as I'd tried to stomp out that fear, it had always lurked just below the surface. I always knew I would be the one responsible for tearing us apart because that's what I did and that's what I was good at. No matter how hard I tried to be something else, something better, I couldn't keep the destructive part of me fully contained.

"Happy trails, Cowboy." Jax flicked a salute down the hallway with that same stupid grin.

My fists balled at my sides. The night had been one sick, downward spiral. Might as well keep with the trend. When Jax glanced at me as I marched toward him, his face ironed out.

"If you don't want to leave the apartment in a body bag, you better get the hell out now."

Next to Jesse, I'd never seen a guy turn and move away from me as quickly as Jax did.

chapter NINETEEN

Jesse

IF I DIDN'T have a calendar to remind me of the date, I would have sworn a decade had passed in those few days since Seattle. I thought I'd known hell for the past month; I thought I'd known despair as a young boy.

I'd been wrong.

The roller coaster of emotions I'd been on the past three days were like nothing I'd felt before. My whole life felt like it was in some state of limbo. Everything felt up in the air; nothing felt certain. I felt like I was losing everything I cared about, one piece at a time. It was like dying a slow death. A quick and clean break would have been so much easier.

Seeing the woman who'd given birth to me had been . . . well, there were no words to describe that. It had been like living one of my nightmares. Five seconds of staring into her face had reduced me to that same scared, lost boy I'd been years ago. Five seconds of being around her had been enough to lose myself. I couldn't even remember how I'd gotten to Rowen's apartment, nor could I recall how much time had passed. Everything from the time I'd escaped Mojo to the time Rowen found me was black. I had no memory of any of it.

Rowen brought me back. She was that one sliver of hope I'd clung to in my darkness, and hearing her voice and feeling her touch had been enough to break through the black walls surrounding me.

She'd saved me in that moment. Only to break me a few moments later.

"Clear something up for me, Walker. Are you most mad at her because she applied to the internship, lied to you about it, might take it, or won't be here for the summer as planned?" Garth asked from across the campfire. We were on night watch again, and I thought he'd been asleep for a while.

"I don't want to talk about it, Garth," I replied, shifting into a more comfortable position. "In case you missed that the past fifty times I've told you that today."

After leaving Rowen's apartment and remembering my truck was a few hundred miles to the east, I'd pulled out my phone and did the unthinkable: I called Garth Black for a favor. He drove straight through the night, picked me up at the gas station I was camped out at, and managed to keep his mouth shut for the first half of the trip home. The second half, he hadn't been able to keep his mouth shut and I'd answered too many of his questions. I had only told him about Rowen's internship, but I regretted giving him even that much information.

He hadn't stopped playing drugstore psychologist since we'd gotten back to Willow Springs. Thankfully, Dad and Mom had taken one look at my face when I came through the front door and not fired off question after question. They let me have the space I needed and let me get back to my everyday routine. But they would pretend with me but only for so long. I expected Mom to be camped out on the porch swing, or Dad to invite me to go fishing, any day. They were fine giving space, but they weren't fine sweeping and keeping dirt under the rug.

"Sure you want to talk about it. You're Jesse fucking Walker. You'd talk your way through the phonebook if you could get someone to listen to you."

"Let me clarify. I don't want to talk to *you* about *Rowen*." I'd avoided saying her name as much as I could. Each time I said it, I felt the way I did then: like a knife had been driven through each of my lungs. I hadn't tried contacting her yet because I didn't know what to say. I'd told her I needed time to work some things out, and I had yet to work anything out. I couldn't call her just to say hi and not expect her to ask questions. So I hadn't reached out to her yet, but she hadn't tried reaching out to me either.

I didn't know why she hadn't. Maybe she was doing as I asked and giving me the space I requested. Maybe she was angry at me for storming out that night—which, by the way, she had every right to be pissed about. Maybe she felt guilty for the things that had happened. Maybe she was done with me. There were dozens of maybes, but the not knowing was the hardest to bear.

"Why not? I'm the perfect person to talk to because I don't talk to anyone else. You don't have to worry about me gossiping like an old biddy. I'm able to offer unbiased, third-party perspective that you, my friend, are not able to get on your own."

I sighed. Garth wasn't first person I'd choose to go to with a problem, but he was the only person for miles, and I knew from experience he wouldn't shut up until I gave him something. "I'm not mad at her, Garth. I'm more mad at the situation."

"What the hell does that even mean? 'I'm mad at the *situation.*' That sounds like some passive aggressive bull-shit or something."

So much for a fair, unbiased opinion.

"I'm not mad at Rowen for applying to the internship. I won't be mad if she chooses to accept it. I won't even be mad if that means we'll barely see each other this summer."

"A whole summer without sex? And that wouldn't straight up make you want to pound something into smith-ereens?" Garth quirked a brow. "Hell, Jess, I'd be mad for you if you got the Charlie-Bravo all summer."

"Charlie-Bravo?"

Garth rolled his eyes. "The dreaded C.B."

"I'm going to need a translation because I'm not tracking."

Another eye roll. "Cock-blocked. Charlie-Bravo equals C.B. equals cock-block. Shit, Walker. Get with the times."

"If that's all I've been missing out on, I'm not sure I want to get with the times."

"Good, because you and your Puritan-ass ways will never catch up." Garth shifted up onto his forearm and tossed a pebble into the dying fire. "You're really not mad about her not telling you about that internship? You wouldn't be mad if she took it, either? Come on, Jess, this is me you're talking to. There's nothing you could admit to me that would made me blink."

"No, I'm really not mad. Present and future tense," I added when Garth's forehead lined. "I guess I'm more . . . worried about why she didn't tell me."

"Are you sure that's worry twisting your stomach and not betrayal?"

I only needed to give that a moment of thought. "No, it's worry. And maybe a little bit of hurt. I mean, was she worried I wouldn't support her wanting to apply? Did she think I'd be disappointed in her if she took the job? What's got me worried is *why* she kept it from me in the first place."

"Maybe she didn't tell you because she was worried of this." Garth motioned at me. "Of you worrying your life away and your tender little heart getting hurt."

"Always a pleasure discussing these kinds of things with you, Black," I muttered.

"Chill your worried, hurt self out," Garth said, tossing another pebble into the fire. "As much as you want to deny it, Rowen and I are cut from the same cloth." Garth lifted his hand when I went to interrupt. "Hear me out. My point in saying that your girl and me are creatures of similar creation is that I understand where she was coming from when she decided not to tell you about the internship."

I resisted the urge to cover my ears or get up and walk away. Garth Black was about as deep as a puddle.

"Deep down, Rowen and me are self-loathing types. We despise ourselves, so when life throws us shit, we accept it because that's what we deserve. The people we let in, the people we love, we're fiercely protective of. Those people are ten times more important to keep safe than ourselves. My guess is that's why Rowen didn't tell you. She wasn't even sure she'd get the internship. Why make you worry about something that wasn't even a sure thing?" Garth shrugged. "I mean, that's what I would have done. I'd keep the truth from someone if I thought it would save them some pain."

That was a lot to process. The wisdom behind the words and the fact that they'd just come from Garth Black's mouth.

"While I'm working that out in my head, tell me one thing, Black. Who in the hell have you ever loved more than yourself?"

Garth rolled onto his back and folded his hands behind his head. "I was strictly speaking hypothetically about myself."

"Didn't sound like it . . ."

"Oh, blow me, Walker. I haven't found my Rowen Sterling yet. I'm still, thankfully, in possession of my nutsac. Unlike someone else I know."

"Two things. Don't ever mention Rowen, blow, and nutsac in the same breath again. Ever. And two, what are you going to do when you find a girl who's able to, miraculously, see past the piece-of-shit facade you keep up?"

Garth chuckled. "I'm going to run, Walker. And I'm not going to stop. Guys like me weren't made for settling down."

That was when a familiar and haunting sound rolled across the valley.

Garth burst up at the same time I did. "Wolves," he cursed, tugging on his boots.

"They're close, too." As I grabbed the rifle we kept for exactly that kind of reason, my heart hammered. To hear wolves howling at night wasn't uncommon, but that . . . hearing their yips and calls as they hunted was something I'd only ever heard once before.

"I'll get the horses ready," Garth called, rushing

toward Sunny and Rebel. They had stopped their grazing to look in the direction of the crying wolves.

That was when I heard the next familiar sound. The one that unnerved me more than hearing wolves. The cry of a cow in distress.

"No time, Garth!" I hollered, running after him. "We've got to go now!"

Garth must have heard the same noise I had because, after pausing, he sprinted for Rebel and was just throwing his leg over him when I caught up.

"Easy, Sunny boy." Both horses were clearly on edge, but they were ranch ponies, chosen because they didn't shy away from just anything—not even a pack of wolves crying into the night. Grabbing onto his mane, I threw my leg over Sunny. Once I had the rifle strap around my shoulder, I sent Sunny after Garth and Rebel, who were already a good fifty yards ahead. Rebel was a tank—he had unparalleled strength when it came to a horse—but all that muscle slowed him down. It didn't take long for Sunny and me to catch up.

The shrill yips, mingled with the low timbered cow cry, was getting louder, so we were heading in the right direction. I pushed Sunny faster until we'd pulled ahead of Garth and Rebel. I didn't have a plan, I didn't know if anything I could do would work, but I heard something crying out for help. That's what propelled me forward.

The sky was clear and the moon was full—just the kind of conditions a rancher wanted when they heard a pack of wolves close by. Being able to see them at fifty yards was better than fifty inches.

There were a handful of wolves, four or five from what I could tell, that had taken down a yearling. One's jaws were locked around its neck while the others tore into it. And the sound? The sound that yearling was making twisted my stomach. It was screaming, its cry muffled and wet from the wolf's hold on its throat.

I knew it was the circle of life, I knew it was nature's way, but witnessing it, hearing the life bleed out of a creature . . . there was nothing harmonic about it. There was nothing but violence and fear.

As a testament to the kind of horse Sunny was, he didn't slow a bit. Garth was still a little ways back, yelling at me, but I couldn't make out his words. All I heard was the animal crying out for help. The helpless creature restrained by its predators, dying at their whim. It was all hitting too close to home.

I slid the rifle off of my shoulder and had the safety off by the time I leapt off of Sunny. I was so close I could smell the blood. The wolves barely noticed me. They were too frenzied ripping chunks of flesh from the still-living animal. I fired off a shot. Then another. By the third one, all but one wolf, the one still at the yearling's throat, had fled. One more shot, and that one let go and sprinted after its pack.

"Why didn't you shoot those sons of bitches?" Garth flew off Rebel and sprinted the rest of the way to me.

I'd kept my eyes on the retreating wolves, but my gaze shifted to the yearling when I answered, "They didn't deserve the quick death of a bullet."

Garth came up behind me. "Damn it all to hell. Couldn't they have waited until the thing was dead before they started tearing into it?"

The yearling wasn't crying like it had been; probably because it was minutes away from dying. The only movement it made was an occasional muscle spasm. Blood covered the ground, and the thing had been so severely mangled, I saw portions of its anatomy. It was a gruesome sight, one that would make any man's stomach churn.

But that wasn't the reason I dropped to my knees beside it. A good quarter of the yearling was, at present, digesting in the stomachs of a handful of wolves, and the rest was coated in its own blood. It looked like any other yearling in the herd, but it wasn't just any other yearling. It was *the* yearling.

The one I'd tumbled down Suicide Ridge to save. The one I'd broken bones and spilt blood to make sure it didn't face that kind of fate. I didn't need to check the tag in its ear to confirm it. I knew it.

"We have to put it out of its misery, Jess." Garth put a hand on my shoulder.

"I know," I said, forcing myself up. I knew what needed to be done. I knew the creature I'd saved last summer was the same one I'd have to put a bullet in that night. I'd saved its life only to have to take it months later.

My hands didn't tremble when I brought the rifle into position. My hands didn't tremble, but everything inside did. My finger had just covered the trigger when Garth shouldered up beside me. He moved the rifle barrel just out of range of the space right between the yearling's eyes. The place I'd always known to put a bullet if one had to be fired, but it was something I'd never had to do.

"I can do this, Black." I butted my shoulder into his and moved the rifle back into position.

"I know you can," he said, moving the barrel aside again.

"I need to do this. It should be me."

"No," Garth said, looking between me and the year-ling, "it shouldn't."

I wanted to argue, I wanted to force myself to take the shot, but when Garth grabbed the rifle, my fight was over. I was spent for the second time that week.

So instead of pulling the trigger, I kneeled beside the yearling and put my hand on what was left of its mangled neck, comforting it like the night I'd found it last summer. That touch had been to comfort the life that was safe; this touch was to comfort the life that was leaving.

The yearling's eyes locked on mine at the same time a shudder ran through its body. And then, it wasn't the year-ling dying in front of me anymore. It was me as a young boy, curled into myself, not making a sound. I was about to squeeze my eyes closed when the image flashed into something else, and it was Rowen curled at my knees. Expressionless, motionless, a shell of the girl I loved. Gone.

My world was falling apart, one tragic bit at a time.

The gunshot ripped through the canyon, vibrating my insides, and after that, the blackness I'd been holding just barely at bay consumed me.

chapter TWENTY

Rowen

I COULDN'T BREATHE right. That's just one of the few symptoms I'd experienced since Jesse walked out a few nights ago. My trouble with breathing normally might not be the worst symptom, but it was the most obvious. Every two seconds, I was reminded that my lungs just wouldn't fill to capacity like they used to.

In addition to the breathing problem, I was unable to sleep for longer than an hour at a time, I'd eaten a total of two bowls of cereal that Alex practically had to force feed me, I couldn't seem to remember jack, I broke out in tears over certain songs or commercials, and I couldn't lift a pencil to paper, let alone actually make something that might count as art.

Oh, yeah. I also looked like shit and felt like shit. Life *was* shit once again, and that terrified me.

To skip the above, drawn-out paragraphs and provide the Rowen Sterling Present Day Cliff's Notes, I was the hottest, messiest, hot-mess to have ever hot-messed the world. Hot. Mess.

Jesse hadn't tried to reach out to me yet. No phone calls, texts, emails, or surprise appearances. I knew that meant he was still working out the things I'd heaped on him, but I really wished he could work them out while still managing to send me a daily text. Just some small measure of reassurance. The events of that night must have taken an overwhelming toll on him. I knew that from the words he'd said, the way he'd looked, and the way I'd feel if I was in his shoes.

I also knew a person didn't just work all that out in a few hours of soul-searching under a blue sky. It was some deep, dark shit that made a person delve into the deep, dark shit within themselves. I knew that from experience. I knew that from wading through my own cesspool of deep, dark shit last summer to come out victorious on the other side. It wasn't a permanent victory—scars like the ones Jesse and I had would never disappear—but it was a victory nonetheless.

I hoped—whatever Jesse was wading through—that he'd emerge on the other side soon, and with the same measure of peace I had from my battles. Or if he couldn't beat it on his own, that he'd let me help him.

My brain knew what the right thing to do was: give him space and let him contact me when the time was right. But my heart wanted something so different. I'd picked up the phone, my finger hovering over his number, so many times I'd driven myself sick from the letdown of forcing myself to clear the screen and walk away from the phone.

The night after Jesse left, I wasn't scheduled to work, but I still went in. I waited at the booth in the front, my foot tapping like I was on speed, watching every figure pass by. I wasn't sure what I would have done if I saw Mar again, but something told me I would at least land myself an overnighter in jail. I'd been nice to the woman, let her into my life. I'd shared my sack lunch with her and sneaked her doughnuts. Hell, I'd found a woman's shelter she could get a shower at and eat a warm meal. I'd trusted her.

I'd been so, so wrong. I'd trusted a person who deserved nothing for what she'd done to Jesse. I'd unknowingly brought the monster of Jesse's past back into his life because I'd been naive. I couldn't have known the homeless woman I'd met in an alley was my boyfriend's childhood abuser . . . but I couldn't help feeling like I *should* have known. How could I not know I was staring into the same eyes that had watched her child suffer at her hands? How could I not know that?

So in addition to the rest of my Jesse-separation symptoms, I felt a guilt so overwhelming I hadn't been able to drag myself out of bed for three mornings. Fortunately, Alex had no problem doing the dragging for me.

And then there was the issue of the internship and Jax's impeccably awful timing. I should have been the one to tell Jesse. I know I should have been the one to tell him months ago, right before I applied. I know he would have been supportive. The thought of spending the summer apart would have killed us both, but he'd never been anything but supportive of me fulfilling my dreams.

Once he'd shown up at Mojo that night, I knew I needed to tell him. I knew I couldn't keep it from him any longer. And then the unthinkable mess with Mar happened . . .

How could I could tell him, the same night he'd come face to face with her, that I'd applied to an internship months ago without telling him and had just found out I'd gotten it? Hell, the internship wasn't even on my radar at that point. Nothing but finding Jesse and comforting him was on my mind. I had been on the find-and-comfort-Jesse autopilot.

Then, barely a minute after Jesse had come back to me, Jax had burst in and dropped the internship bombshell. Worst timing in the history of bad timing.

I'd never forget the look on Jesse's face that night when he looked into the face of the woman who'd given birth to him, and I'd never forget the look on his face when he found out I'd lied to him. Never.

So, betrayal. Yeah, I felt that hardcore, too. Not the betrayed, but the betrayer. After being on both ends of the betray spectrum, I could confidently say being the betrayer was just as bad. In my case, maybe worse. I'd done some serious damage to a person I loved, and that was something I'd hoped to avoid with Jesse. I guess I should have known better.

The past three days had been the worst, having no contact with Jesse being the pinnacle. I could have called Rose or Lily. Even Garth or Josie would have been better than sitting in "radio silence," but I didn't call them either. Jesse had asked me to give him space; calling any one of the four people closest to him seemed like cheating the system.

"Hey, Mopey. Stop crying into your coffee and go get some fresh air."

Who needed to call anyone when I had that kind of support in arm's reach? Yes, that was sarcasm. "No, thanks. I'm planning on wallowing the day away. You have fun with the fresh air, though." I was sitting on one of the three folding chairs staggered around a card table, also known as our dining set, staring at closed blinds. I was back to keeping out the light.

"Please tell me you're not going to wind up being one of those girls who throws her life away because she and her boyfriend got into a fight. Please, for the love of Julio, tell me I haven't been roommates all year with a flake like that." Alex dropped her backpack on the counter and grabbed a cup of coffee. I guess it was morning, time for classes. I'd lost track of time, and when the blinds were closed, I had no way of knowing if it was light or dark.

"I'm not throwing it away. I've just put it on . . . hold for a little while."

"Why?" she asked, dumping a mountain of sugar into her coffee.

"Why? Why, Alex?" I said in disbelief. "Have you really not listened to a single word I've said over the past three days?" She'd been the only shoulder I'd had to cry on since I couldn't call anyone at Willow Springs and Jax was still on my shit list.

"Well, I know what happened between you and Jesse, but why's that deserving of putting *your* life on hold?"

If she had to ask, she really didn't get anything that had happened.

"So what? You fucked up. You fucked up big time," she added when I lifted an eyebrow. "We're human, Rowen. An occasional fucking up big time is written in the fine print. You can't just throw away, pause, fast forward, or delay your life because you made a mistake." She slapped the counter when I lifted the other eyebrow. "When you made a *huge* mistake."

"It wouldn't be so bad if my *huge* mistake only hurt me, but it hurt Jesse in a way I'd taken a silent vow to keep from ever doing. I just can't . . . It's not so easy to move on when you devastate someone you love more than yourself."

"Trust me. You love someone long enough and hard enough, you're going to make an epic screw up or two along the way. Love makes us stupid sometimes," Alex said, pouring a bowl of cereal and milk. "Deal with it."

"I don't feel comforted."

Alex laughed a few notes. "I'm not trying to comfort you, china doll. I'm trying to bitch slap you back to reality."

"Then you're doing an awesome job. I feel success-fully bitch slapped." I rubbed my cheek as Alex dropped the cereal in front of me and gave me the *Eat or else* look. I'd had that look directed my way a bunch of times lately.

"Fine, look at it this way." Alex crossed her arms and looked down at me. "Would you rather have a man like Jesse in your life and have some fucks up along the way, or would you rather stay alone, an old mopey shrew, whose fuck ups only affect herself?"

My immediate answer was one thing, my non-selfish answer the other. After going back and forth a few times, I decided I wasn't in the right state of mind to make that decision. Of course I wanted to spend my life with Jesse—I'd never known life could feel so big and hopeful before experiencing it with him at my side—but after witnessing the damage I'd done to him after my mega "fuck up," I was pretty sure if I had to witness those expressions on his face again, it would kill me.

Apparently my deliberation was taking too long for the impatient person hovering above me because she let out an exaggerated sigh, snagged my phone off the counter, and tossed it in front of me. "Why don't you call him already? Apologize, help him work through whatever shit he's going through, then get back to being the cutest, most nauseating couple on the planet."

"I can't," I replied, staring at my phone.

"Bok, bok, bok," was her intelligent reply.

"Alex . . ."

She grabbed her backpack from the counter and made her way to the door, wagging her elbows and repeating, "Bok, bok, bok." After another dozen boks, she finally closed the door.

Alex's words and encouragement were making me weak. Or were they making me strong? At that stage, it was hard to tell. I couldn't stop staring at my phone, but I managed to keep from grabbing it and speed dialing Jesse.

My cereal was soggy when the will to call him finally tipped the scales on the will not to. My arm snapped toward my phone, and right then, my phone buzzed.

Other than Jax, who I'd ignored, and Alex, who I'd *tried* to ignore, I hadn't had many calls the past few days. I held my breath, hoping Jesse was calling to announce his need for space was over. The number wasn't his, but it was almost as familiar.

"Rose?" My heart leapt into my throat before she said a word. I felt the tension on the line.

"Rowen, it's Jesse. Something's wrong," she said in a rushed voice. "Can you come to Willow Springs? Please?"

I was halfway to the door when I replied. "I'm coming."

chapter TWENTY-ONE

Jesse

I BROKE.

I knew that with absolute certainty because it had happened before. It might have been years since I'd lost my grip on reality, but I'd never forget the way it felt. Feeling like I was holding on by my fingertips, then just barely by my nails, before falling. I fell for so long, I lost track of how long I'd been lost. It was an inexplicable feeling, and the only thing I was more sure of than I broke was my desire to never experience it again.

Given I'd been certain that part of my life was long behind me, but it had managed to creep up and surprise me, I wasn't confident it wouldn't happen again. That was paralyzing. I knew the person I'd been before all of it started, how strong and sure I'd been, and it took all of a month to revert back to the boy I'd been years ago.

I knew control was an illusion. I'd known that for a long time. However, I also knew control was an illusion I could manipulate. I'd been manipulating it for over a decade. I might not have been able to control the people, circumstances, and environment around me, but I could control myself. If that was the only thing I could control, then I'd take it. That was infinitely better than claiming no control in one's life. I couldn't control what happened around me, but I could control what happened within me.

Or . . . I *had* been able to control what happened within me.

After that sober version of a major bender, I couldn't even say that. I had about as much power over myself as I did the rest of the world: none. If I couldn't control myself, I wasn't safe to be around, especially not when I could spiral downward so rapidly. It would be one thing if my span from good to bad was a few clipped words and a night to wake up and feel better in the morning. It was something different when my good to bad was here I am one day, gone the next.

It was too extreme. Too intense. I didn't want anyone to get hurt the next time it happened.

After Garth shot the yearling, I remember about one minute of consciousness, and the rest is a big blank. That night, those wolves, and that yearling had been the proverbial straw that broke my back. Everything had been building up, and when I had to watch an animal I felt a connection with suffer before dying . . . Well, I lost my grip on that ledge I'd been clinging to and fell into the blackness that had been waiting for me for weeks.

I remember feeling like everything I cared about was slowly slipping away, Rowen especially. What I realized when I came out of it was that those things I held dear weren't slipping away from me.

I was slipping away from them.

Maybe it had been my way of protecting them from the storm I felt coming, or maybe it was something totally out of my control, but despite being conflicted about it, I knew one thing: I was relieved it had happened. I didn't want Rowen in the same state as me. Not until I figured out what was happening, why it had happened, and if it could be prevented in the future.

I could imagine only one thing worse than losing her forever, and that was hurting her. I'd take myself totally out of the equation if I couldn't be certain I wouldn't hurt her. In any way.

My break from reality could have been worse, I guess. After jerking awake that morning, feeling like I had the hangover to end all hangovers, I fumbled for my phone and saw I'd only been out a day. After sitting up in bed and looking out my window to see the sun just rising, I realized it hadn't even been a full twelve hours.

But from the look on Mom's face when she came in to check on me . . . I would have thought I'd died and been resurrected. She was still hugging me when Dad and my sisters came in. She was finally thinking about letting me go when Garth and Josie popped their heads in.

What I'd gathered from the party camped outside my door all night was that I'd blacked out and Garth pretty much had to manhandle me up onto Rebel in order to get me back to Willow Springs. Garth left out most of the details, to spare me or my family I wasn't sure, but I was thankful regardless.

After about five minutes of everyone firing question after question at me, I felt like I was suffocating. I asked everyone if they'd leave, using the need for sleep as my excuse, and everyone agreed. Mom was the last to leave. Looking at me with that meaningful expression I'd seen on her face so many times, she said, "That was just one bad day out of the thousands of good ones you've lived, Jesse. One weak day to countless days of strength. Don't let one day set the backdrop for the rest of your life."

Something told me she was right, but something else told me she wasn't. Comparing bad days to good days was like comparing apples to oranges. I couldn't justify having one bad day with having a thousand good ones. They were inherently different things. My concern wasn't the bad days outweighing the good days. My concern was the bad days taking over. If that was a trend I could expect in my future, the good days of the past were a moot point. Try telling a starving person to focus on the fullest their stomach had ever been. Mom's words felt about as encouraging in that moment.

The rest of the day passed in silence. No one knocked at my door, although I lost count of how many times I heard a pair of footsteps stop outside my door for a few seconds before walking away quietly. I couldn't sleep. I couldn't eat. All I could do was think. I thought until my brain felt like it was about to liquefy.

I pushed the thoughts of my childhood and the woman who'd given birth to me aside. I knew from experience that no amount of thinking could make sense of what had happened to me back then. I didn't want to think about the past month either. I'd thought about the torment of my dreams and worries for so long those last weeks that I couldn't do it anymore.

So I thought about Rowen. What it meant for us. What my past meant for our future. If we could have a future at all. And the question that stopped, sped up, and broke my heart every time I asked myself it.

What was best for Rowen?

I could no longer say that I was it. If I stepped back and looked at her life in a neutral light, I couldn't say with certainty that I wouldn't hinder her from living the life she wanted to. As a college freshman, she was already creating what was sure to be a promising career. She'd managed to bust free from the weight of her past to get on with her life. She'd grown, evolved, and was setting the world on fire.

I, on the other hand, was digressing, shrinking, and setting myself on fire.

One year and everything had changed. Everything but the way I felt about her, and that was why I would make the right choice when it came to the hard question. The love I had for her made the decision easy. I was reaching for my phone, about to make the call I couldn't put off, when I heard her voice. Double-checking my phone to make sure I hadn't dialed her yet, I heard her voice again. Getting closer.

I dropped my phone and barely had a chance to stand up from where I'd been camped out on the floor of my bedroom before the door flew open. No knock, no greeting, no words at all. Rowen rushed toward me and threw herself in my arms, almost knocking me off balance.

My arms formed like vices around her as I tucked her head under my chin. For those few minutes when Rowen held onto me and I held onto her, my whole world brightened. Everything didn't seem so gloomy and unsure. Life didn't seem so irrevocably screwed up. I was hopeful again.

But I wasn't a fool enough to believe that feeling could last. It didn't, either. Once I noticed how incredibly fragile she felt. Once I felt her shudder from keeping her tears contained. Once I saw how devastated she was, thanks to me, the moment of brightness was eclipsed.

"What are you doing here?" I whispered into her hair. I knew I needed to let her go, I needed to set her free, but I couldn't execute it quite yet.

"Your mom called me. Then I called Garth. Then I borrowed Alex's car. Now I'm here." Her fingers curled into my shirt like she was afraid I was about to be ripped away from her.

"Why did you come all this way? You're missing school. You're missing your . . . life . . . in Seattle." I paused, having to clear my throat. "I'm fine."

"Don't, Jesse. Please don't." The last time I'd attempted to placate her with the *I'm fine* routine, she'd said those exact same words with so much conviction she had made me a believer. Now, her voice was so small I had to lean in to hear her words. "Garth told me what happened. All of it. I'm sorry, Jesse. I can't imagine dealing with the things you've gone through this month, but even if I can't know exactly, I know enough that it doesn't make a person *fine*. Devastated, sure. Depressed, hell yes. But *fine* . . . I don't think so. Please don't try to sell me on it again."

I sighed. To be known intimately the way Rowen knew me was one of the few special things life allowed us. Right then, though, it only made things harder.

"How are you *really*, Jesse?"

I wanted to be honest with her. I'd made that a priority from the beginning of our relationship, and I didn't want to lose that. "I don't know. I'm not sure."

Rowen exhaled. "Now *that* I believe."

She could still make me laugh, even when I'd hit rock bottom. "That's a relief."

She lifted her head from my chest to look me in the eyes. It had only been a few days since I'd last looked into them, but it had seemed like years. Hers still looked the same, although I knew the ones she was looking into didn't. "I'm not going to ask you what's going on, Jesse, because I have a good idea. A really, really good idea, and most of it's all thanks to me. I know what I did wrong, I just want to know how to make it right."

From the looks of it, she'd gotten about as much sleep as I had the past few nights. She was still beautiful, of course, but everything that had happened had taken a toll on her. "Please, Jesse, just tell me what I need to do to make this right. I messed up, I fucked up big time. I never should have kept the internship from you, and I should have known that sorry excuse for a woman was the one who gave birth to you. I should have called more. I should have just hopped on that bus when the hundreds of whims came up. I should have been here more for you. I should have been everything you've been to me. I should have been more careful to not make such a nasty mess with us like I knew I was prone to do. I should have done so many things differently, but I can't change that. I can't change the past. So, please, tell me . . . how can I change the future? What can I do to make this all right?"

Her words alone were enough to bring a man to his knees, but her expression was what made me feel like my heart had just been ripped from my chest. Her whole face was twisted with agony and one tear fell from the corner of her eye, and I wanted to die right there. I wanted to die before I had to watch another one slip from her eyes.

"You don't need to worry about making anything right, Rowen, because you didn't do anything wrong." I couldn't look at her face and keep talking, so I focused on the wall behind her.

Her head whipped from side to side. "Please don't say I didn't do anything wrong. That's just as bad as you saying you're fine."

"It's true."

"No, it's not."

"It is." I didn't mean to upset her, but I clearly was.

"Keeping the internship from you?"

I stared holes into the wall and answered, "I understand why you did it."

"Bringing you face to face with that woman again?"

I bit the inside of my cheek. "You couldn't have known who she was."

Every word I said appeared to be making her angrier. I didn't understand why. All I was trying to do was lift the guilt she'd taken when I should have been me to bear it.

"And what about the times I missed your calls, or couldn't come out to see you, or had to work when you were in town? What about all of the times I had something else to do when I should have made you the priority?" Rowen's default when she didn't want to cry was to get angry. I still hadn't figured out how to distinguish between genuine anger and masked sadness.

"You were busy. I understand." I shrugged and dropped my eyes.

"Stop it, Jesse. Do me a favor and cut the act out." Rowen shoved my chest and broke free from my arms. "Why are you pretending like nothing's happened? Why are you pretending like none of this is a big deal?"

"Why? Why am I pretending?" I wasn't touching her, and all of the darkness I'd been holding back came flooding in.

"Yes, that's what I asked."

"I'm not pretending for me, Rowen. I've already lived through it all. I'm pretending for *you.*"

"Oh, in that case . . . why don't you stop pretending and give it to me straight? I've been through some shit in my life too, Jesse. Stop protecting me from whatever it is you've been through and what you're going through now and tell me already! I can handle it!" She hadn't started out shouting, but about halfway through, that changed.

I tried to keep my voice controlled, but it quivered instead. "You think you can handle it? You *really* think you can handle it?"

She lifted her arms at her sides. "I'm ready."

"You're ready to hear that the first memory I have of the woman who should have been my mother is her hitting me across the face with a cheese grater? You're ready to hear how my first memory of the man who should have been my father was him stopping his wife from drowning me in a five gallon bucket of water because he didn't want the trouble of disposing of my body?"

To Rowen's credit, she'd started out with her shoulders squared and her chin high, but with each word out of my mouth, she crumbled a bit more. There simply wasn't a way to stay strong when discussing those kinds of horrors. Crumbling was the standard response. I was doing it myself.

"You really think you can handle it, Rowen? Because that's just the tip of the iceberg. That's the first paragraph of chapter one in the five years I spent at those people's mercy."

Lifting her shoulders again, she cleared her expression. "I can handle it."

I cried out on the inside. Why wouldn't she just cry

mercy and walk away like we both knew she needed to? I wasn't sure who it was harder on, me or her, but I knew one thing: that kind of openness would either sever our relationship permanently or forever bind us together.

I was, of course, hopeful for the latter, but I knew it was a false hope.

"You can handle knowing that, on the weeks I was actually fed, it was dog kibble tossed on the basement floor, most of it just out of reach from where I was chained to a water pipe? You can handle knowing that I went without a shower for years, and I was so covered in my own filth that the police officer who found me had to run upstairs so he didn't vomit in front of me? You can handle knowing that the only words I knew until I came here were four letter words I'd never repeat because those were the only words I ever heard? Rowen . . . you can't handle all of this. No one can."

She wiped at her eyes. Oh my god, she was being so damn strong, but I knew she was hurting. I could *feel* the pain sweeping through her. I wanted to wrap her up in my arms and comfort her until my words were erased from her mind. I wanted so much I could never have.

"Neil and Rose figured out a way to handle it. I can too."

"That's right. They did. And there isn't a day that goes by that I'm not overwhelmed with gratitude that those two walked into my life. But the difference is that they knew my background and what they were getting into before falling in love with me. You, though . . . you fell in love with me before you met my demons up close and personal."

"So did you," she snapped back. "You fell in love

with me before you knew what you were up against, and it didn't stop you. Don't act like I'm one of those people who will run at the first sign of a jaded past, Jesse."

"I know. But look at us now. You've moved on from your past, and I'm drowning in mine. And Rowen, mine's the kind that will take us both down if we let it."

"I'm stronger than you think I am." She crossed her arms and stepped toward me.

"And I'm weaker than you think I am." I stepped back. "All of this has proven that. Don't be blind to what's happening. Don't pretend like you can or even want to handle the shit I'm going through."

These words, more than any of the others, appeared to really piss her off. Her eyes narrowed. "I can't fix you. But I'll be here for you while you fix yourself. And I can handle it. I can handle *all* of it."

What more could I say so she got it? I was toxic. I would infect her if she didn't get out. "You can handle knowing that that woman was so convinced I was possessed by a demon that she used to beat me with a wooden cross until I passed out? You can handle knowing I used to pull three-inch slivers out of myself for days afterward? You can handle knowing that I had one special trinket I guarded so territorially that when one of them came within a few feet of it, I charged them, bit at them, behaved like a wild dog so I could keep my one special thing secret? You can handle knowing that I'd gone without food and water for so long, when I was rescued and taken to the hospital, the doctors could tell where and what ribs had been broken without having to take X-rays?"

Another tear slipped from her eyes. I wanted to stop so badly, but I had to keep going. It was the only way to get her to see me for who I was. "You can handle knowing that those people up and left one day, leaving me for dead, and the only reason I was saved was because someone walking by heard a loud sound and reported it? That sound was me, pounding my head against the water pipe, trying to kill myself. I was trying to kill myself at five years old, Rowen." My voice was getting louder, my own tears coming to the surface. "That is the man in front of you."

"Jesse—" she choked out.

"No." I shook my head vehemently. "No one should be expected to put up with a person with the kind of past I have. No one should *have* to." I knew what I had to say, but it didn't want to come out. I had to take a few breaths and remind myself of all the reasons I needed to say it. "You have to save yourself, Rowen. I'm past the point of saving now."

One month had changed everything, one month had upended my world. A year ago, I'd been a person who'd moved on from my horrendous past to claim a hopeful future. A year later, I was a person about to be swallowed up by my past with no foreseeable future. I'd been a fool to expect I could put it all behind me. I'd been an even bigger one to believe I had.

After another tear fell from her eyes, Rowen glared at me. "You know, I recognize a pushing away act from a hundred feet, Jesse. You should know that since you were the one who called me out on it." She marched toward me. She didn't stop until her chest bumped into mine. "Now it looks like I'm the one calling you out on the same thing. So I'll repeat your words back to you . . . Don't push me away, Jesse Walker. I'm not going anywhere."

A woman like her was every man's dream. A woman

who couldn't be shaken and would stand shoulder to shoulder in the face of a storm. I'd found that kind of woman and, beyond all belief, she loved me. And I had to let her go.

I had to let her go because I loved her.

That was what I reminded myself of when I cleared my face and met her eyes. "I'm not pushing you away, Rowen. I just want you to leave."

There was the turning point. There was her resolve crumbling in front of me. She was about to fall apart. I didn't think there was room for it, but I managed to hate myself a little bit more in that moment.

"You're just saying that. You're trying to hurt me and push me away because this is your twisted idea of protecting me." Taking a deep breath, she looked up at me and her hardened expression fell. "I'm not leaving you until you can look me in the eye and tell me you don't want me anymore."

It someone asked me if I'd rather have my fingernails ripped out or look Rowen in the eye and tell her that, I would have slapped both hands down on a table and said, "Do your worst" without a second's thought. I would rather relive a week of my childhood before the Walkers than have to do that. But I couldn't falter. I couldn't fail so close to the end. I couldn't drag her through whatever I was going through. I had to save Rowen since she obviously wasn't going to save herself. Locking my eyes with hers, I set my jaw and got after it. "I don't want you anymore, Rowen Sterling. But I do want you to leave."

Rowen breaking in front of me was exactly what I'd vowed to never let happen. Watching her break before walking away from me for the last time secured the number one spot as the most horrific sight I'd ever seen.

chapter TWENTY-TWO

Rowen

THOSE PEOPLE WHO claim it's better to have loved and lost than to have never loved at all? Yeah, they're full of shit.

The last few weeks, I'd felt like my heart was being sliced and diced every morning when I woke up and realized that Jesse was gone. There was nothing good left in the world. Life was more a chore than a celebration. The ache in my bones, the pit in my stomach, the memory of him that made me wish I didn't have a brain . . . all of it made me doubt the whole loved-lost debate.

Alex and Sid decided to force a night on the town on me, making me certain I'd rather have never loved than lost. Every chump who eyed me like I was a notch to be carved on his bedpost. Every loser who thought a *Hey* and a lame smile was the height of romance. Every man who looked at me like I was something he wanted reminded me of him. The good looks and the bad looks. All of them reminded me of Jesse in some way.

It wasn't just that night, though. Just about everything everyday found a way to remind me of Jesse. The one man who'd been brave enough to love me. The same one who'd looked me in the eye and said good-bye.

That night, the one I'd never forget a single word of, had ripped me to shreds. Not only because Jesse had broken us apart, but because of all he'd shared. I'd known he'd gone through hell before being adopted, but I never had it spelled out for me. Those things he shared with me had seemed unimaginable . . . unthinkable. How could the grinning, happy man I'd fallen in love with been exposed to those types of things and come out of it still able to smile, let alone love? He was a true testament to what the Walkers had done to help him, as well as what Jesse had done to help himself.

People who'd gone through those kinds of things didn't turn into Jesse Walkers. Statistically speaking, people who'd gone through what Jesse had generally went on to spread the same kind of horrors. Jails were over-populated with people like that. Mental institutions too. A small gravestone that was never visited, etched with the dates of someone who'd lived a short life, was another likely outcome for so many people who'd been abused.

So why had Jesse turned out so differently? Why had Jesse been the one to break free of his past? Or why *had* he?

Although I was nowhere as convinced as he was that he was doomed because his past had seeped into his present, the suddenness of it all was staggering. What had been the trigger for it? I didn't have a clue. I didn't need to have one. All I'd needed to do was help him through it. All I'd wanted to do was repay him the favor he'd paid me last summer. I wanted to pull the curtains back for him like he had for me so he could see the person he was in my eyes. Seeing the person I was in Jesse's eyes had done more healing than a lifetime's worth of therapy ever would have.

But that didn't matter anymore. It didn't matter how badly I wanted to walk alongside him in his battle, and it didn't matter how much I wanted to spend my life with him, scars and all. He was gone. He hadn't pushed me away. He hadn't shoved me either. He'd *forced* me away.

There was nothing I could do. He didn't want me. Even at his worst, his rock bottom, Jesse Walker didn't want me. That insecure, guarded girl I'd arrived at Willow Springs as was just begging to be released. I'd managed to keep the lid on her so far. I wasn't sure how much longer I'd be able to keep it up.

"So still no sign of Mar, right?" Alex asked, nudging me. The three of us were crammed into her El Camino, and even though I gave it a lot of crap for looking like it needed to go spend its golden years in a junkyard, it had gotten me to Willow Springs and back. After hanging up with Rose, I'd managed to stop Alex right as she was leaving for school. After I'd explained the situation, she let me take her car and she took my bike. Having good friends was a good thing.

"No sign, and that's okay because a part of me doesn't want to go to prison. It's not okay because I know landing a few punches on her would help with some of this crazy rage I have inside of me."

Sid, bless the dude, did the guy thing and gazed out the passenger window like he couldn't hear a word. I wasn't sure if Alex had told him what I'd told her, but I'd only given her the surface story. I'd told her that Mar was Jesse's birth mother, that she and his birth father had abused him, and that was why he had to be removed from their "care." She hadn't probed for details and that had been a relief because the details weren't mine to share. The details were enough to give a person nightmares for life, like they had me for the past few weeks.

"You realize she's probably sick. Really, really screwed up in the head. Right, Rowen? What she needs is a psych ward, not a smack down." Alex whipped the El Camino into the parking lot of the club they were forcing me to visit.

"No, Alex, she might need a psych ward, but she also needs a serious smack down. She deserves it." I glared out the window and tried not to picture her face. It didn't work. Every time I spoke or thought about her, my blood heated to boiling. The woman who'd done unspeakable things to Jesse had been sitting across a table from me sharing my food . . . and I hadn't known.

The universe had a perverse sense of humor.

"What about his birth dad? Whatever happened to him?"

"I don't know. Mar mentioned once that her 'good-for-nothing' husband had bailed on her and died of alcohol poisoning a few years later. I don't really know. And I don't really want to know either." Whatever had happened to Jesse's dad, I hoped it had been as horrific as the things they'd done to him. I hoped if he did die of alcohol poisoning, it had been an excruciating, prolonged death.

I knew having so much bitterness inside of me was poison. The revenge and rage swelling in my stomach was just as toxic. But there were only two ways to deal with it. One: to forgive, try to forget, and let love and light lead the way. In other words, bullshit. An entire galaxy of love and light wasn't up to the task of taking on what had been done to that young boy. An entire fucking galaxy.

And two: to let the unsavory emotions take over. Obviously, that was my choice.

There wasn't a third. There wasn't a way to move on and play ignorant. Some things I could do that with, but that wasn't one of them. A person who could move on and play the ignorant card on that kind of abuse didn't have a conscience. Or a soul.

Alex found a parking spot at the back of the parking lot and threw open her door. "I can't believe that Jesse came from an abusive situation. He's just so damn . . . happy-go-lucky all of the time. I never in a million years would have guessed it."

"I know." I slid out her side while Sid got out the passenger side. I glared at the club. I wasn't in a club mood. I wasn't in any kind of mood that could put up with loud music, strong alcohol, and dry-hump-dancing.

"He's pretty much got to be the strongest person ever."

I answered with a nod.

"Not to mention he's good looking in a holy-shit-are-you-real kind of way, takes the best care of his girl, has *the* best smile I've ever seen, and has a strength of character that's unparalleled." Alex draped her arm over my shoulders. From the suffocatingly-tight vinyl top she had on, the motion made a strange sound. "You're letting him get away because . . .?"

Jesse was a hard topic for me those days. Like it was hard to talk about a person I'd loved right after burying them. That was the same kind of feeling I had when it came to Jesse. Essentially, I had lost him. He wasn't six feet under, but the five hundred miles of separation felt just as bad.

"I'm not letting him get away, Alex. He broke up with me." I don't know how many times I had to tell her that, but that was the last time. I couldn't say those words again.

"Please. That boy adored you, Rowen. That boy would walk through a fire for you and, when he looked at you, I swore I finally understood what that whole unconditional love thing was all about." Thanks to Alex's six-inch spike heels on her red boots, our journey to the club entrance was slow going. Even though I didn't feel like clubbing, I felt less like talking about Jesse. "And with all of that, you expect me to believe that he had a few bad days and decided to call it off with you? You expect me to believe that right now, that boy, wherever he is, isn't feeling like a damn knife's sticking out of his chest?"

"I don't know. Jesse and I haven't exactly talked in a while, so I don't know what he's up to or how he's feeling. I can give you his number, and you can find out if you're so interested." Cue the bitterness making its way into my voice.

"You really haven't tried calling him? Not even when you wake up in the middle of the night and your finger happens to accidentally bump his number?"

"No, I really haven't. And you know what? He hasn't tried calling me either." I didn't care that she had on stilts; I booked it toward the entrance. All the talk of Jesse made me need a drink. Even though I had a fake I.D., I didn't drink every time I went out. Given my excessive history with alcohol, I figured that was a good policy. But that night, I needed a drink. Actually, I wanted to get rip-roaring drunk because at least then I wouldn't be able to think about Jesse anymore.

Alex wanted to say something else. I could tell from the look she gave me, but that was when Sid suddenly decided to join in on the conversation.

"How's the decision coming along with the internship? You know, if you choose not to take it and stay at Mojo over the summer, I'll give you another raise," he said.

I exhaled. That was a topic I could talk about with relative ease. "I still haven't decided. They said they'd give me another week to make up my mind before offering it to the student behind me. And thanks for the raise offer. I'll make sure to take it into consideration." I shot Sid a little smile. He was a pretty good guy, and I could always use one of those in my corner. There were too few of them out there as it was.

Someone else I'd had little to no contact with over the past few weeks? Jax Jones. First, the little weasel pulled that stunt in my apartment, then later told me it was an honest mistake. Then after finding out through the grapevine about Jesse's and my split, he'd called me, not even a week later, to ask me on a date. After the earful I gave him, he hadn't so much as looked my way when we passed in the hallway. As much as I wanted to give people the benefit of the doubt, some people had reputations for a reason. Apparently Jax was one of those people.

Alex gave me a quick squeeze before we wove through the club's entrance. "Let's have a good time tonight, okay? You deserve one."

I nodded. Not because I thought I was actually capable of having a good night so soon after the break up to end all break ups, but because Alex had gone out of her way to try to cheer me up. I could pretend it was helping as a way to show my gratitude.

The club was very Seattle cool. During spring break my senior year of school, I'd gone to a nightclub in L.A. with my boyfriend of the month. It's a long story . . . Anyways, that club, the L.A. glamour scene, was the polar opposite to a Seattle club. Seattle was full of rich tech nerds who still lived with their moms, gray-suited business women who'd forgotten how to smile, and young hipsters who thought world peace was a possibility. There wasn't a market for glam up there.

The club was understated, the music wasn't too loud, the majority of people had some locally made craft beer clutched in their fist, and there wasn't a single sequin to be found. As clubs went, it was a solid spot to get together and pass the night away with friends. There were worse places I could have been.

There were also better places, much better places, but I tried not to think about that anymore. I could have called any of the Walkers, Garth, or Josie to talk. I knew none of them would hang up on me. They were the closest thing to family I had. But they'd been Jesse's family first. They were his before they were mine, and I didn't want to put them in the awkward position of choosing sides. I would never force them to make that choice, but it was human nature to pick sides. It was hard to be neutral. So I hadn't talked to anyone at Willow Springs in weeks. It wasn't a tenth as painful as not talking to Jesse, but it hurt like hell just the same.

I followed Alex and Sid through the crowd as they made their way to a free table in the back.

"What do you ladies want? I'll go start a tab." Sid pulled out a chair for Alex and one for me.

"Surprise me," Alex answered, tugging on one of Sid's dreads.

"Rowen?"

I wanted a shot. Actually, I wanted a line of them. Hold that . . . How about just bring me a bottle? That's what I wanted. It's not what I needed, though. I plopped into my chair and sighed. "I'll have an amber."

Sid waved his acknowledgment, then disappeared into the crowd.

"So I know this probably isn't a great time to bring this up"—Alex scooted closer to me—"but have you decided what you're going to do when I move out? Are you going to find another roommate or move into something smaller?"

I groaned. Alex had told me a while back that she'd be moving out at the end of the school year. Sid had asked her to move in, and she'd agreed. When I'd told Jesse over spring break that I was pretty sure Alex was making one giant mistake, he'd laughed and said sometimes what we think are the giant mistakes in life turn out to be the best decisions. As usual, thoughts of Jesse delivered a sharp pain to my chest. I tried to bury those thoughts. At least temporarily. They never stayed permanently buried.

"Do you really have to move out? I mean, do you really think Sid's going to be a better roommate than me? I bet he walks around naked and drinks milk out of the jug."

Alex smiled wickedly. "A girl can dream."

"What happens if you move in together and then break up a week later? Talk about hostile living conditions. You really should just stay with me and save yourself the worry." I knew it was a futile argument, but I still had to make it.

Then Alex flashed her hand in front of my face. Her left hand. "If that man calls it off, he is not getting this back."

An engagement ring. A sparkly, emerald cut engagement ring. I felt two things at that moment: excitement for my friend and sadness for myself. I shoved the second emotion aside; that moment wasn't about me. It was about Alex, a girl I'd been certain would never let an engagement ring come within arm's length of her left hand.

But then she found her soul mate and that all changed. I'd found mine, too. And I'd lost him.

I had to force a smile, but I didn't have to force the genuine happiness I felt for her. "Holy crap, Alex. Congratulations." I gave her a big hug before taking a closer look at her ring. Truly, it was lovely. Sid had to have sold a lot of doughnuts to pay for that baby. "Let me guess. The wedding dress is going to be black?"

Alex feigned a look of insult. "With a few splashes of scarlet thrown in."

"I'm so happy for you. My little girl's growing up so fast." I gave her cheeks a pinch before she slapped my hand away.

"We're pretty damn excited about it, too. Sid and I are kind of one giant mess on our own, but when we're together . . . Well, it's a beautiful thing. We're functionally dysfunctional, but somehow, it works, Rowen. It *works*." Alex was staring off into nothing and smiling. She was so happy. I'd give anything to feel that way again. Any. Thing.

I glanced toward the bar, hoping Sid was on his way back because I really needed a good chug of that beer. Then I saw another familiar face coming our way.

"Shit. That *is* Rowen Sterling. And now I can die a happy man because I got to see the face of the girl who rocked my fucking world one more time."

I had to do a double take, but the giant panther tattoo running down his arm confirmed it. "Cillian? Cillian Sullivan? And now I can die a happy woman because I got to do this one more time to your face." I lifted my middle finger at him.

He laughed first, but mine followed shortly after.

"Hey, girl. How's it going?" Cillian gave me a hug, which took me by surprise. Back when we'd "dated" in high school, he hadn't been one for showing physical affection. Or at least, not the fully clothed kind.

"I'm doing okay. How about you?" I asked after he settled into the fourth chair at the table.

"Can't complain. I'm in town because my band's playing a few opening gigs, then it's another town, and another one after that." From what I'd known of Cillian, that meant fresh cities of women who couldn't have heard about the love 'em and leave 'em guy Cillian was.

"Living the dream, eh?"

He nodded, shooting me a wink.

"This is my friend and soon-to-be traitor roommate." I smiled over at Alex, who looked like she wanted to flip me off. "This is Cillian. We went to school together and were . . . *friends*." I'd told Alex enough about my past for her to know exactly what kind of friend Cillian had been.

Cillian tilted his chin at me as if to say, *our secret's safe with me.* "I was the foreign exchange student with an Irish accent who drove the prim and proper American prep school girls wild. Plus, I had a lot of tattoos and smoked."

"Hold up." Alex held out her hands. "You play in a

band, you have tattoos, *and* you smoke? That's, like, a combination I've never heard of. You are a rare find, my exchange student bad-boy *friend*."

Cillian nudged me. "I like this girl. She reminds me a bit of you when we first met."

"What bit?"

Cillian's dark eyes glimmered. "The crazy bit."

"It takes one to know one." I kind of wanted to wipe the smile off of his face, but it was a nice smile. I hadn't appreciated it back in high school. What had turned me on then was a cigarette dangling from his lips, or that unimpressed expression he'd meticulously perfected. A smile meant a lot more to me now than it once had.

"I'd cheers to that if I had a drink."

"Looks like I'm one short, brother." Sid came up behind Cillian balancing three pints of beer.

"No worries. I couldn't drink one even if you'd brought an extra."

"Why not? Did you wear your liver out already?" I asked him. Cillian and I had singlehandedly consumed so many bottles of alcohol that we'd probably kept a tequila factory in production during our high school years. We got drunk together, then had sex in our drunken stupor, then got even more drunk so we'd forget about having sex. Which we'd have again when we'd gotten shit-faced yet again. It had been a vicious cycle, and one part of me always assumed our fast lives would lead to early graves.

But there we were, a couple years later, both alive and sober.

"I kind of had to go through a court-ordered twelve-step program," he answered, shifting in his seat. "If for any reason a cop were to test me and I had even a trace of alcohol in my system, I'd be spending a few nights in a cell."

"That's extreme. What extreme thing did you do to deserve that?" I asked.

"I wrapped a car around a pole because I was drunk."

"Yikes," I muttered.

"Dumbass." Alex's reply wasn't a mutter.

I smiled. "So that earned you court-ordered sobriety?"

Cillian shrugged. "Since it was my second time doing it, yeah."

Sid's face ironed out in surprise.

"And it was a stolen car. Not intentionally stolen," Cillian added, lifting his hands. "I was just so rip-roaring drunk I couldn't tell the difference." Alex shook her head and grumbled another *Dumbass*. "And the pole happened to be a streetlight in front of the police commissioner's house. Whose grandkids play in his front yard a lot. In fact, I think they might have been there that morning." Cillian looked up, thinking.

"That morning? Shit, Cillian, what were you doing drunk driving in the morning?"

"I was still drunk from the night before." I did my best to give him a parental look of disapproval. All he did was laugh. "No one was hurt, Rowen. Insurance fixed the car, the city fixed the streetlight, and the court fixed me by not letting me drink."

"And how's sobriety going for you?" From the looks of it, he'd had a few. Maybe I was wrong, but I knew that lazy smile of his and the way he liked to lean in real close when he was talking to someone.

Opening the flap of his jacket, he reached into one of the inside pockets and pulled out a tiny glass bottle.

"Fucking fantastically." He twisted off the top, lifted it ceremoniously, and downed the whole bottle in one gulp.

"You haven't changed a bit," I said, shaking my head.

"One of us had to. And it obviously wasn't you." Cillian eyed my full beer before reaching in for another bottle.

Through the rest of the night, I surprised myself by actually having a decent time. I was out with one old and a couple new friends, laughing, dancing, and trying to pretend my life was as great as it had been the past year.

Cillian downed a couple more bottles, but really, from what I knew of his tolerance, a handful of tiny glass bottles was like anyone else having a sip of beer. After chatting and bantering, I realized that high school wouldn't have blown so badly if Cillian and I could have been real friends. The kind that didn't only use friendship to cover up getting wasted and laid. Oh, well. There was no going back and, even if there was a way, I'd rather die—not an exaggeration—than relive my high school years of hell.

Sid came back from the dance floor, so sweaty his shirt was drenched, and grabbed Alex's hand. "Come on, woman. I'm ten years older than you, and I've got twice the energy. We're going to need to work on that."

"Yeah, but I've got double the flexibility and three times the stamina so I win." Alex shot me a wink as she let Sid pull her out of her seat.

"Now that right there is an argument I am happy to let you win."

"Finally." Alex elbowed him and waved at Cillian and me. "You kids be good now, you hear."

Cillian lifted his arms. "No promises. Good isn't really my thing."

I chuckled, taking the final sip of my beer. I'd been good and milked the one pint all night long. "No, good really isn't your thing. Not even close."

"From what I recall—some of my best memories actually"—Cillian smiled widely—"good wasn't exactly your thing either."

"It wasn't," I answered matter-of-factly.

"And it is now?"

I shrugged. "I'm not really sure." That was the honest answer. I wasn't sure about much in my life, least of all if good was or wasn't "my thing."

Cillian draped his arm over the back of my chair and leaned in. The look in his eyes was a familiar one. "Why don't you let me help you figure it out? You know, for old time's sake?" Wetting his lips, he studied my mouth, then moved lower. "I've got the old Chevelle out back. You remember? And let me assure you that the back seat is just as comfortable as it was before."

My stomach turned. Once. Then twice. It was a good thing I hadn't had more to drink. I shoved his chest. "And let me assure you that I'm just as confident now as I was then that your dick wouldn't know how to pleasure a woman if its erection depended on it."

Cillian's brows came together. "Someone's turned into quite the downer. You used to be more fun."

"And you used to have more hair." I waved at his hairline, which was still full. That was just the first thing to come out of my mouth. "Why don't you go have a little fun with yourself in the backseat of your Chevelle? Because I'd have more fun getting an enema than joining you."

"You know, they say the longer a woman goes

without orgasming, the moodier she gets. From your moody level, I'd guess the last guy that was between your legs was me."

I resisted the urge to push him off of his chair. Cillian was harmless, unless his ego of mass destruction was considered dangerous. "You did mention a woman orgasming going hand in hand with her mood, right? Because you between my legs and me orgasming are not synonymous."

"Look at you. All smart and shit. When did that happen?"

"When I stopped hanging around the likes of you," I said with an overdone smile.

"Come on, Rowen. We always had a good time, right? I always took care of you? Come on, just one last ride"—he looked devilishly amused with himself—"in the Chevelle, and I promise I will hook you up. I'll make you feel so good you're going to want me calling you up every time I'm back in town."

It was nauseating how highly he thought of himself. It was that much worse because I knew from personal experience what a let-down he was when it came to being intimate. I was considering dumping the melting ice from Alex's empty mojito onto his crouch when something else popped to mind. Something that was eight thousand times better payback. The club we were in might have been one of those easy-going, chill Seattle kind of places, but right next door was a fun and outrageous gay club known for its weekend performances put on by drag queens.

I smiled. My plan hatched. "You know, you're right. I could use a night of total and reckless abandon, and who better to share that with than you?" Cillian licked his lips and leaned closer until it looked like he was about to fall off his chair. "Why don't you head out there now, wait for me in the backseat, and I'll meet you in just a few minutes," I said, getting up.

"Why don't you just come with me now? No sense in putting off a good thing." Cillian's hand dropped to my waist, his fingers skimming the material of my dress. My skin crawled.

"Because," I answered, lifting a brow, "I want to go to the restroom and take my panties off so we don't have to waste any time."

Cillian smiled went higher on one side. "Solid plan. I'll see you in a few."

"See you in a few," I said sweetly. As he turned and rushed into the crowd, I called after him. "Cillian? I hope you don't mind me being on top tonight."

His eyes widened. "Nope. I definitely do not mind."

Good thing because I was definitely coming out on top.

I waited a few more seconds until I was sure he had a good head start before following him. The front doors were as far as I followed him, though, because the parking lot was to the left and the Man's Lady Club was to the right.

On any given night, there were two different types of drag queens around the Man's Lady Club: the ones who performed on stage, and the ones "for hire" who saved their performances for backseats or cheap hotel rooms. Thank my lucky stars there were at least a dozen of the kind I was looking for, dotting the parking lot. I jogged up to the tallest, widest one. Her biceps were as thick as my abdomen. Perfect.

"Hey, sugar," she said, giving me a wide smile. "You lost or something?"

"Nope, not lost at all. I'm exactly where I need to be."

"Oh, well, in that case . . ." She looked me over, the skin between her drawn-on eyebrows creasing. "Female equipment?" Then it was my turn for the skin between my much-needed-to-be-plucked brows to come together. "My rate is double if you've got lady parts because it takes twice as long to get off."

For maybe the dozenth time in my life, I blushed. It didn't last long. "Actually, this isn't about me . . . but thank you . . . This is for a friend."

"Male or female equipment?" she asked, straightening her platinum wig.

"Male. *All* male," I said, winking.

She clapped her hands and smacked her lips. "Point me in the right direction."

"He's in the back of the old Chevelle in the parking lot over there." I motioned in the general area. "Oh, and he's kind of shy, so don't be afraid to take the ropes and show him the way. If you know what I mean."

"Sweetie, if I didn't know what you meant, I wouldn't be driving my fine ass around in a brand new Benz."

"Point taken."

"What does he like?" she asked, already clacking toward the parking lot.

"Why don't you just start by giving him a full kiss on the lips and see where it goes from there?" I wanted to pay Cillian back, not scar him for life.

"Here's my card. You have any more 'friends' who might appreciate me and my line of work, you give me a ring, you hear, sweetie?" She held out the card for me, and I jogged to get it.

"I will keep you on speed dial," I said, glancing at the card. "Lotta . . . Sugar. Sweet name."

"Sweet name for a sweet ass, Sweetie." She shot me a wink then continued on her way.

"Oh, wait!" I called after her, pulling a bill out of my purse. "Here, I'm paying. It's my gift to him."

"You're a good friend." She took the bill and shoved it down her Marilyn Monroe-style dress.

"He's about to find out just how good of one I am, too."

Lotta Sugar patted my cheek then continued on her fierce, Chevelle-finding way.

A few minutes later, I caught sight of Cillian streaking half-naked across the parking lot, screaming his bloody lungs out.

That was the best money I'd ever spent.

chapter **TWENTY-THREE**

Jesse

KNOW WHAT'S WORSE than being at a low point? Having to deal with the aftermath.

The aftermath of wondering if I'd ever get back to being the person I'd once been. The aftermath of having my friends and family throw concerned glances my way when they thought I wasn't looking. The aftermath of looking at all of the pieces at my feet and wondering if I had the strength and desire to build them all back into place. The aftermath and utter devastation of waking up each morning and remembering that I'd pushed away the person I'd wanted to spend my life with in order to protect her from my nuclear fallout.

Three weeks later, and the pieces were coming back together. Slowly, one by one, I was rebuilding myself. I wouldn't have cared if it took a month or a year if I knew Rowen was waiting for me on the other side. But she wasn't. Not after the things I'd done and the words I'd said. Even if she'd found some miraculous way to forgive me, I couldn't let her wait for me.

I couldn't because I might have been climbing my way back up from the fall, but how long would it be until I fell again? It had been over a decade since the last one, but even if I knew it would be double that before the next one hit, I didn't want her around to witness that again. I didn't want that kind of a life for her.

I wanted her to have a stable, loving, and predictable environment. She needed that after the years of chaos she'd lived. One of those three I could give her in unlimited supply, but I could no longer guarantee the other two. I couldn't guarantee a stable and predictable environment if I was a part of her life.

So as the days turned into weeks, I focused on my routine. I kept my head down and worked until my hands were calloused and my muscles were exhausted. I worked twice as hard as every other hand out there so that when I went to bed, I could fall asleep the moment my head hit the pillow. Some nights that worked. Some nights it didn't.

But I kept at it because I didn't want time to think. I didn't want a handful of minutes to unwind. I wanted to be busy or asleep. That was the only way to keep distracted from losing Rowen. It was the only way to keep myself from losing *myself*.

It had been a long month, so when Garth asked if I wanted to come over to his place after dinner and "shoot the shit," I'd agreed. I'd been spending my fair share of time with Garth lately, but he was one of the only people who knew better than to mention Rowen. Everyone else— Mom, Dad, my sisters, Josie—they all brought her up at every turn, wanting to know if I'd talked to her, or if she'd tried calling me, or why I hadn't called her, or why she hadn't called me.

It was enough to drive a man insane. Or drive a man insan*er*.

I got it, we all loved her, but they didn't understand

where I was coming from and I didn't know how to help them understand. I had to stay away *because* of my love for her.

I pulled up to Garth's trailer slowly, stopping a good hundred yards out. I'd killed the lights a hundred yards earlier. I knew from plenty of experience that I did not want to wake Garth's dad, Clay, if he was already passed out from his nightly drinking binge. That was like waking a sleeping bear who could lift a shotgun and make a decent aim.

I stepped out of the truck and shut the door. It closed silently. No squeaks or groans. I'd been driving Dad's truck. Mine hadn't only died on me; it had mysteriously disappeared off the side of that North Idaho highway. When we'd gone back to get it a few days later, it was gone. Highway patrol had no record of it being towed away and none of the impound shops or tow companies had any record of picking up Old Bessie. She was just . . . gone.

Like so much else in my life.

Great. My thoughts were gloomy and, from the feel of it, about to get gloomier. Garth was going to be thrilled he'd invited me over. Speaking of Garth . . . The man in black looked especially pissed off. As I got closer and saw the shattered beer bottles dotted around where he sat in his lawn chair, I understood why.

"Clay asleep?"

Garth glanced back at the dark trailer. "Either that or he's dead. My hope's for the latter."

I stood in front of Garth, checking out the trailer. It had been a long time since I'd been there. Actually, the last time had been . . .

"Shit, Walker. Would you take a seat and chill? You're freaking me out standing there looking all deep in thought." Garth waved to a lounge chair beside him, and my throat ran dry.

That had been the last time I'd been there. When Rowen had been curled up in that chair. I could see her in front of me, her lips parted, her face wrinkled even in sleep, her hand curled around the arm of the chair like it was grounding her.

"Chair." Garth waved at it. "Ass." He lifted his just enough to smack it. "Beer." He pulled one free from the six pack beside him. "Sit."

"Repeat?"

Garth's eyes rolled as he tossed me the beer.

"Well, thanks for having me over for a . . . a . . . boys' night?"

Yeah, that term didn't sit well with Garth. I could tell that from the way his face screwed up. Hell, when I thought about it, the term didn't sit well with me either.

"No, this is not a boys' night. Are you kidding me right now? Did you really just go and call two men in a couple of white-trash chairs, in front a white-trash trailer, drinking white-trash beer . . ." Garth's eyebrows came together as he lifted his bottle in front of his face. "Yep, that's the cheap stuff. This, my friend, is not a boys' night. This isn't a polo shirt-wearing get-together at some club where guys think it's okay to down drinks that are more fruit than they are alcohol."

I raised my hands. "Sorry. Thanks for clarifying."

"Come on, Walker. I mean, shit. Boys' night? Really? *Really*?"

Another reason I enjoyed hanging out with Garth? I

was so busy either trying to or avoiding insulting him that a couple of hours could fly by. "Then what do you call this?" I circled my beer around before twisting it open.

"This is motherfuckin' cowboy game plan time."

"Game plan? Don't we have to be coming up with one in order for it to be a game plan?" I took a sip of the beer and put it down. It was bad.

"That's right," Garth answered as I sank into the lounger.

I leaned back and tried to relax, but it was hard to do when I could have sworn the chair even smelled like Rowen. "And what game plan are we coming up with tonight, Black? The one that addresses and puts together an action plan on how to fix your screw ups?" I smiled and shoved his arm hard enough that he teetered in his chair.

"Not quite. We're going to address and put together an action plan to fix *yours*."

I chuckled. "Yeah, that's funny, Garth. Good one."

"Do I look like I just made a funny?"

Looking at Garth stopped me mid-laugh. He was as serious as Garth Black could get. "What? And you, the guy who wrote the book on how to make a better screw up of your life, is going to give me advice on how to fix mine? Talk about painting the kettle black."

"I don't know about no fucking kettle, but I am kind of partial to black."

I wasn't sure at first, but with every passing second, I realized just how serious he was. "Let me save you the time and effort because nothing you could say could make me feel any worse about my screw ups."

"Rowen."

I winced. "Shit. Okay, you just made me a liar. What

else have you got?"

"You still love her."

My eyes closed as my wince went deeper.

"And she still loves you."

My hands curled around the arms of the chair, bracing myself against the pain coursing through my body. "Uncle. I cried uncle. I've had enough."

"You're living in fairy land if you think I'm letting you off that easy, Walker."

Great. Garth Black had joined the army of people bringing Rowen up at every opportunity. I moved to get up, but Garth moved faster. He shoved me back down and towered over me.

"You're going to listen to what I have to say whether you like it or not, Jess. That's not negotiable. And if you want to kick the shit out of me and run over me with your daddy's truck right after, then bring it on . . . but you're going to hear me out first." Garth lowered his face right in front of mine. "Understood?"

"If I agree, will you get your ugly mug out of my face?"

"Yes, but only if you take back the ugly part." Garth butted his nose into mine.

"Fine. Get your dastardly mug out of my face."

Garth shook his head and moved away. "You should have been a doctor or something as smart as you are. What the hell are you doing working a ranch when you've got words like 'dastardly' in your vocabulary?"

"I like it," I replied, thankful Garth had stopped hovering over me with his beer breath.

"But do you love it?"

I thought about that for a while. Ranching was what I

knew. It was in my veins. I liked it, for sure, but it was tough to say if I'd classify it into the love category. "I don't know. I can't say I *love* it, but it's what I know. It's what I'm good at."

"And what can you say you do love?" Garth asked, shifting in his seat. Probably because he'd said the L word. He wasn't big on mentioning that one.

"I think you know since her name just popped out of your mouth a minute ago."

"So what are you doing here, doing something you like, might sorta love, when something you *know* you love is a few states away?"

I reached for the bad beer. Given where our conversation was going, I'd need a beer, and bad beer was better than no beer. "You know why. I messed up, Garth."

"So you messed up." I lifted both eyebrows. Garth rolled his eyes. "Big time. So you messed up big time. We all do. It's time you start practicing what you preach and forgive yourself. If any guy deserves a second chance, it's you, Jess."

"Practice what I preach? What the hell preaching have I done that you've ever paid attention to?" I wanted to buy what Garth was saying, but messing up big time and what had happened to me the past couple months were two totally different things. I hadn't just messed up big time. I'd taken a vacation in the darkest side of humanity and lived to tell the tale.

I'd lived to tell it, but I'd lost so much.

"You're always talking about taking what you want from life. Having the chance to make a different life for yourself each day. Not letting your past define you. Not pushing people away in an attempt to protect yourself. All that shit you tell everyone else but are obviously too chicken shit to tell yourself."

I was gripping the arms of the lounger again. "First of all, Black, what I'm doing, what I've chosen to do by letting Rowen get on with her life without me, is not the chicken shit thing to do. It's exactly the opposite. If I was a chicken shit, I'd do the selfish thing and beg her back into my life again. A chicken shit wouldn't wake up every morning wanting to send his fist through the mirror so he wouldn't have to look at himself and remember what he'd done. A chicken shit wouldn't let the girl he loved go knowing another man will soon fill his spot. A chicken shit wouldn't take the hard path when there's an easy one. So don't talk to me about being a chicken shit." I was practically trembling from the anger bubbling inside of me.

"Are you done yet?" Garth asked, looking completely unfazed.

"I'm just getting warmed up."

"That was a rhetorical question. I don't really care if you're done yet or not because I've got a hell of a lot more to say before you have the floor."

"A rhetorical question?" I said, taking another drink of beer. It actually made me pucker with each sip; that's how bad it was.

"Yeah, you know, a question that doesn't require an answer."

I threw my head back against the chair. "Dear god, Black, yes, I know what a rhetorical question is."

"Good for you. Now why don't you get up out of that chair, head to Seattle, and tell Rowen what an idiot you've been and how you'll spend the rest of your life making it up to her?"

"I can't."

"Why the hell not?"

"I just can't."

"Jesus, Jess. Man up, grow a pair, and give me a straight answer."

I worked my jaw, fighting to get out the answer. "I have to protect her."

"Protect her? Protect her from what?'

"From myself."

Garth shook his head. "You're staying away from her because you're trying to protect Rowen Sterling from Jesse Walker? Do I have that right?"

"You've got that right."

Garth snorted. "Well, either that's the biggest line of bullshit I've ever heard, or you need to explain yourself a little better."

I could have gotten up and left. I would have if I didn't know that Garth wouldn't let me go without a fight. I'd been in my fair share of fights with Garth Black, and while the scales were pretty level, it was something I tried to avoid. "Sometimes the only way we can protect the ones we love is to protect them from ourselves."

"Yeah, but most of the time doing that just makes both of you want to put a bullet to your head."

I scowled into the dark night. "I'm not kidding, Garth."

"Neither am I."

"Fine, let's say for the sake of argument that I am able to get past my hang up of trying to protect Rowen and I do call her up and apologize and tell her I'll spend the rest of my life making it up to her. You think she's just going to forgive, forget, and get back to loving me right where she left off?" Saying it out loud was more painful than a silent stream of thoughts flowing through my head. More definite or something.

"What I know of Rowen, yeah, she would figure out a way to move on from it all. She figured out a way to do it with her life, right? Seems like she could figure out a way to do it with yours too." Garth took the last swig of his beer and slid the empty bottle back into the case.

"Garth, I'm starting to believe you don't have the full picture of what happened. Did you even hear the rumors? Because, for once, they're not an exaggeration. Hell, you were the one who had to pack me home on your horse after I lost it. I messed up. I lost it. I fucked up." That conversation was heading south fast, but I couldn't take another sip of that beer. It was only making a bad situation worse.

"I don't know much about these kinds of things," Garth started, his voice a few notes quieter. "But it seems like you don't fall out of love with someone because of their fuck ups. It seems like if you really love someone, you love them in spite of their fuck ups."

Those words hit me like a punch to the stomach. Actually, they hit me like each word was a punch to the stomach, every one hitting me that much harder. What Garth said hit me not because I'd never heard it before, but because I'd believed exactly that. To know if I really loved someone, the test was not in loving them during the good times, but during the bad times.

That was the way I loved Rowen, and that was the way I knew she'd at one time loved me.

"You think I've still got a chance?" It was a fool's hope, but I didn't mind being a fool if that's what it took to get a little hope back in my life.

Garth leaned toward me, a twisted smile moving into place. "There's only one way to find out."

chapter TWENTY-FOUR

Rowen

I FOUND THE strangest thing when I was cleaning out my bedroom. Actually, it had been buried in the back of my closet, inside one of the steel-toed boots I used to wear every day. I had the day off last Saturday, and that meant a mine field of thinking about Jesse all day. So I'd decided to clean my room, top to bottom.

After throwing all of my shoes out of the closet, I'd noticed something bounce out of my boot. I had to crawl over to see what it was because it was so small. It was a button, a small round white one with three holes. Nothing fancy or elaborate. It could have been from a man's or a woman's garment. Even though I tossed it into the garbage at first, I went and dug it out right after. As if that wasn't mental enough, I actually slid it inside my pillow case.

I had been sleeping on it for the past week. It was a button. A two-cent, non-descript button . . . and I felt some kind of a connection with it. If that wasn't an indicator of how much I missed Jesse and how our break up had affected me in the cranial region, I didn't know what was.

After working the night shift at Mojo, I was biking my way back to the apartment, feeling like I was going to pass out from exhaustion. I'd hardly been able to sleep for a month straight. Every time I lay down, my mind began racing and I couldn't fall asleep. It was a vicious cycle.

Once I'd made it home and alive in one piece, I locked up my bike, unlocked my apartment door, and stumbled inside. Alex had the night off, and that usually meant she was out living it up somewhere in the city, so I didn't expect to find the lights on and two people sitting at our dining table.

"Man, Rowen." Alex stood and shot me a wink. "How many hot cowboys do you know?"

"One," I answered instantly.

"Aw. I missed you too, sweetheart."

If I hadn't felt so deprived of all things Willow Springs, I probably would have rolled my eyes and tossed another insult his way, but instead I crossed the room, kneeled, and wrapped my arms around Garth. He felt solid; he felt like *home*.

"Um, yeah . . . Are you okay?" Garth patted my back stiffly and cleared his throat.

"Just keep your mouth closed, let me hug you for a little longer, and then I'll be temporarily okay," I replied, inhaling the scent of his dark shirt. It smelled like the laundry soap I'd used countless times in the laundry room at Willow Springs. Garth continued to pat me awkwardly, but he managed to stay quiet as I soaked in a few more moments of Willow Springs. I rubbed my arm over my eyes before pulling away. "How long have you been here?"

"A couple of hours or so."

I settled into the chair Alex had just been sitting in. The shock of seeing him was over, and the questions started. "What are you doing here?"

"I came to check out your apartment. Check out the city. See if it's a place I could live." Garth's eyes flicked around the apartment.

"Garth Black, you'd be more comfortable living on Venus than in Seattle."

His smile stretched wide. "Yes, I think I would."

I waited, but after a few seconds, I couldn't wait anymore. Patience wasn't a strong point of mine. "Are you going to tell me the real reason you're here, or am I to assume you've been kicked off of Willow Springs and need a place to crash?"

"I just might after this . . ."

"After *what*?" The man was infuriating.

"I'll let you two talk. I'll head over to Sid's for the night." Alex grabbed her purse, waved, and took one last longing look at Garth.

"Nice meeting you, Alex."

"Nice meeting *you*, Garth."

"Thanks for your help. And the coffee." Garth lifted his cup.

Alex stopped in the doorway. "You know where to find me if you need any more coffee. Or help."

"Alex," I snapped. "Left hand. Ring finger. Sid. Bye-bye."

She blew me a kiss before closing the door behind her.

Alone together, the air became very thick. Garth and I couldn't seem to figure out what to say next.

"Are you hungry?" I asked.

"I'm all right."

"When was the last time you ate? Dinner? That was over eight hours ago, and I know from experience you guys are ready to devour a refrigerator if you don't get fed every six hours."

"Actually, the last time I ate was lunch. I left Willow Springs an hour or so before dinner."

"Lunch?! Okay, you really need to eat." I headed for the fridge and moved things around to see what we had.

"Don't bother, Rowen. Really. I'm good."

"But you are not a good liar because I can hear your stomach grumbling from here." I lifted an eyebrow and waited for him. His expression and body language looked more uncomfortable than when I'd hugged him.

"Garth. It's a meal and, judging from the contents of our fridge, not a very fancy one. It's not a favor, a bribe, a handout, or something you'll have to repay one day." Grabbing hold of the cheese and butter, I lifted them. "It's a toasted cheese sandwich."

Garth shifted in the chair. "It's never just a toasted cheese sandwich."

I slammed the fridge closed and grabbed the bread. "You're right. It's a toasted cheese sandwich and a little human decency."

"Decency? *Human* decency? That's an oxymoron, right?"

I groaned. "Fine. How about this? I'm going to make two sandwiches. One for myself and one for whoever else in the room might want to have one." If there was one thing about Willow Springs I hadn't missed, it was Garth driving me nuts. "Now that food is out of the way, why are you here, Garth?"

"The question isn't why *I'm* here, the question is why *you* are."

I stopped slicing the cheese. "I live here?" I knew he

was getting at something else.

"I thought you were in college over here. Isn't that supposed to help make you smarter?"

"Black," I warned through my teeth as I turned on the burner. "I know what you're getting at, and that's not something I'm going to talk with you about."

"Yeah, Jesse didn't want to either, but I didn't give a shit then and I don't give a shit now. Because he's in misery and you're in misery and you're making everyone around you miserable."

I slammed the fry pan onto the burner about five times harder than necessary. "I'm not making anyone else miserable."

Garth huffed. "I just sat here talking with your room-mate for over an hour. Believe me, you're making her miserable."

"Fine. Yes, I'm miserable. I'm not trying to make people around me the same, but I suppose it's possible it's been spilling over lately."

"It's definitely been spilling over," Garth added.

"What do you expect? You know about all of the shit I heaped on Jesse. I'm guessing if you talked with him, you know he basically told me to leave and never come back. What else, besides misery, would you like me to feel?" I focused on buttering the bread to keep from looking at him.

"I'm not here to try to convince you that you didn't screw up with Jesse, and I'm not going to deny he screwed up with you, too. I'm here because I can't figure out for shit why the two of you would rather say good-bye to the good thing you had going instead of working it out and moving on."

I slapped the sandwiches into the pan, then leaned into the counter. "He doesn't want me anymore, Garth. He hasn't called once in close to a month."

"Bullshit. Try again."

"There's no way he could move on from the things I did, inadvertent or not, this year."

"Bull. Shit."

"Is that your new favorite word or something? Got anything different?" I snapped before flipping the sizzling sandwiches.

"Not when I'm surrounded by so much of it."

"He's better off without me." I finally spun around to look him in the eyes. "You and I both know that, Garth."

A second passed by. Then another. Finally, Garth opened his mouth. "Bullshit."

I wasn't sure whether to be relieved or not. The profanities and topic were overwhelming me.

"What else have you got for me? I can keep this up all night long."

After plating the sandwiches, I turned off the burner and dropped the two plates on the table. Garth eyed his but didn't touch it. I sighed, then bit into mine as I sat. "I don't know, Garth. It just feels like things shouldn't be this hard. I feel like we're fighting nature or something being together. Nothing for Jesse and me, *nothing*, has come easy."

I was bracing myself for another *Bullshit* when Garth twisted to face me. "Do you really want easy to be the standard by which you measure a relationship?"

If I hadn't been staring at Garth, I wouldn't have believed those words had just come from his mouth. When it came to giving relationship advice, I'd guessed Garth had about as much to offer as an amoeba. I'd been wrong.

"Um . . . no." I set my sandwich down, feeling a little stunned. "No, I wouldn't."

"Good answer."

After a little more deliberation, I asked, "Why are you doing this? Why do you give a shit? You know I think you're a decent guy, but you're not exactly the kind who gives a shit."

Garth's gaze lowered. "I ruined one of Jesse's relationships. I'm not going to watch another be ruined if I can do something to stop it." He paused to clear his throat. "After this, we're even."

So much about those words broke my heart. So much I didn't understand. "Even?"

Garth stood up, snagging his sandwich. "And now you and me are even, too, Rowen Sterling." He took a huge bite out of his sandwich.

He might have had a warped view of being "even" with someone, but Garth Black was quite possibly one of the deepest people I'd ever met. What he'd done to get to me, combined with his words, proved that.

"Where are you going?" I asked as he headed for the front door.

"I've got work in the morning. I'm going to be late, but I'm guessing the rancher's son will go easy on me when he finds out what I was up to." Garth paused with his hand on the doorknob. "Oh, and I left you a present in your bedroom."

"A present?"

"No need to thank me. It's not from me. I was just the delivery boy." Garth popped the last of the sandwich in his mouth and opened the door.

"You really think he can forgive me? You really think he still loves me?" I asked quietly. Garth twisted around, locked eyes with me, then winked. "There's only one way to find out."

chapter **TWENTY-FIVE**

Rowen

THE INSTANT THE door closed behind Garth, I charged into my bedroom. I had no idea what the gift could be, where he'd left it, or how big it would be. As soon as I raced inside my room, all of my questions were answered. I covered my mouth as my eyes went glassy. On the big wall behind my bed was my painting. The one I'd made intending for no one to see and the same one that had turned into a weeks' long bidding war. There was a note propped on my pillow, and I rushed to read it.

I couldn't let this hang on someone else's wall when I loved both of these girls. It's where it belongs now.

I didn't need the *J* to know who the picture and note were from, and I certainly didn't want to know how much he'd spent or how much he'd had to go out of his way to purchase it. Grabbing a pillow, I scooted to the end of my bed and let myself admire it. When I'd been painting it, I hadn't been able to admire it. It had been more therapy and less about art, but months later, the reverse was true.

Jesse'd been right. It was where it needed to be. It shouldn't wind up on someone else's wall when he'd loved both of those girls. When both of those girls loved him.

The painting was a self-portrait, but my face was cut down the middle. One half was the old me. The one who'd shown up at Willow Springs with black hair, dark eyes and makeup, and a vacant, almost dead expression. The other half was me now: lighter hair, light eyes, and lightish makeup. My mouth wasn't turned up in a smile, but my expression was peaceful, my eyes hopeful.

The painting had been less about comparing and contrasting and more about showing how the two people I'd been had made me who I was. It wasn't about what had been but what was. It wasn't about unbalance but harmony. It was my life story in one painting.

I stared at it not with tears in my eyes but a smile on my face. I stared at the painting for so long my eyes became heavy. So heavy, I started to fall . . .

MY ALARM JOLTED me awake. I'd fallen asleep. I wasn't sure if I was more shocked by that or by how long I'd actually stayed asleep. A glance at my phone told me I'd been asleep for almost eight hours.

Whatever dreams I'd been having or, maybe it was just getting a full night's sleep, the fog of confusion clouding my head had lifted. Things were clear. So clear I practically leapt out of bed and ran to my closet.

Thanks to my day of cleaning, I knew exactly where everything was, so I had my duffel packed with the essentials in less than five minutes. After changing and combing the bed-head out of my hair, I was rushing out of my room when I ran back to snag the pillow from the end of my bed. Never go anywhere on a Greyhound bus without a pillow. I was stuffing it into my bag when something flew out of it. That little white button. I couldn't seem to lose the thing, even if I wanted to. I picked it up and tossed it in my pocket before flying out the door.

I knew I had a dozen phone calls to make, and I probably needed to do a million other things before boarding that bus, but they'd have to wait. Everything could wait except for one thing. One person. A person I'd made wait for too long.

When the alarm had jolted me awake, one thing was at the front of my mind. Something Rose had told me at the start of the year, when she and the family had been about to leave after helping me get moved in. She'd taken me aside, given me one of her Rose hugs, looked me in the eyes, and said, "Our priorities aren't what we say they are. They're what we *show* they are."

I knew they were powerful words at the time, but somewhere along the way, I'd lost them. I'd forgotten the power and truth behind them. But I'd found them again, and I was ready to show what my priorities were.

Once I'd grabbed a breakfast bar from the cupboard, I stormed toward the door. I'd decided what I needed to do, and I couldn't move fast enough. Unlocking it, I twisted it open and hurried out. Right into a wide and strong chest.

We both made sounds of surprise.

"I was just about to knock."

"And I was just about to leave," I replied, breathless from all the running around or the person standing in front of me. Probably both.

"Good timing, then." Jesse slid a chunk of my hair behind my ear. His hand hovered at my cheek for a moment after.

"I wanted to see you. I wanted to talk to you."

Jesse shifted his weight. "I wanted to talk to you, too."

"You first," we said in unison.

Jesse smiled. Either that smile or him being a foot in front of me after weeks of separation was going to render me speechless. Soon. I had to get it out quick.

"Okay, how about the person who has the most to apologize for go first?" I said.

"Then that would be me," he interjected. I crossed my arms. "How about ladies first then? Since we can't agree on who has the most to apologize for."

"I'll take it." I uncrossed my arms and kept myself from running into his. "I'm sorry, Jesse. I'm sorry for so many things. Things I could control and things that maybe I couldn't, but it doesn't make me any less sorry." I stopped long enough to recompose myself and my thoughts, then got back after it. "I'm sorry for lying about the internship, and I'm sorry for the way you found out. I'm sorry for throwing Mar back into your life like that, and I'm sorry for what that did to you." The image of the broken shell of Jesse flashed through my mind. I shook my head to clear it. "I'm sorry that I left you at Willow Springs when I knew you needed me. I knew you were pushing me away because you were afraid of hurting me, and I still left you. I'm sorry for this past month and not reaching out just so you knew you were on my mind. Because, Jesse, you were the *only* thing on my mind. And I'm sorry, most of all, for failing you. On so many levels. You were the one person I never wanted to let down, and I did in so many ways." I'd managed to say everything while looking in his eyes, but finally, they dropped. "I'm sorry."

Jesse's hand cupped my chin and tilted it up. He didn't let it go once my eyes were realigned with his. "You know what? I'm not sorry for any of that, Rowen. Not one bit."

I hadn't heard him right. That was the only explanation. "Why?"

"Because here's what I realized. Finally." He exhaled, rolling his shoulders back. "I had to be at my worst, and you had to see me at my worst, in order for us to both know if we loved each other enough to make it work."

I wrapped my hand around his wrist. If he got to touch me, I wanted to touch him, too. "But, Jesse . . . we broke up." We hadn't made it when he was at his worst. We hadn't come through the fire unscathed.

"And yet here I am, standing in front of you right now, asking you, begging you . . . I'll get down on my knees . . ." He did. He actually got down on his knees, which was kind of wonderful in an uncomfortable, what-do-I-do-now kind of way. " . . . to ask you to give me a second chance. Not because I deserve one but because *we* deserve one. We might have taken a break for a while, but we don't need to make it permanent."

Since I couldn't decide what to do and having him look up at me that way made me more uncomfortable with each passing second, I got down on my knees too. That made him smile . . . making me smile. "So you've seen me at my worst, I've seen you at your worst now too, and we've seen our relationship at its worst. You know the only direction from here, right?"

His smile went higher. "I believe I do."

"Since you're in such a divulging kind of mood and I've got you on your knees"—I crept a little closer to him—"mind telling me what changed your mind? What made you decide I wasn't 'better off without you'?" I made air quotes and rolled my eyes. "Because it certainly wasn't anything I said."

He cleared his throat. "I remembered something I said to you last summer."

"You said a lot of things to me last summer." I gave his arm a squeeze and crept closer still. If any of my neighbors were to walk by, I could just imagine the funny looks we'd be given.

"What I said to you about not being afraid to fall. To not spend your time trying to keep from falling, but to spend your time finding that person who would help you up when you did."

"Oh, yeah. That was a good one."

"I found the person willing to stand beside me and help me up if I fell. And when I did fall, when I fell big time, I was so scared of bringing her down with me, I pushed her away to protect her."

I crossed my arms. "You about done pushing?" Everything he said was thoughtful and deep and was making me swoon, but I wanted to get to the point. I needed to know why he was there and if it meant what I hoped it did.

Jesse lifted his finger. "I wasn't quite done yet. There was more than one thing I needed to be beat over the head with to come back to my senses."

I nodded, waiting.

"I wanted to be the best person I could be, Rowen. To prove I wasn't the boy I'd grown up as or anything like the people that gave birth to me. But when I realized I wasn't that person, and that a part of the old me was still there . . . it scared me."

I cleared my throat to fight the ball threatening to form.

"Then someone told me you didn't love me because I never . . . *messed* up." Jesse smiled, I guessed at a private joke.

"I don't. I love you because of the way you love me," I replied, grabbing his hand. It was warm, solid, and responded to mine like it had before all of that went down: with certainty. "I love you for all of your pieces, not just a select few. I love you for your dark, dirty secrets too. I love you, Jesse. I love . . . *you.*"

His eyes closed for a moment as he let out a long breath, almost like he'd been holding it forever.

"So . . . are you about done pushing?" I repeated.

He lifted his finger again, opening his eyes. I waved my hand and let him proceed. He had a lot to say, and after weeks of having next to nothing to say, I wasn't going to stop him.

"I realized that our past never leaves us. We might think we've left it behind, but that's when it sneaks up and beats the hell out of you. Our past is always a part of us. The key is to accept it, acknowledge it from time to time, pay the piper, and get on with your life."

I lifted my hand to his cheek. "You're talking like a philosopher again. You really are back."

His hand came up to cover mine as he crept closer to me. It was the first movement he'd made my way in a long time. It was the first time he hadn't backed away when I'd approached him. It was a little movement that felt like one giant leap. "I just lost myself for a little while," he said softly. "I'm okay now. I'm coming back. I beat this once. And now twice. I don't want my fear of it happening to be the reason I lose you."

He'd never lose me. I was certain of few things in life, but that was one of them. "Fixed. Broken," I said, lifting a shoulder. "I'll love you either way. Just the way you love me."

When Jesse exhaled, it looked like the weight of the world had been lifted from his shoulders. When his eyes met mine, his whole expression changed. It was an expression I was familiar with. One that made my stomach bottom out. "Would it be okay if I kissed you now?"

Tipping his hat back, I draped my arms around his neck. "You'd *better* kiss me now. You've got some serious making up to do."

He moved closer and pressed his forehead into mine before slowly tilting his head until our lips touched. He closed the last bit of space separating us, cinched his arms around me, and kissed me. Not as the man he'd been or the man he hoped one day he'd be but as the man he was. Right there, on his knees in front of me. He kissed me like it was what he'd been born to do, and somehow, I managed to keep up and do the same. If I'd been born to do nothing but practice and perfect the art of kissing Jesse Walker, it wouldn't have been a wasted life. But there was still so much more. So much in store for me and him . . . and us. We'd visited the dark places of our pasts together and had come through on the other side together. Not unscathed, and not as if nothing had happened, but we were together.

When Jesse's mouth left mine, I saw the smile that

was all Jesse, the one I hadn't seen in so long. I knew that no matter what came at us, good or bad, we'd always figure out a way to weather it together. Smooth sailing and easy breezy wasn't our destiny. But we had one, and for me, that was enough.

"Since you've finally admitted that I'm your wing-man, the one to help you up when you're down, dry your tears, and give you a swift kick in the butt when you need it"—I winked at him—"mind telling me what happened for you to go into an emotional nose dive? You know, just so I can be on the look out next time." I wasn't sure if humor was the best way to approach it, but I figured it couldn't have been the worst way.

Jesse stood up, grabbed my hands, and pulled me up with him. "It started with the nightmares, I guess. That's what first shook me. Then when I realized I'd lost something I'd carried around for years, that shook me some more. Really, it was a bunch of small things that added up to something big. Something too big, obviously."

My eyebrows came together. "What have you been carrying around with you? What did you lose?" To my knowledge, Jesse'd never carried around a lucky charm or a worry stone or something of the sort.

"It wasn't anything big or fancy. It was just this little, white—"

"Button." I pulled it out of my pocket and held it out.

Jesse's forehead wrinkled as he examined it. "Yeah . . . that's it. How did it . . ? How did you . . .?" Biting the inside of his cheek, he looked away from it. "Where did you find it?"

"In one of my old steel-toed boots. I just found it the other day. How long have you been missing it?"

"A couple of months."

I turned the button over in my hand. "What's the story? I know there must be a pretty big one."

Jesse cracked his neck and worked to unlock his jaw. "I found that a long time ago. Before I came to live with the Walkers."

"This is from when you were still with . . . with . . . them?"

Jesse nodded. "It was down in one of the old drain traps in the basement. It took me forever to work the screw out, but I had to have it, and at least it gave me something to do. Something to work toward." Jesse went somewhere else for the briefest moment before his eyes cleared and he came back. "Once I had it, I guarded it like you wouldn't believe. At that point, I probably would have given my life to keep it protected and out of their reach."

"Why?" I asked, grabbing his hand. I wanted to understand, but I didn't understand how one button could be so important to a little boy.

"It was the only thing I could call my own. It was the only thing I had that they hadn't given to me. It was something special . . . *sacred.* It's the only thing I have of my life before Willow Springs, and I've kept it with me for years not as a reminder of the life I'd lived, but as a promise of the life I'll never have to live again. A promise of moving on and having a better life. A promise of people to love and to love me." Jesse rubbed the back of his neck. "Now that I just said that all out loud, it seems kind of silly."

"Not silly, Jesse. Not silly at all. Maybe a little sad, but I get it. I totally get it."

"So once this thing I'd loved in my former life left me

. . . I was afraid of something I loved in my new life leaving me. I was afraid of losing you, Rowen, and the thing about fear and panic and possession is that they turn a person into exactly the person they were scared of becoming. I was afraid of losing you, but my fear of that was what ultimately drove you away."

I shook my head, stunned. Stunned at the conversation, at the meaning behind the button, at the whole past couple of months. "I bet you're happy to have this back then." I held it out for him and waited.

And waited.

He studied my hand, the corners of his eyes wrinkling as he concentrated, and then his expression cleared. "Why don't you put it back in those old boots of yours? I think they'd make good companions. I don't need it anymore to remind me of the life I want to live." Jesse wrapped his arm around my waist and pulled me to him. "I've got you to remind me of that now."

"You know that whole lot of making up I was saying you owed me?" I asked, grinning up at him. "You're making a lot of progress in that department. A *lot* of progress."

"Good to know."

"Plus you earned yourself some mega brownie points with that picture I have hanging on my bedroom wall right now."

Jesse's mouth lifted. "There was just something about that picture that reminded me of you. I had to get it for you."

"Despite the thousands of dollars I don't even want to know you spent on it," I mumbled.

"Money wasn't an object."

"Says the guy with no money left in his checking account . . ."

"The guy with no truck and, like you said, no money in his checking account to pay for a new one anytime soon."

Light bulb moment. "Is that so?" I grabbed his hand and pulled him toward the parking lot.

"Rowen? Where are you dragging me? Not that I really care, but am I going to need a change of clothes or anything?"

"Nope. I'll take care of your clothes later. Or at least I'll take care of *removing* your clothes later." I glanced back and winked at him. "But since you got me a present, it's only right that I got you one too. Right?"

"I don't think that's the way it works."

"Well, it's the way it's working right now." Coming around a large pickup, I stopped, grabbed Jesse's shoulders, and turned him ninety degrees.

"Rowen," he said in a rare speechless moment. "How did you . . ?"

"I had it towed here." I shouldered up beside Jesse as he continued to stare without blinking at Old Bessie.

"You had it towed here? From North Idaho?" He tore his eyes away from his truck long enough to gape at me.

"I knew a guy who knew a guy," I answered with a dismissive wave.

"You knew a guy who knew a guy who was willing to tow a broken down, ancient truck to Seattle?"

"Yep. And then the guy I knew knew another guy who . . ." I ran to open the driver's door, searched for the keys I'd stuffed beneath the seat, and cranked on the engine.

Jesse's eyes went even wider. "It's running?" He moved toward the hood. "Wait. Old Bessie's never ran that good. At least not since I've owned her." Unlatching the hood, he lifted it as I came around the front to join him.

Jesse was totally speechless. It was a side of him I hadn't seen much. I'd gotten to know a lot of sides of him I'd never seen before the past couple of months. And you know what?

I loved every single one.

"See? Knowing a guy who knows a guy has its benefits." I nudged him as we admired the shiny new engine and under-the-hood parts as I knowledgeably called them. The guy I'd known was Sid, and the guy he knew was his younger brother. He was a major gear-head who basically just charged me for the parts and a little bit of labor. I'd just gotten Old Bessie back and was planning on delivering it to Jesse when the moment was right.

The moment couldn't have been more right.

"I need to know more of the people you know," he said, still gaping at his truck.

"When he asked if I wanted him to clean up the exterior, I told him that I didn't mind a little mess on the outside, as long as the important stuff's in good working order." I wrapped my arm around him and couldn't stop smiling at that truck I'd hated at first sight, but I had grown to love. The inside, the outside, all sides of it.

"Thank you, Rowen. I don't know if you understand how much this means to me, but . . ."

"I think I do. I think I have a very good idea what it means to you."

Giving his head a shake, his expression changed. "Hey, do you think the apartment manager would mind if it stayed here a while?"

"I don't think he'd even notice. But why? How long are you planning on staying?"

Jesse moved in front of me. "How long do you want me to stay?"

"Forever," I said instantly. It might have been a selfish answer, but it was the honest one.

"That's kind of what I had in mind, too." When his hand dug into his pocket, I was clueless. When his hand came out, whatever was inside of it was too small to be seen. I was still clueless. But when he dropped back down onto both of his knees and held out that gold ring, I had a rush of clarity.

"You know me at my best, and you know me at my worst. You know my past and my dreams for the future. You know *me*. I know the same things about you and I can say with absolute certainty that I will love you every minute of every day, Rowen. In this life, and our next, and our next if there's such a thing as reincarnation. I was made to love you." Jesse's eyes lightened with every word, his face a plane of confidence. "Will you marry me?"

That was what it felt like. The moment when all of my past failures were worth it, when I knew all of my future ones would be, too. That was the moment when life makes sense.

"My answer to your question depends on your answer to mine," I replied, trying to pretend I wasn't totally reeling. Trying to pretend like I wasn't about to grab on to Old Bessie for support.

Jesse didn't even look surprised. He knew me well enough to know I wouldn't be the girl to flap her hands, scream *yes* a million times, and unleash the floodgates.

"What question is that?" He grinned up at me.

Pulling him up until he stood in front of me, the ring still in his hands, I met his eyes. "You know me at my best, and you know me at my worst. You know my past and my dreams for the future. You know *me.* So, Jesse Walker, will *you* marry *me*?"

One corner of his mouth twitched in amusement. "On one condition." He kissed the tip of my nose. "If you'll agree to marry me first."

I laughed a few notes and couldn't get my answer out fast enough. "Yes, Jesse. I'm yours. I guess we might as well make it official."

I'd seen Jesse happy a million different times, but I'd never seen him happy like that. It was happiness in a way that staggered me. Happiness in its purest state. "And I'm yours. So why *not* make it official."

It started raining right as I held out my left hand and Jesse slipped the ring on my finger. I didn't take it as an omen or a sign of what was to come; I took it as a promise. No matter what kinds of storms waited for us in the future, we'd weather them together. Side by side.

"Jesse, there's one more thing I wanted to tell you," I said, needing to get everything off of my chest before we could properly celebrate. "The internship . . . I'm not going to—"

"Take it," he said immediately. "You know and I know that you need to take that internship, Rowen. You *have* to take it."

"But this summer . . . We're engaged now. I want to spend the summer with you." The internship was a phenomenal opportunity, but it was a job. It wasn't a person; it wasn't someone I loved. I was proving where my priorities were. At last.

"And I plan on spending the summer with you too. We're engaged after all," Jesse said with a smile. When he glanced at my ring finger, his smile went bigger.

My forehead lined. "How is that supposed to work if you want me to take the internship?"

Jesse pulled me close. "How's that roommate search going?"

"What? Wait. No. *No*," I said as all the pieces fit together. "Jesse, your dad needs you on the ranch. Summers especially. You can't just up and leave in the middle of it to be with me."

"Actually, I can't think of a better reason to up and leave anything than to be with you."

"Jesse—"

He shook his head. "I've already talked it over with my dad and mom. They're on board with it, and I thought you'd be too . . ."

"I do want you to move in with me, of course I do, but Jesse . . . are you sure this is what you really want?"

"I know we can make it through anything, Rowen. The past couple of months have proven that to me. I know we could make it if we were far away from each other. I trust that. I have faith in that. The thing is . . . I don't want to do it. I want to be near you. Every day. Every night. Why should I settle for you from afar when I can have you near me every morning I wake up?" His forehead pressed into mine. "Relationships are about compromise and sacrifice. I don't want you to have to compromise this internship for me. Or me for the internship. This is my turn to sacrifice something. This is something I want to sacrifice." Drops of rain slid between us, down our faces, and our clothes were becoming wet, but I felt nothing but warmth. "The ranch will always be there. The ranch will wait. I don't want you to have to. Okay?"

I had so many points to argue, so many things that made that such a selfish option, but when Jesse looked at me like that after saying what he just had, I could only manage one word. And it wasn't *no*.

"Okay," I said, feeling a smile moving into place. I didn't only have my boyfriend back—correction, my *fiancé* back—I would get to see him all the time. Every day. Every night.

Life and its proclivities for one-eighties . . .

Kissing me first, Jesse ran to turn Old Bessie off before coming back to scoop me into his arms. "I think you were wrong. I did need a change of clothes for this trip."

I laughed as he ran for the apartment. It didn't matter; we were both already drenched. "You won't need any clothes for a while. You've still got some making up to do." I winked up at him suggestively, and Jesse's pace picked up. "By the way, how in the world did you get here? Since I know it wasn't thanks to Old Bessie."

He smiled as he continued sprinting through the rain. "I took a Greyhound bus."

That right there was what I called a full circle moment.

Just outside the apartment, Jesse lowered me and backed me against the door. His hands braced against the door on either side of my head as his eyes locked on mine. "Thank you for saving me, Rowen. Thank you for coming and saving me."

I lifted my hand to his face and traced each fervent

wrinkle until it disappeared. "I didn't save you, Jesse. I just helped you remember how to save yourself."

"You helped me remember why it was worth saving myself," he said gently, right before covering his lips with mine. We stayed up against that door for a while, kissing and making up for lost time. We kissed until I felt like I couldn't kiss anymore. And then we kissed some more.

There are high points, and there are *high* points. That was mine, having a man like Jesse Walker to love and love me back, and knowing that no matter what came our way, we'd be ready for it.

The rest was up to us.

THE END

ABOUT *the* AUTHOR

Thank you for reading **NEAR and FAR** by bestselling author, Nicole Williams.
Nicole loves to hear from her readers.

You can connect with her on Facebook: Nicole Williams (Official Author Page)
Twitter: nwilliamsbooks
Blog: nicoleawilliams.blogspot.com

Other Works by Nicole:

CRASH, CLASH, and **CRUSH** (HarperCollins)

UP IN FLAMES (Simon & Schuster UK)

LOST & FOUND

GREAT EXPLOITATIONS SAGA

THE EDEN TRILOGY

THE PATRICK CHRONICLES

Made in the USA
Middletown, DE
19 February 2018